SWEET SURRENDER

Before she could change her mind, Jenna quickly shed her garments and scrambled under the covers. As she pulled them close to her chin, she silently willed her heart to quit beating so loudly.

His hand touched her waist and she jumped. "Ticklish?" he asked.

"Your hand's cold."

He touched her again. "Just needs a little friction to get hot."

Jenna sighed.

"You like that, Princess?"

"Yes," she whispered.

"I aim to please. Tell me what else you want me to do."

Her blood pounded thickly in her veins. She closed her eyes and lay still in his arms, unable to speak. She wasn't quite sure what she wanted . . . only that she wanted the man whose arms enfolded her, wanted him in the most primitive of ways. Her lips parted and she felt as though she were melting against him, becoming a part of him, sharing his very breath and the pulsing of his blood.

"Do whatever you choose," she whispered, trembling as she waited for his lips to capture hers.

READERS ARE IN LOVE WITH ZEBRA LOVEGRAMS

TEMPTING TEXAS TREASURE (3312, $4.50)
by Wanda Owen

With her dazzling beauty, Karita Montera aroused passion in every redblooded man who glanced her way. But the independent senorita had eyes only for Vincent Navarro, the wealthy cattle rancher she'd adored since childhood—who was also her family's sworn enemy. The Navarro and Montera clans had clashed for generations, but no past passions could compare with the fierce desire that swept through Vincent as he came across the near-naked Karita cooling herself beside the crystal waterfall on the riverbank. With just one scorching glance, he knew this raven-haired vixen must be his for eternity. After the first forbidden embrace, she had captured his heart—and enslaved his very soul!

MISSOURI FLAME (3314, $4.50)
by Gwen Cleary

Missouri-bound Bevin O'Dea never even met the farmer she was journeying to wed, but she believed a marriage based on practicality rather than passion would suit her just fine . . . until she encountered the smoldering charisma of the brash Will Shoemaker, who just happened to be her fiance's step-brother.

Will Shoemaker couldn't believe a woman like Bevin, so full of hidden passion, could agree to marry his step-brother—a cold fish of a man who wanted a housekeeper more than he wanted a wife. He knew he should stay away from Bevin, but the passions were building in both of them, and once those passions were released, they would explode into a red-hot *Missouri Flame.*

BAYOU BRIDE (3311, $4.50)
by Bobbi Smith

Wealthy Louisiana planter Dominic Kane was in a bind: according to his father's will, he must marry within six months or forfeit his inheritance. When he saw the beautiful bonded servant on the docks, he figured she'd do just fine. He would buy her papers and she would be his wife for six months—on paper, that is.

Spirited Jordan St. James hired on as an indenture servant in America because it was the best way to flee England. Her heart raced when she saw her handsome new master, and she swore she would do anything to become Dominic's bride. When his strong arms circled around her in a passionate embrace, she knew she would surrender to his thrilling kisses and lie in his arms for one long night of loving . . . no matter what the future might bring!

Available wherever paperbacks are sold, or order direct from the Publisher. Send cover price plus 50¢ per copy for mailing and handling to Zebra Books, Dept. 3444, 475 Park Avenue South, New York, N.Y. 10016. Residents of New York, New Jersey and Pennsylvania must include sales tax. DO NOT SEND CASH.

EVELYN ROGERS
SURRENDER TO THE NIGHT

ZEBRA BOOKS
KENSINGTON PUBLISHING CORP.

To Martha Hix, Karla Hocker,
And Pamela Litton,
Great readers, writers, and friends.

ZEBRA BOOKS

are published by

Kensington Publishing Corp.
475 Park Avenue South
New York, NY 10016

Copyright © 1991 by Evelyn Rogers

First printing: July, 1991

Printed in the United States of America

Part One

The Black Horse

Chapter One

Mason County, Texas
March, 1897

"Hi-yah!"

Clayton Ernest Drake's yell echoed through the early evening air settling over the Whiskey Ranch pasture. He gave free rein to his cow pony, a seasoned pinto named Patches who heeded the cry with a burst of speed, muscles bunching and extending, hooves beating like thunder against the hard ground.

Rider and horse flew like the wind across the low grass and scattered wild flowers, their course to the west toward the distant limestone hills and the purple-fingered setting sun. Stretching low across the neck of his mount, Clay felt a surge of excitement, a quickening of his blood.

He rode for the sheer joy of riding across the flat stretch of land. The pasture raced by in a blur beneath the pounding hooves.

He shifted in the saddle, and the pinto canted toward the left on a straight line to a stand of cottonwoods beside one of the Whiskey's half dozen creeks. A well-worn path marked the route, and Clay did not rein to a halt until he was deep in the lengthening shadows beside the narrow stream.

Dropping to the ground, he led Patches to the water, loosened saddle and girth, and grabbed up handfuls of

7

grass to rub at the pinto's lathered sides. A wiry tail flicked and caught him against the neck. He did not take offense.

Clay breathed deep. He liked the smell of the saddle and the horse, of the fresh spring grass on the bank, of the mesquite and sage on the far side of the stream. He liked everything about the Whiskey Ranch. It was his home.

His eye fell to an embossed image on the saddle skirt, and he was reminded of a letter received at the Mason County post office two weeks ago.

"In the nine years since your mother and I deeded the ranch to you, the Whiskey has doubled in size and tripled in value," his father had written from England. "All this came in a time of depression in the Texas cattle industry, of an increasing number of bankruptcies, of reduced herds. While once vast spreads of land have been divided like broken plates, the Whiskey has grown. You have reason to be proud."

The letter had been accompanied by the saddle, a gift in recognition of his thirtieth birthday. It bore the family crest, the heads of three horses on a fan-shaped shield.

Clay fingered the crest. His father had been exaggerating a mite about his accomplishments, but the gift had been right on target, a Western-style saddle marked by the sign of Clay's English ancestry.

In a return letter thanking his father for the gift, he'd written, "Any success I've had came from luck and hard work, not any special smarts."

His foreman put it another way: "You're just too dad-blamed stubborn to let go what's yours."

Clay conceded the man had a point, stubbornness being a family trait on both sides of his family.

Patches snorted, reminding him he was slowing down on the job, and he circled the flat of his hands against the gelding's flank with renewed enthusiasm.

"Feels good, doesn't it, boy?" he asked. "Nothing better than a hard rubdown, for man or beast."

The pinto jerked his head up and down as if in agreement, then returned his attention to the stream.

A rustling in the brush behind Clay yanked him to full alert. A twig snapped. No animal made a racket like that . . . except maybe the two-legged kind. The days when bandits and Indians roamed the country were long gone, but that didn't mean danger was unknown, which was why Clay wore a gun. Right now he was glad to be packing iron. Any man who sneaked up on another without announcing his presence loud and clear was up to no good.

With his left hand rubbing at the horse, his right eased to the handle of his holstered six-shooter. Whirling, he dropped to one knee, gun in hand, and pointed toward the brush.

A lanky figure stepped into view a dozen yards away. "Is that what Emmeline gave you in town, Clay? A good rubdown?"

Clay shook his head in disgust. "Damn it, Andy, you could get killed sneaking up on a man like that."

"You don't never fire less'n you can see what you're aimin' at, Clay. I've rode with you long enough to know that."

Clay stood and dropped the gun back in its holster. "All it takes is one time."

Andy shrugged. "I ain't afraid."

Clay gave up. At twenty-eight, Andy, son of the neighboring rancher Rusty Taylor, was not quite two years his junior, but sometimes he acted like a ten-year-old.

He brushed aside an irritation at the intrusion on his solitude. He'd spent the past two weeks rounding up cattle with Andy and a dozen other cowboys, branding and marking the calves, separating out the stock that belonged to the close-by spreads.

The tradition of joint round-ups was a dying one, but as long as the Drake and Taylor ranches were held by their current owners, both men swore not to put up fences between them. For Clay, that day would never come. Before another name was inked over his on the Whiskey title, he'd be buried six feet deep.

"What brings you out here?" Clay rolled up his shirt sleeves as he talked.

"Orneriness, mostly," replied Andy, his freckled face breaking into a quick grin. "Knew where you'd be riding. Wanted to see if I could sneak up on you. Looks to me like I did."

A ten-year-old, Clay thought again.

Ground tethering the pinto, he ambled a couple of yards upstream, thumbed his Stetson to the back of his head, and satisfied his own thirst before finding a grassy place beneath the trees where he could stretch out his six-foot-two frame and study the rustling leaves. He lay on his back, one booted foot crossed over the other, his head propped on folded arms, and proceeded to do just that. There were times when details like cottonwood leaves needed attention; now, with the roundup drawing to a close, was one such time.

Andy retrieved his roan from the thick copse where he'd left it before sneaking up on his quarry. Tying the horse close to the pinto, he proceeded to sprawl beside Clay, to break off a long-stemmed piece of grass, then chew on the end.

"Surprised you didn't hang around for supper. Cook fried up some mountain oysters. Went down real good."

Clay stared lazily at the broken blue sky directly overhead. He'd wielded the knife that castrated many of the calves, but he wasn't one to enjoy the fruits of the labor.

"Decided to pass," was all he said.

Clay pulled the brim of his Stetson low and silence settled on the men, disturbed by nothing more intrusive than a chorus of crickets harmonizing with the wind in the leaves. Shifting his arms to a more comfortable position beneath his head, Clay listened to nature's evening song, deeply breathing the air that smelled sweeter than gingerbread fresh from the chuck wagon stove. At moments like this, he was at peace with his world.

Or rather, his worlds, coming from two separate cultures as he did. As proof, he bore the monikers of his grandfathers: the first, a titled Englishman whose roots went back to William the Conqueror; the second, a Texas cowpoke who couldn't have come up with the name of his daddy if his ranch had been at stake.

Both were dead and gone before Clay made his squalling entrance into the world, but, as close as he was to his father, an English earl, it was the blood of Ernie the rancher that flowed most in his veins. He realized it at a peaceful time like this, especially when it came after weeks of honest sweat.

The peace of the moment was short-lived.

"Civilization," said Andy without preamble. "That's what's wrong with this country."

Clay ignored him.

"Damned if it ain't," Andy went on.

Clay closed his eyes.

"Don't see how it can be stopped, either."

Knowing Andy as he did, Clay gave up on rest. The problem with his friend was not that he was overloaded with opinions but that he tended to be long-winded about them. In that respect, he was like his father Rusty, one-time foreman of the Whiskey who'd long ago bought his own spread. Once Rusty got wound up, he could extend a Mason County cattlemen's meeting beyond endurance. The sooner Andy got off his chest what was bothering him, the sooner Clay could get back to studying the leaves.

"What brought that on?" he asked.

Andy's freckled face wrinkled into a frown. "Just thinking about our trip to San Antonio last month."

Clay remembered the journey well. They'd been negotiating cattle sales. The prices quoted by the company men, bankers for the most part, had been enough to drive a stockman to drink — or to bargaining, which

11

is what Clay had done. He ended up with a better price than he'd expected when he rode into town.

Andy, trying to learn from him, had not done quite so well.

Clay had no real respect for bankers. Pasty-faced clerks they were, every man jack of them. Men who talked for a living away from the sun. Men who got calluses on their backsides, if they got them anywhere, and not on their hands like any self-respecting Texan. Talking to them for more than a minute left a bad taste in a man's mouth. Before setting out on the long ride back to Mason, which had recently undergone one of its occasional seizures of sanctimony by voting dry, both he and Andy ended up at the Longhorn Saloon.

It had not proven to be a fortuitous stop, at least not for the younger man.

"Civilization," Andy repeated, hard-edging each syllable as he shifted in the grass beside Clay. "It's the ruin of the West."

Clay knew the particular cause of Andy's scorn; it had nothing to do with cattle. At the Longhorn — while Clay was reacquainting himself upstairs with the charms of the proprietor Emmeline — Andy had engaged himself in a poker game with a pair of drummers from New Jersey.

One thing had led to another, as best Clay could figure out later, with a little bragging on both sides of the table, a slur cast upon Davy Crockett and the other heroes slain at the Alamo — "There wasn't any back door to the place, is what I always heard," one of the drummers was quoted as saying — and a wide-scale brawl had ensued.

Andy had ended up in jail; the drummers had gone free. Clay had spent his last morning in town arranging to pay his friend's fine. It hadn't helped the younger man's disposition any when, as they ambled toward the stable to get their mounts, Clay compared him to a fellow Mason County jailbird. "You remember August Schreiber," he'd said, referring to a clerk in

12

Fly Gap. "the one who was jailed overnight last January for working on Sunday? You desperadoes have got to be stopped."

Andy's blunt rejoinder had sent a matronly passerby running for the opposite side of the street.

Weeks later, with the work of the round-up behind him, the young cowpoke was letting the night behind bars get to him all over again, only he was blaming the course of mankind for his troubles, not his own quick temper.

"There was talk at the Longhorn," he said, wound up tight, "about how we'll be putting our horses to pasture afore long and riding around in little wagons that move by theirselves." He spat in the grass between them. "That'll be the day."

Clay was inclined to agree.

"You shoulda' been there, Clay," the younger cowman continued with only a quick intake of breath. "Never heard such palaver. You know, I'll bet those Yankees wouldn't 'a been so quick to use their fists if you'd been at the table instead of humping Emmeline."

Now that, Clay decided, was going too far. "If I didn't know you better, Andrew, I would think you were insulting the lady."

"Lady! Hell, she'd be insulted if she thought you weren't willing to, uh, you know, call on her when you got to town. Won't give me the time of day, but she starts undressing the minute she sees you at the door."

"You tend to exaggerate," said Clay, but the truth was his friend hadn't overstated the case. Emmeline *had* been tugging at the drawstring of her blouse when he first spotted her at the end of the bar.

The saloonkeeper was a lusty one, all right, well endowed and bold the way he liked 'em. A Texas woman who wasn't ashamed of her needs. He'd met women from all parts of the world, but none could match the spirit and looks of those born and bred in the Lone Star State.

13

Texas women fought for what they believed in, whether it was temperance in the sale of alcohol or the freedom to run a saloon. Clay respected their opinions even if he didn't always agree with them, but he had to admit to a partiality for the likes of Emmeline.

In his experience, Texas women were a mighty friendly breed, yet many a cowboy complained he couldn't get a woman if he offered her a month's pay and a gallon of whiskey. It was a problem Clay didn't understand, and he didn't have to make the hundred-mile ride southeast to the city for companionship. Closer to home was the Mason piano teacher, a divorcee whose husband had left her because of childlessness. Having sworn off matrimony, she welcomed Clay into her bed on the nights he stayed in town. He suspected he wasn't the only one, but hell, who was he to complain?

In the spirit of international relations, he occasionally spent time with the Irish lass who served as housekeeper to the Mason mayor. Bridget was earning money to return to Dublin. As she put it, "I'll be taking an Irish stallion as me mate one o' these days, Clayton Ernest Drake, but there's no denying the charm of a Texas bull."

Clay took the comment as a compliment. He wasn't ready yet to settle down to marriage anymore than were the women he bedded. Hard though ranching could be, and sometimes lonely, he liked his way of life.

Hell, he even liked the rambling Texas drawl of Andy, being close to his as it was, and he gave half an ear as his friend and neighbor set about recalling in detail how he'd been spending his time while his good friend was enjoying Emmeline's bed. Clay let him babble without joining in. As much as Andy resembled his talkative father, Clay took after his own. Quiet-spoken, Alexander Drake didn't dissect his adventures like a horse doctor cutting at a carcass to see what had gone wrong.

At last the long discourse drew to a close. Approaching darkness ended the harangue, not, Clay knew, any decision on Andy's part that he'd been talking too much.

They rode their separate ways, Andy to the north toward the Taylor spread and Clay toward the Whiskey ranch house. He took his time, thinking over the good work done and the tough work still to come. He had two thousand head to get ready for market. In the old days he would have been preparing for the long trail ride to Kansas; now all he needed was to make it to the railroad spur close to town.

But there were still long hours involved between the roundup and the final sale. Good hands worked for him, dependable cowmen who thought the way he did and managed ranch operations without trouble when he wasn't around, but there was nothing like joining in the work himself. He'd camped out alongside them since long before the roundup, choosing the thin bedroll to his own comfortable mattress. Except for a few line cabins, he hadn't seen the inside of a house for weeks.

By the time he made the two-mile ride, night was hard upon him, along with a winter-like bite in the air. March was a devil of a month in Texas. Right after a week of sunshine, with a thousand trees and shrubs lulled into sprouting tender shoots, storms could sweep down so strong they'd frost a man's backside if he was caught unaware on the range.

He'd already checked the pecans and mesquite to be make sure the last freeze had come and gone. Sure enough, like all the others, they, too, were in bud. It would get a mite brisk during the night, but that was all; spring was finally under way.

Strolling from the barn where he'd rubbed down, fed and watered Patches, he directed his step toward the stone house his parents had helped build thirty years before, high on a Whiskey Ranch hill. Greeting him on the front porch were a flickering lantern and his great aunt Martha. Once a schoolteacher to the Mason County children, she'd lived on the ranch since marrying Will Poston, a feisty Englishman who had moved to Texas with Alex Drake his friend and boss.

Will had died ten years ago. With Clay's parents spending so much time in England, Martha ran the house and, Clay had to admit, whatever else she could. She was nearing eighty now, her hair white and her brown eyes faded, but she was still a fine figure of a woman, straight-backed and buxom, and she could still tell Clay how to part his hair when she thought the occasion warranted.

He knew by the set of her mouth that now was such an occasion.

She stepped to the porch rail and waved a piece of paper in his direction. "Got a letter from Libby while you were gone. It came all the way from Yorkshire. Brought straight to the house. Rural free delivery, they called it. RFD, for short. Beats anything I ever heard of."

Clay felt a rush of warmth as he thought of Elizabeth Chandler Drake, the fair-haired woman who was his mother. A Texan born and bred, she'd been wooed and won by her blue-blooded Englishman after he took over his family's investment in the Whiskey. Since marrying, she'd traveled far from her country roots, from the once impoverished ranch all the way to the ballrooms of Buckingham Palace. A beauty still, she was at home no matter where she resided.

"A jewel in any setting," was the way Alex put it. Clay planned one day to find the same kind of woman for himself.

"What does she have to say?" he asked as he stepped onto the porch and gave his aunt a welcoming hug.

"She says," Martha replied with a militant light in her eyes, "that with her only son's birthday coming up and considering the Queen's Diamond Jubilee celebrations taking over the country, it's best you get on over to see her and your daddy. It seems to me, she's right."

16

Clay grinned at the way she referred to Alex Drake. He might be known as Clay's daddy around the Whiskey, but in London circles he was known as the Fourth Earl of Harrow, Baronet Trevane, and, of course, husband to the famous Lady Libby.

The Countess of Harrow had picked up the nickname the minute she hit the British shores and charmed everyone with her outspoken, friendly ways. It was a name still used in the two countries she called home.

As for himself, Clay had inherited the title Viscount Parkworth. It was a source of some amusement to his men, especially when he'd done something particularly undignified like step in warm manure.

Clay preferred the designation Libby had bestowed on him: the given names of his two grandfathers. He refused to consider ever being earl. That title belonged to his father.

Clay was a cowboy. It was title enough for him.

Martha took a step back and studied him. "You know, Clayton, you're looking more like Alex every day. Maybe a little taller and leaner but the same black hair and gray eyes." Her own eyes held a glint of mischief, taking ten years from her age. "Not nearly so handsome, though. Too weathered, like those boots you wear."

Clay nodded. "Whatever you say."

"Don't suppose you've had any complaints from the ladies, though."

Clay gave her a bear-hug. "None I'd tell you about," he said, thinking that Emmeline's only cross words, coming when he pulled on his pants, had been a comment concerning his leaving so soon.

Martha pushed away. "Don't try that Viscount Parkworth charm on me, Clayton. I'm immune. What took you so long to get back? Some of the boys have been in the bunkhouse since long before dark."

"Just wanted to check out a few things."

"Don't hand me that malarkey. What you wanted

was to be on the land as long as you could. Never saw anyone so taken with a place the way you are with the Whiskey. Even your mother was willing to leave, once she fell in love."

"Women do that kind of thing. Not me." Clay meant what he said. He couldn't imagine any female trapping him into staying away from Texas on a permanent basis. Only Libby could get him away at all.

He glanced at the letter in his aunt's hand and thought of the summons it contained. Libby didn't ask much of him very often. He suspected that maybe Charlotte trouble was the real reason she was writing, not birthdays or the queen.

Clay and his sister had always been close, and he'd gone to London two years ago for her wedding. The occasion hadn't been especially happy, not with Libby and the earl having a hard time hiding their displeasure with the groom and Charlotte determined to prove they were judging him wrong.

Clay tended to side with their parents. Why Charlotte had chosen that pretty-boy bounder William Rockmoor would forever be a mystery to him. He might hold an earl's title of his own—Earl of Denham—but Clay suspected it was an empty honor with no land and little capital to back it up.

In the interest of family unity, which at the time had been on the shaky side, he hadn't tried to find out for sure.

"I'll go right after the sale's done and the money's in the bank," he said.

"Libby's enough of a rancher to know when to expect you. If I thought these old bones could survive the trip—"

"Those old bones can make it as well as I can, Martha. You come with me and show the women of England how to have a good time. The way I remember 'em, they're all a mite too refined."

Martha shoved at him. "Go on with you. You'll show the women soon enough how you want them to behave."

Clay shook his head. "What I'll do is pay honor to Lady Libby and his lordship, check out the gambling tables and sister Charlotte, then get myself on home. There's not an Englishwoman alive who can make me stay longer than a couple of months."

Chapter Two

London, England
July, 1897

The night Jenna Cresswell took to the streets to try her hand at begging, she had been hiding from the London police exactly one year.

The charge against her was murder; detection and arrest would mean a trip to the gallows, but desperate times required desperate solutions. Jenna was desperate indeed.

She shifted uncomfortably on the hard pavement beside Piccadilly Circus. The location she had selected was supposed to be the best in town for begging or lifting a gentleman's wallet, or so she had heard from the talk at the Black Horse Tavern. She was beginning to think she'd heard wrong. Dressed as a beggar child and huddled as pitifully as she could manage with a single mittened hand upraised, in the past hour she'd received only a ha'penny and, in a grand gesture from a passing swell, a twopence tossed into her lap.

The night further demonstrated what she had learned all too well during the years. Money came with power; it could grant dreams and just as easily take dreams away. She saw clearly the power of the passersby, for in their decision to give or withhold a few coins rested her fate.

The realization was enough to drive a proud and

stubborn girl to dipping, as the profession of pick-pocketing was known among her current social set, though Jenna had not sunk quite that low. The act of begging was humiliation enough, a denial of all she believed about taking care of herself, of refusing to ask the uncaring wealthy for help.

And she was doing it so badly! A twopence and a ha'penny. If she were to risk roaming about the city like this, she would have to show a greater profit. Considering all her responsibilities, she simply must.

With her back against a brick wall and her head and shoulders protected by a worn shawl, Jenna watched the passing parade of feet. Some came so close they almost kicked her ragged skirt.

Maybe it was the unusually cool night that sent them scurrying like cape buffalo out of the theaters and music halls toward their various destinations . . . toward the hundred private clubs and taverns and gambling halls that clustered around Piccadilly. Wherever they were headed, it wasn't toward the poor child she pretended to be.

Jenna wasn't a child, but she was small of stature with fine features and, she had learned in the past year, people rarely questioned what was presented to them as fact. Knowing from painful experience how the deaf behaved and concealing her woman's body beneath layers of rags, even going so far as to bind her breasts tight against her body in case one of the passing gentlemen decided on a better look, she made a convincing picture.

"Move along, there!" a voice called.

Jenna's gaze darted to the bobby in the street. He had been directing traffic near the center fountain ever since she arrived, his shrill whistle cutting through the rattle and creak of the carriages rolling around him. Like a rock in a stream he was, she thought, remembering for a brief moment a far more pastoral scene in a land so far away it might as well be on the moon.

She shook off the memory. This was London, not a

farm near Pretoria. And the bobby could do her infinite harm . . . if she let him get close. That was why he was never far from her mind.

A sudden gust of wind ruffled the dark skirts of the women hurrying past, and more than one gentleman had to grab at his top hat to keep it in place. At the edge of the street a scrap of paper danced in a circle of air, then swept farther into the street, where it fell to the damp ground and was crushed beneath the wheel of a carriage.

Jenna stared at the paper, shivered, and pulled her shawl tight. The damp air was far too cool for July, she thought. July was one of the good months in London. What would January be like?

She brushed aside the question. She would be gone by then.

"Don't touch the creature!"

A woman's voice hung shrill on the late night fog, startling Jenna, and she stared at a pair of sturdily shod feet close to her skirt.

She gave a quick glance upward. The woman, clinging to a man's arm, stared back in disgust.

"Now, now, my dear, she won't bite," the man said.

A browbeaten husband, that's what he was. Jenna could tell from the tenor of his voice. She was as certain of it as she was that the pavement beneath her bottom was hard.

"Don't be too sure," the wife rejoined. "The child could easily be mad."

I'm a woman, Jenna wanted to say, *and probably the clearest thinking person on the block. At least I know the real ways of the world.*

Instead, she stared blankly at the street where the carriages flitted through the night, their lanterns sparkling like fiery insects as they moved away from the lamp-posts, and where the lone bobby hastened them on. The scrap of paper was gone from view.

"She doesn't look mad to me," the man said. "Only meant to give her a coin."

22

Holding little hope that he would actually do so now that his wife had voiced her displeasure, Jenna forced her mittened hand upward.

The woman sneered at the soiled fingers. "How filthy!" she said with a shudder. "She hasn't enough sense about her even to bathe."

I'm as clean as you are.

Indeed, the only dirty places on Jenna were the places that showed. The smudged face and hands, the rags, the cap that covered all of her red hair except for the wisps she darkened and wore masklike against her face, even the tattered shawl she wrapped about her—all were part of her disguise.

"I doubt she has access to a bath, my dear. Probably doesn't have a real home."

Jenna wanted to cheer his brave rejoinder, mild though it was.

The woman gripped the closure of her velvet mantle. "Then it can go to a workhouse if there's need for money. No telling what kind of disease it's carrying. Lice, too, if you inspected close enough." Her shudder was visible. "Shouldn't be allowed out where decent folk walk."

She looked away in disgust and trained her gaze past the carriages and the bobby and onto the flower sellers at the base of the fountain. "Whores," she said.

"Eh, what?" Her husband followed her stare. "Ah," he said, studying the seated female shapes with the baskets of flowers in their laps. Soaring into the night sky from the center of the fountain was the column that bore the statue of Eros. On this night the statue was barely visible in the gaslight drifting upward into the fog.

He made no attempt to argue with his wife's judgment. Thrusting a shilling into Jenna's waiting palm, he said, "I'll hail a cab and we can go on home. Damned night too chilled to walk about after the theater." So saying, he turned up the velvet collar of his coat until it met the brim of his top hat. He gave a sec-

23

ond, studied look to the flower sellers and, wife on his arm, he passed into the throng.

Jenna tested the coin with her teeth and dropped it into the pouch strapped to her waist. If she could find a taker, she'd be willing to bet its full value that her benefactor would be back before long, only this time he'd be spending his money on more carnal pursuits.

She knew the ways of the world, all right, and she had caught the hungry look in the man's eyes.

Once again she took up staring at the passing feet. She ought to leave right now. She wanted to, more than anything else. She wanted to stand as tall as her five-feet-two would allow her, to declare to all that she, too, was a human being with a voice and with a mind. It was only the memory of two pairs of round, trusting eyes staring up at her that had kept her at her post.

That—and the image of a gallows which would not leave her mind.

It had been a long time since she had done what she wanted to do. She wondered if she ever would again.

Half an hour, she told herself, or as close as she could judge it. Right now it seemed an eternity. Still, she would remain, she would make herself look as pitiful as possible, and she would take what she could.

Then she would hie herself to the disreputable tavern she called home. Allowing another quarter hour to get back, she would already be pushing her luck.

She couldn't let it get to her. If she had proven anything in the past year, it was that she could survive in the worst of circumstances and still not lose touch with that inner part of her being which she considered her true self.

The reverend would have called it her soul.

If she managed to escape the predicament in which she was trapped, she swore never, never, *never* to pass an indigent, no matter the age or sex, without leaving some kind of coin.

No—not *if* she escaped; it was *when*.

Five minutes passed, but the only interest she

24

aroused came from a buff-colored dog with prominent ribs and big brown eyes. She never should have looked into those eyes. Her hand stole out and scratched behind one floppy ear. The mutt scrunched closer, whining and wagging his tail.

A couple paused to comment on the dog, and when they departed — their money still firmly tucked out of sight — she shooed him away after them.

Jenna sighed. Animals and children. She attracted them the way she did trouble.

Just when she was about to give up for the night, another couple came to a halt in front of her. This time it was the woman who spoke kindly. "William, look, a child. She needs help."

The voice was soft, cultured. *Aristocracy for sure,* Jenna thought, although there was, beneath the rounded vowels, the hint of an accent she couldn't quite place.

"There must be a thousand of them within a few blocks of here," William responded. "We can't feed them all, Charlotte."

Jenna took immediate dislike to the man.

"But it's cold," Charlotte persisted. "And I'm not trying to feed and clothe a thousand children. Just this one." She knelt on the pavement, ignoring the snort of disgust from the man.

"I've married a Whig, that's what I've done," he said. "You've simply no understanding of money."

His wife ignored him. "Child," she said softly. "Look at me."

Jenna held still, huddled deep in her pile of rags, her open palm held motionless in the air.

"Child."

Jenna gave no response.

"I'm not certain she can hear me." The woman reached for the shawl covering Jenna's head.

"No, Charlotte, I will not have it. There's no telling what you'll come down with." Pulling her to her feet, he reached into his pocket and pulled out a coin. "If

25

you insist, I'll give the little bastard this."

"A shilling?"

"Would you have me give it a crown?"

The question was met with silence. Slowly lifting her eyes, Jenna watched curiously as the finely dressed man glared at his equally finely dressed and beautiful, fair-haired wife. The wife returned the stare without so much as a blink. It was the husband who looked away first.

"Oh, all right," he said and, fumbling in his trouser pocket, thrust a gold coin into the upstretched palm. "Now, I insist we leave. Your brother is expected back at the house anytime. If he's not carousing again half the night."

The woman's response was lost in the high-pitched laughter of a passing harlot, and like the first couple, William and Charlotte disappeared into the crowded night.

Beneath her protective rags, Jenna smiled. A crown. It was a royal fortune. Charlotte was one of the kind ones, a true gentlewoman who gave from the heart. Would there were more of her kind.

Jenna fingered the crown. Deciding she had taken in enough to make a couple of stops on the way home, she stood, careful to keep the shawl and layers of rags about her face and body. Though usually nimble she took a few seconds to stretch the kinks out of her muscles. Even so short a delay worried her. She must hurry back to the tavern. She would be missed.

Like an animal born to the city, she darted through the crowd, down alleyways and streets, narrowly avoiding a collision with a muck cart making its rounds. Once she had to jump out of the path of a motorized wagon—automobiles, they were called. Noisy, smoky beasts in her opinion, and by far too dangerously fast. They would never catch on, she was sure.

She made her way in the general direction of Shaftesbury Avenue, Charing Cross, and at last the edge of the once-infamous Seven Dials. Recent construction had cleaned up the worst of the slum area, but there was still poverty enough in its twisted streets to break the heart of anyone who cared.

The trouble was, no one really did, just as no one paid any attention to her midnight scurrying. Beggars — children and adults alike — were a common sight on the London streets, especially late at night when the upper classes came out to play.

Some of the latter even made it to the Black Horse Tavern. They liked to visit the slums — or at least the edges of them — as though they were on an adventure-seeking safari, with the Dials substituting for the more exotic climes of Africa.

They ought to try living in this part of the city, try breathing in the sour, fetid air that no reconstruction would cleanse. It came from unwashed bodies and stale brew, from desperation and poverty which possessed a stench all its own. Burning Seven Dials to the ground would not remove the smell.

Jenna made her first stop at a Shaftesbury stall, gesturing that she wanted a couple of meat pies, thrusting the shilling into the seller's waiting hand and carefully counting her change. The purchase took less than a minute; not a word had been said.

Her second stop was a run-down lodging house two blocks from the Black Horse. Quickly she climbed the front stoop, raced silently down the hallway and up another flight of stairs, then came to a stop before the last door on the right. She had to move in the dark, since the landlord had declined to provide his tenants light.

She gave the special knock — three quick raps, a pause, then two more. She wasn't absolutely certain the precaution was necessary, but the children took great pleasure in having such a secret to share.

The door creaked open to reveal the solemn faces of Alice and Alfred, as the children were called. Barely six years of age, both fair haired and blue eyed, they were far too thin for Jenna's peace of mind.

27

Nodding in unison, a signal that their father was not yet home, they stepped aside and allowed Jenna to enter. She closed the door firmly behind her.

The apartment, lit by a single lantern, consisted of one small room with a far smaller bathroom at the back. Jenna considered it a miracle that running water was available at all.

The living quarters contained one bed. A pile of blankets in one corner served as a pallet for the twins. Jenna had taught the children the rudiments of keeping their home clean; if their father had ever made mention of their efforts, they had not said.

She doubted that he had noticed. A solemn man she had seen only from a distance, he worked as a street juggler around Covent Garden. The twins said that long ago he had been an actor on the stage. Their mother, an actress, had died from a fever, and the father had developed a thirst. When he wasn't at work, he was drinking. Never at the Black Horse, since he couldn't afford even the low prices Hector Mims, the owner charged. Instead, he got his own bottle, which he consumed sometimes on the streets, sometimes at home.

He went by the name of Morgan — Morgan the Juggler. His primary strength as a parent was that he did not beat his children. But he didn't feed them very well, nor see to their education. It was Jenna's nature to take up where he'd left off, and she brought them whatever scraps that she could. As food for their minds, she had begun telling them tales of adventure; as balm to their souls, she had shown them a tenderness they might otherwise have never known.

By example she taught them to speak well, for she knew, as well as she knew anything, that it was their dropped *h*'s and unique vocabulary which revealed their lower-class status more certainly than did their rags.

In return, when the father was gone, Jenna used the small bathroom to wash her body and her hair. Surrounded by filth, she had become more conscious of her own personal cleanliness than ever before . . . so much that it became almost an obsession. The twins thought she was a little silly to bathe so often or to notice when dirt accumulated on their own floor.

It had become a joke between them, this penchant for water, and, when she could appropriate some from the tavern, this insistence on soap.

In truth, Jenna owed them her life. They had been the ones to find her on that rash flight from the law. She'd been hiding in an alley, the damp midnight air chilling her bones, her mind unable to comprehend the horror of her situation . . . the falling of the body, the whispered advice that she get away fast, the frantic dash into the Dials.

That they had found her on their late-night perambulations was a miracle; along with Hector Mims, they were Jenna's family, the only one she had in the world, and she loved them with all her heart. They kept her in the Dials, but Jenna knew that with recent events she must take them away, and soon.

"Is something wrong?" asked Alice, her eyes trained on Jenna's face.

"She'll tell us if there is," explained Alfred with lofty understanding.

Jenna knelt on the floor in front of them and, unable to resist, threw back the protective shawl and cap covering her head. A tangle of flaming red curls rested against her shoulders, and Alice's tiny fingers reached out to touch.

The child was fascinated by the brilliant shade of red. It had taken Jenna a while to understand that for Alice, locked in a world of grays and browns and blacks, the brightness brought a welcome contrast.

"I can't stay long," she said softly. "But I've brought you something."

She pulled the paper-wrapped meat pies from a pocket in her skirt and placed one in the hands of each child.

29

"I hope you didn't stuff yourselves at supper," she said, knowing full well that they probably hadn't eaten much since morning, when she had slipped them half a loaf of bread and some cheese.

"Thank you, Jenna," said Alice.

"Thanks," said Alfred.

"Eat slowly," said Jenna, watching in dismay as the children bit hungrily into the cold pies.

"I've got to leave," she said when the last crumb had disappeared. "Wipe your hands and throw the paper in the trash."

"We know," said Alfred. When Alice threw her arms around Jenna's neck and planted a wet kiss on her cheek, he thrust out his hand. Jenna took hold and pulled him close, giving him a brief hug that he quickly returned.

This was the most affection they ever showed one another; Jenna figured that anything more would weaken them to the hard world in which they had to survive. But oh, she wanted to hug them long and hard, to kiss them and croon lullabies in their ears. Six years old they might be, and in the Dials considered ready for employment — or for training as thieves — but to Jenna they were just babies.

As she hurried downstairs to the front door, she pulled the cap back in place, tugged the dark strands of hair around her face, and covered her head with the shawl. Before going out on the stoop, she assumed the hunched position that made her look like a submissive child. It took her only a couple of minutes to make her way to the alley that ran behind the tavern.

A year ago, looking for somewhere to stay, a place of refuge close to the twins, she had watched on several successive nights as Hector Mims put out the trash in the alley behind the Horse and brought in the crates and kegs left by the deliverymen. Twice, clad in rags found in the rookery's refuse bins, she had worked up the courage to steal through the back door and peer into the establishment's main room.

At close to seven feet tall, the proprietor had towered over the patrons of the tavern. From the friendly way he welcomed them he had struck her as a kindly man, and somehow a lonely one. Perhaps he was lonely enough to take in a pitiful stray who was willing to work. The idea for her disguise had been born of despair and need; miraculously, he accepted the young deaf and dumb child who scurried in one night and began to clear the tables and clean the floor. He had even provided her a small room where she could sleep.

Strangely, she had not found the life unbearable; or at least she hadn't until six months ago when Hector married.

With the arrival of the beautiful Teresa, all things had changed. Now in the tavern she was considered not only deaf and dumb but witless as well . . . thanks to the gibes of the proprietor's new wife.

For Jenna, trouble seemed to come in bunches. Not only did she have to contend with a selfish, short-tempered woman, but—far worse for her safety—a few weeks after the wedding the police had returned. Not since those dreadful days following the tragedy had she been the object of such a search. The latest stalkers had not been in uniform like the others. They had worn gentlemen's suits and had spoken in the accents of a higher class, but they had the same questions and the same watchful eyes.

"A beauty, with red hair and green eyes," one of them said. As proof, he pulled out a circular containing a likeness of her face, and he passed it around. She recognized it as a flyer that had been widely distributed shortly after James Drury's death.

She trembled as she watched the paper make the rounds of the tables, but she could see no light of recognition cross any of the faces. That night it was to her advantage that many of the Horse's regulars drank to excess.

"Educated, too," the second policeman added. "She worked for a while as a governess. We tried the typing

31

pools and offices where so many of the gentlewomen work these days. Heard she'd tried for employment a few months back, but no luck."

Too well Jenna remembered that almost fatal attempt to find work outside the tavern. She would never try that again.

The policeman looked slowly around the room. "Anyone recognize the lass?"

"Wot's wrong, mates?" a regular had asked. "One o' the toffs huffed and yer blamin' it on 'er?"

"We are not at liberty to say," had been the response, "but she would be advised to make her whereabouts known. The trail we're following ended in these parts, and there are those that believe she never left."

They had soon gone away, leaving a card indicating where they might be reached, but Hector had tossed it into a pile of refuse before Jenna could get a close look at what it said.

Her panic had remained long after their departure. If they had looked more closely . . . if she had been found . . . she would have paid for her crime, undoubtedly with her life. She felt in her heart it was only a matter of time until they returned.

Slipping through the storage area at the back of the tavern, she tiptoed into the dark hallway and turned left into her small room. Hector and Teresa slept in larger quarters on the opposite side of the hall.

She closed the door and listened for the sound of approaching footsteps. Only the tavern noises — clinking mugs and loud voices — came to her.

There was no light in the cubicle to aid her, but she didn't need one. The bed, a thin mattress on a raised platform, was the only item of furniture. There would not have been room for anything else. Tossing her mittens and shawl onto the sheets, she reached under the bed and found the loose board she sought. Dexterous fingers lifted the plank, opened the small box hidden underneath, and thrust the night's spoils inside.

The coins joined the few she had gathered by scouring the floor of the tavern after everyone was gone; occasionally she found a forgotten bit of money, although never enough to do her much good.

The plank once more in place, she stood, fingered the strands of blackened hair to make certain they covered much of her features and straightened the loose cap hiding the clean red hair. Taking a deep breath, she hurried toward the main room of the tavern.

She entered at the end of the bar, behind which stood the hulking figure of the tavern owner. Deep in conversation with one of the regulars, he did not glance her way.

Most of the tables were taken by the denizens of Seven Dials, men and women in shabby clothes with hard and desperate casts to their eyes. There were only a handful of swells in the tavern tonight — men, not women. No self-respecting woman would be seen in the likes of the Black Horse.

Jenna knew she could never again be considered self-respecting. She didn't worry about it anymore. In the dimness she hoped only to slip to work, her absence undetected.

"Simple!"

From one of the nearby tables Teresa Mims screamed the hated name, hated all the more because the tavern roisterers had readily picked it up from Hector's beautiful, dark-haired bride.

Jenna, she wanted to scream back. *Jenna Cresswell.* But she could not. Assuming a posture of submission, she edged deeper into the room.

Chapter Three

"Simple!" Teresa repeated with a louder scream and slammed the chair beside her hard against the floor.

"She can't 'ear ye," yelled one of the customers, a swarthy man who stood across from Hector Mims at the bar.

Teresa laughed contemptuously. With a toss of her dark hair, she glanced at the man. "She knows wot I'm saying, all right. It's the chair that does the trick. She can feel the pounding with 'er feet."

In that, Teresa was right. Jenna could probably have felt the vibrations even if she wore far better shoes than the thin slippers she had found one night by scavenging through a waste bin near Grosvenor Square.

With all eyes in the tavern on her, including those of her husband, Teresa stood, smoothed the low-cut red dress over her ample bosom and narrow waist, and brought the chair down again hard, two times.

Jenna's body automatically curved in on itself, leaving her smaller in appearance than before. As she did every time she came near the new Mrs. Mims, she warned herself to keep her eyes on the floor and to keep her mouth closed. If she made any sound, it could be only an inarticulate grunt or, when the occasion warranted, a high-pitched scream.

Making a wide circle around the impatient Teresa,

she began to clear the tankards and bottles from a table near the front door. She could feel the woman's black eyes bore into her, a host of evil thoughts no doubt directed along the same smoky path, but Jenna ignored them. She could picture the scorn on Teresa's beautiful face. At least, it *could* be beautiful, if only she'd once let a kind thought translate itself into a smile.

Teresa, too, had problems. A short right leg, a legacy from birth, had left her with a lame gait. She had let it distort her view of the world. The fact that middle-aged and homely Hector Mims had taken her from the streets and made her his wife did nothing to gentle her, and neither did the way he gazed at her from time to time, his brown spaniel's eyes warmed by his love.

Teresa had, more than once the last six months, screamed that they were little more than a collection of freaks in the tavern, the hatred bubbling out of her like steam from a crock. Catching the full force of her fury, Hector did not know how to respond, but the watchful Jenna knew the hurt that his wife's ugly words brought to him. All he could do was humor Teresa's ill temper, and unfortunately, when that temper was turned on Jenna, he did not interfere. For the first half of her stay at the tavern she had looked upon him as a protector, but those days were at an end.

Hunched beside one of the tables she had begun to clear, she heard Teresa's shuffling step. She did not cower until the woman's shadow fell across her. A hand reached out and struck a half-filled tankard of ale, sending the stale brew spilling onto the floor.

"Clean it up," Teresa ordered, snapping her fingers close to Jenna's ear. Teresa often issued spoken commands, but they were given for the benefit of the men around her. It was the spilled ale that was supposed to bear the message to Jenna.

35

Feigning a snuffled cry, Jenna dropped to her knees and wiped at the ale. Despite her exaggerated servility, she could not stifle the anger inside, nor the resentment, nor the longing to rebel against this latest injustice. She knew well that rebellion was a luxury too dear for her to indulge in, at least right away, and any thoughts she gave to injustice she could not defend, even to herself.

"Look," Teresa said with a loud laugh, "the fool is good for something."

Laughter met the announcement. No one suggested what Teresa might be good for. Salacious talk concerning his wife was the one thing Hector did not allow, no matter how much she invited it. Given his size and strength, he got his way.

With Teresa standing no more than two feet away, Jenna continued her work, her purposefully childlike strokes doing little more than wiping the ale across the planks of the floor, her thoughts turned in defense to the cache under her bed. As much as she hated to consider it, perhaps another visit to Piccadilly was in order, after the tavern closed. No one cared where she spent the hours when she wasn't looked for to clean and clear. She didn't stand much chance to profit from such an excursion, but at least she would not be wasting her time in sleep.

"She's good for somethin' else, I'll wager." The crude voice came from a table in the corner. She recognized the speaker as Bertie Groat, one of the Horse's regulars, a small-time criminal, a bully and frequent drunk.

When Teresa had arrived as Hector's bride, Groat started bragging to her about his petty thefts, the pickpocketing that gave him coins for drink, the occasional burglary of which he was most proud. Jenna wasn't supposed to hear. But she did, and she remembered.

"Ye want 'er, Bertie?" Teresa shouted out. "Ye

can 'ave 'er!"

"I c'n do better than the likes o' a moron," Groat protested. "I was thinking o' me mate 'ere." He gestured to the man beside him. Slack-jawed, thicklipped, a sloping forehead protruding above his dull eyes, the man grinned back at Groat.

Jenna drew her body and breath inward, wishing she was not only deaf and dumb but also invisible. The fact that she was supposed to be a retarded child would not protect her from the likes of Groat's drinking companion. Usually Teresa was content to ridicule her and drive her to long hours of work. Tonight's suggestion that the pitiful creature who cleaned the tables and slop jars might also provide sex for the customers sent chills of apprehension shuddering through her.

A quick glance at the nearest table revealed a pair of young men in formal dress. Typical swells bent on slumming, she thought in disgust, well into their cups. The slump of their shoulders and the glazed look in their eyes gave evidence she could expect no help from them.

Teresa grabbed out for her. "Let 'im give 'er a try."

Relying on her own skills, Jenna quickly dodged and set up a wail. Even the deaf, she well knew, could make such a defensive noise.

"Shut the brat up," Groat yelled from across the room.

Jenna shuffled toward the bar. Teresa lofted a threatening hand and came after her, the uneven gait more pronounced than ever as she skirted around the tables. With voice raised to an unearthly pitch, Jenna scrambled through the open doorway, down the narrow, darkened hallway, and into the inadequate sanctity of her room.

The door would not lock. Anyone wishing entry would have it soon enough. She thought about the larger room across the hall. To hide there and be discovered would bring a beating and, if Teresa chose to flail her bare skin, her disguise would be discovered.

Teresa was very protective of the room she shared with her husband. Sometimes at night Jenna could detect the sounds of their lovemaking and, often, the ugliness of Teresa's derisive laughter.

Jenna knew what was going on, having averted her eyes from copulations more than once on her night scurryings between the twins' lodging and the Horse. She shuddered at the thought of Bertie Groat's cretin companion coming after her.

From beneath the thin mattress she pulled a knife and slipped it into a pocket of her tattered skirt, then checked to make sure that her breasts were still adequately bound. Good enough, she decided. It would take more than a watchful man to pick out the curves of her body. It would take a personal inspection by hand, and that she would never allow.

Grabbing up the shawl, she wrapped it about her head and shoulders and retreated through the back storage room and into the alley. She made her way quickly toward the lighted street. Her destination had almost been reached when a hulking figure suddenly blocked her way. It was the cretin, so close she could have touched him. A stupid grin split his slack face as he stared down at her. He looked incapable of having found her on his own. He had been sent to the alley. Teresa knew her far too well.

He took a lumbering step toward her. Jenna edged backward, her right hand slipping inside her pocket and curling around the wooden handle of the knife. She had never used it but had known that some day, when crying out would do her little good, she might have to wield it in self defense.

He lunged forward just as she pulled the weapon free. Nimbly stepping aside, she plunged the blade into her attacker's arm, then, with a strength born of necessity, jerked it free.

A shudder raked through her as blood spurted from the wound, covering the knife and her hand, its liquid warmth driving deep into her consciousness the horror of what she had done.

The man cried out in pain and astonishment. Before she could retreat, he grabbed her with one of his huge hands and shook her as he might a doll. The knife fell to the ground close by, landing with a soft, unheeded thud. She was swept with a sense of utter helplessness.

Throwing her against the side of the building housing the tavern, he shoved his full weight against her. Jenna fought against gagging. Rank from accumulated sweat and urine, he smelled worse than all the slop jars she had emptied in the past year, and his breath was strong enough to crack the bricks digging into her back.

Unmindful of his wound, he ground his body against hers. Both hands roamed at will over her bound breasts and he grunted in displeasure, his satisfaction impeded by the flatness that met his probing fingers. He came to her small waist and rounded hips, and his coarse features shifted into an ugly leer.

When his paws groped the fullness of her buttocks, Jenna sank her teeth into shirt and flabby chest until she drew blood, ignoring the foul taste and smell that ravaged her senses and drew bile into her throat.

Surprised by the pain, the cretin lessened the pressure of his bulk, and she was able to free her arms. Her small, tight fists flailed at the fresh cut, sending more and more blood spurting down his sleeve and onto her own rags. At last he gave thought to the wound. With a roar of rage, he pulled away from the damaging hands.

Quick as a cat, Jenna threw herself onto the ground, scooped up the knife and, half crouching, waved it about in threatening gestures that even her

39

stupid assailant could understand, steeling herself against the memory of the first knife thrust that had found its target. If she must use the weapon again, she would.

A clumsy creature, he tripped over his own feet as he sought to get away from the victim-turned-attacker. He fell backward, his head striking the corner of the brick building on the far side of the alley, and he crumpled to the ground. Staring at the inert mass, Jenna took several deep breaths. A wave of dizziness overtook her as again and again the sound of his head hitting the brick echoed in her mind. Try as she might, she couldn't get it to go away.

Her mind traveled far from the alley back in time . . . to the different world where she had briefly dwelled. Gone were the brick walls and trash-strewn ground and the foul smell; in their place she saw a paneled withdrawing room, parted draperies of green velvet, and the flames of a fresh-lit fire.

So real was the room to her that she could smell the acrid smoke from the grate and the roses that grew outside the open window. For all its fine fittings, the second, imagined scene brought her as much pain as the harsh reality of the first.

In despair, she gazed about her at the dark, damp alley. Would she never forget?

She must. Jenna's ability to survive was too carefully honed for her to stand helpless with no thought of escape. For the time being, the cretin offered no threat to her safety. That was the only thing she must consider. Not the past. Only now.

Driven by panic, she fled the tavern to get away from the lusting brute, but with him lying unconscious at her feet, she knew she must return. To delay would be to raise Teresa's ire all the more. The beating — and disrobement — would become an even stronger possibility. Only submission and meekness had saved her thus far from such a fate. She would

40

call upon them again.

With any luck her attacker would awaken with little memory of what had happened or, ashamed that she had bested him, skulk away in the dark to attend his wound.

His wound—the wound that she had given him. She relived plunging the knife into his arm; again the warm blood spurted forth, only this time it flowed like a hellish river over her hand.

Jenna fought back a rare rush of tears as she hurried once again through the tavern's back door. Tears were signs of self-pity, a weakening emotion that served no purpose. Thoughts tumbled in her head . . . what to do . . . what to do.

First she must remove the blood. For that she used the precious drinking water that Hector kept in a small kitchen next to the storage room. Working in the dark, she tore off her outer clothes and dipped the cup into the barrel. She splashed the water over her hands and arms, again and again, unmindful of the puddles she was leaving on the floor.

When she could no longer imagine the red stains on her skin, she used her clothes to wipe up the water at her feet. She would see to cleaning the rags later. Wrapping them about the knife, she returned to the storage room and hid the small bundle in a dark corner behind a keg of ale. If it became necessary, she planned a complete denial of the stabbing—a shaking of her head, a whimper, maybe a piercing scream to show she didn't know what her accusers were talking about. It was to her benefit that the attacker was in actuality as addled as she pretended to be.

A sudden thought came out of nowhere and plunged her close to despair. If the knife had gone past his arm, she might have stabbed him in the chest. She might have killed—again. It mattered not that neither time was there a choice, much less a will to take a human life.

What had she ever done—she who loved children and books and open clean air—what had she done to bring about the terrible fate that sent her to Seven Dials?

She had no answer. Hurrying to her room, she slipped into another of her shapeless garments, a tattered black dress she had pulled from a barrel of garbage in one of the more respectable alleys near Piccadilly. No one would notice the different clothes. Not for the first time she was glad that few paid much attention to what she was really like.

Reaching up to adjust the cap, she felt a stab of pain across her back. The force with which the cretin had shoved her against the brick wall of the alley must have left bruises; she feared she would be sore for days.

So be it. A few aches were the least of her worries.

Hurrying down the dark hallway, she tried to recapture the warm feelings that had comforted her at Piccadilly when the beautiful woman named Charlotte stopped to give her help.

The feelings were gone.

She halted in the doorway to the tavern's main room, which was back to its usual late-night revelry. Teresa, sitting at a table with three grizzled and roughly dressed men who came in on occasion, did not give Jenna so much as a glance. Even Groat, who had turned his brutish companion on her, was closely engaged in conversation with one of the regulars. It was Hector behind the bar who presented her with a welcome smile.

With all the turmoil inside her, she could barely believe the peaceful scene. As much as she wanted to be ignored, she felt a foolish hurt that no one except Hector was glad she had returned to the Horse unharmed.

Grabbing a rag from a bucket near her feet, she

scurried out to earn her keep. Before she could move completely from the shadows at the back of the room, she spied a figure in the door. Her breath caught. Surely it couldn't be the cretin revived so soon.

She let out a low sigh as she realized the newcomer was a dandy, his formal coat and trousers immaculate, a top hat in his hands, his eyes frostily assessing as they moved about the tavern. A typical curiosity seeker, she decided, perhaps a rake who sought a woman for hire. A member of the wealthy class looking to flaunt his power over the poor.

To Jenna, he looked a little weak-chinned and doughy and she had already started to look away when he stepped aside. The man behind him was a different matter indeed.

He stood tall, not so much as Hector, but with infinitely more grace of carriage. Instead of formal evening dress, he wore a simple coat and open-throated shirt, both a rich brown, and trousers that fit his long legs like a second skin. His head was uncovered to reveal thick, black curls of hair; his face was clean-shaven, his skin burnished by what had to be a strong and very un-Englishlike sun.

He wasn't handsome—not in the refined way considered the standard of physical attractiveness for English men. His face was too strong, his features too rugged, his skin too weathered.

Striding into the tavern, he moved surely, with authority and with an angular grace she had never seen before. Like his companion, he let his eyes drift around the room. She caught no sign of frostiness or scorn, but rather an open curiosity, a hint of friendliness as though he considered himself no better than anyone else.

No, he did not look like any member of the gentry she had ever seen.

He did not see Jenna in the protective shadows,

for which she was grateful. She would have had to look away, to take up once again her pretense of withdrawal from the world.

For the time being she much preferred to study him directly. To her mind, the stranger was the most fascinating man she had ever seen.

Chapter Four

Jenna stood transfixed and drank in the sight of the stranger. Her reactions were a mystery to her—a weakening of the knees as though the ground were dropping from under her . . . a churning in the pit of her stomach . . . an inability to breath.

Years ago on her father's Transvaal farm, she had fallen into an abandoned well and experienced much the same rush of sensation on the free-falling descent. As a five-year-old, she had found the experience terrifying. As a grown woman, she did not want the moment to end, even knowing as she did that her inability to think clearly presented as much danger to her as the well.

Accepting the folly of her behavior, she could not look away.

Unfortunately, she was not the only one intrigued by his presence.

"Welcome to the Black 'orse, gentlemen," said Teresa with a flourish of her hand. She was a dozen feet from them, standing beside the table where she had been seated moments before, and she flashed a smile to the new arrivals. Leaning down so that her dress gaped and exposed the full roundness of her breasts, she spoke in low, determined whispers to the three men who had been her drinking companions. Whatever she said, it worked as she must have wanted, for they scattered about the room, taking with them their tankards of ale and stout, as well as their scowls.

Jenna wasn't surprised at the quickness of their response. Many of the men frequenting the Horse did as the proprietor's wife bid, especially when she leaned in front of them and gave them a free view of her charms. Not too long ago, she would have charged a fee for the same.

"Over 'ere," Teresa said, again smiling at the newcomers, adding special brilliance for the dark-haired one in brown. She turned, her sharp eyes darting about like a hungry animal's before settling on Jenna at the back of the room.

"Simple," she commanded over the noise, "get over 'ere and clean up fer th' gentlemen."

"Yer needs t' slam the chair," someone yelled.

"She knows right well wot I want," said Teresa, her voice loud and hard with an ugliness that had not been in her welcome.

I know, all right. You want the man.

Jenna lowered her head and slumped into her usual submissive stance, although the idea of accepting Teresa's abuse under the watchful eye of the stranger loomed as more than she should be required to bear. Purposefully she ignored the order, instead twisting the cleaning rag around and around one hand as though she were lost in thought, as she most definitely was. She was thinking desperately about how she might get away again.

When Teresa snapped her fingers and slammed a chair against the floor, Jenna bitterly accepted the inevitable. If she failed to respond to the summons, she would only call more attention to herself than was wise. To run this time against direct orders from the Queen of the Horse could easily bring one of her minions in quick pursuit.

Hunched in a half stand, her eyes downward, her

face grim behind the veil of hair, she took a circui-
tous route across the dim and crowded room in
Teresa's general direction. By the time she arrived at
the dreaded destination, she could feel the woman's
fury as though it were a blazing fire. She wondered
how long it could be kept under control.

Slapping the rag on the table, she wiped at the
spilled brew left by the departed men. The dangerous sense of rebellion returned. Pulling out one of
the chairs for the stranger, she fought the temptation to slam it down on Teresa's foot.

As things worked out, Teresa did the dirty deed
for her when she pushed her way around the table,
giving Jenna little time to pull the chair out of her
path. The tip of one leg caught Teresa on the in-
step. Before she could stop herself, she let loose a
string of obscenities, and for the duration of the di-
atribe the air of the Black Horse turned blue.

With a glare that promised Jenna impending
doom—and sent her seeking refuge under a nearby
table—the ill-tempered woman shifted her attention
back to the men. The forced smile she presented
seemed as painted on her face as the rouge and
kohl she always wore. With deliberate slowness she
smoothed the red dress over her breasts and settled
her hands on her hips.

Knowing exactly what Teresa was doing—it was
what she always did when an interesting man entered—Jenna quickly peered out to check on the
lone occupant of the table under which she had se-
questered herself. Old Jack, it was, one of the regulars, who was staring fixedly at a glass of ale, no
more aware of her than he was of the nails in the
floor. He'd be staring that way until Hector showed
him the door at closing time.

Good, she thought. She could stay right
where she was and look and listen without being

observed herself.

She gave her attention to the visitor in brown. He was openly studying the woman before him, letting his eyes roam at will. Near Hyde Park, Jenna had seen men study horses much the same way. She was certain he did not seem particularly impressed, not with the tawny skin, nor the black tresses, nor even the dark, smoldering eyes, but she admitted to a prejudice in reaching that conclusion.

Self consciously she tugged at her cap, experiencing one of the rare occasions when she wished she could appear as herself, with her red hair clean and shining and resting against her shoulders, with her green eyes looking boldly around instead of directed toward the floor, with her clothes fitted and fine the way she sometimes pictured them in her mind.

She was, after all, a grown woman and not, she thought, an unattractive one. She was certainly not without a sense of pride.

But like rebellion, pride was a luxury which she could not afford.

Teresa turned toward the bar. " 'ector," she called imperiously, "could we have some brandy for the gentlemen?"

Now *that* was putting on airs. If Teresa called for anything, it was usually ale or, on occasion, a glass of gin.

Hector's coarse features were furrowed into a frown, but he did as his wife bid, grabbing up a pair of glasses and the best, albeit run-of-the-mill, brandy that the Black Horse could offer. When he moved among the tables in the direction of his wife, the floor shook.

Jenna could not help but look upon the giant with affection. He might not protect her from his wrathful wife, but she remembered well that when he had no real reason to do so, he had taken

48

her in from the streets.

She had worked hard for him, and would continue to do so as long as she stayed, but she wished him a better wife.

Teresa ordered that the glasses and brandy be deposited on the table and waved her husband away. Shifting her chair close to her intended flirt of the evening, she pressed her breasts against his arm and smiled into his eyes. The glow from the gaslights on the wall caught in her shoulder-length hair.

Teresa *was* beautiful. A feeling close to jealousy ate at Jenna, and she had to warn herself against such foolishness. She was here to watch the show that was being enacted in front of her, not become personally involved. The stranger was as fascinating as anyone who had ever strolled in for a drink, but a stranger he would remain. The best she could hope for was that he would teach a certain dark-eyed wench she could not entrance every man that she met.

"Clay," said the second man, "you've done it again."

Clay. Jenna said the name several times to herself, then repeated her own, as if in the doing, she was introducing herself to him.

Again she reminded herself this was only a show.

Teresa rubbed against Clay's arms as she reached for the bottle and filled the glasses.

Clay winked at his friend. "I'm here for a few cold ones. Nothing more."

Now *there* was an accent to consider. Definitely American, and definitely west of the Mississippi, but Jenna couldn't get any closer than that. She prided herself on her ability to pick out accents, even of foreigners. It was one of the skills she had perfected in the years before the Black Horse; it came from listening very closely.

She believed she could listen for hours to the drawled words and rich, deep timbre of the stranger's tone. Like his appearance, his voice did not disappoint.

Her place on the floor was perfect for eavesdropping. She realized with a start she was leaning against Old Jack's leg. He must, she decided, be inebriated down to his toes.

For once, fate had given her a good turn by providing her the spot. With the American facing in her direction, not only could she hear everything he said, she could also watch the bend of his head, the flash of his eye, the curve of his mouth when he talked. She had yet to see him smile, yet she could see the light of humor in his eyes. What would his laugh be like?

Deep and rolling, with nothing held back, that's the way. Not the insipid snicker of a gentleman, nor the coarse roar of a Bertie Groat.

"Cheers," his companion said, lifting his glass.

"Same to you," responded Clay.

She watched the tilt of his head as he threw back the brandy, saw the working of his throat as he swallowed, saw the slight grimace as he caught the full, bitter flavor of the second-rate liquor. He was a man who had tasted better, but instinct told her he was also a man who would not complain.

If he would only belch or scratch his privates or do one of the thousand crude things she'd grown used to seeing in the Horse, she could tell herself he was not perfect. Thus far, he'd done nothing that took away from the picture he presented when he first stood in the door.

"Clay"—Teresa, too, had been quick to pick up his name—"I've not seen ye in the Black 'orse afore."

"It's way off my regular path, Miss—"

Mrs. Mims.

"Teresa," the tavern owner's wife responded in a purr. " 'at'll do." She was sitting now with her arms folded on the table, her breasts resting against them — propped up by them, in actuality, making the fullness all the more apparent.

Clay nodded. "Teresa it is."

"Where might this 'regular path' be?" she asked.

"Texas."

Teresa frowned. "That's a wild country, ain't it? Someplace o'er the ocean."

It's a part of the States, Mrs. Mims.

Clay's eyes drifted around the Black Tavern, picked out a few of the more unsavory men and, more closely, the slatternly dressed women accompanying them. What would he think if he could hear the conversations as Jenna was often able to? With only a deaf, slow-witted child nearby, the tavern's denizens frequently spoke of their nefarious activities — bragged about them, about the crimes they had committed and the ones that they planned. Small-time crooks they were, for the most part, but to hear them tell it, they were all involved in great derring-do.

Especially Bertie Groat. From her position, she had to shift slightly to see him. His greasy head was still bent close to another denizen of the Dials. She could almost hear the conversation, dominated by Groat's gruff voice describing the great exploits he planned . . . the property he would steal . . . the people he would hurt.

As if Clay could read her thoughts, he let his wandering gaze linger on Groat, on the flat, scarred face and the mean look in the criminal's black pig eyes. For a moment Groat stared back at him. When Clay did not waver, he was the first to look away.

51

Clay turned to Teresa. "Texas isn't so wild. Just free-spirited with wide, open spaces where a man can let himself go."

He made it sound rather like her homeland near the tip of Africa. Having left there at such a young age, Jenna was always surprised that she could remember it as well as she did.

She felt the vibrations in the floor before she actually saw Hector coming toward the table. He moved slowly, his arms like tree trunks at his side, his uneven pace ending only when he stood close to his wife.

Teresa frowned.

Idly Clay looked up at the man. "Evening," he said.

"Good evenin', sir. Thought t' check on the brandy," said Hector, his voice rumbling out of his broad chest. " 'ector Mims, at yer service. Owner and proprietor. I don't stock the best, not what ye gentlemen is used to."

"The brandy is fine," answered Clay's companion, who had been contenting himself with several glasses to Clay's one.

"Ye've other customers to see to," said Teresa with impatience, attempting to wave him away.

For once, Hector was not to be ordered about, not right away.

"Wife," he said with great emphasis, "ye speak the truth."

A flick of Clay's eyes told Jenna he caught the tavern owner's meaning.

As did Teresa, who shot her husband a look of such hatred that even Jenna, long inured to the woman's temper, was taken by surprise.

Not so Hector, who kept his attention on Clay and thus missed the glare so carefully directed by his wife. "I'll take care of yer needs, gentlemen," he said, "as they arise."

When he turned away, Jenna wanted to cheer his adroit handling of the threat presented by the intriguing Texan. Clay would not know, as did the regulars, that Teresa was off limits, no matter how much she might wish otherwise.

"So your husband owns the Black Horse, does he?" asked Clay.

"Forget 'im."

"Sorry, ma'am." He shrugged. "Can't manage that."

Jenna hid a smile. She also took note of a pleasant warmth curling inside.

A flush of anger brought added color to Teresa's painted cheeks, but she had no ready comeback. As she frequently did when frustrated, she turned her wrath to the one person she knew would not fight back.

"Simple!" she yelled.

Muttering to herself one of Teresa's favorite oaths, Jenna jerked away from Old Jack's supporting leg and began to rub at the floor beside her, as though she'd been doing it for the past half hour. At the same time she considered how to respond. A cry of rage from the open doorway to the street narrowed the number of choices available, cutting off as it did that avenue of escape.

The slow-witted attacker from the alley stood just inside the Horse, his wounded arm held close to his side, his coarse features reddened by fury.

"Simple!" he roared. "I want!"

Hector moved toward the door at twice the pace that had taken him to his wife's side, placing his huge body squarely in front of the enraged bully. "She's but a child. Leave 'er alone."

"She ain't no child." The brute raised his wounded arm, and all eyes in the tavern rested for a minute on the blood-stained rip in the sleeve. "She tried t' kill me."

Jenna trembled. It took all of her self control to continue rubbing at the floor. She was stupid. She was deaf. She could not know the danger close by, could not realize that the one man who threatened her safety was the one man as large and physically strong as the defending Hector who stood in his way.

She shouldn't have taken the knife . . . shouldn't have tried to ward off his attack. But if she had not done so, she would be lying in the alley, raped, beaten, perhaps dead or close to it. For the first time since the two policemen had shown up unexpectedly, she was close to panic, close to speaking out in defense of herself.

Something made her shift her head and she saw Clay staring down at her. For an instant their eyes met; she read speculation and interest as clearly as if he had written them on a slate. She very much hoped he could not read the jolt that the shared look had given her. At that moment she did not feel at all like a child.

Hurriedly she dropped her gaze, her body shrinking deeper into the loose, tattered folds of her dress.

Teresa stood, hands on hips, and glared at her husband. "Let 'im have 'er. She ain't much good t' us."

The attacker's wild eyes sought out his friend Groat and found him sitting at the same table they had shared an hour ago. "She got me wi' a knife," he said.

"You're a fool, Badger," Groat growled. "Simple's only a child."

"Ain't so!" Badger's voice again rose to a roar. "I felt 'er meself."

Jenna had to do something. Edging from under the table, she began to creep toward the back exit of the tavern, her eyes cast downward, her body hunched. She reached the end of the bar and hesitated.

"There she is!"

Badger's roar filled the tavern. Forgetting she was not supposed to hear, Jenna whirled to the noise and saw Badger coming after her. Hector threw up an arm, but the brute caught him on the chin with a lucky punch. He stumbled backward, landing full length across a crowded table, and sent it crashing to the floor, his huge torso lying in the broken wood and shattered glass.

A dozen voices sounded out, some yelling curses at Badger, others encouraging him in his quest.

Like an enraged bear, Badger kept coming, knocking tables and chairs aside, everyone in his path scurrying out of the way. Everyone except Clay. He stood his ground between Jenna and the brute who wanted nothing less than to crush away her life.

The trouble was that the Texan, too, would suffer, and Jenna heard herself cry out, "No!" It was the first word she had uttered in the Black Horse, but in the noise and confusion it went unheard.

As tall as he was, the Texan was no match in size and strength to the maniacal Badger. But such things didn't matter so much when a man was also smarter, Jenna realized, as she saw him step out of the brute's way at the last second, lift a chair and bring it down hard against the back of his head.

Badger halted, swayed, and slowly turned. Clay got him with a right fist to the jaw. Like falling timber, Badger landed with a crash against the tavern floor. As the dust settled, a cheer went up, Black Horse regulars preferring a winner to all else. If there had been time, they would have been laying wagers as to which of the two would remain upright.

The Texan brushed his hands, giving every appearance of one who did this sort of thing every day.

Jenna leaned against the bar in relief. Clay's companion stared in bleary-eyed appreciation, and even Teresa seemed inclined to forgive him for his rejection as she stepped over the fallen Badger, her limp unnoticeable, and brushed a kiss against the victor's cheek.

"See to your husband," Clay said with no more than a glance in her direction, and she backed away, her scowl darker than ever at the public treatment of her.

"Simple!" she screamed. "Where is the fool?"

It seemed to Jenna that all eyes, English and Texan, shifted to the back of the tavern where she stood. Her mind raced. If she turned and scurried out like a frightened rat, someone would run after her and drag her back.

Teresa stared at her with seething hatred. "It's yer fault, fool," she yelled. "Clean up this mess or I'll give ye to 'im when 'e comes to."

Jenna did not doubt her word, and she fought against rising rebellion and panic. She looked quickly around the room. Fearing that the bobbies might be summoned, half the crowd had slipped out the front door, including Bertie Groat. The other half, a more sanguine lot, had already returned to their drink.

Hector, helped to his feet by a pair of burly men, was shaking his head slowly, his eyes too unfocused to see what was going on. As far as Jenna could tell, Old Jack had not moved.

Fearing the bobbies as much as did the petty

56

thieves and whores who had fled, Jenna realized her vulnerability more starkly than ever. For countless days and nights she had evaded detection, staying in the shadows, doing as she was bid, and now suddenly, thrust into the limelight as she was, she was seeing her world fall apart.

She edged toward one of the tables and lifted a fallen a chair. Shoving it under the table, she called herself a fool for ever being drawn to the stranger. He could never, not in million years, be drawn to her. If Badger hadn't come roaring in looking for her, the Texan would have been no more aware of her presence than he was of Old Jack.

For the first time in a long while she saw how truly alone she was. In all the world there was no one to help her, no one to come to her defense.

She hadn't counted on Clay.

He gestured in her direction. "Doesn't she have another name?"

"None that's known," said Teresa, dismissing her with a wave of her hand. "She's stupid. A beggar from the streets, nothing more, and a lazy one, too."

"Did you ask her who she was?"

She glanced back at Jenna. "Wouldn't do much good. She can't 'ear nor speak. Like I said, she's a fool."

"She's deaf and dumb. That doesn't make her stupid," said Clay.

Reaching for another chair, Jenna allowed herself a glance at the tall, dark-haired Texan. He was staring at her, his gray eyes warm with concern, and something tugged at her heart. She knew, without understanding how or why, that if the police came to investigate tonight's brawl, he would make sure she was not involved.

"If you have to choose a name," he said to

Teresa, "why not Child? Or Alexandra or Catherine or even Victoria? Every woman ought to be called something nice."

"She ain't a woman," Teresa growled, no longer trying to maintain a pleasant smile.

Jenna felt Clay's eyes on her once again. She could not resist looking back. His lips were solemn, but she caught a smile in his eyes. The inner warmth returned, far more forceful than before. She stared at his lips . . . she could not look away. Her hands shook so that she had to grip the edge of the table.

"She'll get there one of these days," he said. "If she's given half a chance."

What would his lips feel like on hers?

"There's one thing I'd bet a passel of money on," he continued. "She maybe can't talk, but she's not dumb. Not by a long shot."

He spoke without knowing she could hear, coming to her defense in the one area that she found the most difficult to accept, the assumption that she was not quite right in the head. No one on the streets or in the tavern had ever done such a thoughtful thing before.

Bewildered as she was by his kindness and by his presence, at that precise moment, surrounded by ugliness and danger, Jenna fell in love.

Chapter Five

Clay woke up late the next morning with a head the size and weight of a Whiskey Ranch boulder. Cheap brandy did it to him every time.

It wasn't that, having suffered similar bouts at the Longhorn through the years, he didn't know any better. The problem was that once he got settled in for a companionable drink, he tended to take what was served.

Last night's proprietor had tried to warn him. What was his name? Oh yes, Hector Mims. Tall as a tree, if Clay was remembering right, and a true gentleman, to take such care.

"I don't stock the best," Mims had said.

An understatement if Clay ever heard one, and one that hadn't done much good. He had downed one drink before the fight and, instead of saying an *adios* right away, a couple more afterward.

He was reminded of a dog he'd once owned, a slow-witted hound that went for scrap beans and fatback every chance he got, forgetting what such fare did to his system. Even the toughest cowhand stayed upwind of him until the symptoms passed.

Clay felt a little like that dog, only his downfall was bad booze instead of beans and his primary complaint lingered at the other end. Lordy, but his head hurt, and he had a dryness in the back of his throat that all the creeks of Texas couldn't wet down. He'd rather be bucked into cactus than awake to such torment.

Stretched out in an acre-sized bed at his lordship's Tunstall Square mansion, he shook his head in disgust of himself and let loose a thousand pounding hooves in his head. The disgust multiplied, and he concentrated on holding still. One thought emerged amidst the pain: at least the room was dark.

A door creaked and Clay reluctantly cocked one eye. A shaft of light cut into the darkness from the hallway, then grew to ponderous proportions.

"Good morning, Master Clayton."

Clay should have known one of Libby's servants would have the nerve to come barging in. They were always slipping up on him like coyotes on a calf. Robert was the worst. Clay had known the valet since his first visit to England, when he'd been a young boy, but he'd never seemed to get from him the kind of respect he wanted — the respect of being left alone.

"I've brought you a restorative," Robert said, closing the door behind him with unnecessary force. "It was thought that perhaps it might be welcome." He cleared his throat. "I should point out that it is five minutes of twelve."

Clay could think of a few things that he might point out, as well, such as the importance of letting a man die in peace. Since the valet had been known to have a comeback, he chose the more peaceful path of keeping quiet.

There was no firing the man or even giving him a few weeks off; he was as much a part of the mansion as the overstuffed furniture, there to serve the stream of guests flowing through however he could. Or at least that's what he claimed, and Clay hadn't been inclined to dispute him, things being tentative between them as they were.

After a couple of fractious sessions during that wedding visit two years ago, they had reached an understanding. Clay wouldn't complain when a starched collar was occasionally laid out for him, and Robert would lie low while he dressed himself. Clay figured that any man who could rope a calf from the back of a wild-haired cowpony could button his own britches.

Robert set a tray on the bedside table, then, to Clay's dismay, proceeded to open the draperies to the noonday sun.

For an Englishman, the man was downright uncivilized, a fact that Clay pointed out right away.

"Lady Charlotte thought you would need the restorative. She's in the breakfast room."

Ah, dear Baby Sister. The nickname came to him unexpectedly. He'd called her by it until she was eight, at which time she had taken aim with a slingshot to let him know she was *Charlotte*. In those days they'd explored the Whiskey together; during the next few years, filled with his own adolescent importance, he'd decided she was getting in the way.

When she reached the age of twelve and headed for school in London, he realized how much a part of the Whiskey she really was. He missed her. She had a sense of humor about her that matched his own, as well as an understanding of his feeling about the land, even though it wasn't one she shared.

Clay figured she'd need every bit of humor she could drag up to tolerate the man she had chosen as her mate. William Rockmoor, Earl of Denham. Clay still couldn't believe it, and he knew both Alex and Libby felt the same way.

Sitting up in bed, he reached for Charlotte's "restorative" on the night table. Taken in one gulp, the

61

drink had a kick like a mule; he wouldn't guess at the ingredients. A minute went by before he could catch his breath.

"Lady Charlotte thought that perhaps you would find the potion too strong," said Robert, approaching the mahogany wardrobe that stretched across the wall opposite the bed.

"You neglected to warn me," said Clay as soon as he could get his mouth and tongue working the way they should.

"I assumed, Master Clayton, that any gentleman who can rope a calf—"

"I get the picture." Clay found himself almost smiling, a prodigious change in his abilities considering his condition a moment ago. Maybe Charlotte had something after all with her liquid-cyclone approach to curing a morning-after.

"What about my brother-in-law?" asked Clay, turning to a subject more unpleasant than his aching head. "Is he downstairs, too?"

"Lord Denham is also present, I believe."

Robert had the edge of a sneer in his voice when he mentioned the newest member of the family he had served for so many years. The valet was not without good sense, Clay thought as he hauled himself out of bed.

A half hour later, dressed in open-throated shirt and trousers, he headed down the winding staircase toward the breakfast room. Often the mansion's twenty-four rooms were occupied by guests of Libby and Alex, sometimes even by the earl and his countess themselves. Right now Clay was the only resident. For all the spaciousness and comfort of the house, he preferred the simplicity of his quarters in Texas. A man could use only so much furniture at a time, and he needed no more than a couple of changes of clothes—no matter what Robert said.

Libby, too, had an opinion on the matter, as she did on most things.

"Don't be a jackass," she'd told him last week back in Yorkshire, her Texas twang only slightly modified by the years in England and her vocabulary not changed at all. "Alex and I will be down before long, and we'll be taking you to a dozen balls, the theater, the opera, and Lord knows what all. Don't forget it's the Queen's Diamond Jubilee, and you're still Viscount Parkworth, whether you want to acknowledge the title or not. You'll be needing all those clothes and maybe more."

Clay had not been completely convinced.

He'd gone to the Yorkshire ranch—they called them farms here in England—on the day he turned thirty. The event hadn't meant much to him except to push him closer to the marriage his mother was determined he would enjoy.

But it had meant a great deal to his parents. "We were having a little trouble on a point or two before you came along," Libby had said. "You settled things in both our minds."

Clay wasn't quite sure whether his birth had come before or after the ceremony that united the two in matrimony, both bride and groom being a little vague on the exact date of their anniversary. It made no difference to him, and it certainly hadn't adversely affected the love between his parents.

For all the distance that separated them, he had a great deal of respect for them both. When his father had suggested he look over an experimental herd of cattle in Hampshire, Clay readily agreed, realizing as he did that the earl not only recognized a first class woman when he saw her—even on a remote Texas ranch—but he knew cattle, too. Clay would get down to Hampshire before long.

When he found his way to the breakfast room,

William rose from the table to greet him, informing him with obvious irritation that they had been about to start their third cup of tea, the previous two having been consumed slowly while they awaited his appearance.

He ended the complaint by casting a cool eye at the clothes Robert had finally laid out for his master, beginning with the open-necked shirt and ending with the calfskin Texas-style boots. The valet had shined a year's wear off them, but he hadn't been able to remove all the scuffs.

"I do hope we haven't disturbed you too early," said William.

"We wanted to see how you are getting along," Charlotte explained, pushing back her chair and circling the table toward him. After planting a kiss on his cheek, she tilted her head back and gave him a censorious eye. "It's been a couple of days since you came to call. If you're not going to keep your engagements, Clay, you really ought to use the telephone set. Mama and Papa had it installed just for you."

"I was supposed to drop by last night, wasn't I?" he said with genuine regret, hugging her in return. Until this minute he'd forgotten all about the invitation she extended on a similar visit to Tunstall Square earlier in the week.

He'd have to break down and yank that blasted crank every now and then. Even the servants seemed proud of the thing; to Clay's way of thinking, if it ever really caught on and took to ringing all the time, it could take over a man's life.

Just a little more of civilization intruding, as Andy Taylor would point out.

"You've been sampling the night life of London, I imagine," William said with a sniff. "I told Charlotte you might not welcome visitors

64

before this afternoon."

Clay bristled. There was something about his brother-in-law that irritated him, the way a cheap saddle rubbed at a man's backside. The fact that for once William was right chapped him all the more.

"My sister is always welcome," he said with only a slight twist of the truth. She was welcome, all right, but today she shouldn't have dropped by at an hour so close to dawn.

Charlotte squeezed his hand. Clay held on, keeping her close, and studied her. Tall and slender, she was dressed in a blue gown that matched her eyes, and her golden hair was piled in several loops high on the back of her head. Perched just in front of the loops was a swirl of white felt and feathers that he supposed passed for a hat, although it didn't look nearly as practical as a Texas sunbonnet. Curls of hair framed the face that was so like their mother's.

He felt a surge of pride at Charlotte's beauty and an acknowledgment that he loved her very much.

"I'm sorry about last night," he said with sincerity. "I was on the town. With one of William's friends."

Which was the truth. He'd met him at the private club to which his brother-in-law belonged and had accepted an invitation to see "another side of London." The man had winked broadly, which Clay assumed meant women were involved. Such hadn't been the design; all they'd done was hop from tavern to tavern like a couple of thirsty jackrabbits.

He glanced at William, who was dressed in London's obligatory gray suit, high-collared shirt and wide cravat, his handsome face sporting a neatly trimmed moustache, his full head of brown hair combed into place. There was nothing about his appearance to take exception to, but Clay did so nevertheless. He couldn't bring himself to like anything about the man, including his incessant neatness.

When they were settled around the breakfast table, Clay found himself staring at a plate of kippers and eggs. He took a deep whiff, which he decided right away was a mistake. His stomach joined the protest from his head. No more cheap brandy, he vowed.

Charlotte's eyes glinted wickedly as she studied him.

"It's unfortunate, Clay, there are no calves' testicles, or whatever it is you eat at the Whiskey," she said with mock sympathy.

Her voice, rich with the long vowels of the British, had been smoothed out by her years in England, the way sandpaper smoothed out a rail. It was hard to remember she was half Texan . . . until he took into account what she said, instead of how she said it.

Charlotte, five years younger than Clay, resembled the outspoken Lady Libby in more than just looks.

"Really, Charlotte," offered her husband from across the table. "That is entirely uncalled for. Must you always descend to crudeness around your family?"

Clay caught the frown darkening his sister's face. "Bill's right," he said, trying on the role of peacemaker while at the same time using the name hated by his brother-in-law. "At least call 'em right. They're mountain oysters. Kind of disguises what they are. Surely you fry 'em up for your old man every now and then."

He was joking, but from the quiet, stark look that passed over Charlotte's face, he decided she hadn't caught what little humor there had been in

66

the remark. The starkness was gone so fast he wasn't sure he'd seen it, replaced by a sweet smile that warned she was aiming her sights for someone.

"While I might be interested in testicles in the morning, it is an interest my husband does not encourage."

For all their softness, the words hit the air like a shotgun blast. William reddened above his stiff collar, but Charlotte looked as cool as she had when Clay first walked into the room.

William opened his mouth, seemed to think better of whatever he'd planned to say, and snapped it closed again.

Clay got the message loud and clear. No sex in the morning, and it wasn't Charlotte's idea. There was definitely trouble around the Earl and Countess of Denham's household. Whatever was going on, it wasn't any of his business, and he'd best keep his mouth shut.

Pushing his breakfast plate aside, Clay reached for the tea. One swallow of the bitter brew—and a wry glance at the kippers—made him long for Martha's experienced hand over the Tunstall Square stove. He needed to get her over here for a powwow with the cook.

Still, tea was the best thing offered this morning, and in general he wasn't one to complain.

William leaned back in his chair, once again presenting the picture of a know-it-all. It hadn't taken him long to recover from his wife's slight, Clay had to concede. Either he'd had a lot of practice or he didn't much care. Disliking Bill as he did, Clay leaned toward the latter.

"I imagine you've seen quite a bit of London unfamiliar to me," William said stiffly. "Any place in particular that you would recommend?"

Clay thought of the dingy Black Horse Tavern

with its colorful inhabitants. "No place you would enjoy."

"You went with a friend of mine, you said."

Clay named him.

William's eyebrows raised a mite. "He's a bit of a bounder. Surprised he's still a member of the club. You two must have made quite a night of it, ending, I assume, with some sort of revelry."

Clay started to say that it hadn't been much, just one brief fight and not one blow landed against him. And, of course, one hellraiser of a wife, her seven-foot husband, and a ragged little pipsqueak who was obviously the object of abuse.

No one an aristocratic snob like Lord Denham would be interested in. Charlotte, however, had a great deal more heart and, he suspected, a hell of a lot more smarts. Teresa and Hector Mims would make for little more than interesting speculation if he were given to such palaver; the deaf girl was something else. She was something to get serious about.

"There was a kid last night—" he began.

"A child or a goat, Clayton?" William put in, his upper lip curled.

"Where?" asked Charlotte, ignoring her husband.

Clay decided to do the same. "At a tavern."

"In the slums, of course," said William, undaunted and scornful. "Those people have more children than they can afford and then either abandon them or drag them where they don't belong."

"She was working there," said Clay.

"A little girl. How old was she?" asked Charlotte.

"Couldn't tell," said Clay. "She was so wrapped in rags that all I could see were her face and hands. Not much of her face, either, come to think of it. Mostly just her eyes."

"Like the beggar we saw at Piccadilly," said Charlotte.

"That little brat cost me a crown," said William. Charlotte's eyes flared.

William was getting harder to ignore. Clay's fist curled to match his brother-in-law's lip, which he longed to fatten with a quick right. A brawl at the breakfast table might not do much for family relations, but at least it would shut William up.

He thought again of the pipsqueak.

"She was deaf and dumb," Clay continued.

"How sad," said Charlotte. "I wondered about ours since she didn't say anything, but she responded when I spoke."

"*Ours?* Really, Charlotte. And she most certainly did respond," said William. "You had no more mentioned giving her a coin than her hand shot out like a thief's."

Charlotte drew very still. "That was uncharitable, William."

"I'm not a particularly charitable man, but surely you know that by now. I'm also not a fool."

Clay could read the unspoken words on William's lips: *unlike my wife.* His fist tightened.

"It was only a crown," persisted Charlotte.

"Which probably went for the mother's gin—if the brat has a mother."

"Don't let it worry you," she said, head high and cheeks flushed. "It was my money. And there's plenty more of it to throw away on starving children."

William reddened. Bowing his head, he looked hard into his wife's wide eyes, his own eyes cold with anger.

"Thank you, Charlotte, for reminding me of that fact. When you are around your family, not only does your language deteriorate to the level of vulgarity, but your good sense does so as well." His lips twitched into a tight smile. "The money is now mine, as you very well know, which is a fortunate thing, since you show such poor judgment concerning how it is disbursed."

The Earl of Denham was feeling his oats this morning—or rather the oats he got from his wife's family. Things were just as Clay had suspected at the wedding. Thanks to the Earl of Harrow, William was at last well off. In saying "I do," Charlotte had made her bridegroom secure. It didn't seem to Clay that in turn he was making his bride very happy.

Clay was about to speak when William turned his frosty attention to him. "I seem to remember an engagement at the club which had slipped my mind. Quite unforgivable of me. I really must leave." He stood and gave a cool glance at his wife. "I'll summon a cab. Surely you can handle the carriage, can you not? You're so good at taking charge, my dear."

He was quickly gone, giving no one a chance to respond. Clay's inclination was to track him down in the foyer or in the fashionable square out front or in his club, if necessary, and give him a little down-home lesson in courtesy. One look at the stark eyes and whitened complexion of his sister convinced him that hanging around was the more difficult and more important choice.

Charlotte needed Clay's help—whether she wanted it or not.

"I can always shoot him," he said.

She looked at him, startled. "I beg your pardon?"

"That was a joke."

"It wasn't a very funny one."

"Maybe not. But there's no need to pretend you're happy, Charlotte. Any fool can see—"

"Enough!"

She sounded as imperial as the Queen. Clay realized he had made a mistake, forgetting as he did his sister's pride. Not that it didn't have its uses. At least it had brought color back to her cheeks.

"You can talk to me, Baby Sister," he said.

"Not if you're going to be so stupid. You assume that I cannot handle my problems. That is, if I *have* any. The trouble arose this morning because William and I do not share the same view on giving money to beggars. He believes it encourages them, that it keeps them from applying to the appropriate charitable organizations for help."

"What are these kids supposed to eat while they wait to be taken care of? And don't tell me England's any different from the States. Civilization has caused a lot of problems, a hell of a lot more than it's solved."

Charlotte stood and smoothed the full skirt of her gown where it fell from a narrow waist. "I didn't realize what a wise and benevolent man you are. How many charities have you supported in Mason? Or in San Antonio?"

"I—"

She pushed back her chair. "You must give me a list of them sometime, brother dear, so that I can add to your contributions. In the meantime, please trust me to take care of my own life. I am as much our parents' offspring as you are, even if I am a female and, therefore, good for only one thing. And that, not any too often."

"I never said—"

But Charlotte wasn't willing to argue. He watched her stride from the breakfast room. He followed at a respectable and safe distance, Charlotte being as he recalled rather good with her right fist, for all her lack of weight. He doubted a London

71

school had erased that natural ability, even if it had taken the twang from her speech. He was damned sure, no matter what she said when her pride kicked in, that almost two years of William's company had sharpened her urge to fight.

She had asked him to trust her, he reminded himself as she exited the house, not bothering with so much as a nod of good-bye. Trust her, he would— until events told him to do otherwise.

He watched from the front stoop as her footman helped her into the open carriage that had been a wedding present from Libby and Alex. Just as he had expected, she took up the reins and whip with ease and headed down the street at a fast clip, the footman running behind to catch up.

Perhaps, given her determination and strong will, she could change William into a thoughtful, loving husband.

It shouldn't be any harder than teaching a rattler not to strike.

He turned back to the house.

A few of Charlotte's jibes ate at him. Well hell, maybe he did think women were good for sex. No maybe about it. They *were*. But that didn't mean they weren't good for something else.

As for not being "wise and benevolent," that one was harder to handle. A list of charities he'd given to would be mighty short. But he wasn't given to cruelty or meanness, and he *had* defended that child last night. She'd been on his mind off and on since he was forced out of bed.

As to *why* he'd come to the pipsqueak's rescue, he couldn't say. Sometimes in life a man had to go with his instincts. And it had seemed right defending her . . . from both the brute that hauled after her and the viper-tongued wife of Hector Mims.

It was Mims who handled the fallen body after

Clay sent the chair crashing down on him.

"We'll put 'im in one of the rookery alleys and by the time he comes to, 'e won't be remembering a thing, or 'ow in 'ell to get back 'ere," the proprietor had said. "Not one o' the regulars, this un."

Clay had stayed around to make sure Mims was right, and to see as best he could that no retribution was taken against the child. And, unfortunately, to drink some more of the brandy.

The police had not appeared, for which everyone expressed relief, proving that in some ways London's Black Horse was not so much different from the Longhorn Saloon back home.

The picture of a huddled, ragged figure flashed across his mind — specifically of a pair of wide, green eyes staring up at him from the midst of tangled hair. Simple, was she? Something in her frank stare said otherwise. He'd bet his best mare that she was sharp as Aunt Martha. All she needed was the right kind of schooling for the deaf, and she'd be able to find a better place in the world.

But that was like saying all she needed was to be crowned Queen of England. She was likely to get the one as much as the other.

Maybe he ought to look in on her again. The idea surprised him at first, but the more he considered it, the more it seemed right. Just his instincts working again, most likely; maybe he was wise and benevolent, after all, no matter what Baby Sister said.

The truth was, Charlotte had riled him just the way she used to. Worse, she'd got him to thinking. Tonight he'd mosey by the Black Horse, this time without his companion and definitely without ordering anything stronger than ale. Somehow he would try to communicate with the girl, to get through to the sharp mind he suspected was lurking

73

beneath that ugly cap.

So what if he didn't know how to talk to someone who could not hear. It certainly wouldn't cause him any trouble if he tried.

Chapter Six

Jenna was washing glasses behind the bar and considering exactly where she might try her hand at begging again when the Texan returned. She saw him right away, standing in the open doorway, the cool dark air of the summer night behind him, the tavern light falling across his lean, sun-burnished face.

One of the glasses slipped from her grasp, bounced against the floor and, leaving a watery trail in its path, rolled to a stop against her foot.

Her heart pounded in her ears as she bent to retrieve it. Slowly, unable to breathe, she stood upright, or as upright as she allowed herself to stand, her head barely clearing the four-foot-high bar.

Scrunched as she was, she could still see well enough to spot the full length of the tall Texan from his loosely worn black tousled hair to the tips of his American boots. She felt a rush of pleasure that she could not remember having felt before, and a comfortable sensation that all was right with her world. Which, of course, it was not, but it was nice to think so for a change.

Clay. She must have said the name a million times since last night.

He was dressed much as he had been before, in shirt and trousers that revealed a broad chest and long, lean legs. She especially liked the boots. Polished though they were, they still lent a foreign, open-air look to him that was refreshing in the staleness of this city hovel.

He seemed to bring the outdoors in with him, and definitely not the outdoors of Seven Dials. When she looked at him she could imagine the scent of rich fields of loam freshly turned, of red grass on the veld, of orange groves in the spring.

Clay's eyes moved about the half-filled room, and she ducked. She didn't want him to see her; she just wanted to see him — and she had been so certain she never would again. Perhaps there was a God in Heaven, after all.

She refused to wonder why the Texan was back in the Black Horse tonight a scant twenty yards away. The answer might involve Teresa, who had made it amply clear throughout his earlier visit that she hoped his intentions were entirely dishonorable.

For now it was enough that Jenna knew he was near and available to look at whenever she felt the urge. She would be content, having learned as she had through bitter experience not to expect a great deal out of life. At least she would *try* to be.

If only he could get a little closer . . .

"Cap'n threw that bos'n overboard," wheezed the old man leaning on his elbows at the end of the bar.

Long wisps of gray hair covered his bent head, the spotted skin of his scalp showing through, and a full gray beard hid half his face. His rheumy eyes had a distant, inward look as he spoke. In the smokey quiet on this slow late night, his asthmatic voice carried well across the wide room. "Just pitched him into the storm, that 'e did, sure as I'm standin' 'ere, mate."

Hector, standing close to Jenna and providing the old tar a captive audience of one, nodded and continued to wipe at the glasses she set beside him from time to time.

The man's story was one he had told a hundred times before. His youth had been spent at sea and he liked to relive those days on the "briny deep."

Teresa, clad in the red dress she had worn the previous night, sat at one of the tables with a couple of whores who were complaining about the slow night.

"They're dirty old men, 'at's what they are, wot'll gi' ye the pox," she said in a lull while the sailor drank from his tankard of rum. "Don't 'ave nothin' to do with 'em. Take my advice."

Teresa was full of such wisdom lately. Six months ago she, too, had been on the streets. But she was a married woman now with a place of her own, and she never let the women of her former profession forget it.

The two recipients of the wisdom stared into their jars of ale, an expression of shopworn fatigue on their painted faces that matched their tawdry clothes. Neither was much older than twenty, Jenna had overheard them say one night, a couple of years younger than she, but the flat look in their eyes, their haggard faces and bodies slumped with weariness, made them look twice the age. They could never pass for children. She suspected, knowing as she now did the debilitating life in the slums, that even as children they had probably looked world-weary and old.

Teresa spotted Clay a couple of minutes after Jenna. So did the whores, who stared openly at him, their boredom gone as quickly as a shot of whiskey served to one of the Horse's regulars. A whispered comment from Teresa sent them back to their drinks.

Abandoning the table, Teresa fluffed her black hair, moistened her lips, and began to make her way toward the front door. She looked, Jenna decided, as though a light had gone on inside her, and she walked slowly, deliberately, so that her limp was barely detectable. Jenna knew how much effort that took, and she could admire her strength of will if the entire purpose of impressing the Texan had not been to cuckold her husband.

Did you really come back because of her?

The question rang in her mind.

Last night she had tried to convince herself he wasn't interested in the obviously available woman, but that was last night, when Jenna had wanted to believe that *she* was the only female who had caught his eye. She in her ragged disguise. An hour of listening to the moans and cries coming from the opposite bedroom, to the bedsprings creaking, to the voices calling out unintelligible words, had reminded her all too well that Teresa was a desirable woman.

Jenna's lone experience with a man was a single kiss and brief pawing — and then disaster had struck.

Of course Clay was here because of Teresa. What other reason could there be? Certainly not the friendly atmosphere in the Black Horse, considering the near brawl he'd been involved in, nor the quality of the tavern's brandy. More than one of the regulars, none of them exactly connoisseurs, claimed it tasted like "piss from the black 'orse 'isself."

Jenna was fast losing her sense of pleasure.

The two would laugh and talk, Teresa openly flirting and Clay responding the way all the men clearly wanted to when she turned her attentions to them. Then Hector would object and there would be another fight and this time the bobbies would come and . . .

A thousand worries assailed her. Most of them boiled down to one. Teresa and the Texan. What if he stopped Hector the way he'd stopped Badger last night? What if Teresa looped her arm in his and took him directly to the large back room?

Her mind running wild, her hands working furiously in the water, Jenna imagined them making the kind of noises she had heard last night . . . the mating noises she'd been listening to throughout the six months since Teresa's arrival.

Hearing them like this in her mind, with the deep-voiced Texan as Teresa's partner in the coupling, filled her with unexpected rage.

Jenna cast her eyes to the wash water, shocked that

she could think such wanton and violent thoughts . . .
she who must always have complete control of herself
. . . she who had so little experience of her own with
men . . . she whose desperate plight had been caused
by a man with the same urges that brought the Texan
back.

What had possessed her? For a moment she had
wanted herself in the bed with Clay.

The strength of her emotion last night as she had
gazed at him—the warm glow and kind thoughts that
she had ascribed to love—these were lofty feelings far
removed from carnal considerations. Clay had been a
kind and forthright protector. He had looked at her as
a human being and not a creature to be shunned. Her
regard for him was noble and pure. She had called it
love, but perhaps it was gratitude and respect.

So what was this strange warmth in her nether re-
gions as she stared at him? She had never experienced
such an insistent feeling before. It spread up her stomach all the way to her lips, which parted of their own
volition. Even her breasts were tingling and with
warmth heading likewise in the other direction, her
toes were curling against the floor.

Worst of all, she couldn't turn her eyes away. The
longer she looked, the more she was filled with hostil-
ity over the nearness of Teresa Mims. She recognized
the feeling as jealousy; she had experienced it last
night and now it was returning with amazing vigor.

It was a foolish emotion, wasting her energy and
causing her to abandon the self possession that had
kept her free and alive. But it would not go away.
Wouldn't the Texan get a laugh if he knew what turmoil he had set loose in the heart and mind of the ragged little beggar? Especially since all he had done was
walk in the door.

The devil in her wanted to interrupt the whispered
tête-à-tête that had started as soon as Teresa got to his
side, wanted Clay to hear the way Teresa still called her

79

Simple, despite his pointed suggestion to the contrary. The woman must have used the name more in the past twenty-four hours — ever since Clay departed — than she had in the past three years.

Simple, get yer arse over here and clean this mess.

Simple, yer the lowest, vilest, dirtiest, ugliest creature ever put on this earth.

It didn't matter that Jenna wasn't supposed to hear. Teresa's aim had been to show everyone else what a fool she had to contend with.

Teresa was not a kind woman, nor, in truth, a very smart one. She would not know that anyone with a tittle of sense or sensibility would see the ugliness of the remarks reflected onto the speaker. Occasionally some such person wandered into the Black Horse.

But never anyone like Clay.

He was as ruggedly appealing as she had remembered him, with his ruffled black hair and probing eyes. His features were strong — prominent cheekbones, straight nose and chin, and lips not too thick and not too thin. For a moment her eyes lingered on those lips. Staring at them was an easy habit to form.

The old sailor erupted in a fit of coughing. Jenna sent a sideways glance to Hector; with his coarse features drained of their normal relaxed humor and his wide brown eyes alert, he was as intent on the couple as was she. It was not a situation that portended a peaceful night.

This time, she just *knew,* the bobbies would come.

Lifting the last pair of glasses from the tepid wash water, Jenna nudged the tavern proprietor with her arm to get his attention and placed the cheap barware, dripping wet, in his hands.

He took them absent-mindedly, his eyes still on his wife and the Texan. It would seem he was not to be distracted by anything so inconsequential as a deaf child.

Teresa, holding on to Clay's arm, was gesturing to-

80

ward one of the tables in the far corner of the room. He shook his head. Teresa pouted. To Jenna's amazement he removed her hand from his shirt sleeve and began to stride away from the tavern entryway . . . straight toward the bar . . . straight to her.

Jenna ducked her head, self-consciously tugging at her cap and shaking her head from side to side in a gesture common to the deaf. With no more than a dozen patrons in the tavern, he could still call unwanted attention to her just by standing near.

Far worse, he had a way of looking at her that seemed to see right through her disguise.

As pleased as she had been before, so was she terrified now. She felt like a birdie in a badminton game, bounced from a state of calm to chaos and, she prayed, eventually back again. Too much attention and she could easily be exposed for the fraud that she was. All she had really wanted was to look at him again. Perhaps she had wanted too much.

Go away, she wanted to scream.

He was almost directly in front of her, not three feet away. Again she tugged at the cap and twirled her fingers through the darkened wisps of hair that rested against her face. Muttering to herself a sampling of the oaths she had overheard in the Dials, both scatological and profane, she began placing in a straight line the glasses that Hector had dried.

"Mims," said Clay with a nod of his head. "Good evening."

"Evenin'," Hector returned, his eyes never leaving the Texan's face.

Clay's arms rested on the bar, his shirt sleeves turned back at the cuffs. Jenna stared at the tanned skin and the fine black hairs revealed, and then at the strong brown hands. Clean they were, down to the blunt nails, but she could see the calluses on his palms. A working man, not one of the fops who usually came slumming. She liked him all the more.

81

She could feel a pair of gray eyes on her. A tingling began at the back of her neck.

" 'ow 'bout another brandy?" asked Hector.

"No, thanks," was the quick reply. "I didn't come by for a drink. Just wanted to make sure the girl was all right. The polecat who was after her didn't show up again, did he?"

Oh, that voice. Fearing the expression on her face, Jenna turned from the two men and picked up a half-empty beer bottle that she had been meaning to throw away. She held the bottle to her breast as tenderly as if it were Clay's hand. Ever since the long-ago illness during which she really had been deaf, she dearly loved the sound of a pleasant voice. In the Black Horse, she heard so few. And none as rich and deep and thrilling as Clay's.

"I told ye," shrilled an all-too-familiar female, "that she was all right."

Teresa, it seemed, had arrived at Clay's side.

"So you did," said Clay. "Just wanted to check out things for myself."

"The child works 'ard enough," Teresa added with more sweetness. "But not too 'ard so as to do 'erself 'arm. The problem with 'er is that as dim-witted as she is, there's little I can ask 'er to do. She disappears sometimes at night and we have no idea where she's gone. Always returns."

Teresa didn't sound particularly happy about the last.

I go out to care for the twins . . . and now to beg . . . to get money for those I love. Someday soon we will leave.

"I pray that the poor dumb bas—, uh, baby, has not, you know, taken up wi' men," Teresa continued.

Hector growled, and Jenna almost dropped the beer. Unable to keep her back to the conversation a moment longer, she half turned and twirled the bottle on the bar, knowing full well that those gray eyes were watching her with care.

Teresa stood with bosom and elbows resting in front of her, a circumspect space between her and Clay that Jenna would fit into. "She's ain't old enough, o' course," she said, "but w' someone o' 'er kind—"

She broke off with a shrug of her slender shoulders and a fluttering of her lashes.

Teresa might not be smart, Jenna thought, but she was definitely wily. She took consolation from the fact that they were speaking about her, a topic that Clay must have introduced at the door. But why?

At that moment the old sailor who had been humming a shanty under his breath asked for another tankard of rum. Hector, muttering about having to go to the back for more, shot a warning glance at Clay before he left.

Teresa immediately edged closer to her prey and smiled.

"Perhaps if you gave her more responsibility," suggested Clay. "Seems to me school might do her some good."

Teresa's smile died. "School! For that idiot?"

Jenna caught the displeasure on the Texan's face, as did Teresa, who immediately tried to make amends. "I don't believe she could ever learn t' read," she simpered.

It's something you've never mastered, Teresa.

"Surely there's a school in this big city for children like her," said Clay.

The Deaf and Dumb Asylum. Jenna could have filled him with details.

"Not much good as it'd do 'er," said Teresa. "Like I said, she's just too dim-witted."

Jenna had heard the insult one too many times. In her anger, she set the bottle of beer down with such force that it overturned, spilling its stale contents across Teresa's amply exposed bosom, beading on her white breasts and staining the red cloth

83

almost to black.

"Bloody bitch!" Teresa's voice was not a pretty thing to hear.

A long-nailed hand swung out, and Jenna barely backed away in time to keep the cap from being jerked from her head. But escape was short lived. She got the definite feeling Teresa planned to come over the bar after her. Doubting that Clay would fell this latest oppressor with a chair, Jenna did the one thing she knew how to do. She ran.

Darting the length of the bar and directing her feet to the back hall, she collided with Hector, who stood in the doorway, a pitcher of rum in his hand. The pitcher went straight up, Jenna went around, and the darkly odorous liquor spilled across the already damp bosom and down the skirt of the pursuing Teresa as the pitcher landed on the floor with a crash.

Jenna could have sworn she saw Clay put himself in the enraged woman's path, but she did not tarry to watch the rest of the scene. Indeed, she did not stop until she had flown out the back door and separated herself from the tavern by a distance of two blocks, her steps instinctively taking her toward the lodging house of the twins. Darting into the alley close by their building, she stood in the shadows away from the street light and caught her breath, her arms wrapped around her middle to still the trembling inside.

She had not perfumed the rancorous Mrs. Mims on purpose, but she would never be believed. Never had she seen the woman quite so enraged. It might be as long as a day or two before she could safely return, and even then it would be to scenes of increased abuse.

The one consolation she had was the look on the Texan's face when the beer hit its target. A smile had definitely been on his lips, a half grin that was as charming as she knew it would be.

Something tugged at her skirt. Her mind flew to memories of rats and she jumped.

"It's only us, Jenna," two voices said in unison.

She glanced down and was barely able to make out the dirty faces of Alice and Alfred staring back. As glad as she was to see them, under the circumstances she really would have preferred they not find her.

She shook her head solemnly. They knew the signal; it told them to pretend she wasn't there. They backed away toward the lighted street.

How small and defenseless they looked, standing there in the patched and oversized clothes she had bought for them at a second hand exchange. Jenna knelt and motioned them back. In a flash they were in her outstretched arms. She gave them a big hug.

"Why are you two out so late?" she whispered, trying to sound angry. "Wasn't the food I brought you this afternoon enough? Not getting greedy now, are you?"

She couldn't resist running her hands over their backs. Both pairs of shoulder blades were painfully prominent.

"We heard something," whispered Alice.

"She got afeared," added Alfred with great importance, "and I had to get her outside."

Jenna looked at them with solemnity. "Your home is safer than the street because you keep the door locked, isn't that right?"

One after the other, they nodded.

"It's not good for you to be out here."

"I tried to tell her," the boy said with wounded pride.

"You did not!"

Jenna stroked a curl from Alice's face. "You must not argue with one another. Didn't we agree on that?" She included Alfred in her smile. "You need each other and I need you. Right now, I need for you to go back inside and lock the door and not open it until your Papa gets back. Can you do as I ask?"

They both nodded, but Jenna saw the worry in Alice's round brown eyes.

"I'll tell you a story tomorrow if you'll meet me

85

down by the river in our special place."

The worry vanished.

"Now go."

She watched the departing figures until they had rounded the end of the alley. How much she wanted to run after them and tuck them into bed. But she could not do so every night. They must be independent, or as independent as two such very young children could possibly be.

Jenna felt a rush of love for them. She would take them away, and soon. If, that is, she could continue to evade arrest. If her grandiose plans did not work out, if the unthinkable occurred and she found herself in jail, she vowed to see that they were taken care of, although she had no idea just how she could manage such a feat. Her love for them was not unselfish. In truth, they gave more to her than she gave to them. They helped her keep a hold on sanity.

Footsteps on the street sent her deeper into the alley. A figure passed beneath the block's lone streetlight. She recognized Clay right away. He passed so quickly through her limited line of vision that had she blinked, she would have missed him altogether.

It was obviously fate that had sent him down the same path she had taken when she ran from the tavern. Jenna was a great believer in fate—and most of it bad.

But she also believed that there were times when people could help shape their destinies. Was she to let the Texan walk away from her tonight without knowing more about him? If she let him go, she knew she would never see him again. Idle curiosity might have brought him back tonight to see if the Black Horse was really as he remembered it. He would not come again to see another installment of her continuing and, it would seem lately, farcical woes.

He had shown consideration for her. The least she could do was make sure he made his way back safely to his hotel or wherever he was staying, although just how she could protect him, she had no idea.

Months of scurrying through the streets of the Dials had prepared her for this night stalking, and she found, once she had hiked her skirts clear of the pavement, she could move in silence at the long-stride pace that Clay had set. Or at least she could for the first mile; the second was a great deal more forced. But Jenna was motivated. She did not let him get long out of sight. Occasionally she could guess the route he had chosen — which generally was away from the worst streets of the slum — and thus take shortcuts. Only once did she fear she had guessed wrong, and for a few heart-stopping minutes she thought he was gone.

When he hove into view on the far side of the street, she almost revealed herself with a whoop of joy.

Jenna fully expected him to be on his way to a clean, middle class hotel. When it was clear he was heading for Tunstall Square, one of the richest and most exclusive parts of London, she tried to reason things out. He must have more money than she had supposed, although he hadn't looked wealthy. And there were those calluses on his hands.

Maybe he just had wealthy friends.

He stopped at one of the fanciest of the fancy places on the square, Number 32, walked right up the front stoop as though he owned the place, and let himself in with a key.

Crouching behind the shrubbery across the street, Jenna stared. He had wealthy friends indeed.

Somehow she couldn't put him in with the rest of the Quality. His calluses, for one thing — and he had chosen to walk the two miles from the Horse rather than summon a cab.

Or maybe she simply didn't want to. She wanted him to be different in all things, not just in the way he looked and walked and in the kindness he had shown. Foolish thought though it was, she didn't want him to be rich, for that would put him beyond her even more than he already was.

A terrible thought struck her. Maybe he had a wife and six children waiting inside. He had been without a wedding ring, but that was no certain clue.

She stood in the damp night air with no more than a layer of thin rags to protect her and focused on the ornate brass knocker of the door. Caught in the glow from an electric street lamp directly in front of the stoop, it seemed to put out a beacon light of its own.

She waited a long time and was at last rewarded by a light going on in one of the upstairs rooms. He walked in front of the bared windows, raised his arms and stretched. It seemed to her he could very well touch the ceiling with those strong brown hands, if he tried. But then he could do just about anything he set his mind to.

Half expecting a woman to join him in front of the window and wholly praying that one would not, she stared up in rapt attention. She breathed a sigh of relief as the seconds slipped by and he remained standing alone.

She pictured the rippling muscles under his shirt. What if he took it off right now? It was an interesting question and gave her pause for thought. She was beginning to fill in a few details of the imagined scene when, to her sharp disappointment, he pulled the draperies closed.

Good-bye, Clay.

She turned to leave.

No!

Hadn't she just been telling herself lately that she never was able to do what she really wanted? And hadn't she been feeling just a wee bit sorry for herself?

What she wanted was to know more about him . . . that's all. It wasn't that she would do anything except look if she got the chance. Maybe she could find a way to thank him for his kindness. He truly had been kind.

By the time Jenna reluctantly took her leave of the

mansion, she knew what she had to do and she set her path toward a stall halfway to the Dials. Tradesmen gathered there in the early morning hours; if there was anyone in London who could tell her about Number 32 Tunstall Square, it was one of those gossiping men. For once she would speak and listen, taking a chance that she would be recognized. The chance was not too great, given the large number of ragged children on the streets. On her side, too, was the fact that to her knowledge none of the stall's regulars had ever made it to the Horse.

Depending upon what she found out from them, she would lay out a plan for keeping up with Clay. Of course what she considered doing was foolish, but the admission didn't change her mind.

"Man does not live by bread alone," the reverend had often intoned.

And a woman cannot live with only fear. As much as helping the twins gave her sanity, thinking about seeing the Texan again gave her hope.

Chapter Seven

Jenna spent the next twenty-four hours avoiding Teresa whenever she could, stealing away for a couple of hours to meet the twins by the Thames as she had promised last night, and when she returned, working very hard in the once again busy tavern.

Slipping out during the evening to beg was out of the question; she would only provoke Teresa's ire all the more when she returned. Instead, she concentrated on her work, scurrying so fast, clearing and wiping and washing, that she had Old Jack, normally the most preoccupied of men, glancing at her from time to time.

With so many customers to talk to, Teresa paid scant attention to the upstart child except to scream orders, pound chairs and call her ugly names a half dozen times. It was, Jenna thought, a typical night at the Horse. She hefted the slop jar that was kept behind the bar. If there was anything she could say in the night's favor, it was that Badger did not return, and there was no other to look upon her with the same lustful eye.

It was well past midnight, after Hector had sent the last carousers out and barred the front door, that she was able to find solitude in the back alley. Pacing in front of the piles of refuse, she came to a halt close to where the alley opened onto the street and considered what to do about the information she had gleaned at the stall shortly before dawn.

"Number 32, is 'at wot yer askin' fer?" one of the men had said. "The earl 'o 'arrow owns the place, 'im and 'is missus. She's a right good 'un, so me own missus says. From the States, she is. A rare countess, 'at's wot the

90

missus calls 'er."

"From the States? You wouldn't happen to know where exactly, would you?"

"You'd 'ave to ask me wife. Keeps up with the aristocrats, she does. Don't mind since it don't cost nuffin."

"Do you know anything about the earl?" Jenna had asked.

"Ain't in the city much. Lives som'air to the north, 'im and 'is countess. Stays up there mostly. Not that the 'arrow 'ome on the square ain't a busy place. Seen lots o' toffs goin' in an' out. Uses the bloomin' place like a 'otel, they does."

Which was exactly what Clay was doing, Jenna thought, and she contemplated how such knowledge could possibly affect her. When she had sought the information in the early hours of yesterday morning, she thought perhaps to act on it, to return to Tunstall Square, to see Clay again, to learn why he of all the people who wandered into the tavern had shown her compassion. She wished, if nothing else, to learn his last name.

Could she really be that much of a fool? She had far more vital matters to think about, such as gathering as much money as she could to take herself and the twins away from the Dials. She would, of course, have to talk to Morgan, their father—perhaps even make a small payment to him, buy them if that was the way he put it. She was too used to the ways of the rookery to worry about niceties such as how the necessary transactions of life were labeled.

If she were anything other than what she was, she could leave the two and take care only of herself. But she had seen too much misery, too much heartbreak during her years of growing up, and she could not wish even worse for those brave tots.

Mostly, she had to protect herself, for she could do them little good if she were thrown into jail, and she swore to herself that she would follow a sensible course.

91

But oh, how she wanted to see Clay again.

Teresa's brittle laughter startled her to the present, to the dark alley where she stood, to the dank air lying oppressively against her ragged clothes, and to the ghostly clouds floating across the nighttime sky. A man's deep answering laugh drifted from the side of the tavern around the corner, eclipsing the woman's high pitch. Somehow Teresa must have unlocked the main entry to the Horse and had slipped through to meet someone. Jenna couldn't identify whoever stood beside Mrs. Mims, but she knew it was not Mr. Mims.

Jenna leaned against the alley wall of the tavern, letting the darkness of the night protect her.

"Bertie, yer a nasty man," said Teresa throatily. Again the man laughed, the sound thick and guttural as though it were forced from lungs coated with smoke.

"It's me charm," he answered. "Why don't ye come down the way w' me a bit? I'll show ye a nasty trick or two."

Jenna held her breath. Bertie Groat, braggart and thief and loaf-about in the tavern, was not much of a conquest, but Teresa did not sound inclined to order him away. The two must be at least a dozen yards away from her around the corner, but she could hear every nuance in the woman's voice, as well as the man's suggestive response. So clear were the sounds they made in the still night, both could have been standing by her side.

The brick wall cut into her back, reminding her of the bruises from Badger's attack, but she did not move. Any second she expected Hector to come roaring out of the tavern and enforce the unwritten law that around the Horse his wife was to be left alone.

"Bertie, ye haven't the scratch," derided Teresa. "I'd go no place w' ye wi'out a bit more reason than wot ye got 'anging a-tween yer legs. Or wot ye claims t' 'ave."

Toughened by her year in the rookery though she was, Jenna blushed.

Bertie growled. "Yer problem is that Texas bloke wot come aroun' an' got ye thinkin' o' betterin' yerself. 'e likes the moron better 'n yer."

"The fool likes little girls, 'at's what 'e does. There's plenty o' 'is kind comes slummin' aroun' 'ere."

"Takes the business clean away from old wimmen likes yerself, don't it? Goin' after the tykes 'at way."

Jenna felt sick inside, and dirty, just listening to them talk. In some obscure way it seemed she was betraying Clay by not stepping forward and defending him, although of course she knew she could not.

"Otter teach the blighter a lesson, 'at's wot we otter do." Teresa's voice was hard, ugly, filled with anger and bitterness. From around the corner Jenna could feel the hate radiating from her like stench from the sewers beneath the Dials.

" 'ow yer plannin' on teachin' 'im anything? 'e don' gi' ye no more 'n a nod."

"Now who said I'd be the one t' do it? Yer al'ays braggin' about yer mighty deeds." Teresa's voice was taunting, needling, scornful. "Seems t' me yer could do more 'n talk."

"I'd lay 'im out right soon enough iffn I got the chance't."

"Talk's cheap, Bertie."

"So it is." His voice turned wheedling. "Wot's it wort' t' yer if 'e comes aroun' agin an' I do wot yer wants?"

"Depends."

"On wot?"

"I fancy those boots o' 'is. Like 'em for meself, sorta souvenirs, like the gentry buys when they goes abroad."

"I fancy a souvenir o' me own, an' it ain't no boots." Groat laughed again, the same deep, dirty laugh Jenna had heard at first, but she could not pick out what he was whispering. She didn't have to. Teresa's returning cackle told her more than she wanted to know.

"I best be gettin' back in," Teresa said after a moment of silence. " 'ector'll be roarin' out 'ere and yer won't be able to do nothin' about those boots or nuthin' else, fer that matter, onc't 'e gets 'is 'ands on yer privates. 'e won' be atter a good time, I can tell yer that, and neither'll ye, not fer a long while."

" 'im an' who else?" Groat's words were brave but they lacked conviction and hung lifeless on the night air.

" 'e don't need no one else. Remember wot I said, Bertie. The boots."

Jenna heard the shuffle of Teresa's uneven gait as she hurried away toward the front tavern door. Shrinking back into the alley, she watched Groat's swarthy figure lumber by in the dim streetlight.

She closed her eyes and listened to the pounding of her heart. Teresa had no more interest in those boots of Clay's than she had in an empty jar of ale. She was after revenge; the Texan had spurned her charms in favor of a filthy, stupid child, and for that he must pay, especially since she had someone willing to avenge her injured pride.

If Clay came around again. Surely he would not.

But if he did?

Clay could take care of himself, even against the likes of a cutthroat like Bertie Groat.

Or could he? Groat wouldn't fight fair; he'd sneak up in the dark, a knife in his hand, a sudden slash, the blade buried in cloth and flesh, Clay falling . . .

Jenna swallowed hard. He must be warned, but how? Only she could do that and she had vowed to stay away from Tunstall Square.

She wrapped her arms around her middle and held on tight. She must honor that vow . . . she must.

A tiny whispering voice deep inside reminded her that Clay had not hesitated to come to her defense.

She remembered Badger lumbering through the tavern's front door, his flat, crude features distorted to greater ugliness by lustful rage. Clay had stood his ground and felled him.

94

And Clay might very well return.

As much as she felt her emotions wrapped up in him, she did not understand him in the least, but she understood herself and what she had to do.

After a fast trip into the Horse to get her shawl, she headed out through the twisting streets of the rookery, past the sleeping drunks and the whores leaning against lamp-posts, their sisters-in-kind slumped in open doorways, past the fetid piles of refuse and the occasional muck cart moving slowly along.

She did not wander down the safer, meandering route that Clay had selected last night for his walk from the tavern to Tunstall Square. Instead, she chose a quicker course, and within half an hour she was standing where she had stood the night in the shadows of a row of trees across from the Earl of Harrow's mansion. Behind her lay a wall of thick shrubbery; before her, an empty cobbled street lit with the harsh glow from an electric lamp-post, and beyond, a row of brick facades — the impenetrable, unwelcoming homes of the privileged class.

She was swept with the sensation that since leaving the Dials she had traveled to another planet, not simply another road.

The tall house directly opposite rose forbiddingly, dark and austere, and she wondered how many others besides Clay were availing themselves of Harrow's ready hospitality at the present time. She had seen no one enter or leave; perhaps he was staying alone.

She waited impatiently another half hour for him — or for anyone — to appear, but, with the exception of an occasional passing carriage and one noisy automobile, all was quiet in the square.

What if he had returned to America?

She didn't care for the thought.

No doubt, she assured herself, he was upstairs sleeping — by himself, of course, since she had chosen to believe there was no wife — in a large feather bed, unaware of the huddled figure watching his window from the street.

Now that was a pitiful picture, and it was one Jenna could not abide. She tapped her foot impatiently. Despite the work she had put in at the Horse, she was filled with a restless energy. Standing here was driving her wild. She had brought herself to this place tonight for a specific reason which must be acted upon; that there were other reasons more deeply hidden, longings she couldn't name, was not the issue now.

Palms damp, Jenna forced from her mind all thoughts of her own safety. Her eyes focused on the brass knocker that gleamed from afar in the eerie and artificial light. Whether Clay was inside or not yet returned, there would be a servant to answer the door . . . someone to take a whispered warning to him if she made it convincing enough.

One foot edged out of the shadows, and then another, and she knew that she must act quickly or she would not act at all. Crossing the street, her shawl placed over her head and shoulders as though it were a protective shield, she quickly took the steps to the door. Three short raps of the knocker brought no immediate response, and she waited a full minute, then rapped again.

Footsteps shuffled on the other side of the door. Struck with a need for caution, she scurried down the steps and stood in the shadow at the side of the entryway away from the light.

The door opened a crack. "Who's there?" a man asked sharply. A young man, by the sound of him, a footman wakened from his sleep.

Caution made Jenna affect the speech of the Dials. "I've got a message for one o' yer toffs." She spoke far too softly, and added with greater conviction, "a warnin' as it were for the American."

"What's goin' on?" The young man stuck his head out the door and looked around. "Who's there?"

Heart in her throat, Jenna edged deeper into the shadows. "Tell the bloke e's to stay away from the Dials. There's danger about fer the likes o' 'im."

The footman, clad in trousers and a partially buttoned shirt, his fair hair ruffled, stepped outside. "Whoever's out here, step up where I can get a look at you."

That Jenna could not do. "Are ye listenin'?" She had no trouble sounding angry. "Tell 'im what I said."

He turned toward the sound of her voice and took the top step. "Come on out of there and show yourself. What's the likes of you doing at the square this hour?"

"Jimmy." A harsh, authoritarian voice rang from behind him in the darkness of the house. "What is the meaning of this standing half dressed at the door in the middle of the night?"

Jimmy glanced over his shoulder. "Mr. Randolph, sir. I heard a knock. Thought maybe it was Parkworth come home late without his key."

"You think too much, Jimmy." The voice grew louder. "And you speak with impertinence. Besides, he returned long ago. Is there someone there?"

"Just a . . ." The footman threw a look of disdain in her direction. "A beggar of some sorts."

"For heaven's sakes, get rid of it."

Anger and humiliation warred within Jenna. She might be many things Jimmy and Mr. Randolph would not approve of, but she was not an *it*.

"Tell 'im —" she began, her voice raised.

"Get on with you. And don't be knocking again or you will be in real trouble." With that, Jimmy stepped back inside and closed the door.

A sudden and chill gust swirled a cloud of dust around Jenna, and she sneezed. Indignities piled on indignities, and all because she had been trying to do what she knew was right. She turned in a flounce, her head held high despite the ragged shawl covering it, a militant light in her eye.

So she was turned away at the front door, was she? There was always the back. If she had anything to do with it, Clay — Mr. Clay Parkworth — would receive the warning that he needed and deserved.

Calling upon her skills of stealth, she made her way down the length of the house and around to the servants' entry off the alley. Away from the electric lamp-posts on the street, she had to rely on the full moon for her light.

The rear of the house itself was L-shaped, but a tall wooden fence extended from the near wall across to the corner of the property, squaring off the back and forming a solid, impenetrable barrier to anyone who might choose to enter uninvited. The door opening onto the alley was locked tight, as was the gate in the fence. Standing in the shadows cast by the moon, she stared up at what seemed acres of brick and stone, broken by occasional dark, arched windows and a cornice near the roof.

There was not so much as a vine or gutter that looked substantial enough to hold her weight, even if she had been athletic enough to scramble toward the second floor if she had been so inclined, which she most certainly was not. Driven as she was to complete her mission, she could hardly do so with a broken neck.

She was startled to hear footsteps in the alley, and a woman's low laugh. A refuse bin near the back entryway offered sanctuary, and she scooted toward it. She barely tucked herself behind its solid protection and away from the moonlight in time to avoid detection by the couple hurrying along.

She fully expected the man and woman to walk on by. They stopped by the gate, the woman's back not three feet from where Jenna crouched.

"Nellie, when'll I be seein' you again?" asked the man as he nuzzled her neck.

Nellie giggled. "Stop that, 'arry. I'll be found out and let go."

Harry spread his bare hands on Nellie's buttocks and began to circle his palms.

Why was it, Jenna asked herself, she always ended up a witness to the intimate moments of others?

"Come on, Nellie girl. You know what you wants, and so do I."

Again Nellie giggled. At least, Jenna thought, Teresa was not given to such an unfortunate laugh. It was the first charitable consideration she had sent in that direction since the marriage ceremony.

The couple proceeded to whisper and kiss while Jenna debated whether or not to interrupt and pass on the message that needed to be conveyed inside.

Somehow she did not think Nellie could be counted upon to complete the task — if for no other reason than the fact the servant could not possibly reveal how she came by the information without revealing her own late-night escapade.

Forced to abandon that line of thought, Jenna concentrated on the cramp which threatened to cripple her right leg. Her endurance died just as the lovers' long farewell came to an end.

"Ye won't be havin' no trouble w' the brute, will ye?" asked Harry as Nellie pulled from his embrace.

" 'e knows me right well enough. I gives 'im 'is food." Idly Jenna wondered which of the manor's servants Nellie fed; surely she didn't mean one of the guests.

With fervent promises to "get out again next Thursday if the 'ousekeeper ain't around," the girl let herself in through the back gate with a key. Over the muffled footsteps of the departing Harry, Jenna heard Nellie secure the lock from inside the fence.

Another lock was undone and a door opened and closed. She listened for the sound of the door being secured once again, but all was quiet. Had Nellie perhaps been thinking of Harry and neglected to take care of the final locking?

Jenna waited awhile, but the question would not go

away. When she decided to try the back side of the house, she had been possessed of a vague plan to roust someone other than the uncooperative Jimmy, but another idea, one far more devious — and dangerous — occurred to her and would not go away.

Hiking her skirt, she climbed atop the refuse can and stared down into the wide open area behind the house. Much of the ground was taken up with a garden; at the far end a greenhouse extended from fence to brick wall. Around the base of the house were flower beds crowded with roses, their petals silver in the moonlight, like ghost flowers for the midnight world.

She took a moment to breathe in their sweetness.

With her agility, it took little effort for her to vault over the fence and land in a patch of freshly turned dirt. Her feet tingled from the impact, but otherwise she was all right.

She felt the ground pulsating under her. Startled, she looked toward the greenhouse and saw what appeared to be a pony bounding her way.

The pony barked, and she realized her mistake. Her welcomer was a very large dog . . . with a very deep bark and a set of clearly visible and very large teeth. The recipient of Nellie's largesse, no doubt. Harry's brute.

Jenna swallowed. It was only a dog. And dogs were her friends.

"Good boy," she whispered and held out the back of her hand.

The dog halted three feet away. A light went on in one of the rear windows. Jenna held very still, and the dog tilted his massive head. She recognized the breed as Bullmastiff. The short hairs bristled on the back of his neck. Jenna knew that her well being depended upon her hiding all fear.

"Good boy," she said again, her voice full of a confidence that she did not particularly feel. The dog continued to stare. All was quiet and the light went out.

"Good boy," she said, hoping the third time would be the time that charmed.

The dog put one giant-sized paw in front of the other and slowly closed the distance between them. His head dropped low and came up under her palm. She stroked and crooned the magic incantation "good boy" several times; the dog's head was as hard as a Black Horse table and almost as wide.

She caught the definite wagging of his tail, and she kneeled in front of him, putting her face on a level with his tongue. He proceeded to anoint her with a friendly lick on the cheek.

She stood and whispered, "Sit." To her amazement, the dog did as she bade. If only Jimmy had been half so cooperative.

A very well trained animal, she thought as she patted his head, although he was not overly qualified as a keeper of the watch. He couldn't be earning the five pounds of food he must consume every day.

"Stay," she commanded and stepped toward the door. The dog whined. He was little more than a puppy, she decided. With one more ear scratch and a second order to "stay," she turned and stopped at the back stoop. Cautiously she reached for the handle. The door opened. Naughty Nellie, she thought. Anyone could be breaking in—even someone as low class as the beggar dismissed with such disdain at the front.

She dropped her head back and looked up the towering expanse of the brick wall, past the arched windows, past the corniced roof, all the way to the sky. Pale clouds wafted across the inky abyss. She felt completely alone.

Not since that hateful night a year ago had she been inside a proper home, and never one so grand as this. Her hand shook and she thrust it inside her shawl.

Perhaps she could find paper inside and a pen with which to scratch a message to Clay.

Or perhaps she could march right up to the second

floor, find his room, and tell him what she had come to say.

No, that was absurd. No woman with any morals at all went marching into the bedroom of a man who was not part of her family.

She thought of Bertie Groat and the evil she read in his eyes. Perhaps it was not so absurd after all. Perhaps the real immorality would lie in allowing Clay to be hurt.

Closing her eyes, she weighed what she could gain by slipping inside against everything she could possibly lose. The second list was by far the heavier, but to stop now would be to admit that she had failed in her mission, and that she had failed Clay. In her heart of hearts, she knew, too, she wanted to be near him again.

She could not leave . . . not yet. For all her acquired caution, she had also gained a certain boldness on the streets, a daring that she would never have known in a more ordinary life. It was that boldness that had sent her into the Black Horse for the very first time; it was that boldness that had sent her begging two nights ago for extra money for herself and the twins. And it was that boldness that kept her standing where she was right now.

If she were caught . . . well, she would say that she had been grateful to the stranger for his help and wanted to help him in return . . . or better yet, if someone other than Jimmy found her, she would write out the message, pretending to be deaf and dumb.

She opened her eyes and once again gripped the handle. This was utter madness, complete stupidity, foolishness beyond compare. Nevertheless, she slipped inside.

Chapter Eight

Jenna's eyes adjusted to the dark. With little more to guide her than the moonlight drifting in through a lone window, she crept forward, deeper into what appeared to be a pantry.

She came to a bench and sat, willing her heart to stop beating so loudly and her breath to slow. Had her entry been detected? Around her the house creaked in answer, but she heard no other sound. Nellie had obviously scampered on upstairs to her room to sleep the few hours left before another day began. Everyone else must be abed, Jimmy and the redoubtable Mr. Randolph included.

Which is where Jenna ought to be, back in her own cubicle in the Dials. Panic seized her. For the life of her she could not remember the exact nature of the threat against Clay . . . Something about losing his boots.

Then she thought of Bertie Groat's laugh and the knife he must certainly carry, and she pictured Clay standing in the doorway of the tavern as he looked around for her.

Jenna stiffened her spine.

Time after time she had proven herself resourceful, and she put her practical mind to work. Somewhere around there must be paper and pen. She would write a note and somehow get upstairs to that bedroom he used, put the message where he would be certain to see it when he awoke, and leave again.

There would be lamps in ample supply to light her way if she chose to use them, but she was afraid that in doing so she might call attention to herself. Something smaller and less obtrusive was called for. She felt around on the pantry shelves until she found a box of candles. In an adjoining scullery she located the matches. A single light in hand, she set about looking for the writing supplies she required.

She found them in a drawer just inside the kitchen door. Someone, the housekeeper or the cook, had begun a list of supplies for purchase. She tore off the bottom of the paper and, using the small stub of a pencil she found beside it, proceeded to write.

BEWARE OF SEVEN DIALS AND THE BLACK HORSE. DANGER AWAITS. YOU MUST STAY AWAY.

It seemed rather dramatic to Jenna, but then her being here at all contained more than a hint of the same.

With the light shaded by her hand, she found her way to the back stairway and proceeded to take it one step at a time, the folded message in her pocket, her slippers making not a hint of noise on the carpeted floor. Several times she paused and listened for the sounds of someone stirring, but she was met by nothing more sinister than the creaks of the dark, forbidding house.

The stairway continued up to the servants' quarters, but Jenna turned left at the first landing and found herself at the end of a wide, paneled hallway. Slowly she stepped forward, light from her candle flickering along the polished walls and across a pair of paintings and, halfway down to her right, a tall pedestal supporting what appeared to be a very valuable vase.

It all looked so rich and beautiful, far beyond what she had ever seen before, even during that brief period in her life when she lived in the house of a member of the gentry.

What a lot of rooms there were and several hallways leading off to the right and the left. She pictured the outside of the house and the window to the room used by the visitor Clay Parkworth. His room had been over and slightly to the left of the front door. A bedroom facing onto the square was what she sought.

She eased down the hallway toward the window at the far end, passing the head of a winding staircase that appeared to lead to the front foyer, feeling more like an apparition than a flesh-and-blood person — except for the pounding of her heart and the cold fear that cut like a knife into the pit of her stomach. Just as she had figured it would, the hall window looked out onto the street; she was almost directly above the mansion's front stoop.

Which meant the door to her right led to the bedroom she was looking for. She blew out the candle, placing it on the hallway rug. The door creaked like a banshee when she opened, then closed it at her back.

"Robert?" a deep, sleepy voice asked.

She stood without moving, her back to the wall, and listened to the terrifying rustle of bed covers. Several minutes slipped by. Quiet descended, and at last she was rewarded with the sound of deep and regular breathing. Only then did she allow herself to draw a breath.

Drop the paper and run.

The order from her mind was clear enough, but neither her hands nor her feet would move. She had traveled a long way from the alley behind the Black Horse and she could not leave so soon. After all, she was telling Clay that he must never see her again. The thought struck her with such force that she actually swayed toward the remembered sound of his voice.

The room was disgustingly dark, the moon being on the far side of the house and the draperies being closed anyway to whatever light might make its way inside. Several more minutes crept by before she could make out the dark shapes of furniture, the wide bed on the side wall to her left, and the lone figure stretched out beneath the covers. Directly opposite her were the shaded windows; to the right, a huge wardrobe.

As quiet as a floating feather, she tiptoed toward the bed. One hand clutched at the paper in her pocket, but she did not pull it out as she knew she ought.

At her destination, she could see nothing but Clay's outline alone on the bed, which should have been enough. But it wasn't. She thought of the street lamps outside, then thought of the draperies blocking their light.

So what if he caught her? She would gesture, pretend ignorance of what he asked, and then press the note into his hand. He had said she was more intelligent than people assumed. She would simply be proving him right.

At the most she would be sent out again into the night. That's what she told herself as she made her silent way to the drapery cord. One slight pull brought an opening sufficient to let in a shaft of light. It fell directly across the bed and onto Clay's chest, which was uncovered. Completely uncovered. Unless he were wearing underwear bottoms, he slept in the nude.

Tiptoeing back around the bed, she knelt beside him. His face, turned toward her, wasn't in the light the way his body was, and so she concentrated on the latter. He lay on his back, one arm flung across the pillow beside him, the other on top of the covers at his side. The short curls of hair that she had seen at his throat continued down his chest, thickening where the covers began at his waist.

His upper arms were muscled and sinewed, as was his neck. She wished she could see his face better, but she did not dare open the draperies further—not unless she truly wanted detection.

She sat back on her heels. Is that what she wanted? In her heart did she wish him to open his eyes and see her, to take her into his arms, to kiss her long and hard? Was that what she had been thinking about all along? Not warning or protecting him—at least not entirely, but pressing her lips against his?

Her mouth grew dry, and her breath halted once again. Jenna wasn't a child with a child's fantasies of romance. She was a woman. And yes, she wanted very much to kiss his lips, his throat, the palms of his strong brown hands. Her desires opened within her like budding flowers, and she felt the giddiness that came with spring.

Two nights ago she had decided that she loved him. In the ensuing days she had almost convinced herself that what she felt was a simpler gratitude and respect. But she wasn't feeling grateful or even respectful right now. What she was feeling was decidedly more dangerous than the fear for his safety that had driven her to his room. That she of all people should harbor such longings was truly absurd, but even more absurd would have been an attempt to say they did not exist.

She commanded herself to be cautious. But she had come too far, had risked too much, just to drop the message and then leave.

She sat up. He shifted to his right side and lay with his face close to hers. She could just barely make out the features. Dark lashes curled against his cheeks, and his lips were slightly parted. She concentrated on the lips.

Leaning forward, she brushed her mouth against his. Stunned, she sat back, her lips tingling and her mind in a whirl. Where was the feeling of disappointment she might have expected, the reminder of another similar yet far different encounter that had turned her away from men? They were not to be found . . . no disappointment, no reminders, just sweetness and warmth and a yearning for another kiss.

What a gentle touch it had been, no more forceful than a light breeze caressing her cheek, but it had made all the difference in her world.

Clay stirred, and Jenna panicked. Stumbling to her feet, she ran to the door. She reached for the handle.

"Who's there?" Clay's deep voice sounded like the snap of a whip.

She looked over her shoulder and saw him sitting up. She was completely away from the illumination of the window and knew it would take a few minutes for his eyes to adjust to the dark. She held perfectly still, caught by his awareness of her the way a creature of the night is stunned by a sudden light.

Tossing off the covers, he sat up and she saw that he did indeed sleep in the nude. In the dark she blushed, and she averted her eyes.

He shifted his weight to his feet.

"Please don't move," she whispered. She was amazed, and equally relieved, when he settled back on the bed. She also admitted to a flutter of irritation that he seemed so little surprised to find an unknown woman in his room.

"Who are you?" he asked. "One of the servant girls?"

She rounded her vowels like the highest toned lady in town. "Is that what I sound like, Clay?"

He laughed in the dark and the sound, as rich and deep as she had imagined it, caressed her like a warm western wind. "Not any I've heard." He paused, making no attempt to cover himself. "Is this some kind of joke?"

"No."

"Not a joke, huh? Then you're a thief."

"If I am, you don't sound afraid."

His square shoulders hunched into a shrug, then once again relaxed. "Should I be?"

For some inexplicable reason, Jenna felt her tension ease. "I'm not going to hurt you. I promise."

"Now I can hardly take your word for that, can I? Mosey on over here, and I'll check to see if you're armed. Then we'll decide how I ought to feel." He paused, and when he spoke again, his voice was serious. "It might be I'll have to pull my gun on you."

Jenna started, all relaxation gone. "You have a gun?" It was one contingency for which she had not planned.

Again he laughed. "In a way. At least, I'm armed with a loaded weapon. You get on over here and I'll show you exactly what I mean."

Jenna wasn't sure what he was talking about, but she figured that she was better off remaining by the door. She clutched her hands together. One thing was clear. Clay thought she had appeared in his room for reasons far from the truth, and she found she could not disabuse him of the error right away. Under anything approaching normal conditions, he would not give her a second look, even if she were dressed in something better than the present rags. But in the dark he gave every evidence of finding her more than a little interesting, and she felt a sweet-sad yearning inside that just might match his own feelings, at least in part.

This was the way she had felt when she watched him in the tavern. She felt truly obsessed, and she could not simply toss down the note and leave.

"I am a thief, in a way," she said, keeping her voice soft and warm. "I stole a kiss. Nothing more."

"It wasn't a dream?"

"Not to me."

He paused. "Then not to me either. Maybe I need another sample to make sure you're the same one."

Jenna's heart raced. "You must have a great many women visiting your room at night."

"There's always room for one more. By the way, how in hell did you get in?"

"I have my ways."

"You sure do, honey. You sure do." He snapped his fingers. "I know. Someone sent you as a birthday gift. I've been shooting my mouth off saying English women can't compare to the ones back in Texas. Someone wanted to prove I was wrong."

Relief flooded her. A birthday gift. It was a perfect masquerade and she must seize it right away. And she must most certainly forget her disappointment because he was inordinately at ease.

She managed a gentle, controlled sigh. "Happy birthday, Clay."

"Is that it? One kiss in my sleep?"

"You wouldn't want to get all your gifts at one time,

109

would you?"

"Can't think of why not. I'll tell you what. Mosey on over here and we'll talk about it."

Jenna swallowed. He was getting harder and harder to turn down.

"You keep saying that . . . you know, 'mosey on over here.' Is that how a man talks to a woman in Texas?"

"I don't know about anybody else, but I've been known to use it a time or two."

"And do the women usually mosey?"

"Usually. If you do a little of it, I'll show you why."

Jenna suspected she already knew why. Clay must be a charming man in bed. At least, she supposed he must be. In truth, she did not know what she meant. He had her very confused.

"I brought a message to you," she said.

"Other than happy birthday."

"Your friends know you've been going into Seven Dials."

"It was one of those friends who took me there. So what's the problem?"

"You've made enemies."

"I'm not surprised. Got anyone particular in mind? Maybe someone unhappy over a poker game?"

"Your friend overheard talk. Threats against you, was what he said. At a tavern called the Black Horse."

"So why didn't he tell me himself what he heard?"

Jenna thought that one over. "He thought I might be a more effective messenger."

"Whoever he is, he's got a point. At least you've got my full attention. The Black Horse. I had a little trouble there the other night."

"And you'll stay away?"

"To tell the truth, I'm not much on doing what someone tells me, especially if he doesn't tell me to my face."

"Then you won't stay away."

"Maybe all I need is a little more convincing about why I should."

"I see. Are you often warned by women in the night?"

"Warned? That's not exactly what I'm used to women doing."

Jenna knew she was swimming toward deep waters, and it took all her concentration to keep to the shallows that she understood.

"I'd really like for you to stay out of the Dials. It's not a very safe place."

"You seem mighty concerned."

"I am."

"Then why are you staying so far away?"

"Because I haven't got your promise," Jenna said, determined to be as stubborn as he.

"It's part of the deal, is it?" asked Clay. "I'm still not convinced."

"Leave the back gate and door open after midnight and I'll return tomorrow." She spoke softly and, she thought, rather seductively. "We can talk about it then."

"Won't work. Unless you're a hell of a lot bigger than you sound and a lot tougher, you couldn't get past Theodore."

"If you mean the Bullmastiff, don't be concerned. Theodore and I are friends."

"Friends?" He sounded truly surprised and, she didn't think she was reading too much in the word, truly admiring.

"That's right." She grew reckless. "He wasn't nearly as fierce as he tried to appear. Like most creatures of his gender."

"Does that include men?"

"They offer me no trouble." It was easy, she decided, to prevaricate in the dark, as well as to flirt.

"Honey, I'll just bet they don't." He paused. "Who in hell are you really? I don't even know your name."

"Someone sent to intrigue and advise you. As you said, to show you what English women are really like. My identity isn't part of the . . . arrangement."

111

Jenna was having to think very fast, but thus far, Clay hadn't commented on whether she was making sense. She found, once her heart quit threatening to pound its way through her breast, that she very much liked talking to him this way. So it was nothing more than another masquerade, but it was one she could throw herself into with all her heart — at least as far as the talking was concerned. Unfortunately, Clay would not be content to just talk for very long. It was a game to him right now, but it was one he wanted to win. It was time, she knew, for the game to end. Another minute and he'd have her 'moseying' before she knew what was happening.

Especially if she continued to taunt him the way she was doing. She was playing with fire, and she had retained sense enough to know that if she stayed any longer she would get badly burned.

"The gate and the door. Don't forget. If I learn you've gone back to the tavern, I won't return."

She slipped into the hall and without taking so much as a deep breath, flew like the wind toward the back stairs, abandoning the candle by his door, praying that one of the early rising servants didn't catch her. Or perhaps one of the earl's other guests. She still didn't know if Clay was the lone visitor in the house.

Luck stayed with her. Outside she saw the first rays of daylight over the neighboring house. Theodore was lying close to the back stoop, as though he had been waiting for her return. He lumbered to a stand, tail wagging, and allowed her to scratch behind his ears once again. What a watchdog, she thought.

Getting back over the fence proved more difficult than she had realized. At last she called the dog over by the gate, and with repeated assurances that he was truly a "good dog," she stood on his powerful shoulders and hiked herself over.

Well, she thought as she darted down the alley, she had found another benefit to being small and light.

She took her time getting back to the Horse. Tomorrow night . . . even if she went solely to protect Clay from harm, would she actually return? And if she did, what exactly would she do when she slipped into the protective darkness of his room?

He had struck her as a strong and good man, even kindly, but she didn't think he was one to take rejection two nights in a row.

Upstairs, Clay stretched out in his bed. He should have followed the mystery woman and found out just what in tarnation was going on. Or grabbed her when he had the chance. But she had him going, he had to give her credit, she had him doing what she wanted him to do. And damned well liking it.

She did her job well. He appreciated a professional who acted like one.

Tamed Theodore, had she? He looked forward to her trying to tame him.

Would she have a figure and a hunger to match that voice? Whoever had sent her must have chosen carefully. After all, Clay had done a lot of bragging about Texas women. And Englishmen didn't seem to take much to that kind of talk.

He brushed aside the talk about Seven Dials. Someone's idea of a joke, more than likely. The area wasn't one he would care to visit any too often, but on each trip to the tavern he had made sure to stay out of the worst streets and away from where more than two men were gathered at a time.

That was about as cautious as he needed to be. Besides, it wasn't the men or the slums that he wanted to give thought to.

Knowing Robert would be along to haul him out of bed before long, he dropped his head back on the pillow and began to contemplate the following night.

Chapter Nine

"I'll be hogtied," Clay said. "This thing really works."

He spoke into a wooden box on the wall of the Harrow library, where he had been summoned shortly before noon by the stone-faced butler, Randolph.

"Of course the telephone works, you cowboy!"

His sister's voice came to him over the earpiece scratchy and thin, as though she needed to clear her throat, but he could still hear every word even though she was three miles away in her Barrister Place home.

"All I want to know is if I can expect you for dinner tonight."

"Tonight?"

"I know this is a late invitation, Clay, but I hope you won't tell me you have plans."

Clay didn't much care for the pleading tone of his sister's voice. She was practically begging him to come by for dinner, and he wasn't used to Charlotte begging for much of anything. He didn't believe it was his company alone that she was after. Somewhere brother-in-law Bill figured in.

He shrugged, as if Charlotte could see him from her own comfortable drawing room.

"I do have plans, sort of."

The particulars he decided to keep to himself, especially since he wasn't certain of them himself. In the cold light of day he was tempted to believe his unseen visitor had been one of those English ghosts they seemed so proud of around the country.

Except for the soft voice that could tie a man in knots just with a word or two. No ghost he'd ever heard about came equipped with a voice like that. It was for sure she wasn't a dream; he'd had some powerfully interesting ones since he first noticed little boys were built differently from little girls, but none with the effect of last night's session.

"Bring her if you want," suggested Charlotte.

"What makes you think it's a woman?" He tried to sound offended.

She laughed sharply. "Don't be insulting, Clay. Are you trying to tell me it's *not?*"

He decided not to comment, one way or the other. If the woman in his plans was real flesh and blood — and if he could somehow manage to get the dinner invitation to her — she wouldn't be the kind to sit down next to William Rockmoor for a bowl of soup and a little discussion about the state of the British Empire.

"What time?" he asked.

"Seven," answered Charlotte. "Should I expect another guest?"

"Just me."

"Clay, when are you going to find a suitable woman and settle down?"

"What makes you think this woman you've dreamed up isn't suitable? And suitable for what?"

"Men," said Charlotte in disgust. "I'll see you at seven."

Still feeling awkward talking to the wall, he hung the earpiece on its hook and set about getting through the next few hours, most of which he spent riding one of the fine stallions his lordship had provided for his visit. In late afternoon he read through some hog feed literature that he found in the library. At seven sharp he was standing at his sister's door, his hand hovering over the brass knocker, his mind conjuring up how the evening would go.

If Charlotte needed him to do battle against husband Bill, he was more than willing. More than likely, all she wanted was a little friendly talk.

He'd try his damnedest to comply, but he'd probably be thinking of getting back to bed . . . back to his birthday gift.

One of his drinking buddies in London must have sent a woman to him; she'd said so, and he couldn't see she had any reason to lie. Probably been sent to warn him, too, about the rowdy parts of town. The least he could do was receive politely whatever she had to say.

Oh yes, he wanted to be back home as soon as he could, wanted to start talking to her nice and easy the way he had talked before, taking his time before he began to unwrap his gift. Taking his time would be a novelty, neither Emmeline or the piano teacher being big conversationalists, but then, they were women he knew.

If he was any judge of the female of the species, he was right in thinking this one would like to tease and taunt a little before getting down to the serious business of having a hell of a good time. It might just work out that he could even discover how she got past Theodore.

But first for dinner with the battling Rockmoors. Out of respect and affection for his sister — and to surprise her for once — he had put on a cut-away coat, stiff-collar, and a silk cravat. Practice, he'd told Robert, for when Lady Libby got into town.

"A wise course, Master Clayton," the valet had said with what appeared to be a smile, although it was so faint, Clay couldn't be sure.

He brought the door knocker down sharply and was promptly escorted into the Barrister Place parlor by a sour-faced butler who made Randolph look like a rodeo clown. Both Charlotte and William were waiting. Like himself, William was dressed in black. Stiff-backed as a picket, he stood by a low fire on the grate, his full head of brown hair combed back slickly, his eyes as usual faintly disapproving as he regarded his brother-in-law. It was Charlotte, seated in a nearby chair, who was a sight to behold.

She wore a yellow gown, and there must have been a mile or two of ruffles and lace added to the strategic places women seemed to think needed decorating. With all that golden hair piled in curls on top of her head and a warm smile of greeting on her face, she reminded him of the sun.

When she offered him a glass of sherry, he figured they would be corralled in the parlor for a while. And when he got a closer look at the lines around her mouth and the flat look in her eyes, he figured that, proud though she was, she was having a hard time keeping the clouds of worry from rolling in. All was not well at Barrister Place.

"You're going down to Hampshire, aren't you, Clay?" she asked when he settled into the chair beside her. William kept up his guarding of the hearth.

"That's my plan."

"Hampshire?" William's neat eyebrows rose to his neatly combed hair and his moustache twitched.

"The earl wants me to look over some cattle," Clay explained. "They're doing some experiments with breeding down there he thought I might want to look at."

"Ah yes, he still dabbles in that sort of thing, doesn't he?"

It would have taken a deaf man to miss the amusement in William's voice. Clay felt his hackles rise.

"He's done some damned fine work getting fatter beeves to market at less cost."

"How interesting," responded William, a slight smile on his lips.

"You'll have to pardon my husband," interjected Charlotte with a wave of her hand. "He's not quite

117

sure where milk comes from, so don't expect him to talk about cows."

William flicked a cold glance at his wife. "I know the quality of fine roast beef. That's all a gentleman need concern himself with, Charlotte. And certainly all that a lady needs to know."

Clay saw that a curled fist was going to be a regular thing if he stayed around his brother-in-law very long. The surprising thing was that Alex or Libby hadn't gotten angry and shot William before the wedding ceremony. Charlotte must have pitched one whale of a fit to get her way.

He concentrated on her. As if she could read his mind, she curved her lips into a smile, but the grip she had on her sherry was enough to shatter the glass. Clay expected any minute for the crystal to snap in half.

"We saw the Queen yesterday, Clay," she said, deftly changing the subject. "She was riding in the royal carriage just outside Buckingham. We'd gone for a walk in St. James' Park, and suddenly she was right there. For someone close to eighty she looked in remarkably good health. One of the grandchildren was with her. There are so many, I have a hard time keeping up with them."

Clay knew that in all that rattling on, she was playing the part of peacemaker. He wished her good luck in the chore, since he'd made a mess of it at the breakfast table yesterday.

"If Libby has her way," she said, "I expect I'll be seeing her myself before long."

"I'm sure we both will," said Charlotte.

"As is only right," William said, directing his words to Clay. "You are, after all, Viscount Parkworth, and in this sixtieth year of Victoria's reign it's particularly proper that all members of the peerage pay her honor."

Clay shot a glance at William. The title held little importance to him personally, although for his father's sake he respected it. What got him now was the realiza-

118

tion that his brother-in-law respected him solely because he could attach it to his name. Not because he raised cattle, which was far more important since he had to work hard at it, but because he was titled. For that, he had needed only to be born.

Clay would never understand the British, even though he was half British himself. Laced stiffer than an old maid's corset, most of them. Too much attention to pomp and circumstance and not enough to open skies, maybe was the problem. A few weeks spent looking at miles and miles of prairie and limestone hills wouldn't do them any harm.

Wouldn't much hurt him, either, come to think of it.

William was not through, warmed to his subject as he was. "There's nothing quite like the British Empire. Nothing in the history of the world. I do not imagine that we will ever see another country to match ours."

"I'd have to agree with you there, Bill."

Wound up as he was in his words, the way Andy Taylor got sometimes, William didn't give him so much as a frown. "At any given moment of the day or night — right this very moment, in fact, Victoria's Diamond Jubilee is being celebrated some place in the world. India, Canada, Australia, or anywhere in the vast stretches in between. I was reading in the *Times* that they have opened a Jubilee Mine in the Transvaal. Not for diamonds, mind you, but for gold. And a fitting tribute it is."

"They've tried digging for iron ore around Mason, and even looked for uranium," Clay remarked, unable to resist a little digging of his own, "but it's not in honor of the Queen. Don't recall so much as a cup of coffee being raised in her honor."

"What else should one expect in the colonies," William snapped back with a sneer.

"Not meant as disrespect. She's just not a household name in the county."

"As a citizen of Great Britain, it is up to you to see

that she is."

"Could be." Deciding not to rile his brother-in-law more, Clay kept his mouth closed and listened while William went on about the royal family, Transvaal gold, and in general the London social scene. Charlotte seemed to be listening, too, but her eyes were directed to her half empty glass and Clay couldn't be sure. When talk turned to the Marquess of Salisbury and his term as Prime Minister, he poured himself a second glass of sherry, which was usually not too high on his list of recreational drinks. Tonight it tasted good.

At nine o'clock they finally got around to shifting to the dining room, where Charlotte stuffed him with cucumber soup, broiled whitefish, baked capons, and an overcooked slice of roast lamb, the latter dressed up with a mess of vegetables that would have made the nutrition-minded Aunt Martha proud of her niece.

Talk was still dominated by William, and Clay found it easy to let his mind wander. There was only one thing he could give genuine attention to, and that was the intruder with the sexy voice. Once Charlotte caught him with a grin on his face and asked right sharply why he thought the Crimean War so amusing. He didn't come up with an answer that seemed to settle her mind.

After a large serving of raspberry tarts and whipped cream, which she would not let him decline, he grudgingly admitted they were thicker and tastier than any ever produced in the Lone Star State. Charlotte ordered him back into the parlor, put a glass of brandy in his hand, and asked him what he'd been doing lately.

Clay got the definite feeling she was trying to postpone his leaving. Settling back in his chair, he shrugged.

"Really, Charlotte," said William from his standing position at the hearth. "Leave the man alone."

She did not give her husband so much as a glance.

Clay studied his sister from over the rim of his glass. As before dinner, she was seated in the chair next to his, only now the fingers of both hands were drumming on the carved wooden arms. The lines around her mouth seemed deeper than ever, and her eyes had taken on a light that didn't have much to do with something so simple as trying to have a good time.

She was strung tighter than a barbed wire fence after Andy Taylor had been working it over for a while, but it wasn't a condition Clay could bring up in her parlor. Yesterday she'd told him right smartly that she could handle her own problems. Unable to work things out, she had turned to handling his.

"I haven't been doing much of anything," he said.

"Come now, Clay, you are most definitely preoccupied tonight. William and I could take off our clothes and copulate right here on the carpet, and you wouldn't notice."

"Charlotte, really!" said William.

"I'd probably notice," said Clay.

"It's a woman, isn't it? The woman you told me about when I rang you on the telephone."

"I don't recall telling you about anyone. You were doing most of the talking on that thing."

"Don't bother to deny I'm right. You barely touched your food, and after all the trouble I went to."

The edge of self pity in her voice startled him.

Wound up as much as her husband had been at the dinner table, she went on. "I should have remembered your usual diet of beans and fatback —"

"Not *my* diet," interjected Clay. "You're thinking of that dog we once owned. Never cared for fatback myself."

Charlotte's nose wrinkled. "Oh, yes, the dog." Her lips twitched and Clay thought she was going to break out in a smile.

"Give me a thick steak any day," he said. "Good Texas beef. Not that I didn't appreciate all the trouble you went to."

"Don't hand me that malarkey," she snapped, for a moment sounding like the old Charlotte, the one he caught a glimpse of now and then. "All evening you've been a million miles away. Especially at dinner."

Not a million miles, he could have answered. Only the three it would take to get back to his room.

"Maybe it's just that I don't like cucumber soup."

"I doubt if you've ever *had* it before. And you didn't taste it tonight. What's really on your mind?" Her fingers rested on the chair arms, and her brow furrowed. "There's not anything wrong, is there? Have you heard from Alex or Libby?"

Clay shook his head. If Baby Sister was going to imagine all sorts of worries, he would give her something real to think about. He would tell her the truth.

"I've got a woman waiting for me back in my bed."

William's eyebrows shot up, and his moustache shook like a nervous caterpillar.

"Liar," said Charlotte.

"No, really," continued Clay. "I don't mean she's exactly there—"

"I didn't think so." Charlotte sounded satisfied. "It's one thing to meet someone at one of your taverns, but to—"

"She's supposed to be there sometime before long."

From the corner of his eye, he caught William watching him carefully, apparently far more interested in the current topic than he had been earlier in Hampshire beeves. And he had thought his brother-in-law bored with talk of sex.

"Just who is she?" asked Charlotte. "One of the servants? Really, Clay, I thought you had more sense than that."

"She's definitely not a servant. Sounded more like a lady. I got the feeling she'd never been in the house before she showed up last night. She slipped in while I was asleep and kissed me awake."

122

Charlotte rolled her eyes. "I see. A woman—a *lady*—appeared in your room last night and woke you with a kiss. Aren't you getting your story mixed up with one of those fairy tales Martha used to read us? Not that your version isn't a shade more lurid than anything the dear woman ever picked out."

Clay took a swallow of brandy and let the warm liquid ease its way down his throat. Definitely several cuts above the Black Horse brand, he decided. "You asked and I'm telling you. We talked and she promised to come back."

Charlotte considered him a moment. "She just walked right up to your room—"

"That's what she claimed. Sometime early in the morning. Three, maybe four. Woke me out of a deep sleep." He could see he continued to have William's complete attention, as much as he had his sister's.

"And who let her in?" asked Charlotte. "Or perhaps she had her own key. Maybe she kissed the entire staff awake before going upstairs. Have you asked Robert whether or not he had a visitor?"

"Robert said the back door was left unlocked. One of the servant girls slipping around, he thought. And there were signs someone had been tromping around in the new flower bed by the gate."

"Which means she got past Theodore. Clay, you are full of b—"

"Now, now, Baby Sister. Mind your language."

"I was going to say you are full of bald-faced lies. No one can get past Theodore except someone he knows. She must have been built like a Hereford bull."

"But without all the usual equipment, you mean." William choked on his drink.

"That's what I mean," said Charlotte.

"I didn't get a look at her, what with the room being so dark," explained Clay, "but I'll find out the details tonight."

Charlotte was not subdued. "What I think is that

123

you don't want to tell me what you've really got on your mind. It probably involves a woman, all right, and that's certainly your business. Just don't tell us any more fairy tales."

So much, Clay thought, for spilling the truth.

"Good brandy, William," he said, lifting his glass.

"Thank you," his brother-in-law said, his self control returned, his nod as stiff as the collar on his shirt.

When Clay glanced back at his sister, he could sense a change in her mood.

"Clay," she said, her hands resting in her lap, "William and I are riding down to Brighton tomorrow. Some friends have a home near the water and have invited us to stay there while they are in France." She glanced briefly up at her husband. "We thought it would be good to get out of the city for a week or so. Why don't you come with us? You could take a few days to look at that cattle in Hampshire and then come down to the coast."

At last, Clay thought, the reason for the invitation to dinner. Charlotte might have wanted his company for the evening, but she also had another, more involved invitation to present to him.

He cogitated on it and decided it was one he could decline . . . even if the seaside town had been high on his list of sites to see. He'd caught the pleading look in that glance Charlotte had given her husband. They weren't much more than newlyweds, their second anniversary being only a few weeks past; in the event they were getting away to work things out between them, they needed to be alone, whether Charlotte thought so or not.

And if that wasn't the reason behind the Brighton trip, they still didn't need a big brother poking his nose into their lives every time they turned around.

"Maybe I can join up with you later," he said.

Charlotte protested, and William echoed her words, although with a mite less enthusiasm, but Clay stuck

124

to his guns. A half hour later he was making his hurried way back home, his thoughts torn between where he'd been and where he was heading.

Blood relatives or not, women had a built-in power to keep a man in turmoil. He'd been sent on his way with a request from Charlotte to tell his mysterious visitor hello.

When it came to sarcasm, Baby Sister didn't know when to quit.

Chapter Ten

Midnight had long come and gone by the time Clay let himself in the Tunstall Square home. He barely made his entry before the butler Randolph, fully and neatly clothed, arrived in the foyer a half minute too late to perform the job of opening the front door.

"Evening, Randolph. Anything going on?" Clay asked as he headed for the curved stairway.

"If I might ask, what did Lord Parkworth have in mind?"

"Anybody drop by to visit recently?"

Randolph hesitated. "No one has come to call."

Clay stopped at the bottom of the stairs. "Something wrong? You don't sound like your old self tonight."

"Nothing is wrong, m'lord. It is just that there was an incident last night. I did not mention it at the time, but perhaps I should have."

"Was it around back?"

Randolph's gray eyebrows lifted a fraction. "Why, no. Oh, of course, you refer to the maid Nellie's unfortunate behavior."

"You didn't fire her, did you?"

"No, m'lord, but I most certainly gave her a stern warning not to do anything so scandalous again."

Clay shook his head. "These maids don't lead much of a life, do they?"

The butler sniffed. "I hope they do not."

Servants, Clay decided, were more rigid in their behavior and expectations than the so-called gentry.

"What was the incident you referred to?" he asked.

"A . . . person came to the front door. Long after you had retired."

"A person?"

"I did not see the caller. The footman answered the summons, and he said it sounded like a woman. She, if I may refer to the caller as such, she kept to the shadows, and he did not get a good look at her, although she sounded like one of the Cockneys. She tried to say something about you, m'lord, or so Jimmy thought, but at my suggestion he demanded that she leave. Of course she did so."

A Cockney? Not if she were the Princess, which she must be. Clay couldn't convince himself two women would be seeking him out in the middle of the same night to see to his safety. Hell, even *one* would have seemed impossible a week ago. At the front door she must have been affecting some kind of accent. If he got around to it, he'd have to ask her why.

Clay fought a smile. Randolph was about to bust with pride for having saved the family home from invasion, and all he'd done was send the desperado around to the back.

She must have liked coming in that way—or preferred staying away from Jimmy and Randolph as much as possible, because she'd asked to come in the same way tonight. He'd made sure the back door and gate were unlocked before leaving for the Rockmoor manse. Theodore had been his usually friendly self, all two tons of him, and Clay had warned him to be careful who he let in the yard.

As a precaution, he had warned Robert to make sure the back entries remained unlocked. Robert had

127

not asked why, merely commenting that surely Theodore would serve in the place of a half dozen bolted doors.

He had also asked Robert not to drop by his room until he was called. Again, Robert had not asked why, strengthening Clay's growing conviction that the valet was a gentleman's gentleman in the best sense of the term. Both of them had decided it wasn't absolutely necessary to let Randolph in on everything that was going on.

Clay hoped all his care had paid off. Waving goodnight to the butler, he took the steps two at a time. The door to his room was closed, but there was nothing unusual about that. Most every door in the house, and there were dozens of them, were usually kept shut. The upstairs hallway reminded him of the second floor of the Longhorn Saloon, although it might be considered a tad fancier with its Oriental carpet, the Constable landscapes hung in the center of each paneled wall, and the pedestal holding the porcelain vase from one of the Chinese dynasties. Clay never could keep those dynasties in order, but he figured that's why Robert and Randolph were kept around.

The minute he slipped inside his room, he knew she was there, even though he couldn't make out so much as the footpost on the bed. It was something maybe about the electricity in the air that told him, or an unfamiliar flowery scent, or maybe it was just that he wanted her so much to be waiting, he could accept nothing less.

"Hello," he said to the dark.

"Hello," she said.

Her voice, drifting to him from somewhere near the window, was soft the way he remembered it, and sexy. She put more into the one word than most women managed to fit in a whole conversation.

She'd placed herself as far from the door as she could manage, with the bed separating them. Clay, a sense of relief rushing through him because she had really returned, figured they could meet in the middle.

"So you got in all right. No trouble with Theodore?"

"He's a wonderful dog."

"He's a mighty poor guard."

"Don't blame him. I happen to get along well with dogs and children."

He figured she also did right well with men. Somehow the thought irritated him. And come to think of it, he felt damned foolish standing here talking in the dark. He stumbled for the bedside lamp.

"No."

"What do you mean, *no?*

"I mean no."

"I hope it's not a word you're planning on using very much."

"Whatever plans I have do not include striking that lamp."

"I have to see you."

"No, you don't. If you insist, I'll leave." There was a hard edge to her voice that had not been there before.

"You'd never get past me."

A pause, and then he heard a soft, "Please."

Clay would give a woman anything if she said "please" like that. The light would be a negotiable point later, when she was in a more agreeable frame of mind.

"Mind if I get undressed? I've had this mule collar on for about as long as I can stand."

Her laugh was as soft as her voice, but he heard in it a nervousness that surprised him.

"You may . . . get undressed."

Clay stripped down to his trousers and stretched out on the bed, shoulders propped against the pillows at the headboard, and directed his words toward the window. "Are you going to stay over there all night?"

"You're an impatient man, Clay."

"That's one way of putting it. Let's just say I'm ready for my gift."

Which was an understatement, the British half of him talking. His body had been ready for her the minute he heard her voice. He had to remind himself he had been looking forward to some beforehand talk.

"I'd like to know a little about you first," she said.

"I'm planning on letting you know a lot more than that. Why don't you—"

"Mosey on over to the bed?"

Clay laughed. "Yeah."

"In a little while. First, let's talk."

"I'm better at talking afterward."

"After—? Oh, of course."

"Sometimes during, if the spirit moves me."

"Oh." The word came out more like a sigh.

For a woman who made her living as she did, she sure as hell gave signs she wasn't quite up on what was going on, or, for that matter, exactly what she was supposed to do.

He came down hard on his impatience. Baby Sister had accused him of thinking of women in only one way, and he'd been quick to tell her she was wrong.

If Miss Birthday Gift wanted to talk, that's what they would do. For a while, he'd let her call the shots. He'd get his turn later.

Besides, he had to admit to a curiosity that was getting as strong as his other, more expected itches.

"You behaved yourself tonight," she said.

"How's that?"

"You didn't go into the Dials."

"Now how did you know? You got someone on my tail?"

"I don't understand."

"You got someone following me?"

"I just know."

"I've got it. You're that tavern owner's wife. What's the name? Oh, yeah, Teresa."

"No!"

Now that was a definite response. He was glad she could work up so much feeling, even if it was put to saying his least favorite word.

Shifting to his side, he tried to pick at least her outline from out of the dark, but all he could see were shadows. "You know, honey, I'd be a mite more comfortable with this situation if I knew what to call you. I accept you're not Teresa. Didn't really think you were, anyway. Don't take this for an insult, but you've got too much class, and I can't get a handle on Mrs. Mims ever saying 'no' the way you just did."

"I'm not insulted. On the contrary."

Clay grinned. With every word his mystery woman uttered, she sounded better and sweeter and more intriguing. "For all I know," he speculated out loud, "you could be one of the Queen's kin."

"It's possible. She does have rather a large family, doesn't she?"

"Then why don't I call you Princess?"

"Princess?" she asked, and he heard the laughter in her voice. "I have no objections."

Whatever the joke was that pleased her, it pleased him, too. "At least that's taken care of. Now then, Princess, what do you want to know? I'm not a very complicated man."

"Can you tell me about Texas?"

The question surprised him and hooked him, too.

131

Every woman he'd met in England had wanted to tell him what she thought about his home. Most of them had it all wrong.

"Hard to know where to start. It's a big state with a lot of people and even more cattle. It's got mountains and rivers and an ocean and miles and miles of flat land that can either make a man feel small as a prairie dog or big as a god."

"What about your home? Do you live on a mountain?"

"It's hard to run cattle on a mountain."

"Then you have a farm. Is it yours?"

"I own a ranch. Never say 'farm' to a stockman. It's considered a cuss word."

"A profanity, you mean."

"Yeah, that's what I mean." Lordy, but she had an entertaining voice. Even ordinary words sounded sweet when she said them. Damned if he wasn't enjoying talking this way. Eventually, when she crawled under the covers beside him, he'd like to have her whisper a few of what women called "sweet nothings" in his ear. He'd be more than happy to oblige her if she wanted some of them whispered right back.

The more he thought about all that close-up whispering, the warmer he became. Playing her game was getting downright uncomfortable, what with the tight fit of his trousers and the effect she was having on him. Still, he'd give it a few more minutes. She wanted to know about Texas, and he was just gentleman enough to comply—and enough of a Texan to enjoy the brags.

Before long, he'd put his own wants to her. And maybe, when he got around to it, a question or two of his own.

"Farms don't have cattle," he explained, settling back on the bed, "at least not an entire herd, unless

132

it's a dairy. My place is called the Whiskey Ranch. Named for a drunk that gambled it away to my grandfather. Old Ernie had to fight like hell to keep the place going. Gave his life's blood to the ranch."

"He was killed?"

"Someone wanted his land. The bastard didn't get it."

Clay had no idea why he was telling her so many particulars, considering that he normally spoke about his family's past about as much as he discussed the ocean floor.

"Do you have a wife and children that are waiting on the Whiskey for you to return?"

"No wife. No kids. Just rolling hills and creeks so beautiful it could make a grown man cry to think of them."

"You love it, don't you?"

"You might say that."

He waited a long time for her to speak; he could almost hear her thinking in the dark.

"I lived on a farm once." She spoke hesitantly, as though she had to force out each word. "It was a long time ago. And it was a real farm. No cattle, except for a milk cow. Just orange groves, mainly, and corn."

"So you're a farmer's daughter."

"Does that have some significance?"

Except for an off-color story or two he'd heard around the campfire, it had no significance whatsoever. "Just an observation," he said. "The thing is, you don't sound like a country girl. What part of England was your place in?"

"It wasn't." She paused so long that he wondered if she'd managed to slip out without his knowing. "My father and I lived in the Transvaal thirty miles from Pretoria. Do you know where that is?"

"Yep. I have a great aunt who is hell on geography."

"Actually, we lived in an area called Witwatersrand."

"Aunt Martha wasn't inclined to go into that much detail. What about your mother?"

"She died when I was born. I was her only child."

"My condolences. Your father still there?"

"He died when I was six."

He caught no self pity in her voice, just a telling of the facts.

"So how did you get to England? Relatives send for you?"

Again came the hesitation.

"Look, Princess, if you don't want to talk about yourself, then don't. We can probably think of something else to do."

"It's just that I never talk about myself. I don't suppose it could do any harm. You'll be going back to Texas soon."

"You trying to get rid of me?"

"No, I'm not trying to get rid of you."

He caught the urgency in her voice and almost came off the bed after her, feeling a little of that same urgency himself. Why in hell he was finding her so vulnerable, he couldn't figure. She'd been sent as a one-time gift. He had to give her credit. She had him completely bamboozled, and after only one brief kiss when he'd been half asleep.

Clay admitted it wasn't the kiss that had got at him. It was the way she talked, asking questions and listening to what he had to say, then telling him about herself as though he were the only man in the world she had ever confided in . . . as though she knew him outside of this room, as though she cared.

Whoever she was, she was special, and the way he was feeling right now, he'd like the night to go on

134

forever.

"So tell me about England, Princess, and how you got here. I'd like to know," he said, and realized he wasn't handing her a line. But he also didn't plan on spending the entire evening simply throwing words back and forth.

"And then," he added, just so she'd understand how things were, "it will be time for you to crawl into bed."

Chapter Eleven

Crawl into bed.

Clay expressed himself clearly enough. Jenna sat huddled on the carpet in the dark by the window draperies, knees pulled to her chest, and thought of the words she wished he had said.

My darling, come to me and make me the happiest man on earth.

Or: *I have long dreamed of this moment. You are the woman I desire above all others.*

The truth was, she was the handiest woman at the moment and she'd given not the slightest hint she wouldn't pounce on him like a kitten on a rubber ball and play the night away.

She was also a fool, an imbecile, an idiot to wish their situation was otherwise. She loved him and he didn't know who she was.

Which didn't keep him from wanting her in his bed.

It was an extraordinarily poor time to discover that she, cautious and practical and even calculating when she had to be, was also a romantic at heart. As her troubles had worsened over the past months, she'd given up all plans of someday having a home and a husband, of sharing that home with the twins and, if fortune shone upon her, with children of her own. For her, the twins would have to be enough.

She realized now how important those abandoned

plans had once been. Though they were dreams that could never come true, they had never completely left her.

"England, remember?" Clay's voice was darkly insistent and pulled her from her thoughts. "You're supposed to be telling me how you got here."

"England, yes," Jenna said.

She wrapped her arms tighter around her knees. She knew exactly how and why she had traveled to this land from her South African home. And she knew why she'd returned to this room—not because she had promised to do so, but because she could not stay away. She had felt yearnings impossible to ignore. She had felt so alone, more so than she had felt in all the months before Clay strolled inside the Horse.

Ordinary common sense, it would seem, was best saved for those with ordinary lives.

At least he was a little interested in her as a person. That interest would have to satisfy.

"When I was six, my father sent me with a nanny," she said.

"Now that sounds downright English."

"He *was* English, but he'd gone to the Transvaal as a young man to make his fortune. After a few years he had invested in a diamond mine and made a little money, more than he ever made from farming. Not nearly as much as he had hoped, of course, but then one rarely does. With the trouble between the British and the Boers, and the Africaners, too, he was saving to buy a home in Portsmouth. That's why he sent me on ahead, so that I could begin my education in an English school. He planned to join us there in a year, perhaps two, depending on how things went financially."

"So what happened?"

"He went into Pretoria on the wrong afternoon.

There was a riot—" Her voice broke.

"He was killed."

Jenna appreciated his bluntness. It eased the hurt in the telling of the long-ago tragedy.

"Yes, he was killed. Before my ship even docked."

"And what happened to his little girl?"

Jenna could not tell him everything . . . even knowing he was soon going back to that strange place called the Whiskey Ranch.

"Nothing very dramatic," she lied.

There was no point in telling him about the solicitor in Portsmouth who had informed her of her father's death, and of her poverty, all John Bailey Cresswell's money having disappeared. There was no need to tell him about the train ride into London, where she had planned to stay with the nanny's family until something could be decided about her . . . or about the screeching wheels on the track just south of the city, the sudden jolt, the tumbling of bodies, the screams.

Nanny, her one link with the past, her lone hope for the future, had been killed in the wreck; a blow to the head had left the six-year-old Jenna unable to hear. The condition had proven to be temporary, but her hearing didn't return for a long, long while.

"I ended up in school," she said simply.

The Deaf and Dumb Asylum had been its name, on Old Kent Road, London, a charitable institution run by the Reverend Joseph Cox, a good and generous soul. How strange it was to have lost all touch with him, after all he had done for her. One of her great regrets was that she had not repaid him in kind, but to communicate with him would only bring them both shame.

One brief letter was all she had allowed herself, and that almost a year ago.

Would he approve of what she was doing tonight? He would find it impossible to do so, considering his deeply held beliefs of right and wrong. But he was a kind and sensitive man, a widower who had on occasion expressed loving memories of his wife.

"Someday, Jenna, you too will find someone to share your life," he had told her shortly before she left to make her way in the world. "I wish you the happiness I have known."

The wish was not to be; whatever happiness she could find would have to be temporary, a stolen moment in the arms of a man who would not tarry long.

". . . And you grew up," said Clay.

Jenna nodded, though she knew he could not see. "I grew up. It's not a very interesting story, I'm afraid." Not when she had left out most of the particulars. There were some details she could never reveal to anyone, even someone about to sail away.

"Why is it I get the feeling you're holding something back?"

Clay could be a difficult, stubborn man, and much too clever for Jenna's peace of mind.

"I don't think you really want to know everything that brought me here tonight, do you?"

She wanted to add that she wasn't sorry in the least to be in his room . . . to be talking to him this way . . . to have him so near. She forgot the words of love she'd been craving. For the first time in a very long while—except for those occasional hours with the twins—she did not feel isolated from the rest of humanity.

"You're right. I don't want to know." Clay's voice was flat, dismissive, as though she had disappointed him in some way. "It's a strange coincidence, but my father did the same thing with my sister, only she was twelve."

"Did what?" she asked, startled.

"Sent her to an English school."

"All the way from Texas?"

"He wanted her to get the best education she could, and he felt that would be here."

"And what about you?"

"I'm too ornery to benefit from one of your public schools. Aunt Martha did all right by me. I don't make a fool of myself more than three times a day."

Jenna's heart warmed to him all the more. She liked a man with a little humility, especially when it was so misguided. "That's more than I can say about some of our British gentlemen."

"I'd rather not hear about any of them."

Again she heard the disappointment. He had misunderstood. He thought she meant the other men she had known, the others she had visited in the night, the ones who had come before him. She would have laughed out loud at his error if she hadn't felt such a heaviness in her heart.

"You're stalling, Princess."

That she was. The irony of the name he'd chosen struck her anew. If Clay only knew he had anointed as royalty a resident of the Dials.

"Come to bed."

His voice was deep, husky, and altogether compelling. More, it reminded her more sharply than ever of the way things really were. He didn't think of her in actuality as a princess. He thought she was a whore.

It was what he *wanted* her to be.

Jenna gave a brief, bitter thought to her dreams of someday escaping from London, of having a home and a husband. They were not the stuff of real life, at least not hers.

Real life consisted of Teresa's taunts, of questioning police, of the wide, fearful eyes of Alice and Alfred.

And real life was also Clay Parkworth of Texas, lying stretched out only a few feet away and waiting to show her a few truths about the ways of the world as he saw them.

Since the age of six, when she bade good-bye to her father for what was to be the last time, she had known little joy — Until she met Clay. She loved him, with all the fervor of an innocent heart. Nothing having to do with him could be less than magnificent, and that must also include the act of loving. Since his appearance in the Black Horse, he had made her days endurable simply because she had begun to contemplate the nights when she might see him again.

More than anything else, he had made her forget the unhappy events of the past.

There was a quality about Clay that drew her as nothing else ever had, a strength of purpose, an inner reserve of power that drove him to acts of kindness and courage when all around him cowered and mocked. He was also, she suspected, capable of great passion.

Her only problem was that up until tonight passion had been an emotion completely disconnected to anything pleasurable she had experienced in her own mind and body, an excuse humanity gave for grapplings in the night, an expression read in a book. Or worse, an ugliness, a kind of violence one human being inflicted on another. This violence she understood very well.

The reverend might have spoken of love and companionship, but he had not gone into the physical side of such relationships. And neither had the ladies of quality who volunteered their time at the school.

141

She trusted Clay would teach her what she did not know. Jenna was no coward, no matter what else could be said of her. He was right; she *had* been stalling. But no more.

Heart pounding, she stood and slipped off her tattered clothes, from the cap atop her head to her ragged underdrawers. As terrified as she was of approaching him already undressed, she was more frightened that he would feel the coarseness of her gown and know her for a fraud. Whores, at least the kind he would be offered by his friends, would wear satin and silk against their oft-touched skin.

Her hair, even the wisps about her face, was as clean as her body, shining with the glow of a fresh-lit fire. It hung loose and thick about her shoulders.

He would not see its sheen, of course, or its color, but he would touch it. She very much wanted him to touch it. As she had stood brushing it earlier in the twins' lodging room, she had imagined him stroking the curls over and over again. It was the one specific image she had allowed herself when she was picturing the possibilities of the evening.

She had gone so far as to steal a small vial of wool grease from Teresa's room. Lanoline, it was called, to soften the skin. Jenna had rubbed it liberally on her hands and arms, hoping to disguise the roughness she'd gained from her hours scrubbing the Black Horse floor.

Stripped of her rags, she was struck with a sensation of vulnerability. She had done a great deal of rationalizing, but she hadn't actually imagined herself crawling naked into bed. Right now the thought was unavoidable, and very, very daunting.

Clay pulled back the covers. "Let's get started, Your Highness. I'd say you could make a man feel like a king."

She took a step toward the bed and her knees

142

gave out from under her.

"Are you all right?" he asked. "I won't bite." He chuckled. "Well, maybe a little. But only where you want me to."

If he thought to encourage her, he was going about it the wrong way.

"Clay—"

"Now don't tell me you're a tease. I won't believe it." He sat on the side of the bed facing her.

"I'm—"

The words caught in her throat. He was removing his trousers. He finished with amazing alacrity. "Are you certain you don't want a light?" he asked.

He sounded proud of what she would see; the thought unnerved her even more. So maybe she had imagined violins playing and a surge of adoration welling inside her, and Clay, swept with the same feelings, confessing to the same deep emotions, the same sweet longings, the same intense waves of love.

What she was getting was a very determined and very naked man crouched on the side of the bed a few feet away and expecting a good-time girl to pounce upon him and do things she did not truly think she could do. Even if she knew exactly what those things were.

She had wanted to know the joys of lovemaking, but she also needed to know a few more practical details. All she really knew from her unwanted observations in the rookery alleys was that a woman spread her legs, and part of a man's body entered a special place, jerking violently for a moment or two before pulling away. Both man and woman made animal sounds, and in the case of Mr. and Mrs. Mims, the bedsprings creaked a great deal.

For the first time in a long while, she turned coward. A mistake, that's what this evening was, a terrible misunderstanding on her part and on Clay's.

At the moment Jenna would have preferred a confrontation with the London police.

She edged toward the pile of rags on the floor. Knees bent, she reached down. She dropped her eyes to try to find her underdrawers. Without warning steel fingers gripped her shoulders and lifted her back to her full height, and she was pulled against a wall of flesh.

"You're a small one, aren't you?" Clay asked, his hands stroking her shoulders and her back, thumbs trailing against the back of her neck. A thousand shivers shot along her spine.

The top of her head came just to his chin, and her breasts were crushed against his body, which felt hot and hairy and hard. She tried to push away, and her own hands came up against his chest and encountered slick skin pulled taut, and wiry curls covering the smooth skin. Most startling of all, she felt the beating of his heart. A sharp intake of breath and she was assailed with new scents, musky and forbidden, that set off another wave of chills.

"This is all a mistake," she said. "Let me go."

"You give a lot of orders." The words were blunt, and he made no move to do as she asked. "Must be the British approach."

"You're not paying attention to me."

He laughed, and she felt his breath stir her hair. "Still playing games, Princess? I've got a couple in mind we might try."

He bent his head and brushed his lips across her cheek, at the same time he rubbed his hips against her. A solid object pressed into her stomach, and she realized with a start exactly what the object was.

Jenna's mind was in a whirl, and her body was going through such strange transformations involving heat and tingling nerves that she could not think straight, could not imagine anything she might say that would make him stop. Except—

"Get in the bed," she whispered and was relieved when he allowed an inch of air between them.

"Now that's an order I'd be glad to obey."

He released his hold on her. She stepped away. "Clay, there's something—"

"Whoa, Princess. Enough palaver."

His hand gripped her upper arm and slid down until he had her by the wrist. One tug was all she was aware of, and then they were both at the edge of the bed, and he was seated, pulling her down onto his lap, down onto that very hard part of his anatomy. It pressed against her bare buttocks and for a moment was all in the world she could think about.

Two urges tugged at her, one to pull free of all contact with him and the other to wrap her arms around his neck and kiss him long and hard.

She shifted, he moaned, and then she felt herself being pulled onto the bed. How he managed to bring it all about so quickly and so smoothly, she wasn't sure, but all of a sudden she was stretched out beside him in the bed, the covers tossed over them both, one of his legs pinning her down so that she was powerless to move. His head hovered above hers in the dim light, and she could make out the outline of his sharp-hewn face.

His eyes she could only imagine, but she knew they would be like burning coals.

Nothing was as she would have ordered, not the heat of his flesh nor his unyielding presence nor the frightening demands her own body seemed to be making on her.

She had no more begun to contemplate those demands than she had something far more insistent to think about: Clay's hand on her breast.

"Nice," he said.

He was stretched out on top of her so fast she did not have time to roll away. With his arms propped on either side of her shoulders, pinning her arms to her sides, he loomed over her, his face close to hers.

She fought a sudden panic. Try as she might to remind herself he was the same man who had defended a child in the tavern, she failed. The man holding her hostage against a feather mattress was consumed by thoughts other than charitable, kindly ones. In that, he was no different from other men.

As she stared up at him, all she could make out was the shape of his head, the tousled hair and the angular edges of his face. He leaned down to kiss her, and she felt her breasts flatten against his chest.

He shifted one hand to the side of her breast, his thumb stroking its tip. Ripples of pleasure went through her, their intensity so overwhelming that she shivered beneath him.

"Not cold, are you, Princess? I'll have to do something about that. Can't send you out of here ailing, now can I?"

His hand moved slowly down her side and beneath her buttocks. More than ever she felt his hardness against her abdomen, and more than ever she felt a sudden heat building between her legs.

Freeing one of her hands, she pressed against his chest and tried to push him away. Her fingers encountered coarse hair curling over tight hot skin. Shoving her palm harder against the wall of muscle, she discovered how strong he actually was. She might as well have been pushing against a Texas mountain for all that he moved.

His own broad palm circled her buttocks and she

146

realized with a start that she was actually moving her body in the same rhythm as his hand. What's more, she had no inclination to stop. Incredibly the heat built, concentrated and yet spreading throughout her body.

His lips and tongue moved the hair from her ear and he whispered, "Too soon. You're not going anywhere, are you? No second parties for you tonight."

His tongue outlined her ear, and his breath burned against her skin. As mortified as she was by his comment, she was also thrilled by everything he was doing to her. The heat built to the force of an explosion, frightening her with its potency.

His mouth took command of hers, and he raked her tongue with his own. A moan caught in her throat, and she was suddenly not afraid. If this was passion, then it was the most irresistible emotion she had ever felt. It was not ugly or violent; it was glorious, at once tender and untamed.

One free hand was suddenly not enough, and she tugged until her other hand was free. She stroked the powerful upper arms that were so unlike her own. In the dark she could feel the ropey sinews and hard, taut muscles flexing beneath her fingers. She shifted the hungry inspection to his shoulders and then, as he broke the kiss, back to his chest, finding his nipples and teasing him with her thumbs as he had teased her.

"Right, Princess," he said huskily. "Right."

His fingers made their own survey, starting with her hair. "Tell me what it looks like," he whispered into the curls.

"Black," she managed.

"Like the night you came from. Does it shine?"

"It shines," she said in truth.

He shifted to her forehead, trailing gently down to her closed eyes. "What color are they? I want to

147

picture them in my mind."

"They're . . . blue."

"Black hair, blue eyes. Nice. And full lips. I'll bet they're red, aren't they? Red and wet and hot."

She could not answer, could not breathe. She wanted to be all those things that he wanted her to be. He liked black hair, she could tell. And blue eyes. For him, in the dark, she could be exactly what he wanted. But not in the light; only in the dark. Somehow, she would do what her instincts told her to do and be the experienced woman he expected.

Remembering how his tongue had penetrated the recesses of her mouth, she caught her fingers in his hair and pulled his head down, covering his lips with hers and imitating the penetration, brushing her tongue against his, hearing the growl in his throat and answering with a soft moan.

He shifted, moving his body aside and caressing her breast once again, his palm and fingers drawing fire wherever they touched. He broke the kiss, leaving her for the moment bereft, her mouth wet and cold and abandoned in the darkness. The cold was forgotten when she felt his lips tracing the curve of her throat and the rise of her breast and at last circling the hard tip.

All thoughts splintered under the tender assault.

His tongue played back and forth while his hand stroked her abdomen, gradually moving lower as her body pulsed in supplication for his caress. Willful deliberations of what he was going to do to her ceased; whatever he did would be wonderful. When he reached the triangle of hair, his skilled fingers looped around and around, closer and closer to the insistent throbbing between her legs.

A small cry escaped her lips, a plea as much as a sigh, as she lifted her hips, too overcome with eagerness to be embarrassed by what he did to her, or by how she was asking for more. She was under the control of her own instincts, long-buried desires that were as old as time and as new as tonight.

The throbbing spiraled close to the point of pain. His fingers probed deeper, circling, arousing her to madness. She knew she was wet against his hand, a strange occurrence she could not explain.

"Almost, baby, almost," he said, with such intensity that the sound was like fire catching in her veins and thickening her blood.

"Hold me." The words were an order. For one wild moment of panic she didn't know what he wanted her to do. She *was* holding him, caressing his arms, his shoulders, his broad back, loving each place that she touched, wanting to lick the sweat from his skin. But that wasn't enough for Clay. He urged her to do something more, to hold him somewhere else.

She knew of only one place he could mean.

He made it so easy for her to find the object of her search in the dark, his hardness pressing as it did against her leg. Tentatively she touched it, waiting for him to respond in some way, to let her know she was doing what he wanted. He lay still, as if waiting for something to happen.

All right, she thought, and she gripped him with great firmness, rubbing her hand up and down from the widened, moist end to the thick hair at the base. Again and again. This time she got a definite moan.

"That's right, Princess."

She quickened the process. Suddenly he pulled her hand away. "Let's ride."

He shifted his hips against hers, his strong thigh parting her legs. He lay between her, his hand beneath her buttocks, and it seemed the most natural thing in the world to hook her heels around him.

She knew what would happen next, but didn't know its impact. Burying her head in the crook of his shoulder, she embraced him tightly, her arms around his neck.

He plunged inside. The shock ended all pleasure, and she stifled a cry, holding it deep inside so that he would not know he had hurt her.

He hesitated. "Are you all right?"

She nodded.

"You sure? You're mighty tight."

She found her voice. "Let's ride, Texas." She even managed to undulate her hips. She did not love him quite so much at the moment, but it was a disenchantment that could be no more than temporary.

He chuckled. "That's my Princess."

Slowly, surely he began to pump inside her, his body moving up and down, his arms embracing her, his lips pressed in her hair. Her heart pounded, and as the pulsating sensations quickened, she found her eagerness and her love for him returning. She held on with all her strength, matching his rhythmic thrusts, the soreness gradually giving way to the pleasure of before.

Without warning she was seized with an imperative need to go faster, faster . . . the explosions coming so fast that they became one immense eruption which shook her to her soul.

She was barely aware of Clay's own frantic pounding, of his cry, of the burst of hot liquid deep inside her. She clung to him, too stunned by the force of rapture to let go. She thought her heart would burst from her chest as waves of pleasure washed over her, again and again, slowly diminishing into a sweet afterglow that translated itself in her flustered mind as the peak of happiness.

If this was what passion was all about, no

wonder it had captured the attention of the world.

Gradually she became aware of Clay's sweat-slick body against hers, of his labored breathing, of his lessening caress. He shifted away, and she clutched the covers to her throat, glory trailing into an unexpected embarrassment over his knowing the most intimate things about her.

What a foolish thing it was to feel shy at such a moment when she had opened herself to him with such complete abandon. But since meeting him, she had done several things which the world would consider foolish. Shyness after her first lovemaking surely would be understood.

Of course he didn't know it was her first. And if she had done everything that he expected, he never would.

Lying under the covers beside her, Clay slipped his arm around her waist and pulled her toward him, her back against his front. "Now that," he whispered into her ear, "was a damned fine birthday gift."

Jenna squeezed her eyes closed. Desperately she tried to recall the thrill of only a moment before, but all such sublime feelings seemed lost to her. She felt used, which was of course senseless because she was the one who had come to him.

And she felt sore. Never had she known that lovemaking could hurt. Clay had shown concern when she cried out, but she could not admit to him what she was going through at the time. She tried in vain to remember something—anything— that Teresa and the whores who frequented the tavern might have said to indicate the pain that she had encountered. Would it be this way every time?

"I guess I'm just not used to a little woman like you," Clay said. "Not complaining, you understand.

151

If I didn't know better, I'd think this was your first time."

Jenna fought a fluttery panic. "But of course you do know better." She tried to sound worldly, and calm. "As you pointed out, I'm a little woman."

"Yeah," he said, snuggling closer. "But not too little. I'd say you're just right."

He let out a contented sigh. "Promise me one thing, Princess. Promise this won't be the only time I'll see you. Not that I saw you exactly, but you know what I mean."

"You want me here again?"

"Or I'll sneak in your back door, if that's what you prefer. Just tell me where you hang your hat." He kissed the side of her neck. "That's a Texas expression, but maybe you get the drift."

Jenna was fast catching on to his language. "I get the drift." She thought about where she hung her hat—in a small back room of the Black Horse.

"We'll have to trade promises," she said. "I'll return if you stay away from Seven Dials."

"Back to that again, are you?"

"Back to that again."

"Whoever sent you must have been a little loco on the subject."

"Whoever sent me was very loco, as you put it."

"Okay, I promise." His callused thumb brushed against the tip of her breast. "Your turn."

"I promise," she whispered. Even as she said the words, she wondered if she lied.

His hand settled once again at her waist, and gradually his breathing grew steady. In less than a minute she felt the rise and fall of his chest and heard a low, sonorous snore.

She tried to cling to the glorious feeling of completeness that he had brought to her, but she found it slipping away, replaced by a return of loneliness.

How that could be, with Clay's arms around her, she did not understand.

If she were swept with a momentary feeling of desolation, it could be only because she knew she would never have his love. But then, he hadn't offered it and more, he had no hint of how she felt.

She found her eyes hot with tears. Gently she used the top blanket to dab them away. Crying—if she gave into it—would be the most foolish thing of all that she could do.

Chapter Twelve

Clay woke up the next morning to a knocking at his door. He opened his eyes to slivers of sunbeams breaking through at the edges of the draperies, not enough to light the room but sufficient to tell him day had arrived. It took him a minute to get his bearings, to remember last night. He was alone in the bed. His Princess had gone.

The knocking continued. "Come in, Robert."

The valet entered and set a tray on the bedside table.

"I thought my sister was headed for Brighton. Don't tell me she took time to send up another restorative."

"No, Master Clayton," Robert responded as he opened the draperies a fraction, allowing only a narrow shaft of light into the room. "Lady Charlotte has not made an appearance. I decided that perhaps coffee would be in order this morning."

To Clay's surprise, he turned and left, easing the door closed behind him. Robert, it would seem, had a greater understanding for the peccadilloes of a man than Clay had credited him.

If the Princess could be called a peccadillo. He lay back in the bed and stared at the ornately plastered ceiling. What he would like was for her to become a habit. He hoped she'd been listening when he tried to tell her just that.

154

He stretched his muscles. This morning, as good as he felt, he was ready to take on the world. A woman at night—especially one as cuddly and co-operative as the Princess—could make a man feel that way.

Clay pulled himself up short. There was no comparing the Princess to any other woman. He'd never met anyone quite like her, and that included all those females in Texas he'd been bragging about. Small and soft but with the power of dynamite to set off a man. At least that was the way she had affected him, and that was all he would let himself consider.

Last night was one he was not likely to forget, and half of it had been spent in talk. If anyone had told him he would be ambushed by a woman's soft voice as much as by her soft curves, he'd have attributed the prediction to an overdose of locoweed.

But he would have been wrong.

From Pretoria to Portsmouth to Tunstall Square, his mystery woman had lived a varied life. She didn't seem much inclined to tell him all the details—he'd caught her hesitation on a point or two—and that was all right by him. The important thing was that before he lit out for home, the two of them had crossed trails. Whatever reason had brought her to his bed, including that ridiculous warning about the Dials, he got a strong feeling that she enjoyed the proceedings as much as he.

And she had promised to return.

So maybe she wasn't pure as the driven snow, as the saying went, but hell, neither was he. And she wasn't planning on setting up housekeeping with him anyway. They made a right fine couple, limited though their relationship would have to be. He wished she were here right now to share a cup of coffee and maybe a little more of that talk, and then whatever else they could think up.

The main trouble with last night, aside from the fact he hadn't got a good look at her, was that the time had passed too fast. And he'd pulled the dumb fool stunt of falling asleep.

He plumped pillows behind him and sat up. For a moment he rested his hand on the bedsheets where she had lain. Something on the white linen caught his eye . . . a long strand of hair. He picked it up and held it to the light. The hair was unmistakably red.

And she had unmistakably said her hair was black.

He threw back the covers, wondering what else he would find. Another strand of red hair—another bit of proof that she hadn't been completely truthful with him.

Now lots of women colored their dark hair red, but he'd never heard of a redhead wanting to disguise her natural color. Not that his knowledge on the subject was vast, but he didn't much think he was wrong. Even Emmeline had talked about a henna rinse one night, but he'd assured her he liked her just the way she was.

He pondered the point but came up with no ideas, except that maybe English women had different preferences concerning the way they looked. Wanting nothing to mess up the good feelings he'd been enjoying, he set to making excuses for whatever else she had told him that might not be the truth. When he saw the bloodstain on the sheet, he forgot about the hair.

He felt like a damned fool. Blood on the sheets. He knew what it meant.

She'd been small and tight, all right, that much he noticed as soon as he entered her sweet flesh. Not having that much experience with doll-like

156

women, he'd even jawed about her size and about how maybe it was the first time for her, and then he'd gone on to believe what she'd said about just being little and everything was fine.

The bloodstain said different.

At the time he'd been liking everything too much to put too many questions to her. She certainly hadn't done anything to make him think she was inexperienced. The way he remembered it, she'd been urging him to ride. Under such circumstances, Clay was never one to tell a woman no.

Not even a redheaded virgin who had claimed to be a black-haired whore.

What the deuce was going on?

Clay felt dumb as an armadillo and just about as thick-skinned. Not a sensitive man, not old cowpoke Clay.

He didn't have much trouble going over the short time they'd been together. Lordy, but she had been a sweet armful, and he'd bet the Whiskey barn that she had told the truth about the death of her father and about the ocean voyage.

After that, there hadn't been much said. School was all she mentioned in particular, and then she'd hinted he might not want to know exactly how it came about that she was what she was.

Only she wasn't.

Clay scratched his head. The Princess had given him a lot to think back on with pleasure, and a riddle he couldn't get out of his mind. Without a word of protest or a claim about how much she was sacrificing for him, she had handed over a gift women always prized — and men, too. In most quarters, first-times were a big deal. The Princess must believe otherwise.

Once he got going, the puzzles came at him fast, questions about whether someone had sent her or whether she had come on her own, and just how much she really knew about the Dials.

Not being a man for surprises and damned uncomfortable with riddles, Clay yanked at the pull beside the bed. Before he could stir his coffee, Robert was at the door.

"Yes, Master Clayton?"

"Randolph was telling me about someone who came knocking at the front door night before last. He mention anything about it to you?"

"I believe he did indicate a caller, although I cannot add anything other than what you have already said."

There Robert went, avoiding a simple *yes*.

"Seems he said something about a footman answering the knock."

"That would be Jimmy. A young employee, Master Clayton. An impetuous lad."

"Would it be too much trouble for me to talk to him?"

If Robert was surprised by the request, it was impossible to read it on his face. "I will have him sent up immediately."

"Thanks."

After the door was closed, Clay stretched out, took a long draw on the coffee, and tried to get his thoughts in some kind of order. First he'd talk with the impetuous Jimmy and try to figure out if the two callers had really been the same, but he wouldn't end his investigations there. Somehow, no matter what it took, he'd find out just who his royal visitor really was, and what was going on.

Jenna waited two nights before returning for a third time to Tunstall Square. During that time Clay had remained away from Seven Dials, or at least away from the Black Horse, just as he had promised. Despite her answering promise to visit him again, when she arrived at the elegant street in the middle of the dark, misty night, she did not rush around to the alley behind the Earl of Harrow's home and up the back stairs.

She had some problems to work through first.

In truth, after she had slipped away from the tavern close on an hour ago, her long evening of work at last at an end, she had not known her steps would bring her to this shadowy street. Wrapped in her beggar's rags, the front fringes of her hair sooted again and obscuring her face, she had planned only to find a busy corner where she could seek alms.

It would be only her second such foray; as much as she hated to beg, she had been remiss in not forcing herself onto the streets every night. She knew full well how much she needed the money so that she and the twins could get away. In a curious way, she had been living a charmed life over the past twelve months, scurrying about the Dials and, lately, points beyond. Every moment brought the danger of discovery. Surely she had used up all her good luck.

And so tonight, when the tavern closed, she had ordered herself to the hated task of soliciting coins from the rich.

Instead, with her slippered feet taking her along pathways she did not consciously choose, she went to the one affluent place in all of London where she could not call attention to herself. In search of refuge from curious, unseen onlookers, and there were many that she imagined peering out from behind their shades despite the deserted sidewalks and street, she stood in solemn silence opposite the earl's mansion, the shawl her main protection

159

against the vapory night.

With branches of a broad elm tree stretching overhead and a wall of thick, pine-scented shrubs at her back, she waited, but for what, she did not know. A welcome sign in the upstairs window seemed no more likely than a brass band to greet her at the door.

What she sought was far more personal—perhaps a sense of urgency that would draw her inside the house, whether or not she was completely comfortable in going, or an equally compelling sense of shame that would send her back to the Horse.

Neither emotion stirred her to action; all she felt was a restlessness that she did not know how to allay, and a sense of irony about her relationship with Clay, especially about the soiled-dove view he held of her.

Until their mating, she had been a virtuous woman, and determined to remain that way for a long while, perhaps forever, no matter the baseness of her surroundings. For Clay, she had given up her virtue willingly, although, until she saw the blood-stain on her leg—in the early morning hours when she'd been in her small tavern room—she had not realized that there would be physical evidence of the fact.

Ignorant as she was about her own body, she could not believe there would be bleeding any time but the first. It was another burden for a woman, this proof she was no longer pure.

Despite her assurances to the contrary, would Clay know of her lost virginity? She prayed he would not. He was not the sort of man to learn something like that and leave it alone.

Thinking of him only brought her torment, and she concentrated on the house. In stark contrast to the surrounding gloom, the electric street lamp near

160

the Harrow front door cast a flat, cold light on the expanse of brick that held her attention. The facade's arched windows, dark at this late hour, reminded her of closed eyes. It was a distressingly uninviting picture that rose before her, all the more so because it housed such judgmental people as Jimmy the footman and the butler Randolph.

If only they had not turned her from the door—if only they had listened to what she had to say . . .

Jenna stopped herself. If such had been the case, she would not have lain in Clay's arms and, tormented as she was by the memory, she also admitted to the feelings of great joy that he had shown her. Wrong though it might be, she could not in all honesty claim unalloyed regret.

For the past two days and nights the image of that house had stayed in her mind, and more, the shadowed image of an upstairs room. She had shuffled through her duties without fear or even weariness, removed from the barrenness of her surroundings by the remembrance of heated touches and whispered words. Not even Teresa's screeches and Bertie Groat's growling taunts had disturbed her private thoughts.

But she had remembered more than the thrill of the night. She had remembered the resultant despair, which had lingered far longer than anything else.

A damned fine birthday gift. When all was said and done, that's all she was to him. Determined to grab a moment's happiness, and rationalizing about the morality of what she did, she had not thought such a condition would matter. But it mattered very much.

She shivered, but not because she was cold. The air clung to the exposed areas of her skin like wet cloth, but the discomfort was as nothing compared to the raw wounds of memory. If only Clay were less than he was—if only he were truly selfish, an animal concerned with his own needs—she could call herself a fool and push him from her mind. But such was not the case.

At first she had been aware of no more than the black-haired Texan's captive and ruggedly handsome presence, of his deep, drawled words, of the intelligent, watchful look in his eyes. The power of his being, of his decency had come more gradually when, time after time, he helped a slum child he knew only by the demeaning name of Simple.

No one realized better than Jenna what a rare thing it was to find charity in the heart of a stranger, especially one from a gentleman's world. Such men were far more inclined—if they were inclined to any act of kindness—to drop a coin in an upturned palm and hurry on, their conscience clear and their thoughts turned to far more important concerns.

Clay was different. With nothing to gain for himself, he had cared.

If his goodness had been all, then she could have appreciated him from afar and let the memory of him get her through the difficult days until she could make good her escape. But she had looked at him again, in the tavern and in his bed, and she had wanted more. She had yearned to touch him, to hold him, to share his kiss.

And she had needed to warn him of the threats against his life.

She called herself a fool. The written message shoved under the door might have served the only important purpose very well. After all, if she disregarded the powerful feelings he set off inside her, she hardly knew the man.

Why are you a guest in the Earl of Harrow's home?

What are you doing in England?
When do you plan to leave?

Those were questions she should have asked.

The clip-clop of horses' hooves on the brick street sent her deeper into the shadows. She watched a matched pair of blacks come into view from out of the mist, behind them a large and elegant carriage, a top-hatted coachman perched high at his post. The carriage came to halt beneath the street lamp in front of the Harrow mansion. A man emerged from the far side. She caught a glimpse of his bent, hatless head, of his broad shoulders and long arm which stretched to the open carriage door. She recognized him right away.

"Thanks for the ride," said Clay to a seated figure inside. His voice echoed in the night, loud and distinct.

"Tomorrow night, remember." The response was muffled but adequately clear, and Jenna was certain she recognized the voice of the man who had been with Clay when she first saw him at the Horse.

"You promised to give me a chance to win back some of my coin," the man added.

So Clay had been gambling. She pictured him in an elegant hall, tables far grander than the Horse's scattered beneath crystal chandeliers, black-suited men with none of the characteristics of Bertie Groat tossing money away as though the supply would never end. As much as she preferred to think of Clay riding about his ranch, she knew he would fit into such a room.

Had he once thought of her? Or had he been with another woman, a voluptuous, perfumed figure in fancy dress who leaned against him much as Teresa had done and vowed to bring him luck? The scene flashed across her mind with incredible detail, right down to the light in the temptress's dark eyes,

163

and roused a fire of jealousy that heated her blood.

She watched as the driver of the carriage snapped a whip over the rump of the horses, setting them in motion. Clay paused at the door, turned, and looked across the street and straight at her. It was impossible that he could see her, hidden as she was by the shadows and by the distance of misty night, and yet it seemed that his eyes were seeking her out.

She hugged herself tightly to still the trembling that one look from afar had aroused.

He was dressed in a black cutaway coat, a white ruffled shirt and a wide gray cravat, his top hat carried carelessly in one hand. She always pictured him in more casual clothes, an open-throated shirt and fitted trousers and those wonderful Texas boots. Tonight he looked as elegant as any English gentleman she had ever seen. She felt shabbier than ever and somehow more alone.

At last he turned and let himself inside. Five minutes passed and then she saw the light go on in his room. Another twenty minutes or so went by before all was darkness once again behind the closed draperies.

It didn't take a great deal of imagination to see in her mind's eye his naked body stretched out beneath the covers. It was true that with the light extinguished last night she had not gotten a good look at him, but her hands had done the looking for her. There was much that she remembered of hot skin and long legs and muscles.

He'd had those muscles in the most unexpected places; she remembered in particular the flatness of his abdomen and the inside of his thighs.

You're hopeless, Jenna told herself and admitted she could have thought far worse.

There was, she decided, one way to find out if he expected her to slip into his bed a second time, as he had said he would. Making her way to the alley at the back of the house, she checked the gate and found it unlocked. He must be waiting for her upstairs. Standing in the alley, her hand gripping the cold metal handle, she thought about him lying naked in bed.

She heard Theodore's paws striking the ground as he lumbered in the direction of the fence.

"Good boy," she said through a narrow gap in the slats, and was rewarded with an excited, welcoming bark.

A light went on in a back window, and Jenna whispered cautions for Theodore to hush. The dog fell silent.

"Theodore," she whispered, "you're not earning your keep."

He responded with a clearly audible swish of his tail.

She stood in the darkness, without so much as a hint of moonlight penetrating the damp air, but she could not make herself go inside . . . not with her hair dirty and her body clad in the worst rags that she owned.

Women were prone to such stupid affectations, she decided, especially when they wished to be pleasing to a man. Clay wasn't interested in her clothes; she would take them off right away, and as for her hair, he wouldn't even see it.

The truth was, she was more afraid than she had been before. She fingered the gate handle. Clay expected her to return.

A damned fine birthday gift.

True, but the realization did not fill her with pride.

Hurriedly she took her leave, before she changed her mind about going upstairs, and retraced her steps to the tavern, where she somehow made it

165

through what was left of the night. In the familiar surroundings of poverty, she also made it through the following day, snatching bits of rest when she could, thankfully in the absence of Teresa who had disappeared after declaring to Hector that she needed a new dress. Jenna even had time to visit with the twins, who informed her their father had found a new place to perform his juggling act.

"He says we may be leaving here soon," Alice said, her voice filled with distress.

"And he weren't . . . wasn't drunk," added Alfred, a note of surprise and pride in his voice. "Not that we want to go."

The eyes of both children glanced around the shabby dark room that was their home, then returned to Jenna, who knelt before them.

"He hopes to find you better lodgings," she responded with a reassuring hug, hiding the distress that the news had provoked. She ought to wish them a far better life than the grim one that stretched before them — and she did — but she could not contemplate with unmixed relief their taking up residence some place far away, some place where she might never see them again. The very thought hurt.

Neither Alice nor Alfred seemed impressed by her explanation, and as a way of distraction she settled them on the pallet that served as their bed, their backs braced against the wall, and read them an especially adventurous story from a book she had bought for a precious penny at the second-hand exchange. When she left to go back to the tavern, they were reenacting the scenes.

At work Teresa was too busy flaunting herself in a new red dress to pay any mind to the child she continued to call Simple. Jenna caught sight of the two prostitutes who frequented the Horse, the tired and shabby young women who were often the recipients of Teresa's unsolicited advice. For the first time Jenna wondered just what had brought them to their occupation. Could it have been unrequited love?

It was a foolish idea. People did what they did in the rookery in order to eat, in order to live. Love was an emotion better saved for the gentry, for the aristocracy at Tunstall Square.

Hector Mims had dared to let the tender emotion snare him, and he seemed none the happier for it. Jenna understood just how he felt. The irony of her situation struck her once again, clanging like an iron bell in her somber thoughts. For love, she had given herself to Clay. A year ago, to keep from giving herself to someone else, she had done the worst thing a human being could do to another. She had taken a life.

The memory of both events would haunt her forever.

As bad as she considered her situation, worse trouble came in through the front door just as Hector was preparing to close for the night. Jenna was behind the bar washing glasses and Teresa was sitting at a table with the whores in the middle of the otherwise empty tavern when a pair of men in dark suits and bowlers strode in from the rainy night.

She had not seen them in six months, but she recognized them immediately. They were the policemen who had questioned the Horse's patrons about a redheaded woman that must be found. Something had brought them back to the tavern. They had come to take her away.

Chapter Thirteen

"Look wot's come in from the rain!" Teresa's shrill voice rang out in the empty air of the Black Horse.

The prostitutes who sat on either side of her straightened their slumped shoulders and forced a smile onto their painted faces as they stared at the two men.

"We're fixin' to close, gents," said Hector. He was standing in the middle of the room, a half dozen empty glasses in his hamlike arms.

"We've not come for a drink," one of the men said, doffing his bowler hat and brushing the dampness from his coat.

The prostitutes' smiles broadened.

"O' course they ain't," said Teresa scornfully. "This time o' night a man's lookin' fer something better to warm 'im than a glass o' ale. Ain't that right?" she said as she studied the newcomers with bold regard.

One was a short, stocky man, the other tall and thin, but their misshapen suits and sour countenances were the same. Both could have benefitted from a haircut and a shave.

The second man, the tall one who had not spoken, gave a careful look to the whores, a brief smile softening his features, but before he could speak, the first one said, "Not right at all." He turned to Hector. "Name's Primm. Matthew Primm. This is my colleague Ebeneezer Crock. We were here once before. Must have been six months ago. Anyone remember?"

Crouched behind the bar, Jenna concentrated on the gray, tepid water and the glasses she was washing and, most of all, on the route that would take her down the hallway and out the back door.

"Coppers!" Teresa said in disgust. "Might 'a known."

The two prostitutes shrank into themselves as though they wished very much to be somewhere other than the Horse.

"Ye was lookin' fer someone, best I can recall," said Hector. "Told ye then, couldn't do ye no good."

"Maybe you can and maybe you can't." Primm settled the bowler on top of his unkempt hair and patted it in place. "There's a reward now for the woman we're seeking."

Jenna held very still.

"A reward, eh?" asked Teresa.

"A substantial one."

Her scorn gone, she shot a sharp look at her husband. "Gi' the gents some ale and let's 'ear wot they 'ave t' say."

"Mr. Primm," said Crock, "it wouldn't do no harm to take away a bit o' the thirst, now would it?"

Primm scowled in disagreement, but after a moment's hesitation settled down at one of the tables. Silently, Hector turned toward the bar, and Jenna could have sworn he sent her a warning look.

Teresa stood.

"Keep your seat, miss," said Primm. "We won't be staying long."

The prostitutes turned their attention back to the last dregs in their glasses, their shoulders once again rounded, their eyes once again flat.

Hector set the dirty glasses he had been carrying on the counter behind the bar, close to Jenna, and picked up two that she had cleaned and dried. Half

169

filling them, he moved slowly toward the men.

"On the 'ouse," he said.

"No need." Primm pulled a coin from his pocket and set it on the table. He took a swallow of the ale. "Thank you, my good man. Now to the business at hand. Which of course, I'm sure you will agree, is the money."

" 'ow much?" asked Teresa from her nearby table.

"A thousand pounds."

"Scratch me arse!" Teresa howled, and the prostitutes once again were on the alert.

The sum was beyond anything Jenna could ever have expected, even if the announcement of a reward had not come as a surprise. She remained very much a wanted woman. The family of the slain man must have put up the money; in the past year they had neither forgiven nor forgotten. To a resident of the Dials, a thousand pounds was a royal fortune, equal to the holdings of kings and sultans, a sum unknown to common men.

With eyes widened and head shaking slowly in disbelief, even Hector seemed impressed. "Where'd the police get a bloody bundle like that?"

"Didn't say it came from the police," said Crock.

"Didn't say otherwise," Teresa pointed out.

"We're not at liberty to divulge the source of the money," said Primm.

"Don' 'e talk fancy," said Teresa. " 'ow we supposed t' know the money's fer real?"

"I assure you it is most certainly real."

" 'ow do we gets our 'ands on it, then?"

"Tell us where we can locate Miss Jenna Cresswell, born in the Transvaal, raised in England, former governess to the late James Drury, disappeared these past twelve months."

"Wot makes yer think we'd be knowin' the likes o' 'er?"

"Because, as we said when we visited this establish-

170

ment some months ago, we believe she's hiding somewhere in the city. And she was last seen entering Seven Dials."

"And," added Crock, "no one's seen her leave. We've been asking around and all we've learned is that if they tried hard enough, an army of women could hide in this rabbit warren and not be seen again."

"Somethin's not right 'ere," said Teresa. "Why would someone wort' a bloody fortune be 'idin' out i' the Dials?"

Shut up, Teresa.

"Seems t' me yer ain't tellin' all yer knows."

"We're telling all you need to hear. It's not known for sure if she's in Seven Dials, and the reward will be offered in other parts of the city. We can reveal, however, that the woman is in trouble. We're trying to help her if we can."

Jenna believed the last part about as much as she believed Teresa was a saint.

"Miss Cresswell's an educated woman," continued Primm, "with red hair and green eyes, not much above five feet tall, and she's been on the run for a year. Now she can hide the education and maybe the red hair, but the eyes might give her away, and the size. And the time she's been around. One year, remember. She would have shown up around the summer of '96. All we're asking you to do is consider who among you matches this description. And let us know. We'll do the rest."

He pulled out a card. Teresa rose to get it, but Hector was at the table first.

"Primm an' Crock, it says," Hector read. "Wot's the numbers 'ere fer?"

"A telephone set in our office. There is someone there who will take down whatever information you wish to give. Or, if you prefer, we will come in person to listen and investigate."

171

"Now 'ow would the likes o' me get a telephone?"

"For a thousand pounds," said Crock, "you'd find a way."

"Don't tarry long," advised Primm. "Not if there's anything at all you wish to tell us. This tavern is not the only place we have visited, and there will be others who find the reward as interesting as the woman here." He gestured toward Teresa.

There were others who would kill their mothers for that much money, Jenna thought, and in truth for far less.

She squeezed her eyes closed. Here she was, watching and listening and breathing like any ordinary mortal and her heart was busy pumping the life's blood through her veins, but she considered herself a dead woman.

In this moment of panic she was tempted to give up . . . to stand straight, pull the cap from her head, and stride to their table, announcing her presence and putting an end to her misery. She was a second away from doing just that when she heard the scrape of chairs. Her eyes flew open and she saw the men stand.

"We hope to hear from someone soon. Do not lose that card."

"Ain't likely," said Teresa with a sharp laugh.

The men were halfway to the door when Primm turned back. "Who's that?" he said, gesturing toward Jenna. "Didn't see her back there before."

"Simple," said Teresa with scorn. " 'at's wot we calls 'er. A fool who cleans up the place. Don't expect no 'elp from 'er. Deaf as a post."

"Deaf you say?" asked Primm.

"A child is wot she is," said Hector. "Been 'ere most o' 'er short life."

Jenna could not believe what she heard. Hector surely hadn't forgotten how long she'd worked for him. So why had he lied? Unless he knew—

172

The idea was impossible. Never had he given the least sign that he considered her anything other than what she seemed. Maybe he just didn't want to draw unnecessary attention onto her, but that didn't seem quite right, either.

Whatever his reason for lying, Primm and Crock apparently believed him, for they left without another word.

But, oh, the fear they left behind them. When word spread about the reward, every female who was under six feet in height would be subjected to suspicion and, worse, to inspection. Even the giant Hector would not be enough to protect her, especially when he wasn't able to protect her from his wife.

Jenna made short work of the rest of the glasses and, leaving Teresa in deep conversation with the prostitutes and Hector locking the front door, she hurried back to her room. Quickly she counted the money in the cache beneath her cot, but it was a pitiful store for all her months of searching after lost coins and her one night at Piccadilly Circus. She could not regret one farthing that had gone for the care of the twins, but she could regret waiting so long to take up the hated begging.

Cautiously securing the small box once again beneath the loose floor board, she huddled on the bed, afraid to remove her cap and let her red hair fall upon the thin pillow beneath her head. She pondered what to do. Many times during those first weeks she had packed her pitiful belongings, determined to flee, only to think of the twins and realize she could not yet leave.

Perhaps she ought to pack now. Jailed, she could do them little good.

Her thoughts went back a year, to that period in her life that more than any other she wished she could change. How proud the Reverend Cox had been of the education she had received at the Deaf and Dumb Asylum, and how proud he had been of her.

"You've been here most of your life, Jenna. Fourteen years. As much as I dislike saying good-bye," she could hear him say, "we both know it's for the best."

In her mind she caught the resonance of his voice, and the kindly tone that had brought her such peace during her growing-up years. "You're like a daughter to me, but there's no future for you here. You must find your place in the world."

Your place in the world. The phrase echoed in her head until it was all she could think of. Her place, her new home. Even now she could feel the horror that was to come in this supposed sanctuary — the fine home of the redoubtable James Drury, wealthy member of the gentry who dabbled in banking, a husband, father of two boys she was hired to tutor . . . James Drury, the lecher. The last had proven the most important of all.

Usually she thought about him only in her nightmares, when she was unable to turn her contemplations to a subject less troubling. Tonight she was wide awake, and she remembered everything . . . the attic garret in the Drury estate where she had been given not much more space than she had at the Horse, the two young hellions she was supposed to civilize, the pale and whining Mrs. Drury who declared that any problems arising in the classroom were Jenna's to handle, although she most certainly advised against chastising the delicate young charges with anything stronger than a word or two.

Mostly she remembered Mr. Drury. A short, middle-aged man of prodigious girth, he had a booming voice that was given to barking orders and a diamond stickpin in his cravat that proclaimed he had the wherewithal to enforce any demands he might bark.

Jenna had taken one look at him on that first day she reported for work — especially at the glint in his

174

eye as he centered his attention on her figure—and knew he was not a man like Reverend Cox.

"You look mighty young to be taking on two active boys like my sons," he had said. "James the Younger and John have minds of their own."

"I'm twenty," Jenna had said, her chin lifted proudly. "I've handled a dozen children at the asylum when they couldn't hear a word I said, and they learned their letters and geography to the most exact standards. It's in my papers that the Reverend Cox mailed to you last week."

"So it is. Should have seen you in person, of course, but too busy, much too busy. There are those who prefer men to tutor their sons before sending them off to school. I disagree." He took his time looking her over. "You'll do. Very nicely, if I'm any judge."

He hadn't, of course, indicated exactly what he meant by the 'very nicely,' and she had assured herself he meant in the education of his sons. She got the first inkling of his proclivities when she saw the parlormaid coming out of his study the next afternoon, her apron untied and her cap askew. Polly was her name, and she wore a militant look in her eye.

"What're you lookin' at?" Polly snapped. "Don't be mindin' anyone else's business but yer own."

Jenna had entertained no intention of doing otherwise, and for the next few days she had stayed well away from both the master and the mistress of the house, choosing to take her meals either in her room or in the downstairs servants' hall. Neither did Mr. and Mrs. Drury approach her, leaving her to believe either that she was doing an adequate job of keeping their boys at the appropriate tasks or that they simply did not care, as long as they were not bothered.

The reality was that she was having a difficult time. James the Younger and John did indeed have minds of their own, as their father had said, if they had minds at all. Poor at their studies, they were well equipped with mouths and lungs and vocal chords, which they put to frequent use, one of them barking like the father and the other whining like the mother until Jenna was ready to turn in her notice.

At the end of her exhausting first week, as she was sleeping soundly in her attic room, she was awakened by a loud knock. It penetrated her sleep like the shot from a canon, and she sprang from the bed, heart pounding, and threw open the door.

Polly, her face twisted into a scowl, thrust a note into Jenna's hand. "He wants you." Turning on her heel, she disappeared down the narrow hall, taking her candle with her and leaving Jenna in the dark.

Head reeling, Jenna fought for a clear thought. It took her a moment to realize she was holding the piece of paper, and another to light the bedside lamp.

My dear Miss Cresswell, several things have come to my attention and it is necessary for us to talk. Please come to the withdrawing room at once. It was signed *James Drury.*

Experience was soon to teach her exactly what those things he mentioned were, but at the time she could believe only that she had done something terribly wrong. Having come to the conclusion that she would have to resign, she did not want to find herself in the embarrassing position of being dismissed. Dressing hurriedly, she rushed downstairs.

She found her employer standing by the hearth, surrounded by the opulence his money had bought — green velvet draperies, paneled walls, and delicate brocade furniture resting on an Aubusson carpet. Full bellied and balding, his suit pulled tight across his shoulders, he looked out of place in the room.

When he turned to face her, she saw there was a half-filled brandy snifter in his hand. She also noticed the leer on his ruddy face.

"Ah, my dear Miss Cresswell, do come in. Sorry to

176

bother you at such an hour, but there are so many demands upon my time that I have simply had no other opportunity for us to speak." He swallowed most of the liquor. "And I have meant to do just that since I first watched you walk into this room."

Disliking the look in his eyes, she remained close to the door.

"Have I done something to displease you or your wife?" she asked.

"My wife?" His hand waved in dismissal and brandy sloshed in the glass. "Mrs. Drury concerns herself with little more than her sickly mother. She's in the country right now seeing to the old fool."

He finished the drink in one gulp and set the empty glass on a table.

"And as for me, no, my dear, you have done nothing to displease me. On the contrary."

"I thought, because of the lateness of the hour—"

"You will find, Jenna—you don't mind my being so familiar, do you? We'll get on much better if we call each other by our first names, at least in private, you understand. Well, Jenna, you will find that sometimes I conduct my affairs in the middle of the night. It's what men of my class do, but then I don't suppose you've had much experience with men like me, have you? Nor any sort of men, really. Can't say that I'm sorry. You're a real beauty."

His eyes lingered on her breasts.

"I really must insist—"

"Now, you're not in a position to insist on much of anything, are you, Jenna? This is your first position, is it not? Come to the sofa and I'll tell you exactly what's expected of you."

"Mr. Drury, there's been a mistake—"

She turned from him. She would not have thought so large a man could move so fast, but he was beside her in an instant, his hand gripping her wrist as she reached for the handle of the door.

"I repeat, my dear, come to the sofa. It's far better to do what I say. Ask any of the girls."

Jenna twisted to free herself. Outweighing her by ten stone, he had no difficulty in dragging her to the middle of the room and shoving her down against the sofa.

"A drink?" he said as he hovered over her. "It might help you to relax."

Jenna shook her head.

"It is time we got better acquainted. Surely you would not disagree, not a girl in your situation. I want to know that my sons' governess is suitable for the post."

Jenna shuddered, tried to stand, but he stood in front of her so close . . . so close. He cut off all light, all air, but still she could see his sunken gray eyes and bulbous nose, his jowly cheeks and thin, slicked-back hair, and the shiny red skin that looked as though it could not grow a beard.

Suddenly he was jerking her to her feet . . . covering her mouth with soft, damp lips . . . she shoved . . . he grabbed for her dress, caught his fingers in her sleeve and she heard a ripping sound as once again she shoved against his portly body.

He fell. The crack of his head hitting the hearth obliterated all other noise, even the cry that escaped from her throat. Jenna waited for him to move, but his sprawled body lay inert on the carpet. She forced herself to feel for a pulse in the folds of his neck; his skin felt scaly like a snake's, already cold as a fish, despite the heat from the fire not three feet away. A year later she remembered the feel of that skin, remembered it in great detail.

"Saints preserve us!"

Jenna twisted her head to see the parlormaid standing in the doorway, her eyes wide with horror.

"Is he dead?" Polly asked.

Jenna nodded, too filled with sickening desperation to put the truth into words. Slowly she stood, her eyes returning to the hearth and to the twisted body, more bloated in death than it had appeared in life. There was no blood beneath the head, she thought. How could there be no blood?

Polly walked to her side. "He was a bastard, that he was. Deserved what he got."

"It was an accident. He came at me—" Jenna's voice broke.

"Think the police will be listening to anything you have to say? He's the wealthy one. He's the important one. Or at least he was. Don't look too important now, do he?"

Jenna closed her eyes and for the first time thought beyond the immediate horror. She thought about the consequences of the night, thought about the police. More than once during the years uniformed officers had come by the asylum to make sure the children were not operating as thieves and pickpockets on the surrounding streets, and Jenna had seen that anyone poor and downtrodden was automatically suspect in their eyes. She hugged herself. Having little more than the clothes on her back, she would certainly fit the description of poor.

"You'd best get out of here," Polly urged. "I'll tell 'em I found 'im this way. Got to raise the alarm, you know, so suspicion won't fall on me."

"But where will I go?" Jenna had asked stupidly, unable at that moment to think for herself.

"Away from here. Find a place you can't be found."

Polly had pushed her through the door. "Get out. I'll cover for you."

And Jenna had got out. Later, despite her closeness to the twins and her acceptance at the Horse, she grew to regret the decision. It was not her habit to run from trouble; she knew that in her moment of confusion, with her employer sprawled at her feet and the parlormaid's voice the only one to be heard, she had acted foolishly.

Two weeks after the tragedy, clinging to the belief that it might not be too late to turn herself in, she had risked arrest by tracking Polly to a rundown lodging house on the edge of the Dials. She queried the former parlormaid about what happened after she had run.

"Just as I said," Polly responded, her eyes flat, her once starched clothes dirty and in need of patching. "They found you was gone and talked about how you would be hanged once they caught up with you. Which ain't much worse than what's happening to the rest of us. The old lady won't give references to none of us girls, says we're lying about the way her husband couldn't keep his hands to hisself."

She stared in hopelessness around the dingy room with its cracked window and peeling walls. "Don't know what's to become of me, seeing as how I can't get decent work. You're best off wherever you are. They've got your picture on one o' them flyers. All over the city, it is. I ain't blamin' you, mind, for what happened. Wouldn't 'a minded doing the same to him meself. 'Sides, it wouldn't 'a been long anyways before that bitch of a wife found an excuse to let us all go. Just get back to wherever it is you're hiding and don't come around here again."

But Jenna had been unable to return to her underworld existence without taking a hand in her own fate. She had sought employment at an agency specializing in domestic help. Lacking the proper papers, she had been met with hard looks and guarded questions. When the interviewer mentioned calling the authorities, she had known she was recognized and she had fled.

Like Polly, she could not find decent employment; unlike Polly, the alternative for her was more than just bleak poverty; it was a trip to the gallows, and she had slipped back to the tavern, accepting the twins and Hector as her new family and her plans to leave with the children as her only dream.

Deafness had been a natural subterfuge. After her first two years at the asylum, when she was barely eight, her hearing had suddenly returned, but she had been fearful of expulsion to a workhouse and had kept her newly restored ability a secret for months.

When she had at last admitted the truth, Reverend Cox said he understood. Eventually, arrangements were made for her to teach the other children and to translate for them the communications of the hearing world, understanding as she did their special needs. She had met with nothing but kindness from the reverend and from a few members of the gentry who donated their time and money.

Most of the latter, however, expected instant returns for their largess. They wanted humble gratitude and constant flattery. They wanted to be made to feel good. It was no wonder Jenna had come to resent their power and their arrogant ways. But she hadn't resented the manner of their speech, and she decided to learn for herself their fine accents. Not always would she be taken as a charity case.

All her fine talk had not helped her in the Drury home, nor had it helped her at the Horse.

But it had helped her convince a certain Texan that she knew the members of society he called his friends, or at least she knew one such man who had sent him a birthday gift.

Strange how her thoughts kept returning to him when she knew he could not be more than just a foolish hope . . . a dream . . . except that for one night when he had been all too real. Desperate for consolation, she had no place else to turn.

"Clay."

She whispered his name in the dark of her small

room.

"Tell me what to do."

No answer came to ease her troubled mind.

A thousand pounds. Men like Bertie Groat and women like Teresa, numerous as cockroaches, would be scouring the streets looking for green-eyed redheads who stood not much above five feet tall. She would, truly, rather turn herself in than see the money go to one of them.

Perhaps if she did so, she could ask that the reward go to Alice and Alfred Morgan. Perhaps, but that part of her hazy plan seemed more fairy tale than possibility.

One thing was certain. If she did decide to end her hiding, she could not do so before she saw Clay one more time. No matter what he thought of her, or what he had surmised, she must return to Tunstall Square. This time she would not remain on the street.

It was just possible that he *could* advise her on what she should do. He thought she was getting paid for her services; maybe she could take the payment in advice.

Tomorrow, she told herself. She would risk one more day in the Dials, and tomorrow night she would go once again to the square. She would tell him everything that she could manage to put into words, and she would hear what he had to say.

Chapter Fourteen

Jenna spent the next day scrubbing out a corner of the storage room; she had never undertaken the task before, but Hector gave her only a passing glance when he saw what she was doing and Teresa was so busy searching the surrounding slum for someone— anyone—to hand over to the officers Primm and Crock that she had no time for the Horse, even after the sun had fallen behind the last abandoned building in the neighborhood.

All night the tavern was crowded with men and women alike talking about the money. It loomed like a shining prize, a winning ticket at Ascot, an inheritance from a long-lost aunt. And all they had to do was find a woman with red hair and green eyes who, unknown to them, was washing glasses behind the bar.

Even the few dapper gentlemen who drifted in seemed caught up in the talk, their eyes gaining a mercenary gleam as they contemplated the thousand pounds.

Midnight came and went. At last Teresa strolled into the Horse, sullen and uncommunicative, which was the way Jenna liked to see her. An hour later, with the tavern at last empty of customers, Hector locked the front door, turned down the lights in the main room, and went with his wife to their bed. Jenna had already retired. The moment she heard the creak of the mattress springs, she knew she could not lie there for another minute and listen to what she now completely understood. Besides, she had business of her own to take care of.

Rising from her own thin mattress and tucking the best dress that she owned under her arms, she sneaked down the hallway, through the storage room, and out the back door.

Two blocks away the twins, used to her strange hours, let her in, and she performed with dedicated thoroughness the simple ablutions that were available to her, slipping into the dress and folding her older rags under the pallet. Once again she lathered her hands with lanoline.

Not knowing whether she would ever see the children again, she allowed herself a long, firm hug and a kiss on their cheeks.

Alice held on tightly and returned the kiss.

Alfred looked at her in puzzlement. "Something's different tonight, Jenna. You ain't — you never done — you never did nothing like that before."

She let the grammar go uncorrected. "Never did what?"

"Kiss us," his eyes turned toward the floor.

"Well, you know how mushy women can be. Did you mind?"

"I didn't," said Alice quickly, her fingers tangled in Jenna's sleeve.

"I suppose it wouldn't do no — wouldn't do any harm from time to time," said Alfred, who had taken a manly step backward.

"Good," said Jenna, looking away before they could see the moisture in her eyes. "Now you two get into bed and say your prayers and get a good night's sleep. You never know what the day has waiting for you."

On the street outside the lodging house she passed their father, the juggler known only as Morgan. A slight, fair-haired man, he carried in his hand a heavy canvas bag containing the tools of his trade — the wooden pins and balls used in his performance. She had seen the bag once when he had left it in the room.

Never had they spoken, and she did not believe he knew of her existence. She hoped he never would until it was time for her to leave. It was risky enough having the twins know she was an adult with all her senses intact.

As she passed unseen by him in the dark, she did not catch the whiff of cheap ale that she expected, and he was coming home far earlier than he was wont. Perhaps he really was trying to be a better parent to his children, as Alfred had indicated. She wondered what had brought about the change, and what it might foretell.

But he was soon gone and likewise forgotten in her mind, which turned to other matters. A fog hung over the city, so thick it pushed her along on her journey to Tunstall Square. She took extra cautions to avoid anyone who stood without help from lamp-post or companion at this darkest hour of the night, and she kept her shawl pulled tight over her head and face.

At last she arrived at her destination. Marching through the back gate with only a whispered greeting to Theodore, she scurried up to Clay's beckoning room.

He wasn't there. As she had done before, she secreted herself in a dark corner next to the draperies, only this time she remained standing. She had only a short time to wait, and to worry, and to plan, before he strode into the room and closed the door behind him.

He remained by the door. She listened to him breathe in the dark.

"You're back," he said. "It's been close to a week."

"Four days. Or rather, four nights."

"Close enough to a week. I had about given up."

"You did that before," she said, feeling herself slip into the strange comfort of a situation that should have been terrifying. Perhaps it seemed comforting only because the rest of the world had turned more hostile than before. Or perhaps she owed the pleasant

185

feeling entirely to Clay.

"What, given up?"

"No. I meant the way you knew I was here. As soon as you walked in."

"Yeah, I guess I did. The room's different with you in it." He hesitated a moment. "Tell me something. Are we going to have another argument about the light?"

An edge in his voice worried her, and she could not attribute it solely to his irritation over her delayed return.

"I didn't come to argue," she said, her voice barely above a whisper.

"Good. I've got a powerful urge to look at you, Princess." She heard him move toward the bed. "Come to think of it, I've got several powerful urges."

"No!"

"No urges?"

She caught her breath and found that her hands were squeezed together tight. "I meant no light. Not right away. Maybe later, if — well, maybe later, that's all." She sighed in exasperation.

"You're a tough woman to figure, anyone ever tell you that?"

Jenna had no answer for him, and she kept silent.

"Honey, don't ask why I'm giving in so easy, but just get in the bed and I'll forget the light. For a while."

"That's direct enough."

"It is why you came up here, isn't it?"

I came for advice. Or at least so she had told herself.

"Tell you what," he went on. "You get undressed and I'll get undressed and we'll meet in the middle. Does that sound fair enough?"

Fair? Jenna had forgotten the meaning of the word. "I'm already undressed," she lied.

"You're also about to get attacked on the floor." His voice was husky. "Get in the bed."

Maybe she deserved the order, slipping into his room as she was doing, but she didn't like it. Tonight, unlike their last time together, he reminded her of the autocratic visitors to the asylum who had expected to be entertained. Maybe he'd been too long associating with the people of the Earl of Harrow's class; maybe he was wealthy in his own right and came by his arrogance naturally. Or maybe she just hadn't notice earlier that he liked to have his way.

"You're still standing out there in the dark, Princess."

"So are you."

"Not in the mood to mosey?"

Jenna sighed. As much as he was irritating her with his manner, she was very much in the mood. She needed to talk to him, needed to confess, but she didn't want to speak of her tangled problems with each of them standing on opposite sides of the bed, and she immediately began to rationalize. It wouldn't hurt to lie beside him and talk. It wouldn't hurt to ask him to hold her while she asked him what to do.

Here she went being an idiot and an imbecile again, but around Clay she should have expected nothing else. In bed it was possible they wouldn't talk . . . at least not right away. Her private troubles were not high on any priority list — not his, even if he had known they existed, and it would seem, not hers, not when his presence in the room aroused familiar yearnings and his voice set her blood coursing warmly in her veins.

She would do her confessing later, when he seemed ready to listen. She acted before she could change her mind, quickly shedding her garments and tossing her cap aside, then scrambling under the covers. As she pulled them close to her chin, she silently willed her heart to quit beating so loudly.

He made equally short work of his clothes and lay beside her. His hand touched her waist and she jumped.

"Ticklish?" he asked.

"Your hand's cold." She spoke the truth.

He circled her stomach with his palm, his fingers splayed wide. "Just needs a little friction to get hot."

187

Jenna sighed.

"You like that, Princess?"

"Yes," she whispered. With all the heat building inside her, *like* seemed a foolishly inadequate term. Spineless, that's what she was. When he touched her, she couldn't think, couldn't worry, couldn't imagine a world outside this room.

"I aim to please. Tell me what else you want me to do."

Jenna did not know how to respond. Despite his caressing hands, she felt a brusqueness in him that she had not experienced before. What she wanted was for him to be the same man whose tender loving had brought her back to this bed, but it was a yearning she could not put into words.

"Whatever you choose," she said. "I trust you."

"Now that's a start in the right direction."

He brushed his lips against hers, lightly, tantalizingly, leaving her hungering for more. In the dark his hand found hers, and he stroked her palm with his thumb.

"Kinda rough for a lady's hand," he said.

So much for the lanoline.

"Don't Texas women ever build a callus or two?"

"They do if they ride often enough."

Jenna, who had never been on a horse in her life, said, "What makes you think I don't?"

"I'm talking about horses, Princess."

"So am I."

"Maybe we can mount up sometime and go for a long gallop."

Jenna swallowed. "Maybe."

His hand abandoned hers and trailed down the valley between her breasts, his fingers at last making small circles on her abdomen and dipping into the thick thatch at the juncture of her thighs. A soft cry caught in her throat.

"Is it black? You said you had black hair."

His voice had not lost its hard edge, but this time she

was too dazed to give it much notice. Everything he did to her was like an opiate, dulling her mind to unwanted thoughts and entangling her in a world where only sensation had any import. How splendid it was not to think, but only to feel.

"Uh huh," she said lazily, nestling herself against the cool linen sheets in delicious abandon.

The circling strokes quickened. "Is this what your customers usually do to you?" he asked. "Being from Texas, I don't know much about the ways of English gentlemen or what their women want. You'll have to tell me if I'm doing something wrong."

"You're not . . . doing anything wrong." The words came out thick and low. She was dimly aware that he seemed to be telling her something she ought to heed, but all she could concentrate on was the touch of his hand.

His fingers trailed lower, touching with seductive insistence the high inside of her thighs, then continued their hot movement through her parted legs, rubbing against the beginning fullness of her buttocks. Her hips rose from the soft mattress to meet his explorations, and she massaged her own pulsating nub against his hard wrist. Behind her closed eyes she saw only black velvet, but her body felt wildly hungry with need.

"Is this good?" The question was insistent, forcing its way into her conscious thought. "You're the expert. You'll have to tell me."

He did not sound kind.

His hand stopped its wanderings and moved away, slipping back through her legs without touching her, leaving a chill within her where only an instant ago there had been fire.

She felt a rising panic. She stared up at his face, wishing she could make out his features. "Let's not talk so much, Clay."

His stretched-out body was resting against hers, but it brought her no comfort right now.

"I don't ordinarily have much to say to a woman in bed, but you kinda taught me to look at things differently."

"That was the first time," she said, fright mixing with her panic. Tonight could not go wrong. She wouldn't let it.

"We don't have to talk right away." She touched his face. He gripped her hand, imprisoning it against his chest.

"Oh, but we do. I was kinda wondering where you were the last few nights. You have another gift to deliver? Introducing yourself the way you did to me?"

"Clay—"

"That's who I am, all right. The question right now is, who are you?"

Jenna held very still, unable to speak, unable to draw in a single breath.

"I spent the last couple of nights asking around town for the answer to that puzzling question. Couldn't get it out of my mind. It didn't take more than a few hours each evening. Got around to everyone I could think of who might have hired you. And you know what I found out?"

She listened to his even breathing and the pounding of her heart. A thousand ways to answer him flitted through her mind; she rejected every one.

"I don't care what you found out."

"You should, Princess. I didn't find out a damned thing."

Her one free hand gripped the covers tightly, holding them protectively at her throat. "Maybe whoever it was didn't want to be found out." His breath stirred against her cheek, so close was he to her. Even where their bodies did not touch, she could feel the heat rising from his skin.

"Or maybe you lied," he said. "The question I have to ask myself right now is why."

She did not want the night to go this way, not at all. She wanted, and needed, a tenderness from him, a few gentle words that told her he looked upon her as a person and not just another woman in his bed. He had shown her such tenderness the first night, and she very much wanted it again, as much as she wanted everything else.

But there was nothing gentle about him right now. She should have known things would not work out as she desired.

An attempt to shift away ended when he edged an arm beneath her shoulders and held her tight, one leg stretching over both of hers and locking her securely against him. Letting go of her hand, he touched her stomach just as he had done long minutes ago when she thought his only purpose was making love. This time he moved upward, stroking and fondling first one breast and then the other, giving equal attention to each extended tip.

It was exquisite torture, but it was torture, nevertheless.

"I've met a lot of women, you know, on both sides of the ocean," he said. "I've even been with whores who tried to tell me they were virgins, but never once has a virgin tried to tell me she was a whore."

She had been right to worry. He knew, at least part of what she had to say. She squeezed her eyes closed. Denial would be futile. If only he would quit touching her, perhaps her mind would clear and she could think of exactly how to respond.

"Now a woman can lie all she wants to about some things. Like how a man's pleasing her and how he's the best she's ever had. We kinda like to hear that stuff. Some of us even sweet talk right back. But if there's one thing a man doesn't like, honey, it's being made a fool of. Not in bed."

Behind her closed eyes, the tears burned. "I didn't mean to make a fool of you." A sob escaped. "That's not what I meant at all."

"Now don't cry, Princess. I can't stand it if you cry. All I want —"

As miserable as she was, and as much as she hated that sob, Jenna caught the defensiveness of his tone.

"All you want is everything I have to give."

"Don't turn my words on me."

"Clay, please let me go. I can't think with you all over me like this."

"Now why is that?"

"You know exactly why. You're the expert in bed, remember? Isn't that what all these accusations are about?"

He gave no answer, and she was surprised when he did as she asked. Making certain that no parts of their bodies touched, she sat up and brought the cover to her chin.

"You think I'm playing some kind of game, don't you? Making a fool of you, I believe you said. How a woman can lose her virtue in a man's bed and be accused of nefarious purposes is more than I can understand. I don't expect anything from you. I haven't asked."

"I have to give you credit. Whoever you are and whatever this is all about, you have a way of putting things that makes me sound like a heel. Remember, I was the one who was lied to. I just want to know why."

"I really did come to warn you about trouble in Seven Dials. People have seen you there, and I've heard talk. It's all right to go slumming once in a while, but you have to know that there's danger in the rookery. I didn't lie about that."

"Wouldn't care to tell me exactly how you know about this danger, would you? And why you'd care about what happened to me?"

"I told you, I overheard talk. I'd seen you and you interested me. I . . . live there."

"You have a house in the Dials?"

"A room."

"I'm not much on the way folks talk around here, not a linguist you might say, but you don't sound like someone from the slums."

"Well, I am. I wanted to warn you to stay away."

"Because I interested you."

"I'd never seen anyone quite like you. There aren't many Texans wandering the streets near my room. When I heard those schemes to watch for your return, I followed you and, well, you know the rest."

"That the only reason you came around?"

"It was the reason I told myself, but when I got upstairs, things just happened. I didn't know you could tell I was a—"

"A virgin. You can say it, Princess. It's not a dirty word."

"From the way you've been treating me, I would have thought it was."

"There you go again, putting me in the wrong. Okay, let's say I believe you. You live in the slums and you're not overly much informed about your own body and you got this craving for old Clay here. Anything I left out?"

With desire for him fast receding, Jenna felt a wave of irritation take its place. "I was worried about you."

"Oh, yeah, I forgot that part. You were worried about me, a rank stranger. So you bested a Bullmastiff, broke into the Earl of Harrow's home—"

"—the back door was unlocked."

"All right, you walked right in, delivered your message, then hopped into bed and became a slave to love. Now, have I got everything right?"

She got up from the bed and began to pace, kicking aside her clothes to keep from tripping. He made no move to stop her. If the night air was chill on her bare skin, she did not notice. He wanted the truth. That's exactly what he would get, just not in the bit-by-bit way she preferred to tell him.

"In case you were wondering why I returned, just in case you decided I was still this slave to love, perhaps I should confess everything. There's a reward out for me and I wanted to ask you just what to do."

"A reward?"

"A thousand pounds."

Clay whistled. "That's more than they were asking for Jesse James, and he robbed trains. Just what is it you're supposed to have done?"

Jenna was so angry at the sarcasm in his voice that she forgot her shame and misery. "Killed a man. In self defense, but try telling that to the police."

"Have you?"

"I panicked and ran. Stupid, I know, but it seemed the right thing to do at the time. I've been hiding out for the past year."

"In Seven Dials."

"Yes, in Seven Dials."

The realization of what she just had revealed brought her to a halt. She had told everything, except about her masquerade as a child and about the twins that she looked upon as her own, and about how she had fallen in love.

Somehow those details were too close to her, too personal for her to tell . . . especially the last. Only the twins would she mention later.

He laughed.

Jenna couldn't believe she heard right.

"Princess, that's the damnedest story I ever heard. You ever thought about writing a book?"

She stood very still. "It's the truth." Couldn't he hear the anguish in her voice?

"At least it's what you expect me to swallow as the truth."

No, he most certainly did not hear the anguish, nor anything that she said. She had revealed secrets that she had never told another living soul, and he had kicked them about as he might kick fallen leaves. Who was he anyway to set himself up as her judge? She had done nothing to harm him; on the contrary, even he admitted she had brought him great pleasure.

"All right, Clay Parkworth," she threw back at him, "why not tell me just who you are? What gives you the right to stay in the Earl of Harrow's house night after night and eat his food and welcome women into your bed?"

"Why, I thought you knew all about me, Princess. In the first place, my moniker is Clayton Ernest Drake, Clay for short. And in the second, the earl's my daddy."

And Clay accused her of lying!

"Of course he is. And I'm really the Queen of Spain."

"No, you're a killer, remember? Keep your story straight."

"I'm just after one you will believe. I gave up on the truth long ago."

"At last you admit it. Enough of this foolishness, Princess. Damn, I'm getting tired of calling you that."

"I'm a queen, remember? Your Highness will do."

He came out of the bed so fast she had no warning of his attack, his aim for her unerring. Dragging her back under the covers, he laid his body on top of hers. "I've never done it to a queen before. I'm going up in the world, wouldn't you say?"

Filled with anger and panic, Jenna shoved against his shoulders, twisting to free herself from the imprisonment of his hot, hard body. She would not be abused this way, she simply would not.

"Keep fighting, Your Highness," he said, his lips close to hers. "Whether you realize it or not, you're rubbing me just the right way."

Chapter Fifteen

Jenna couldn't believe this was happening. She felt assaulted, and she reached for his face, wishing she had the nails to scratch him, but he caught her wrists and forced her arms back to the pillow on each side of her head.

"I don't know what's going on here, but you make me crazy," he said, his voice thick, his breathing fast and shallow. His head loomed close to hers, and his heat burned its way through her skin.

Jenna warred against her seething emotions as much as she warred against him. Did he think that, unlike him, she was completely sane? Most certainly she was not, not with his body pinning her to the linen sheet and her aware of each hard plane, each taut muscle from his shoulders down to where her toes touched his ankles. Not when she wanted to hurt him and love him at the same time.

Still she fought, but all she managed to do was increase the friction that he had spoken of, and the result was a spark of desire. As her skin rubbed against his, her breasts tight and full against his chest, her thighs rising to meet his long, strong legs, she felt every nerve ending tingle into electrifying life. Her blood pounded thickly through her veins and she realized that instead of shoving against him she was hungrily massaging the tight flesh of his shoulders and the back of his neck.

How quickly her panic became passion, and her anger an equally turbulent need. No longer did she want to get away.

He responded in kind. With a hard, deep sigh, he covered her mouth with his and their tongues danced wildly together, their breaths intermingling. His hand caressed her breast, kneading and stroking and flicking, and her own trembling, eager hands slipped under his arms, pausing to finger the thick hair that she found. She heard his moan and felt the tightening of his body.

Her hands moved on, exploring the wide expanse of his taut back and lower to his narrow waist and hips. At last, arms fully extended, she touched his buttocks; remembering how he had massaged her body, she massaged him in the same firm manner with her palms.

He broke the kiss and pressed his mouth against her ear. The rough dampness of his tongue and the heat of his breath drove her deeper into ecstasy.

"Yes," he whispered. His tongue stroked. "Harder. Good." Each word came out in small explosions; with each, her ardor increased. She brought her hands up slowly against his back. He lifted his hips and she knew he wanted her to hold him once again.

Tenderly she slipped one hand between them and gripped him, sensed his impatience, and began to stroke the length of him, letting her fingers drift to the fullness at the base. All her inhibitions burning away in the heat of passion, she explored that most intimate part of his body, the extraordinary area between his legs that was so different from hers, then brought her hand back to the stroking that she knew he enjoyed.

"Easy," he said, then covered her mouth with his. She writhed beneath him, breathing in a scent of musk and sweat that was sweeter than any scent she had ever known. The only sounds she heard were his heavy breathing, the rustle of the sheets, and her own eager moans.

He entered quickly, with none of the pain she had felt the first time of their joining. His warm lips pressed against her neck and his arms embraced her tightly as their bodies flailed together with compelling need. Holding him with equal fervor, she lost all sense of time and place. Swept by surges of passion, she squeezed her eyes closed and clasped herself tightly to him, letting his own rapid thrusts carry her to ecstasy.

It seemed an eternity before the world began to form around her once again. When she could think clearly, she opened her eyes and saw the outline of his head bending close to hers. She knew that in the dim light which managed to squeeze in around the closed draperies he could see no more than the same vague outline of her.

Perhaps on this last night together she should let him strike the lamp. Then she could tell him again the story of the past year, only this time without the rancor of the first aborted telling. With dispassion she could recount in detail the scene at the Drury home and her ill-considered escape.

It all seemed so logical to her, so right . . . except that the words caught in her throat. The time for such a calm confession should have been when he first walked into the room. She had known it when she first arrived and she knew it now, but Clay had made her forget her resolve. She had spit out the words before, and he had not believed her. He would believe her now.

She called herself a coward, but perhaps that was being too harsh. To confess her crime and risk immediate arrest — for she truly did not know how he would react — would be to admit the loss of all hope, to accept that she would turn herself in, or allow him to summon the authorities if he so chose. That, she was not quite ready to do. Not just yet.

If only she trusted him to care for her. But he had been harsh in his judgment of the one subterfuge to which she had admitted—the story of the birthday gift.

A man doesn't like to be made a fool of, especially in bed.

So she would postpone the inevitable. She had been doing little more than that for the past year.

Making love to Clay in the dark had a magical aura about it, and she could pretend things were other than they were. The light was the enemy; the truth was the enemy. She closed her eyes and lay still in his arms.

Lowering his head, he pressed his open mouth against her throat and licked her skin. "You taste salty. And sweet. Your heart's still pounding. Did you know that?"

"I know. I thought it was going to burst."

He chuckled. "Never known that to happen. If you get scared the next time, let me know and I'll try to take it easy."

"You seem quite sure there will be a next time."

"It would be a shame to lose what we've got. You think loving is always this good? Not for me, and I know damned well not for you. All you gotta do is tell me what's going on with you, and I don't mean about any thousand-pound reward. Only a country fool would believe that kind of malarkey."

"The story's true." She felt him ease away. "It is," she said, her voice rising a pitch. "I heard it yesterday. Two men spoke of the money, said they would announce it around the city."

"And you decided it would make a fine tale to spin tonight."

"I guess that's what I thought."

Heartsick, Jenna looked away from him into the dark. Clay was not all that she had supposed. For all

199

his loving methods and his natural Texas charm, he could at times fit well into the English ruling class — judging, questioning, wanting his way. He could be kind, all right, but when and where he chose.

As hard as it was to lie to him, it was harder to lie to herself. As much as she loved him, and there seemed little she could do about feeling differently, she did not deserve his sarcasm and he did not deserve the truth.

He wanted a believable story? That's exactly what he would get, if she had to invent plausible situations all night long.

She shifted away from him in the bed.

"I saw you at a party. Never mind which one. I didn't know who you were and decided to make a game of finding out. I followed you here and eased inside."

"Weren't you afraid of getting caught? Maybe getting thrown in the hoosegow?"

"The what? Oh, you must mean prison. Yes, that was a concern, but more than anything I wanted to get to know you better, and what quicker way than by crawling into your bed? I tried the front door first, but the sentries down there wouldn't listen to anything I had to say."

"At least they were more alert than Theodore."

"All they did was challenge me. I've never been one to ignore such a thing. I was not dressed as myself, of course, and I suppose they decided I meant you harm. By the way," she said, hurrying on before he could interrupt, "I really did hear rumors about your going into the Dials. That part I never lied about."

"So who are you?"

"My name isn't important."

"We've been around this track before, and I wasn't wild about it the first time."

"I can't tell you. Uncle Thomas would not understand."

"Ah, a name."

She had pulled it out of the air.

"Now we're getting somewhere," he added. "Your father's brother?"

"That's right. My father is no longer alive; that part was the truth. And the rest of the truth is, I saw you and I wanted you and I decided to do something about it."

"Without payment."

"I don't need payment. I'm really very well off."

"Sounds like a spoiled rich girl talking."

"I've been called that before."

She fell silent and waited for him to tell her how much he believed. All in all, it wasn't a bad story, even though she had invented it as she went along. A creative mind was her legacy from reading all those fanciful tales to the twins . . . that and needing regularly to avoid the truth.

He sat up. "Still don't know why we can't get a look at one another."

Jenna bounded from the bed and scooped up her clothes, clutching them to her bosom. "No, Clay. I asked you for darkness."

"As my aunt used to say, you'll have to come up with a better reason for getting something than just asking."

"All right, how about this? You accused me of playing games. If that's the truth, then I've won. You couldn't find out anything about me, you said. Light that lamp and you're admitting you're giving up."

"You're the one that likes challenges, Princess, not me."

She knew that even as he accepted her latest lies, he had come to the end of his patience. He shifted to the far bedside table. Holding tightly onto her clothes, she darted around the bed and came at him just as the fire was struck. Without thinking, she grabbed for his wrist and the lamp dipped dangerously. Immediately she let go of him as he righted the lamp.

She blew out the match, and the night around them seemed darker than ever. "No, Clay, no. It mustn't be."

"You'd set the house on fire, wouldn't you, to get away?"

"Never," she cried, turning from him. "I would do nothing to hurt you. Please let me go. Otherwise you can only hurt me."

"Damned if I can see how."

He attempted to come at her, but she could tell from the sound of thrashing that his legs and feet were tangled in the bedcovers and she hurried out the door, slamming it behind her and dashing down the long hall, her clothes still clutched to her naked breast. In a flash she was down the servants' stairs and out the back door, taking a moment to pull on her clothes. With the cap firmly in place and the shawl wrapped tightly about her, she ran down the alley.

She did not take so much as a second to tell Theodore goodbye.

Clay slapped the reins against the stallion's sweating shoulder and leaned low, giving the horse his head. Hooves pounded against the narrow dirt road that wound south of London into Surrey, and the tree-lined miles slipped by fast.

As fast, Clay thought, as the Princess making an escape.

The comparison didn't exactly catch him unawares. He'd been pondering a great deal about the woman who had twice warmed his bed. It had been a week since he'd caught a glimpse of her face as she leaned toward the flickering match, but she'd been lingering in his mind. He wanted her back more than

202

he would have believed possible. He missed her, as much as he missed riding the Whiskey. It was a hell of an admission to make, but it was the truth.

She wanted to play games, it would seem — the good kind that called for snuggling her hot little body against his, and the bad kind that kept him in the dark, in more ways than one. If he hadn't tangled himself in those damned bedcovers, graceful man that he was, he might have caught her in the hall. She'd been so frightened he would do something like that, he was almost glad she had got away. Almost.

She was sleek and fast all right, a fine filly who was playing him for a fool. The only thing he couldn't figure was what she was getting out of it. He'd like to believe she wanted nothing more than his body, but hell, he wasn't so proud of his manly endowments that he could take that idea seriously. The whole situation had been eating at him so much, he'd taken to the road.

He rounded a bend and came directly upon the rear of a hay cart making its slow way along in front of him. Twenty yards away, thundering directly toward him in a cloud of dust and occupying a goodly share of the narrow road, appeared an oncoming carriage and a team of four. Moving fast from opposite directions, they would be passing the cart at the same precise moment. Walls of wilderness to right and left offered no quick route for passing the cart, and Clay saw no alternative but to charge into the carriage's lane.

He gave a Texas *hi-yah* and dug heels into the stallion's flanks. The mount responded with a burst of speed; rider and horse hurtled past the cart and back onto their own side of the road just as the carriage whipped by, its four horses lathering and straining, leather traces creaking, the coachman yelling an indistinguishable oath and shaking a raised fist in the air.

Pulling back on the reins, Clay glanced over his shoulder at the cart. The driver, an old man with long, graying hair, a battered hat resting on the back of his head, waved a sign of approval at Clay's horsemanship and gestured for him to keep riding. The nag that was hitched to the cart, bobbing head in blinders, kept up her plodding pace as though disaster had not skirted so near.

Directly overhead the noonday sun beamed down its silent heat, strong and welcome when Clay considered the past damp, cool days in London. Around him he could hear only the labored breathing of the stallion, the rustle of leaves, and the song of a bird from somewhere in the woods to his right, and it was all music to a country boy.

In silent penance for riding so recklessly—and to give his horse a well-earned rest—Clay settled down to a sedate pace, one more appropriate for a viscount who was out for an afternoon's ride. He needed the practice, what with his parents planning a visit filled with society get-togethers for them all.

Wiping the sweat from his brow, he settled his hat low on his forehead and brushed at his riding coat. He must remember he was not galloping across an open pasture or along a flat, wide Texas road. He was in England, where there were unexpected turns and unannounced perils that could sneak up on a man.

But Lordy, he wanted to cut loose again. Breathing all that city air had tied his muscles in knots, and it felt good to get out on the road again. In the country, he was as close to the Whiskey as he could get, and he could think.

The trouble was, when he started cogitating, thinking about the two countries which claimed him and the ways they were different and alike, shadows of a woman kept taking over—just the way they did when he was in London.

Clay knew the problem. After three visits, two

spent mostly in bed, shadows and a story or two were all he had—one he couldn't believe and another which might have a touch of truth. A spoiled rich girl who wanted his body. Maybe—maybe not.

Over the past week he'd been looking for her, determined to find out exactly how knowing who she was could bring her to harm. Hell, he didn't want to hurt her. Something about her brought out his protective nature, and he was determined to discover why. Instead of tromping through brush to find her the way he hunted in the Hill Country, he'd been dressing up and attending society doings. He was operating under a major handicap, though. In Texas he could spot a deer or a wild turkey fifty yards away, mainly because he knew their habits and looks. He couldn't say the same for the Princess, even after knowing her in ways of the most personal kind.

His hands and body had learned many things. The Princess was small in stature—when her toes were teasing the tops of his feet and rubbing against his ankles, her head was resting right under his chin and her breath was tickling the hairs on his chest. At times like that she would stroke his nipples with her tongue, a remembrance that gave Clay a jolt of heat in his loins.

No, the Princess might not be able to stretch out the length of the mattress, but she had enough curves to satisfy any man.

Spoiled rich girl, was she? She didn't make love like one.

And there was her voice. In England it told a lot about a woman. Hers was low and sexy, throaty and somehow gentle the way he thought a woman's voice ought to be. In the dark, listening to her, he thought of unexpected things—shallow creeks running over limestone beds, a summer breeze whispering across a Texas pasture, the good feeling he got when he'd walk into the Whiskey ranch house and hear his aunt singing in the kitchen.

The Princess and his aunt were about as different as two women could get, and yet he linked them in his mind. He'd have to think on that one awhile.

The voice told him more about her than just her gentleness. She was also a lady, in the British sense of the word — a dyed-in-the-wool member of the upper classes. He'd figured that from the start, though maybe there would be some among his English acquaintances who would disagree. She was a lady, all right. It wasn't only her voice and the way she chose her words so carefully — he knew it from the considerate, restrained way she had about her. Which didn't mean he wasn't almighty grateful that she occasionally forgot to mind her manners. He figured a lady, even the English kind, didn't always have to be restrained.

Mostly she was a lady who didn't want to be found out. Didn't want anyone to know she was even interested in Clayton Ernest Drake, Viscount Parkworth, only son of the Earl of Harrow and heir apparent to the title. As if being interested would shame her in some way.

Funny the way she'd gotten confused, switching his title with his real name. Clay didn't care for all the malarkey that went along with this peerage business, but he sure as hell wasn't ashamed of it, either. He owed his father respect, and that meant respect for everything about him.

She had to know who he was since she'd seen him somewhere around town and found out where he lived. She'd tried to throw him off with a few questions about why he was imposing on the earl's hospitality, but he figured that was her way of throwing him off her trail, the way a fox would take to the creek to get away from a hound.

He couldn't believe it was his position that bothered her. There might be a few women on the island

206

who'd be aiming their sights higher than a viscount, but he couldn't see her angling for a duke—or maybe he just didn't want to see her that way.

One thing was for sure, she'd lied about riding. Instinct told him she wouldn't know how to get on a pony, much less a full grown horse.

A servant's rough hands and a lady's soft voice—a paradox he'd have to contemplate.

He spied an inn just off the road, and decided to stop. Paying the stable boy to care for the stallion, he went inside and ordered an ale from the burly man behind the bar. With no more than a passing glance at the dark-haired barmaid standing close by, he carried the tankard to a corner table, dropped his hat and gloves beside the ale, and settled back in the chair, his long legs stretched out in front of him.

He stared at the ale, but all he saw was a pert little nose and a pair of full red lips—all he'd been able to see before the match went out. He had to give her credit. Coming on with the plea about how he could hurt her, she'd got clean away without leaving a trail. He wondered just how far she'd gotten naked.

Hellfire, she had him turned inside out, and he couldn't so much as identify her if she walked into this tavern and sat right beside him.

Unless she wasn't dressed—he'd have a shot at it then.

He settled back to enjoy the ale and the picture that came to his mind.

"Can I serve your lordship another drink?"

He opened his eyes to the woman from the bar. She was standing in front of him, hands on broad hips, her lips wet and parted in a smile. Black hair thick and wavy rested against her shoulders, and her black eyes gleamed with a clearly recognizable light.

"Perhaps your lordship would be wanting somethin' besides ale."

"No, thank you. No food. I'm not hungry. I'll

just finish the ale and head out."

"An interestin' accent you have. A Yank, right?"

"Right."

"Well, Yank, there's hunger and there's hunger." She glanced over her shoulder at the bartender, who was busy serving another customer. "Bertram don't much like me talking to the men familiar like this way. A straightforward man, Bertram is. But I always say, what he don't know won't hurt him."

"Is he your husband?"

She threw back her head and laughed. "Don't he just wish. Now take a handsome man like yourself. You must have several appetites that call for satisfying on a heated day like today."

She stood back and grinned. "If you sees anything that looks good to you," she added in case Clay hadn't already got the message, "it's necessary only to ask."

Uninterested though he might be, Clay couldn't resist smiling back at her. Whether riding or relaxing in a bar, he might as well give up on any attempt to act the part of distinguished viscount. He just wasn't cut out for the role.

The truth was, he couldn't work up interest in anyone besides the Princess. "Just the ale, thanks all the same."

The barmaid did not take kindly to rejection. "I'm as good as her," she said sharply, backing away no more than a couple of feet.

"As good as who?"

"The woman on your mind."

"So I'm thinking of a woman, am I?" Clay said.

"Only one thing'll bring a light like that to a man's eyes. Less'n it's another man, but you don't seem to be that sort. She be from London?"

It was a question he couldn't rightly answer.

"From outside Pretoria," he said thoughtfully, more to himself than the woman.

208

"That around here anywhere?"

"Africa."

The woman blinked, still uninformed.

An orphan from a farm in the Transvaal. A desirable, passionate redhead who had given him her virginity but not her name. These were details he kept to himself, along with a few memories of exactly how she responded to him in the dark.

The woman departed, leaving him to his thoughts. They didn't give him much peace, and he made quick work of the ale, then went to claim his horse. By the time he had made the long journey back to town, he was ready to find the Princess pacing the floor and eager to get things started. But he really didn't think she would show up again, not after the hard words that had passed between them and her abrupt departure.

That left him only one thing to do—find wherever she was hiding and flush her out, the way he flushed out quail.

Well, maybe not quite the same way, since he wouldn't be looking at her through the sight of a gun.

He made it back to Tunstall Square in late afternoon. Robert met him in his room and took the riding clothes he stripped from his body, the valet's eyes lingering only for a second longer than necessary on the scuffed boots.

"How was the ride, Master Clayton?"

"There's some beautiful country around here. A man needs to get out of the city once in a while. You ever manage to get away?"

Robert shuddered. "I have lived my life in London. I do not choose to do otherwise." He gestured toward the bedside table. "While you were away, a letter arrived from America."

It was from Aunt Martha. Clay read it fast, looking for indications that things weren't running too smoothly, convinced as he was that he was the only one who could manage the ranch as it ought to be managed. She claimed otherwise, writing general news with a few particulars added by way of the Whiskey foreman and Andy Taylor. Andy had promised to check in with her from time to time.

"Is there a problem, Mr. Clayton?"

Clay realized he must have been frowning. "No problem. They're getting along all right without me." He grinned crookedly. "Kind of knocks a man in his esteem."

"Which is not, I assume, where a gentleman wishes to be knocked."

"Not as a rule, Robert. Not as a rule." Clay caught a glimpse of wicked humor in the valet's eyes, but he paid him respect by not mentioning it. Robert would not want to be accused of acting like a clown.

When he had settled down to a hot bath, Clay did some thinking. He needed to get back to the ranch. No, he told himself. He *wanted* to get back. Didn't he?

What he ought to do was get on over to Hampshire and look at those cattle his lordship was interested in, strike a deal for a breeding bull if he liked what he saw, and get back to London. There were a few of his parents' friends he hadn't gotten around to visiting yet, and he wanted to do so before the earl and Libby arrived in town week after next. He'd go to the parties with them, the last of the Diamond Jubilee celebrations, and then, after checking in with Charlotte and brother Bill, wherever they had set up headquarters, he could get back to Texas.

That pretty much summed up what he ought to do, what he had been planning on, too, but he'd never been one to stick by an intention just because he had settled on it once. Flexibility, he'd told Andy, could be a man's best friend.

So maybe he wouldn't go back right away. Not

until he knew more about the Princess. Otherwise, the mystery would be eating at his craw the rest of his life.

The idea settled his itchiness, and he turned his thoughts toward how to spend the evening. He had plans for early on, the opera, which he had taken a liking to, if it didn't go on too long. Those Italians, Puccini especially, sure could cause a ruckus on the stage.

As for later, he didn't much care for coming back here and waiting for the door to open and a naked woman to slip inside. A man couldn't count on things like that more than a few times in his life, and Clay had already had his times.

As best he could recall, there wasn't much going on after the opera. He'd had his fill of Claridge's and the gambling halls, and he'd been warned to stay out of Seven Dials.

Now that gave him an idea. He hadn't been to the Black Horse in a long time. Maybe he'd drop by and see how the little girl was getting along. What with the Princess and all his social obligations as set out by Lady Libby, he'd been neglecting her lately. She seemed the kind to take care of herself, no matter what that witch of a woman who helped run the place claimed, but it wouldn't hurt to check and make sure.

Yep, the opera and the Black Horse. He'd decide where else to go from there.

Chapter Sixteen

Jenna couldn't believe her eyes.

Clay was no more than a dozen yards away, standing in the open doorway of the Black Horse looking as handsome as she had ever seen him, once again in a black cutaway coat and wide silk tie. Tonight he truly could pass for the son of an earl, especially since he wasn't wearing his Texas boots.

And here she was on her hands and knees with a bucket of wash water and a brush, trying to clean up the blood a couple of roisterers spilled before Hector had thrown them into the street not ten minutes ago.

Peering at the door through darkened, disheveled hair, she felt a cold, sick knot in her stomach. No matter how she looked at the situation, it was not her finest hour.

The reality of the scene struck her. Clay was here! Boots or no boots, he could be killed!

She allowed herself a daring, quick glance around the room. No Bertie Groat. No Teresa. At least not yet. Neither had been seen much around the Horse since Primm and Crock had announced the reward, although the other denizens of the Dials, unable to find their prey in the first hours of the hunt, had lost interest in claiming the money.

Jenna would not have sworn that Teresa was in

truth out searching for a diminutive redhead with green eyes, but since her absence provided relief from the regular barrage of insults and orders she threw around, Jenna did not complain.

Except that she worried about Hector, who seldom smiled.

She tugged at her cap, then turned her mind once again to scrubbing hard at the floor, white-knuckled fingers wrapped around the brush, her mind racing faster than her hands could move. This was the first time Clay had returned since she issued her warning. She knew why he was here. Ignoring her claim to be a wealthy woman out for nothing more than a man, he had accepted her challenge to learn her true identity. Somehow he'd had her followed, maybe hired investigators for all the females he'd had dealings with since arriving in London. Whatever he had done, he had met with extraordinary success.

No other explanation seemed possible. He had come to make her admit publicly to her masquerade and to the way she had spent several early morning hours, thrusting herself on the good graces of a man she barely knew.

She ceased her work and sat back, the worn soles of her shoes hard against her bottom. Maybe, rather than shouting at her in the middle of the busy Horse, he wanted to confront her privately. The idea offered little comfort.

A week had passed since she had made her rapid exit from his room, a long, cold, lonely week during which she worked at the tavern, forced herself to beg on the streets, and all the time strived to convince herself she could not go to him again.

But he had come to her.

Catching a glimpse of him from the corner of her eye, she saw he was still standing in the door, more than six feet of elegant black and white that somehow managed to look at home in the shabby tavern. She knew without staring into his wondrous gray eyes that he was looking at her. Nervously she splashed wash water from the bucket, wetting the front of her skirt more than the floor, and set the brush in rapid motion.

Reason took over. He couldn't possibly know the truth. Each night she had ventured forth to gain capital for her escape, she had been extra cautious to see she wasn't followed.

The conclusion was obvious: he wasn't investigating his Princess. He came to check on the pitiful child who had attracted his attention and his sympathy, which wasn't a whit more comforting, and she went back to scrubbing furiously. He needed to leave, and right away. The danger awaiting him was real.

Why wasn't he able to ignore her the way the rest of the world was able to do?

"Clay!"

Teresa's high-pitched screech came from the opening to the back hallway. Whatever her activities had been, they were ended early tonight and she had made an unexpected return. And, it would seem from the welcoming sound in her voice, she had decided to give the Texan another chance.

Jenna muttered an oath under her breath, scrubbing so hard she splintered the floor. A thin sliver penetrated the pad of her forefinger and she dug it out. Sucking away a drop of blood, she tried to decide what to do. She didn't much think Clay would be charmed by Teresa, but she also didn't want him to get close to her. He was a clever man. He might detect something about her, some aura, that would give him a clue as to who she really was. She was scented with scrub water, not lavender wa-

214

ter, but the fear lingered.

The truth was, she didn't know just how much he had seen of her face before she'd extinguished the match. Surely he wouldn't recognize her now, but the worry lingered. He was a very clever man.

Without warning, she spied his patent leather boots close beside her tattered skirt. So shiny were they that she could almost see her reflection in them, which would have been unnerving indeed.

Another pair of shoes, these black and worn at the heels, also came to a halt within her line of sight, along with the hemline of a dirty red dress.

The two had come from opposite ends of the room, but their destination had been the same.

"Glad t'see yer back at the 'orse," Teresa tittered. "Don' worry none about t' child. 'er's just doin' 'er work. No 'arm in 'at."

Clay kneeled. She could have touched his trousers if she just reached out . . .

She braved one quick look at him through her tangled, darkened hair. He flashed her a smile of such sweet concern that her throat constricted, and she cowardly squeezed her eyes closed. He might not be able to recognize her aura, but his was driving her to the point of panic.

She remembered his painful sarcasm when she had been in his arms. Now, when he thought she was a slum child, he was treating her with great respect.

She didn't understand him in the least.

His hand covered hers over the brush. Red and rough though it was from the harsh soap, it must be recognizable as the hand he held so often, the hand he guided to—

Closing off that line of thought, she whimpered and cowered; in the privacy of her mind she cursed and wished him away.

215

He tossed the brush aside. "Let's see how you're doing, Child," he said, and placed his hands under each of her elbows. Strong and comforting he might have been to someone truly abused, but he was terrifying to her.

Jenna knew her luck was fast running out. She had been getting by with fooling the drunken crowd in the Horse, and Teresa who wanted to believe she was a freakish fool, and even Hector, who was not one to judge another closely unless it was a man nearing his wife. But she was terrified that perhaps she could not fool Clay. If he hadn't got a clear look at her face that last night in his room, it was possible that here in the tavern he might not recognize his Princess, at least not right away, but he would know she wasn't a child, know for certain that she wasn't slow-witted, and figure out soon enough that she wasn't even deaf.

He would speak out, pulling off her cap as he did so, and there would be those in the Horse who would pounce upon them both, taking whatever action was necessary to remove Clay from the scene and dragging her to Primm and Crock for the reward.

She very much feared for them both, and all of her survival instincts came to the rescue. She jerked away, knocking the scrub bucket over and sending gray water washing over the shiny patent boots and the run-down shoes.

"Bloody bitch," Teresa screamed. Whatever comment Clay had to make was lost in the laughter of the crowd.

Jenna scurried around him and made a dash for the door, keeping her body low to the floor and her head tucked down. She hit the outside pavement running, darted down the first alley she came to, emerged on another dingy street little different from the one in front of the Horse, and kept on going, barely aware of the huddled figures in the doorways and the sleeping bodies lying next to the unlighted buildings, keeping clear of the horse droppings in the street even as she kept up her pace.

When she came to a halt in the shadow of an abandoned glove factory four blocks from the tavern, she gasped for breath and waited for the stitch in her side to go away. All was quiet around her. No one had followed. She was safe.

If Clay had half the sense with which she credited him, he would find his way safely back to Tunstall Square. If only she could be certain of the exact location of Bertie Groat.

Her relief lasted until she caught sight of a pair of figures walking toward her through the dim light cast from a lamp-post, one tall and thin, a top hat tilted on his head, and the other short and burly and bareheaded. Though they came from the direction opposite the Black Horse, instinct told her they offered danger, and she had learned not to ignore her instincts.

For a brief, terrified moment she considered falling to the ground right on the spot and pretending to be asleep — or dead, whichever the two men chose to believe if they considered her at all. But she could not bring herself to remain so exposed. Shelter was what she needed — walls and a roof to protect her from prying eyes.

Her wild glance ended at the factory directly behind her, and she hastened up the half dozen steps leading to the closed door. The handle turned and she slipped inside, then listened, her ear pressed against the edge of the partially opened door, as the footsteps of the two men gradually grew louder and echoed in the quiet night.

Too loud. Whoever they were, they were following

her up the steps. The hallway where she found herself was cloaked in darkness. She threw herself into a corner behind the door and huddled, arms clasped to bent legs, her head low and eyes wide.

If only she had the knife she kept hidden away beneath her mattress. Not once had she even glanced at it since that terrible night when she had been forced to draw blood, but she felt the same panic now that she'd felt when the cretin Badger had tried to force his attentions on her. She hadn't seen him since, just as Hector had predicted, but he was far from being the only threatening scoundrel on the streets.

She watched in horror as the door opened and the two men came inside. In the pale light, she could make out little about them except to confirm her original thought that one was indeed short and the other tall.

A single inhaled breath added the information that one was perfumed with oils reminiscent of the royal rose garden and the other had not bathed in quite a while.

"I tell yer, all will be well. Just as yer wants."

She recognized the harsh, guttural voice of Bertie Groat.

Bertie Groat! The short and smelly man was Bertie Groat! The realization of his presence, coming as it did several seconds after he spoke, hit her like the report from a gun. She had grown so used to seeing him huddled over a jar of ale in a corner table at the tavern most every night, and bragging to anyone who would listen, that his presence here was more of a surprise than her own.

At least, she told herself, he was not out harming Clay in return for Teresa's special kind of reward.

She held herself tightly. Whatever the miscreant was up to, it was certainly nothing that would benefit her. And it was nothing the law would condone.

She kept perfectly still, willing herself not to breathe.

"It had better be well," snapped the second man, the perfumed one. "I'm paying you a good price for your services."

"As I been tellin' yer, guv'nor, all 'll be well."

Their footsteps gradually receded down the dark hallway and took them into a nearby room. She heard the snap of a match. In a minute the soft glow from a lamp filtered through the open door and into the hall.

Groat's voice continued, lower but clearly audible in the stillness. "I snatch the tyke and make a right fine distraction, as yer put it. Yer'll have the Queen's necklace in yer pocket afore they knows what's 'appenin'. She's an old 'un, shoulda kicked off long afore now. Won't put up much o' a fight."

"It's a fight I'm trying to avoid, you fool. If I am forced to harm her in any way, you will be the one to suffer. I promise: you will suffer a great deal."

Groat's companion, a gentleman at least in his speech and scent, uttered the words with authority, but his voice had a peculiarly thin timbre that made him sound like an aged woman. The voice didn't rob him of conviction, however. If Groat didn't believe the threat, Jenna certainly did.

"Won't be no fight 'cause o' me," Groat growled. "Got a distraction o' me own that'll keep the blarsted rozzers busy."

"You had better know what you are doing, Groat. If you don't—"

"Don' worry. The stupid bloke I've got in mind ter 'elp 'll do wot I say. 'e don't know nuffin 'bout the partic'lars, but 'e's got responsibilities wot'll keep 'im from askin' too many questions." Groat paused. "Mind ye, I'm not

219

claimin' the boy won't be 'urt."

"I don't care what you do with him. Just get him away. He's an adventurous sort, as I told you. Likes to wander around. Catching him away from the others shouldn't present too much difficulty."

"I gets yer. They all starts to 'owlin' when they see 'e's gone. An' that's when yer moves in fer the jewels."

"What I do is no concern—"

Something slithered over Jenna's foot, and a small cry escaped her throat.

"What's that?" the gentleman asked sharply.

Jenna pulled inside herself, willing herself invisible or far, far away. In her mind's eye she could picture the two men standing in the flickering light of the room, the tall aristocrat looking toward the hall like a snake searching for prey, and Bertie, blinking and scowling, hunched beside him.

"Wot's wot?"

"In the hallway. I heard something."

"Jus' yer mind playin' tricks, guv'nor."

"Get out there and investigate. Now."

Jenna knew that the barked orders would not be ignored. Terror-stricken, she scrambled from the corner and flung open the door, stumbling down the stairs with Groat lumbering somewhere behind her in angry pursuit. She caught her balance on the pavement, but she knew there was no escape . . . no protective portal for her to run to, no alley, no open door. All she had was a wall of clammy brick to one side of her and a dark street on the other, and all around her the foul-smelling air of the Dials. She did not have even the protection of her shawl.

For one horrible instant she was frozen with terror. Necessity thrust the terror aside, and she crouched on the filthy pavement next to the factory steps. Groat's booted feet halted beside her. She lifted her hand and whimpered.

He gave an ugly laugh.

"Who is it?" the man called from the shadows inside the open door.

"It's the brat from the Black 'orse Tavern."

"Get rid of him."

" 'im's a 'er, guv'nor."

"Fool, it matters not whether it was a boy or girl who overheard us. Do what I say."

Groat muttered something under his breath, but even Jenna's sharp ears couldn't pick it up.

"No need to do 'er in," he said more clearly. "Deaf as a post, she is. A moron, too. Wouldn't unnerstan' even if she could 'ear."

"I would rather err on the side of caution."

"I'll toss 'er in the river if yer likes, but wot difference it'll make I dunno. The brat knows 'ow to clean the slop jars, but little else."

Groat studied the front of the factory. "Teresa— she works at the 'orse—Teresa sez she runs off from time t' time. Dunno where. Looks like we know now. 'ides out here, likely as not."

"That is no concern of mine. It is late." The gentleman exhaled a breath of impatience. Peering at him as best she could, Jenna could see only a pair of gloved hands, raised in an elegant pose that went with his voice and his scent and the fine top hat. She watched him smooth the white gloves.

"Do what you want," he continued. "But be forewarned. If anything goes wrong because of her, you will pay. Do not be more stupid than necessary, Mr. Groat. I do not make idle threats."

Jenna tried to get a look at the man's face as he hurried down the stairs, but always he was turned from her and he directed his step in the opposite direction. As he hurried away, she saw only his tall, thin figure and the long tails of his coat flapping

221

about his legs. At the moment he passed under a lamppost, he lifted his hat to straighten it and she caught a glimpse of a bald pate surrounded by a fringe of hair—brown, she thought, but she couldn't be sure. Hat in place, he continued on his way without breaking stride.

From her view he looked like thousands of other gentlemen out on the town. Despite the baldness, she put his age in the late thirties, but it was only a guess.

From the corner of her eye she caught a heavy boot directed at her head. She fell away, and the heavy toe missed her by no more than inch.

"Get on wi' ye," Groat growled. "I gots t'ings to see to. Yer can wait yer turn."

Reacting to the boot more than to his words, she cowered for a minute more, then tucked her skirts about her and scurried down the street. Never once did she look back.

Groat was as bad as his gentleman partner when it came to issuing threats, and Jenna did not take them lightly. The only benefit she could see at all from the night's business was that the rascal would be too busy with his other concerns to bother with Clay.

As disturbed as she was by the thought of Groat wishing her harm, she could not forget the rest of the overheard conversation. It worried her more than she would have believed. She knew a crime was to be committed, a terrible offense that involved a child and the Queen's jewels. To know and not to reveal what she knew must surely be against the statutes of the crown. And what was far worse, to know a child might be hurt and do nothing to save him was most surely against the dictates of her battered conscience.

Something must be done, and she was the only

one who could do it. But what?

She encountered no more adventures on her way to the tavern, and she allowed herself to go over all that she had heard. Groat had bragged often about his expanded criminal activity. It would seem that the bragging had not been simply talk. No wonder he had not been seen around the Horse the past few days. He had business to attend.

To steal a necklace from the Queen seemed far too grandiose an undertaking for the likes of Bertie, but of course he was following the instructions of an aristocrat. There was nothing said as to the boy's identity, just that he was a wanderer. It wasn't a description that distinguished him from other boys.

Jenna knew painfully well the course of action that lay before her. The police must be told.

She also knew painfully well that she could not walk to Bow Street and relate everything she had heard, not if she wanted the police to take action preventing the planned crime. Once learning who she was—and they would, right away—they would forget what she had to say.

If only she knew the identity of the boy, then perhaps she might warn him or his parents. She tried to imagine an elegantly dressed child cavorting about a carefully tended lawn, his thin legs in short trousers and high socks, the buttons on his shirt made of pearl.

All she could see were the round, sad eyes of Alfred Morgan staring up at her in the alley beside the lodging house. For all she knew, the six-year-old Alfred could be the same age as the threatened child, but yet that was all they could have in common. It was a curious confusion, yet she couldn't get the image from her mind.

In her heart she knew the truth. For all his wealth, the unknown boy deserved as much protection from crime as the dear lad who lived in the Dials. That protection had fallen to her. She should have appreciated the irony of the situation, but lately she'd had all the irony she could handle.

She soon arrived at the alley behind the tavern. Letting herself inside, she stopped at the door leading into the main room. Clay had gone, as had most of the customers. Teresa sat at a table by herself, and Hector was wiping the bar. Neither gave a sign that they had heard her return.

She crept back down the hallway to her room. Two plans opened up to her. Somehow she must get paper and pen and write to New Scotland Yard, telling in detail all that she had overheard. It was the only thing that she knew to do. If she learned any more, she would write them again. Otherwise, she would pray that whoever opened the letter paid heed to what she wrote.

The second plan was equally important. She had to stay away from Bertie Groat. He had threatened to take care of her later, and she knew that he would.

A heaviness settled on her that she could not shake off. It was time to leave the Dials, which meant saying good-bye to the twins. Somehow she would have to find the strength. Perhaps their father really was trying to accept his responsibilities as a parent. If he chose not to, maybe she could talk to him about sending for the children later, once she found another place to hide.

She would have to be careful. There were those who still yearned for the thousand-pound reward; Morgan the Juggler could very well be one of those.

Wearily she sat at the edge of her cot and thought about Clay. Once she had tried to take her problems to him, and had been met with scorn. She

GET
FOUR
FREE
BOOKS
(AN $18.00 VALUE)

ZEBRA HOME SUBSCRIPTION
SERVICE, INC.
P.O. Box 5214
120 BRIGHTON ROAD
CLIFTON, NEW JERSEY 07015-5214

could not return again.

Despair threatened to overtake her. Tonight, she knew, she had seen him for the last time, and she did not know how she would find the strength to go on. He couldn't possibly mean so much to her, this long-legged Texan with his sometimes kindly, sometimes aristocratic ways.

But he did.

In her darkest moments, Jenna had begun to lose her conviction that no matter the circumstances, life was worth living, that the pursuit of freedom was worth tremendous sacrifice. Clay had walked into the tavern and revived that belief.

A person had to believe in something in this world — the reverend had told her so often enough and she knew he was right — but she also knew that the something he spoke of must be more substantial than a few stolen nights of love. In the final analysis, that was all she and Clay had really shared.

She would forever remember that in their last moments together, she had anointed his polished shoes with dirty scrub water. The memory would have brought laughter to her lips if she had not already begun to cry.

Chapter Seventeen

Early the next morning, having decided that Groat was still deep asleep in whatever hovel he called home, Jenna ventured onto the streets and made purchase of a small packet of stationery and an envelope. She spent more than she had planned, but she knew the letter must look presentable if it were to be taken seriously by the authorities.

Back in her tavern room, with Hector and Teresa still asleep across the hall, she labored long and hard over the contents. At last she was through, having related exactly what she had heard and the general location in which she had heard it.

She also described both men, giving particular attention to Groat. She would have preferred accusing him to his face, with the authorities looking on, but she knew that was not possible.

She also would have preferred knowing the gentleman's name and the exact date of the planned robbery. She didn't think it was far off.

Once the correspondence was posted, she went to the lodging house where Morgan and his children lived. To her surprise, the juggler, normally a daytime sleeper, was not home, and she spent a while visiting his children, expressing pleasure over the new clothes each had been given by their father and even more pleasure over the food he had bought.

She did not linger over a long goodbye. They

would know something was wrong—especially Alfred, who let little escape him. Besides, to stay longer would have meant breaking into tears.

Alice and Alfred had been her strength during the past months that she had known them, her reason for going on, and she knew that she had been theirs. They must all remain so for each other.

Thus, when Alice asked her if she would return later in the day, she lied and said that she would try. She also assured them that they were not to worry, that if something unforeseen occurred and she could not get back right away, they should know that she was all right, and that she would be with them again as soon as she could.

It seemed a poor farewell, but it was all she could manage. At least she had been able to see them for the last time and part with a gentle hug and loving thoughts. Later, when she found a new place of refuge, she would write to Morgan. Somehow, she vowed, she would see that these precious children were all right.

She concentrated all her thoughts on the twins. If for one moment she let her thoughts wander, she would find unthinkable memories and bitter regrets drifting through her mind.

Slowly she made her way back to the Black Horse, her eyes on the lookout for Bertie Groat, her thoughts in a tumble. Knowing she would not return for possibly a long time, she had lied to the twins. And she had repeatedly lied to . . . to someone else. The fact that this someone had lied to her in turn with a wild story about being the son of an earl did not lessen her feeling of guilt.

She had been born into the world a loving, truthful person. Whatever had happened to turn her into such a conniver who played light with the truth?

The answer came right away: Pretoria politics, a train accident, and one fatal shove. They were not exactly ordinary events in a woman's life.

Ordinary events were marriage to a loving man and motherhood. For Jenna, things had not worked out quite that way.

It was with a heavy heart that she eased inside the tavern's back door and made her way to her room. She heard Hector slamming pots about in the small kitchen beside the storage room; Teresa must be asleep, resting for the night to come.

She needed sleep herself, but knew it would not come. Pulling her small store of clothes from beneath her cot, she bundled the rags and one good dress on top of the thin blanket. The dress was the one she had worn on her mad flight from the Drury home; it seemed appropriate that after a year it was still the best by far that she owned.

Last she took out her cache of coins from beneath the loose floorboard. Her week of begging had proven profitable and she had enough money to buy some sort of simple transportation out of town—if she could decide on a destination and if she knew what she would do when she got there.

She could only hope that the posters featuring a drawing of her face had not gone before her and were not still remembered. Danger awaited her in the world, but then, it also awaited her in the slums.

When she had everything assembled for a departure, she lay down on the bed and waited for night to come. If Teresa behaved as she had done so often lately, she would be leaving just as the tavern got busy. If Hector sought her out to help him, she would pretend to be asleep. He would think her ailing and would leave her alone.

Her conscience smote her. Hector deserved better than he was getting from the women in his life, but on this last night under his roof she could not risk going out where Bertie Groat would see her.

Someday, she vowed, she would make up to Hector for any inconvenience her leaving might have caused. When she could, she would tell him how much his kindness meant to her and how she always viewed him as her friend.

The sound of loud voices awakened her from a deep and dreamless slumber in the middle of the night. She sat up, startled. A moment passed before she realized exactly where she was. The fog in her mind gradually cleared, and she remembered lying restlessly in her room during the busy hours of the tavern's operations and then, as the last customers left, drifting off to sleep. She had planned to rest only until Hector and Teresa had settled down, but the nights of begging and the past hours of emotional turmoil had taken their toll. She had been exhausted.

The voices that had awakened her grew more animated. Still dressed in rags, her hair sooted and covered with the cap, her money strapped to her waist beneath her clothes, she crept to the sound of the talking. It came from the tavern's main room. Hector, shirt half tucked in and feet bare, was standing by the door. Teresa was standing behind him wearing little else but a sheet.

"Bertie dead. 'ard to believe," Hector was saying.

Stunned, Jenna halted by the bar.

" 'appened at one o' them fancy parties fer the Queen. This afternoon, as it were." The speaker was one of the Horse's regulars, a ruddy-faced man who claimed to have once worked on Fleet Street. He was always one to spread gossip, and he could often be seen hawking the one-page scandal sheets that came off the presses with scurrilous stories the more reputable papers refused to print.

"A children's garden party, la dee da, ye knows wot I means, w' the ole girl 'erself in attendance. Lots o' gents 'n ladies all about, 'n tykes runnin' all over the place."

" 'ow you know so much about it?" Teresa asked.

"I 'as me sources at *The Times*. Don't ye worry yer pretty 'ead, Miz Mims. I know wot I know. They sez Bertie was tryin' to rob one of the toffs, mebbe even the ole girl 'erself."

"Always did think 'e was better'n the rest o' us," Teresa put in.

" 'e ain't better now, lyin' as he is at the morgue. They got the one wot was workin' w' 'im. Morgan. The juggler. Lives down the street aways. A couple o' brats 'e 'as. Don' know what'll 'appen to 'em now. The workhouse, I'm afeared."

Alice and Alfred! Jenna collapsed against the bar. A long moment passed before she could take in the full import of what she heard, and then her heart broke at the realization of what the twins must be going through. Their father arrested for a crime and those precious children doomed to a workhouse. It simply could not be.

Especially when for the first time since she had met them, the children had harbored such hopes that he was coming around.

The new clothes . . . the food. Jenna understood now where they had come from. Morgan had been paid by Bertie Groat to be the distraction he had bragged about in the glove factory, the one that would draw attention away from the kidnapping and away from the theft.

From all that Groat had said, Morgan had not been part of the robbery. The gentleman conspirator had not known of his participation until last night. The man at the door had said there were children at the party, which fit in with what she had overheard. As a juggler, Morgan might very well have been hired to entertain them, but not to kidnap one of them . . . not to steal.

Somehow he had been caught in the passage of events. He must be in some horrible cell at Holloway . . . maybe even Newgate. She had heard suspected felons were kept within its notorious walls while they awaited trial. And the children—

Groat dead, Morgan arrested, and the children—

Jenna shook her head against the horror of it all. She had a million questions she wanted to ask, but of course she could not ask so much as one, could not appear to know anything was wrong.

Morgan arrested, and the children . . . what had happened to them? The workhouse had been mentioned, but Jenna suspected that an orphanage would be their actual destination. Not that it made much difference. One was about as terrible as the other. Little food and rest, long hours of work, young fingers forced to tasks that nature had never intended for them, bodies subjected to deprivation . . .

Her mind worked frantically. She must remain calm and she must find them. She must somehow convince the police that their father was innocent of anything other than working for Bertie Groat.

If he really was innocent.

She could not let herself believe anything else.

But what to do? She was the only witness to the planning of the crime and had already told everything she knew. The letter could not have arrived yet, but when it did, she doubted it would be taken seriously.

Could she identify the finely dressed culprit if she saw him again?

No, she could not. But she would readily know who he was if she heard him speak. And there was that strange scent that he wore, attar of roses as she recalled. It was unusually sweet for a man.

She forced herself to breathe deeply, even as she wrung her hands. She needed a plan. She needed to find the two little children and make certain they were all right. Leaving London was beyond the realm of possibility. Not yet was she to be free of Seven Dials.

She thought for a moment about going to Clay for help. But only for a moment. What if once again he did not believe her? Her thoughts ran wild. He might even insist on calling the authorities to listen to her story, and she knew too well what they would say and do.

The thought of him brought her to the point of breaking. She forced into the forefront of her mind the recognition of how she needed to stand alone, to take care of herself even in the darkest of times.

And this was, indeed, the darkest of times. Whatever she decided to do and however she tried to bring it about, she would, as she had done for so long, work out her problems for herself.

Part Two

Whitecastle Street

Chapter Eighteen

London
September, 1897

"Clayton Drake, you ought to be ashamed of yourself." The young woman with the auburn hair piled on top of her head laughed up at Clay from behind a fluttering pink fan.

"Could be. You're not the first to suggest it," he responded, trying to remember the woman's name.

"What do you mean by asking if I ever slip out at night?" She giggled. "No respectable lady would do such a thing."

They were standing at the edge of a crowded dance floor in the home of the Duke and Duchess of Castlebury, music from a ten-piece orchestra drifting around and between them, but it wasn't enough to tempt Clay to ask her to waltz.

"She wouldn't? Not even if she was sweet talked?" he asked. Laura, maybe. No, Belinda. Linda.

She folded the fan and struck his arm. "Not if she's a real lady." She edged the width of a saddle horn closer. "You naughty man. You know I couldn't be sweet talked, as you so charmingly put it, into anything I considered wrong."

Clay couldn't catch any censure in her voice. Maybe a little challenge, but nothing that told him to take his fox hunting elsewhere. The only reason he sought her out at the crowded gathering was because of her hair color and because she'd been eyeing him across the wide room all night.

Now that he got a close-up view of her and a few minutes of her flirting, he figured that no matter what she claimed, this particular lady might be talked into a few late nights if a man wanted to put his mind to the task, which Clay was not inclined to do. He shouldn't have gone so far as to put any questions to her in the first place, except for the looks she was throwing him and except for her hair.

And there was also her height. He let his eyes trail slowly down her silk-clad figure. Yep, if she snuggled up to him in bed, her toes could just about tickle his ankles while her lips played against his chest.

But he didn't care to give her a chance to prove it. To begin with, the color of her hair was a shade too dark — and the pitch of her voice was too high. Breasts too low and waist too thick, and lips a mite too thin. Truth to tell, she had either too much or too little of a lot of things. She wasn't the Princess.

"You know what they say about the handsome Viscount Parkworth?" she asked.

"There's no telling."

She wafted her fan and hit him again. "They say he's only interested in women — that is, *ladies,* of a certain coloring." She plumped up her already amply plumped up hair.

Clay studied the roots. Definitely dyed. And that had not been the case with the Princess. A few of her more personal curls, the ones that most observers would never see, had been left behind on the sheets. They matched the strands she'd left on the pillow. A natural redhead was the Princess. Miss What's-Her-Name most likely had personal curls as dark as her roots.

Which was maybe not the kind of speculation a peer of the realm ought to be making about a lady,

236

but then Clay figured he wasn't the first one to do so.

Armistead. Lucinda Armistead. That was her name. How would old Lucy respond if he told her what he'd been thinking? She'd hit him with more than her fan, pretend shock, and if he persisted, maybe suggest they vamoose to a more private room. What he deserved was a knee to the groin.

Habit drew Clay's eyes to the dance floor and to the women whirling by. He knew he was loco to be looking for his mystery woman after four long weeks, but he couldn't stop just yet.

He felt a hand on his arm and stared down at the short fingers and long painted nails resting against the sleeve of his black cutaway coat.

"Clayton, you're not listening to me."

He managed to return a smile in Lucy's direction. "Downright rude of me, wouldn't you say?" he said with an attempt at gallantry. "My mama taught me better."

She tittered in response. "Lady Libby is quite delightful. No one knows what she will say or do next, but it's always so . . . interesting. Like arriving in London at the wheel of a motor car with the earl by her side."

"She always did like to make an entrance."

"Rumor has it she drove all the way from Yorkshire."

"Rumor is wrong. She bought the Daimler on the outskirts of the city and was practicing how to drive. Wants to join the Royal Automobile Club, she says."

"Another club? We already have so many."

"I don't think it's the kind you're thinking of."

"Well, I know most of the clubs in town, and I never heard of this one."

"Neither had the earl until she mentioned that it had been started this year. My father is a very patient man."

A lot more patient than his son, Clay decided. He

grew restless to get away.

"Are the earl and countess still in London?" asked the intrepid Miss Armistead.

"They've gone to Paris for a few days."

"My, they must lead an exciting life."

"Most of the time they're on the Yorkshire farm. I'd call that exciting, but it wouldn't be for a woman like yourself."

He could tell she didn't quite know what to make of the remark. He took advantage of the momentary pause in the conversation while she thought it over, excused himself, and drifted around the edge of the crowded floor. He rough counted almost a hundred people dancing. Fifty women to study. Not a one that looked possible.

The ball tonight was one of two dozen affairs he had attended since returning last month from his cattle-buying tour of Hampshire. At most of them he'd been with Alex and Libby. It had been good to see them together, to watch his mother charm everyone in sight and to watch his daddy watching her, too. Seeing the way the earl and his countess were so different and still a matched pair made him feel proud, but for once in his life he'd felt a mite lonely, too.

Contrary critter that he was, he blamed that on the Princess. Couldn't look at another filly long without thinking of her. She hadn't shown up the few nights before he left for Hampshire, not that he'd expected her to considering the way she left, but that hadn't kept him from looking for her when he got back, itching as he was for a sweet welcome home.

Hell, he'd been more than itching. He'd been hotter than a pistol and ready to do a little shooting of his own. He'd wanted to talk to her, too, to tell her not to get so worked up over his questions. He wanted to win her game and find out who she was. He had a strong urge to hold her tight and feel her eager little hands doing a few of the things

238

they did so well.

But it was more than just wanting her in bed. He'd been lonesome for her company, for the sound of her sweet voice, and he'd wanted to let her know how much he missed her. Across Hampshire he'd had a hard time concentrating on those bulls.

A passel of plans for the two of them had been roaming around his mind, but one by one he'd shoved them aside. The one remaining involved a few questions about why she had panicked like a rabbit running from the hounds, and just because he wanted to light the lamp. If she was disfigured in some way, hell, that wouldn't bother him, or he'd like to think he was man enough not to let it get to him.

His Lordship and Lady Libby, surprised that he was hanging around England so long, had stayed in town a couple of weeks, then left for a trip to Paris that they'd been planning. He'd hated to see them go, but it was probably for the best. His mother knew something was eating at his craw, which was exactly the way she had put it. If she'd stayed around very long, she would have forced it out of him.

It was just as well Charlotte was still with old Bill in Brighton, otherwise she would be questioning him, too, and there were some things he was just as glad Baby Sister did not know. She'd never let him live them down, and besides, they were private things between him and the Princess.

The orchestra played on, and the dance floor was a whirl of dresses in every color he could imagine. Penny-plain, the ball was called, because it wasn't a masquerade, but he couldn't see how there was anything plain about it.

Watching the ladies, he thought of the fields of wildflowers back in Texas. It would be a long time before they started blooming, but he wanted to see the fields, brown though they would be until spring. It was way past time he started on his voyage home.

239

Just a few more days and he'd give up.

"Parkworth, good evening."

He turned to the portly, gray-haired gentleman who had sidled up close.

"Evening, Sanders," said Clay, regarding the man with care. The last time they'd been together was two nights ago over a deck of cards at White's. Poker had been the game, although Sanders had expressed a preference for bridge. Clay had lightened the Englishman's wallet by a couple of hundred pounds.

"Ripping good time, isn't it?" Sanders said with enough enthusiasm for the two of them.

"Ripping," replied Clay.

"But then, of course, a man of your tastes might prefer something a little more . . . shall we say challenging?"

Clay wasn't quite sure what he was getting at, but he could take a guess. "Like a hot game of bridge."

Bulls-eye. Sanders smiled. "I swear, old chap, if you give it a try, you'll find it gets in your blood."

Clay figured he had enough bad habits as things were without adding another card game to the list.

"I'll stick with poker."

"Not sporting of you, Parkworth. Not sporting at all. You should give me the opportunity to recover my losses."

Clay felt guilty. Sanders was an abominable poker player, and Clay had chosen the game. Sanders was also of a mature age, he reminded himself, and should have known not to play cards with an uncouth Texan who didn't have any more class than to take every shilling that was thrown on the table and then leave.

Still, he felt guilty. "There a card room around here?"

"Sporting chap, Parkworth. Knew you were. Wouldn't be Harrow's son otherwise. I believe there's an area set aside for those of us more interested in sedentary pursuits. Never could see the fascination with all that running around a dance floor. Give me a good card game any day."

Clay wondered why it took the British a couple of dozen words to say *yes*.

"Show me the way," he said.

"I'll need to find two more players, of course. Is there anyone you might suggest?"

"It's your game."

"Give me a half hour. I'll meet you in the card room to the right of the front stairs."

With a predatory gleam in his eye, Sanders departed, looking, Clay assumed, for another two victims with pockets full of cash. Like Texans, the Brits took their gambling seriously. He just hoped he could work up enthusiasm for the particular game of the night.

Idly he let his eyes roam around the room. Nothing much to interest him, just a lot of men in suits much like his and a lot of women decorated from head to toe in flashing silks, glittering diamonds, and gleaming jewels. A rich assembly it was of peers and peeresses, of diplomats and politicians, of financiers and merchants.

Some of 'em even worked for a living. Probably not enough calluses among the lot of them, though, to match one Whisky Ranch cowpoke.

For their pleasure the orchestra worked hard on the raised platform across the dance floor, and an army of servants distributed glasses of champagne or fruit punch. Most of the servants were men as stiff-backed as any hand in Tunstall Square, but he also saw a few women toting trays.

"Good evening, Clayton."

Clay turned to the smiling face of his hostess, Her Grace, the Duchess of Castlebury, leader of society and close friend of Libby's. She was dressed in lavender; the famous multiple strands of Castlebury pearls

241

rested against her throat, and the sharp gleam of intelligence for which she was equally famous shone in her eyes.

"Good evening, Your Grace," said Clay.

"I'm surprised a strapping young man like you isn't out there on the floor taking away the breath of some smitten young girl. There's enough of them available who would readily forsake their current partners for the chance to be whirled around by the handsome viscount from Texas. You're considered quite an oddity, you know."

"I've been told that a time or two."

"I meant it as a compliment, of course. Oddities — if they're not offensive or insulting — are quite the thing in London this year."

Clay grinned. "Then I'm here at a good time. I've been hoping to lead you in a polka. Any chance of that?"

"I'm afraid not. Pulled something in my back. It's not very pleasant this getting old."

Clay looked her over. Early sixties, he figured, but she was still a slender and handsome woman, her face bearing only a few smile lines around the mouth and eyes, and her once dark hair not yet completely turned to gray.

"Maybe I could get you a rocking chair. You could sit here and watch the dancing and rock in time to the music."

Her brown eyes glinted. "Watch your sauciness, Clay. I'm not so old I can't take you to task when you need it. Libby left instructions for me to do just that."

"I'll bet she did."

"Besides, I wouldn't have been able to put together such an evening if I were as decrepit at you suggest."

"And I thought the servants did all the work."

"Humph! You are an impudent one. It's not like the old days, you know. Not many of us keep the full

242

complement of servants we used to." She waved a jeweled hand around the room. "Most of these are temporaries, and I can tell you, they are a mixed lot."

"I haven't noticed any of them pouring champagne over your guests or belching—" Clay caught himself. "You'll have to pardon my manners, Your Grace. Or maybe I should say my oddity."

"Perfectly all right. The same physical necessities occur in England, only we rarely admit to them. Tell me, Clayton, just how much longer will we be treated to your presence?"

"Running me out of the country?"

"Of course not, but you didn't stay half this long when your sister was wed."

"I'll be leaving soon. Maybe run down to Brighton for a few days to visit Charlotte. Then it'll be back to work."

"How is your sister, by the way? Haven't seen her in the past few weeks."

"Charlotte's fine." Clay let it go at that and turned his attention to the servants. He'd barely given them much more than a glance, having grown used to the presence and occasional intrusions of Robert and Randolph and the rest of the hands at the Harrow home.

He particularly noticed a short and slender woman who was turned away from him halfway around the dance floor. Twenty yards separated them, but he got a good look at her. She wore the usual uniform of the serving girl, longsleeved black dress with white collar and cuffs, a white apron and a white cap, the latter perched atop a mass of red hair.

Red hair. Funny he hadn't noticed her before, but he'd been too busy looking at the guests. The Princess had made clear from the first visit that she wasn't a servant, despite her rough hands, and later she'd said outright she wasn't hurting for money. This particular woman could not be the one

243

he was after.

But he could not look away. He gave her the quick toes-at-his-ankles, lips-on-his-chest test to see if she was the right height, and as far as he could tell from a distance, she passed.

The servant half turned, and he could see she was carrying a tray of glasses. Examining her in profile, he was struck by her loveliness. Her lips were full and her chin was firm, and her cheekbones high, but somehow they all went together to form a soft and very pretty picture.

She turned farther, and her wide eyes caught with his. Abruptly, she again gave him her back and began making her way slowly through the throng in the opposite direction.

"What about that one, Your Grace?" he asked, gesturing in the departing redhead's direction.

"Which one? Oh, her. A temporary, I believe. Why? Has she done something wrong?"

"Not that I've noticed."

"Ah, I understand. The color of her hair. More than a few people have remarked on your proclivity to seek out our titian-haired young women. But a serving girl, Clay? You'd have the poor thing in a tizzy and talked into whatever you wanted. Not unusual, of course, among our class, but in your case it hardly seems sporting." She hesitated. "Perhaps I shouldn't be mentioning such things."

"Libby left instructions."

Her Grace nodded. "She would not be pleased."

Clay knew that Libby wouldn't much care whom he took an interest in, as long as he treated the woman fairly, but then he wasn't sure whether she would consider his relationship with the Princess exactly fair. In fact, he wasn't sure just how she would view the whole thing, and he'd just as soon she not find out.

He turned away from the servant. "I think I'll mosey outside for some fresh air. I've got a hot bridge game coming up in a few minutes. Wouldn't hurt to steady my nerves."

"Sanders caught you, did he? He said he would."

It took him fifteen minutes to get outside, stopped as he was by a couple of women who hinted that their dance cards were not filled. Clay played the bumpkin Texan and pretended he didn't catch on.

He exited the ballroom through an open French door and stood on the outside steps in the spilled light from the ballroom. The night was clear and cool, and stars lit the sky as though they'd been ordered special by the duchess. Taking a deep breath of the sweet English air, he nodded to several men who had come outside for a smoke.

At the base of the steps, which extended along the wall of the house, was a narrow lawn and then a bank of shrubbery that marked the beginning of the Castlebury gardens. Even Clay had heard about the gardens; they were supposed to be among the best in all of London.

Gas lights sparkled like jewels along the pathways that webbed the famous flowerbeds and tall, maze-forming shrubs. Aunt Martha would like a stroll down a few of those paths, he thought. Several couples were drifting toward them, to smell the roses, more than likely, and maybe take advantage of the dim light and privacy. If he'd had a woman he was interested in, he would be doing the same thing.

He ought to be getting on back to the card room, but it was easy to postpone his first lesson in bridge and he found himself heading down one of the paths. He couldn't make out much detail except that both beds and shrubs were neatly laid out, not at all like a Texas wildflower patch.

As he followed the winding route, Clay found his mind wandering over a lot of things—the two countries that claimed him . . . the restlessness to return to one while the other still had a hold on him . . . the Princess . . .

"No!"

The speaker, a woman, was standing on the opposite side of a thick wall of seven-foot shrubs. He'd heard that particular word before spoken in just that tone, more than a month ago while he was in bed. And, he would swear, it had been spoken by that very same voice. But maybe he just wanted to hear it again.

"Don't be acting so innocent with me," a man answered. His voice was slurred, and he was angry. "You didn't come out here just to look at the moon."

"Let me go! I'll scream."

"And who'll pay any attention to a servant who came alone out in the garden? You know what you're here for, and so do I."

"You chose the wrong woman this time. Get away."

A servant, was she? A redheaded servant, that was for sure. Clay heard the distinctive sound of a slap.

"Why, you little bitch," the man growled. "You'll pay for that."

Clay waited for no more. A grim look settling on his face, he lit out down the path to find a way to the scuffling pair.

Chapter Nineteen

Jenna straightened her cap and her shoulders at the same time as she sought an effective defense.

"You presume too much, sir," she said with dignity.

Mild words they were, considering the boiling anger she felt inside, and she kept her eyes downcast lest they give away the power of her fury. She did not want to goad this pompous lecher into further affronts; she wanted him to let her go. Lowly servant that she was, already she had gone too far with the slap, but she had not been able to resist.

He stood inches away on the garden path, his barrel-shaped body blocking her path, gaslight casting harsh shadows across his jowly, leering face, decidedly unimpressed by her rejection. Having followed her on her ill-conceived dash from the ballroom, he did not want the journey to be in vain.

Jenna swallowed. Hedges loomed on either side of her, and to her back stretched a crowded bed of roses, behind which loomed still another wall of greenery.

She seethed with frustration. The garden was to have been her place of refuge, far from the ballroom and from Clay's sharp eyes; instead it was a trap. The only satisfaction she could draw, and it was little enough, was the ugly red mark she had put on her assailant's cheek the moment his hands began wandering. In the flickering light she could see the outline of her hand.

"Getting a bit above yourself, aren't you?" he growled. Once again he gripped her arms and pulled her roughly against him. Foot raised, she tried to aim the point of her shoe at his calf, but he jerked her about with such ferocity that she had to abandon that line of defense.

His bruising fingers cut into her arms and she watched with horror as his fat, damp lips moved in on hers. Maybe she ought to let him take one quick kiss . . . she shuddered at the thought.

His mouth had no more than touched hers than she felt him propelled backward.

"Wha—" he said.

The figure of another man towered behind him. Someone, she thought with a rush of relief, had come to her rescue.

Her attacker spun around. She heard the smack of a fist against the oaf's jaw. For all his girth, one smack was all it took to send him in a crumpled heap to the ground.

Jenna gasped, hand to mouth, as she watched him fall. It had all happened so quickly. Her attacker, a moment ago so rude and threatening, was suddenly a still, dark mass at her feet. She looked up in gratitude at her rescuer.

Clay returned her stare.

She froze, unable to believe that he was here, staring down at her with a determination that took her breath away. But he was real all right, tall and dark and determined. Having believed she would never see him again, she was torn between throwing herself into his arms and making a dash past him toward the house. Since her feet refused to move, she stayed in place.

He brushed his hands, paying no more attention to the fallen man than if he had been another shrub.

"Good evening."

He smiled while she was struggling for breath, but it was not a smile filled with mirth. Surely he could hear the pounding of her heart.

Jenna blinked. He waited for her response. He couldn't possibly recognize her . . . could he?

She dipped into a curtsy. "Thank you, sir." Terrified as she was, she had no difficulty pitching her voice high. "I came out for a bit of fresh air, and the gentleman here took it upon hisself to follow, if you know what I mean."

Clay frowned.

Her fingers fumbled at her cap and at the strands of hair that had fallen loose during her struggles. The high white collar of her dress choked, but she resisted loosening it, fearing he would take the action for something that it was not.

He watched her in silence.

"Gentlemen ain't always gentlemen, if you know what I mean."

The man lying between them moaned, then returned to silence.

Jenna was talking too much . . . far too much, while Clay watched and waited, his eyes darkened to obsidian. The power of him enveloped her, beckoned her, weakened her. She felt his presence to the very center of her bones. Using all of her will, she managed to edge a step backward, and then another. Her foot sank into soft, damp dirt.

"No more games, Princess," he said. His voice was deep and insistent, and the forbidding expression on his face was indelibly inked in her mind.

Jenna's heart stopped. "Go on with you, sir," she said, far too brightly, "I ain't no princess, that's for sure." She took another step backward. Both feet were in the dirt. A thorny rose bush pressed uncomfortably against her rear, but she ignored it. "I best return. They'll be missing me inside."

"I've missed you, too."

The words caressed her with unexpected potency. Knees weakened, she swayed toward him. She hadn't slept well, had barely eaten, had not known a moment's peace since she last saw him. With all her other problems and with all her vows never to see him again, she had been unable to keep him from her heart and mind, and here he was, so close she had only to reach out . . .

"I'd say it's about time you told me just what in hell is going on," he added, his voice turned harsh.

The words and the tone in which they were delivered brought Jenna to her senses. Clay was blocking her path just as effectively as the boor at her feet had done. He'd been playing her, the way her father taught her to play fish in the Transvaal streams, and he'd decided it was time to reel her in.

"You must have me mixed up with someone else, sir." She tested the firmness of the soil with another slight step. The rose bush caught in her coarse woolen skirt. The sweet scent of flowers filled the air, and she could hear the strains of the music drifting out from the ballroom.

"I don't think so. Your voice came through loud and clear, Princess, over the hedge. I'd know it anywhere."

"Go on with you, sir."

"You've already gone on with me, now haven't you? Let's go some place where we can talk. I've been looking for you a mighty long time, and we've got a few points to clear up."

She shook her head with vehemence. "I've heard invitations like that one before. I'm a nice girl, sir."

His eyes rested on her lips for a moment, then slowly moved down to the shoes and back up again. She'd taken great care to see that she was properly dressed, hang the expense. She had to be to get inside the right homes. Proper though it was, the uniform

250

was also by far too fitted to her body, and it was a body he knew well.

"I'm sure that you are a nice girl," he said. "Very nice."

She could read doubt in his mind, but she also read determination. One thing was certain. Nothing she said was convincing him to let her go.

"I might point out, however," he said softly, "that you are standing in the duchess's prize rose bed."

Again the man on the ground moaned. This time he stirred.

Clay glanced down. Jenna took advantage of the moment and twirled away from him, putting her feet into motion as fast as she could, the spiny stems of the waist-high bushes tearing at her gown and apron. She paid no mind to a ripping sound, or to the painful scratches inflicted on her bare hands by the harsh thorns. Dancing around the plants, she covered the six-foot width of the bed in a trice. When she came to the wall of shrubs that formed a backdrop for the roses, she threw her hands over her face and plunged forward.

Miraculously, she hit a space between two bushes and shot through to a pathway on the other side.

She could hear Clay cursing the thorns. He would have to take care of his own problems; she had problems of her own. She hurtled forward, making a dash for the lights of the house. Her shoes had picked up so much mud that they slowed her maddeningly, and she took a moment to untie their laces and toss them aside. Remembering what they had cost, she retrieved them quickly and resumed her flight.

Certain that Clay would soon be close behind, she took a sharp right at the first intersecting path she came to and then a sharp left at still another, determined to choose a twisting route that would confuse him. Passing a couple clinching quietly in an alcove, she kept going, turning right, then left, then right again.

When at last she emerged from the maze of shrubbery, she paused in the shadows and stared at the steps leading into the ballroom. To enter by that route would bring impossible attention to herself. She must not be found. Pausing only long enough to knock the mud from her shoes and put them on, she darted away from the lights and made her way around the back of the house and toward the servants' entry at the side. Just as she stepped through the door, she heard hurried footsteps somewhere in the dark. Clay was close behind.

Inside she was met by a bustle of activity, servants scurrying back and forth too intent on their work to pay attention to her. She eased down a back hallway, past the kitchen, her destination the small room that had been set aside for the use of domestics employed for the evening. She would gather her purse and coat and somehow find a door that Clay was not watching, and she would hurry back to the twins. No real harm had been done, at least not yet.

A footman barred her path. "Here," he said, thrusting a tray of wine-filled glasses in her hands, "see that these are served, and be quick about it."

He gave her no choice. She carried the tray up the stairs to the entry that opened onto the evening's festivities, but instead of moving among the guests, she set the glasses down on the first table she came to, shoving aside a vase of chrysanthemums to make room.

She made a quick withdrawal back through the entry, her mind racing. Clay would be inside the servants' area by now, looking amongst the maidservants for her now all too recognizable face, causing a great stir. She had to outmaneuver him, and instead of retracing her steps downward to an unavoidable encounter, she took the back stairs to the next higher floor. She emerged onto a long, wide hallway lined on either side with closed doors. In front of one stood a serving girl, in position to guide the ladies to the bedroom set aside as a powder room.

For once Jenna was in luck. No one else was in the hall besides her and the wide-eyed girl. Motioning for her to be quiet, Jenna threw herself into the room on the right, leaned back against the closed door, and fought for breath as she looked around. Light came from a pair of sconces flanking a marble fireplace on the opposite wall. She was in a small, and blessedly empty, sitting room. Resting in the center and facing the hearth, its back to the door, was a brocade settee, on either side of which were matching chairs.

She tiptoed forward and caught sight of a large white bearskin rug covering the carpet in front of the settee, a forbidding bear's head still attached. From the expression on his countenance, she gathered that the animal had not quietly given up the fight for life.

She had heard that the Duke of Castlebury was a noted hunter. She shouldn't have been surprised by the trophy, but something about the snarling face and sharp teeth unnerved her.

Considering her circumstances, a sleeping kitten would have done the same.

Silently she sent a plea to the girl guarding the powder room, begging with all her heart that no report would be made concerning just where she had gone. The sound of someone running echoed in the hallway. She heard a door open, then slam, and then another. Beyond any doubt she knew it was Clay, hot in pursuit. She had not outmaneuvered him after all.

But he was searching quickly . . . too quickly, she prayed, for thoroughness, and she took heart.

The room offered no egress other than the hallway door, and she threw herself onto the settee and huddled in shaking silence, not daring to breathe, praying the high back with its fancy scrolled edge would effectively block her from view. The door to the sitting room opened. She pictured Clay's tall figure poised, his sharp eyes casting about the room, his mouth firm and determined. She could feel the power of his will and she trembled.

At last the door closed, and she was once again by herself in the small room. After a full and agonizing minute, she sat upright and gazed into the cold fireplace. Indeed, she felt very much alone.

Slowly she stood. She *was* alone, but then that was nothing new, and she forced her mind to the more mundane matter of how she would get away. Ruefully she stared down at her once pristine apron, at the white cuffs that were soiled and ripped. Somehow she would have to get every spot removed and mend the tears, or she could never again seek temporary employment in the right kind of house where the gentlemen of the city gathered.

If she wasn't able to be close enough to the gentlemen to hear them speak, then she couldn't find the real culprit behind the aborted jewelry theft and she couldn't rescue Morgan from jail and she couldn't help the twins.

She had known going into the world outside the rookery would present grave danger, but she'd had little choice, not if she were to complete her critical mission. At first she had tried the parks and the churches, anywhere crowds gathered, always searching for a thin, balding man with a high-pitched voice and a scent like a rose garden, but she had met with failure.

Domestic work became a necessity, only this time she had gone with forged references, unlike that frightening time in the early days of her hiding when she ventured to the agency empty-handed and was recognized. She had still feared recognition and an appearance by the police and, worst of all, she had feared running into Clay. Until tonight she had found only men like the one who followed her into the garden, imperious men with sly hungry looks about them and fingers that liked to pinch.

Knowing she would meet such boors again, she would keep up her search. Not that she knew exactly what she would do when she found the culprit; she planned to watch him, to follow and hope he would incriminate himself in some way.

Jenna was willing to risk everything because the twins trusted her. They were the cause she believed in, the reason to keep going against overwhelming odds. They missed their father more than she had expected. With her plan to take them away to a new life looking more unattainable she had vowed to do all she could to free him from jail.

Confessing all to Clay was out of the question; she didn't trust him to hear her out this time anymore than he had the first, when she'd gone to him about the reward. She admitted to herself how preposterous her latest story was, and she could not begin to imagine how he would take it—except that he would declare she needed to come up with something more believable.

Jenna had no more lies to tell. She was stuck with her role as a servant, and to that role she would cling.

Her attempts to repin her hair beneath the servant's white cap proved futile, and she collapsed on the settee, her gaze directed toward the bear. The light from the sconces gleamed in the brown glass eyes and reflected off the sharp fangs. He would be growling in perpetuity, as it seemed that she would be on the run forever.

Thoughts turned to the man searching for her whereabouts. Tears burned at the back of her eyes, but she blinked them away. She must learn to accept heartbreak.

Why, oh why, hadn't Clay done what any normal, uncaring man would have done and sailed for home weeks ago? But no, he had to stay around and try to find her, or at least that was what he had implied.

I've missed you.

She could hear him saying the words. She knew exactly what he had missed.

Well, she had missed him, too, but for a far more critical reason: her heart and soul were inextricably bound to him. She had no idea why. He could be as maddening as any member of the aristocracy, as arrogant and self-possessed, as demanding and judgmental. But in a dingy tavern he had looked at a beggar child with tender concern, had defended her against abuse and returned more than once to make certain she was all right.

And when an unknown woman invaded his room, he had spent long stretches of time in talk when other men would have taken the satisfaction she offered and then turned on the light, no matter how she asked for the dark.

He had been loving in ways Jenna had never known existed, concerned about her pleasure as well as his own. Thinking she was taking a few moments of happiness in a life that had held so few, she had willingly joined in that lovemaking. She had little known that the temporary pleasure they enjoyed would bring her lasting pain.

A tear escaped and she roughly brushed it from her cheek. Why did he have to come to this particular ball? Why did he have to be so close to the dance floor the one time she was passing drinks? Why—

The handle of the door turned, making no more than a whisper of sound, but it snapped her to full attention. She stood, turning to watch as Clay entered and closed the door behind him.

His eyes locked with hers. "In your other lives, do you always make such dramatic entrances and exits?"

She brushed at her apron. "Whatever do you mean, sir?"

"You're a stubborn woman."

"You frightened me, sir."

"Stop it, Princess. Give up. You've been found."

She lifted her chin. She could be stubborn, all right, as stubborn as he. "As I said, sir, I don't know what you be talking about. In the garden you tried to take advantage, you and that other gentleman. Me mum taught me to run from the likes of you."

She even managed a sniff of disapproval.

He took a step toward her. "You're doing this very well. Almost makes me think you're an actress. And I thought you were a spoiled rich girl. There's just no telling where you'll show up next."

He was as sarcastic as ever and, unfortunately, just as appealing. She was struck again with how wonderful he looked, so at ease in the white shirt and black coat, and he moved with a masculine grace that was entirely natural. A lock of black hair rested carelessly on his forehead, just above thick brows and dark gray eyes. How many nights had she imagined those eyes peering down at her as her head rested on the pillow? How many times had she pictured what he must look like when he was caught in the throes of passion?

"Princess." His voice was husky. He must have read her thoughts.

She pulled at a strand of hair that had fallen against her cheek and shook her head, but she could bring no words to her lips.

He walked slowly toward her, rounded the settee, and halted so close that her apron brushed against his trousers. She breathed deeply and wondered inconsequentially how he always managed to carry on his person the clean, enticing scents of the country.

His eyes burned down at her. She inched backward and dropped her gaze to the tips of her shoes that peeped from the hem of her gown.

He lifted her chin, forcing her to look back at him.

257

"I heard the real you speaking in the garden, remember? You have a lovely voice, Princess, even when you're angry." His thumb stroked her cheek. "And a lovely face."

She squeezed her eyes closed. "No," she whispered, knowing her response was weak but unable to say more.

His fingers stroked her tangled tresses and she felt him remove the pins and cap, loosening the few thick curls that had remained in place.

"Lovely," he said.

He continued to stroke her hair, and she swallowed a moan of pleasure.

"There's one way to prove who you are," he said, bending his head to hers, his hands resting lightly on her shoulders.

She opened her eyes and stared at his parted lips. To kiss him in the light . . . to tickle her lashes against his cheek and watch the muscles of his face twitch . . . to break the kiss and see his lips move away, moistened by her own tongue . . .

Her body ached for him, and he had touched only her chin. She was truly trapped.

But having sworn never to give in to him again, and remembering all too well where she was, she could not allow herself such luxury, and she whirled away. With her back to him, she willed her breath to slow. "It's not proper to take advantage of a servant girl."

If she expected a gentlemanly response, she was mistaken. Firm hands turned her back around to face him.

His eyes flared with anger. "Since when have you been concerned with what's proper?"

She tried to protest, but her cry was stilled by his lips covering hers. The shock of their warm insistence spun through her. Feebly she pushed against his chest, but his arms enfolded her with such steely power that she was no more effective in her efforts than if she had tried to hold back the dawn.

His probing tongue teased her lips but she refused him entrance. How dare he assault her this way? She did not want his lovemaking, not like this when all he wanted was to prove that she lied . . . to prove his dominance . . . to prove he was right.

Right now he seemed little better to her than any man who would assume his right to find pleasure with a servant girl, and she twisted to get free. Locked in his powerful embrace, she managed only to pull her lips away from his.

"Too late," he whispered. "I know you far too well to think you really want to escape."

"Let me go," she ordered, her chest heaving with ragged breaths.

"It's my turn to say no."

His lips were upon hers once again, savaging her with a fierceness that frightened as much as it inflamed. She shifted her hips away from him, desperate to get away, but a firm hand clamped against her buttocks and held her hard against him. Through the layers of clothing, she could feel his swollen manhood pressing against her abdomen. He lifted her buttocks and his knees bent, and the protuberance teased the juncture of her thighs.

Jenna tried to swallow a moan, but the telltale sound escaped and she knew he heard. He answered with a growl, and his hands stroked, probed, taunted with inexorable thoroughness the length of her spine.

This was a new Clay, a more demanding man than she had realized he could be, one who would not listen to any protestations she might try to make. She felt as though she had roused the inert bear she'd been contemplating. She was caught in his feral clasp, only this was no animal of the wild that held her. It was the sometimes-gentle Clay gone wild with lust. He would not be appeased by a kiss or an embrace, no matter how tight he held her, and he would not be put off by her pleas.

Crushed as she was against him, encircled by his arms, she felt her own desires explode. She did not know herself; she was an untamed she-bear responding on instinct and she forgot where she was or why she was there; she knew only that she wanted the man whose arms enfolded her . . . she wanted him in the most primitive of ways.

Her lips parted and she danced her tongue against his. Her heart pounded wildly, and she felt as though she were melting against him, becoming a part of him, sharing his very breath and the pulsing of his blood.

He drew her into his warmth and into his power. His hold on her was more than the touches of his hands and lips. She was back where she belonged, in the only home she had known for so many years — Clay's embrace. Forbidden to her though it must be, it was grander than any royal palace, more sacred than St. Paul's. No mere building could compare with the glory that enveloped her now.

He broke the kiss and pulled her to the rug. Jenna had no idea how he managed the maneuvering so smoothly, but somehow she was stretched beside him, her skirt and apron pulled high around her hips, her high collar unbuttoned at the throat, his hand on her petticoat.

She forgot the ragged state of her underwear or the absence of any underdrawers or suspenders. She simply had not been able to afford them, and she had not imagined that anyone would learn of the omissions.

She had not imagined Clay.

Now she was glad that so little would impede his reaching her throbbing core. Simple elastic bands held up her stockings above her knees. His hand found them. He rubbed at the naked thigh above the band. Her skin burned against him, and she felt her legs parting to meet his questing fingers. Through the thin protection of her petticoat, the furry rug tickled sensuously against her bare buttocks, and her feet pressed against the back of the growling bear's head.

She sighed into the mouth that came down on hers. She tasted as much as heard the groan that sounded in his throat when he discovered just how naked she was.

Always she reacted this way to him, always gave in to the primal urges that swept over her. All thought dissolved to pure feelings, to the arousal of every nerve ending, to the sweet mouth and rough tongue, to the hard body pressed against her, to the strokes and caresses of his magic hands . . .

"Clayton Drake!"

A woman's voice boomed out over her.

"Make yourself presentable at once! And let that girl alone!"

"Damn!" Clay whispered in her ear as Jenna tried to assimilate in her confused mind exactly what was happening.

His fingers ceased their probing and he embraced her. He held her tight, as if to protect her from danger, then put his hands to work, swiftly smoothing down her skirt and apron, caressing her once again for a brief moment, then, while her head still reeled, pulling her to her feet. There was, of course, nothing about his person to make presentable except perhaps for a wrinkled tie and ruffled hair.

Trying to get her legs steady underneath her, her hand resting for support against Clay's arm, Jenna looked past him and into the scowling face of Her Grace, the Duchess of Castlebury.

Chapter Twenty

Jenna stood mortified, wishing she could crawl beneath the rug. Shock and shame overcame her, and all the passions that had been rising within her settled into a cold dread that lay like a rock in the pit of her stomach.

She forced her eyes upward. The Duchess of Castlebury stared back without flinching.

"Your Grace, I can explain," said Clay.

The duchess's attention focused on him, and Jenna got the feeling she was no longer of any importance. "I doubt it. Did we not discuss only an hour ago the unsuitability of sporting with servant girls? Especially since you could have your choice of any woman in the room under the age of seventy."

Jenna's cheeks burned with humiliation.

"I called you an oddity," the duchess continued, cutting off his response with a dismissive wave of her hand, "but really, this was not the sort of thing I had in mind. Sanders is waiting in the card room and I told him I would seek you out, but I hardly expected such a scene. You have surprised and distressed me greatly, Clayton."

Her Grace's eyes flicked to Jenna. "Perhaps it would be best if you left. Please gather your belongings and draw as little attention to yourself as possible, girl. It goes without saying that you are no longer in the employ of this household."

"I'll be leaving with her," responded Clay. "After I clear up a few points."

"No!" Jenna stared up at him in open horror. "There's nothing for you to say. Absolutely nothing that could possibly be of concern to Her Grace." She cursed the tears blurring her eyes.

"Princess—"

"Haven't you done enough?" Her shame hardened her to the distress on his face, and she turned back to the duchess. "I most sincerely apologize for causing any embarrassment to you, Your Grace. What happened here was—"

But there was no way she could possibly explain what had happened. The specifics were all too obvious, and the reasons behind them too complicated and private for her to put into words. Let the duchess believe she was a wanton serving girl who lost her senses and her virtue to a dashing gentleman. She wouldn't be greatly wrong.

Foreswearing any attempt at dignity, she picked up her cap, brushed her hair from her face, and hurried around the settee, around Her Grace, and out the door, leaving behind her a frustrated man, an offended peeress, and the skin and stuffed head of a once ferocious bear.

She also left the fragments of her pride.

She closed the door quietly and tried to pull her thoughts into some kind of order. Vacillating from embarrassment to anger to despair, she felt a trembling inside that would not go away.

But she did not blame herself alone for her shame. For the first time since he strolled into the Black Horse, she was able to direct real fury at Clay. Tonight, eager to find her out, to claim her body once again, he had thought of little else. He'd been distressed when the duchess walked in but only because he'd been interrupted.

263

An oddity, Her Grace had called him. That he was, a cowboy from Texas who slept in the beds of earls and socialized with duchesses, a rugged man who attracted women of all ages and classes and who openly sought the attention of a maidservant.

There was only one way that any man, Clay included, could manage such feats, and that was to be very wealthy indeed.

Once he had called himself a stubborn mule. She was inclined to agree with him, and the worst thing of all was that he didn't show an overabundance of concern about how much that stubbornness hurt anyone else. But then that was not unusual among the upper class.

She'd had it proven often enough, beginning in the asylum and reinforced in James Drury's withdrawing room and then over and again at most every place she had worked the past few weeks. Outside of the stunning tragedy that had taken place in the Drury home, tonight was by far the worst. Was there no place a common woman could be safe from assault?

Clay would dream up some story that would at least get him out of the room, then he would be after her once again. He must not find her.

Down the hallway she caught sight of a trio of ladies staring at her in open curiosity from the door to the powder room. Jenna turned quickly away, refusing to be the object of their ogling for one second longer, and hurried down the back stairway that led to the kitchen and to the room where she had left her belongings.

As she hurried, she tried to straighten her clothes, to put her hair and cap once again neatly in place, to assume once again the role of a proper maidservant, at least until she could get outside. Once again she would be Mary Roberts, which was the name she had put on the forged papers for the hiring agency. But

264

her hands would not stop trembling and she could imagine the shock that must still register on her face.

Giving up on a presentable appearance, she crammed the cap in her pocket and walked quickly down the back corridor, past the larder, the wine cellar, and the huge kitchen with its three gas-burning ovens and forest of pots and pans hanging from racks along the walls.

It was all so grand, even down here where the servants labored, so much better than where she currently dwelt, the air redolent with the odors of baking meats and breads instead of the foul scents of the slum.

But where she was going she would find a pair of friendly faces and no one to judge who she was. As she slipped around and past the half dozen cooks and servers who scurried about, she attracted only one curious glance that she could see, and that from a footman who was about to lift a silver tray loaded with sliced beef. His attention seemed caught by her loose and tangled hair. She hurried past him, her head held high.

The temporary servants' room was deserted. Donning her coat, she pulled the collar high, secured a scarf about her head, and with her small purse tucked under one arm let herself out the side door. Standing in the pathway that ran the length of the Castlebury mansion, she contemplated the food she had hoped to take from the enormous piles of leftovers and of the money she had planned on earning for her night's work. It would not do, she knew, to seek out the duchess's pinch-nosed butler and request even partial payment on the wages due her as a temporary domestic. She would have more luck begging on the street.

Only she wasn't dressed for it. In the world in which she lived, at any level, appearance was everything. You were what you looked like, and right now she looked like what she was—a servant girl who had been enjoying a little tickle and slap.

The lighted street at the end of the pathway was crowded with carriages belonging to the Castlebury guests. Standing around in groups talking and smoking, the drivers were numerous enough to resemble a small army. Having far less to do than the kitchen help, more than one offered to keep her company as she hurried past.

She took an intersecting street, this one dark, and when a block away she heard footsteps behind her, she slipped into an alley and huddled in the dark. She could barely make out the figure of a man hurrying past in the street, and she had no idea whether or not he was Clay.

When she could hear the footsteps no more, she headed out in the opposite direction, took several turns, and managed to hop onto the back of a lorry that was headed in the general direction of the Dials. She concentrated on the sound of the horse's hooves clopping along the cobblestone streets.

By the time she jumped off the back of the wagon, the night had turned cold and a fine mist was drifting down on her dampened scarf. As she made her way along the narrow, dank streets of the rookery, she pushed all thought from her mind save returning to the place that had become her refuge.

That place was no longer the Black Horse. There was no room for the twins in her small room at the tavern, and even if there had been, Teresa never would have let them remain there in hiding. She had wanted to take them away from the area, to a cleaner neighborhood, to a better room, but she had used much of her money on her workclothes and more on food.

And she had not known exactly where to go, a

short redheaded woman with green eyes who had a reward on her head and two children who were also the object of a search.

In desperation she had tried the asylum, taking them there in a hired carriage after a particularly unpleasant afternoon spent serving tea in one of the homes of the gentry. Two women, both finely dressed in velvet capes and feathered hats, had emerged onto the front stoop just as the carriage arrived. Jenna recognized them as a couple of less-than-charitable sorts who had known her before.

The reverend would have to hide her from such as they, as well as hide the twins, and she could not ask him to do so. He would be harboring a criminal under the roof of his beloved institution. If she were discovered, he might very well lose his position, and she could not ask him to risk all for her sake. They had returned to the Dials—just as she was returning on this late, unfortunate night. Her hurried steps took her to the door of the glove factory, where she gave her secret knock.

She heard chairs pushed aside and bolts turned, and at last the door creaked open. Alfred stepped aside and let her enter. A small gas lantern resting on the floor behind him gave her light.

"You're early tonight," he said, sounding like the man of the house.

He proceeded to reform the complicated system that she and the twins had designed to make the abandoned factory secure, part of which had been the painstaking procedure of removing one of the bolts from an inside door and affixing it to the front.

"I'm home early," she explained, removing her scarf, "because there was not as much work as I had hoped."

Alice bounded toward her down the hall, in her hand a tin plate holding a flickering candle. She came to a stop in front of her and stared up. "Did you find the bad man?" she asked in a rush. "Did you?"

As she had done every night since hiding the twins in the factory, Jenna slowly shook her head. "I think he must have gone abroad for a while. You know, until all the to-do over the robbery is past."

Alice's tiny features twisted threateningly.

"She's going to cry," Alfred announced matter-of-factly. "She's been doing that lately."

Jenna knelt before her and took the candle from her hands, setting it on the floor. With difficulty she refrained from touching the precious little face so close to hers. How pale the child looked. She needed the kiss of the sun.

"Well, it passes the time, doesn't it?" Jenna said in much the same tone the boy had used. "But it doesn't do much else except make the eyes burn and stuff up the nose. I'll just have to teach you to make your own handkerchiefs, now won't I?"

Alice snuffled, but there was interest in her damp eyes. "Would you do that, Jenna?"

"Of course I would. I'll bet there's some embroidery around here somewhere. We found needle and thread, didn't we? And didn't you help me sew my dress?"

Alice giggled. "I made a mistake."

"You made a mistake, but that was all right. We repaired it and no one will ever know you pinned the sleeve on upside down."

"Alfred will tell."

"I will not," her brother shot back from his position at Jenna's elbow. He was a brave lad, indeed, but when she was in the factory, he never got far from her side.

"Besides, who would I tell?" he went on. "Nobody knows we're here, and that's 'cause I helped cover the

268

windows so light won't get out at night."

"And you did a fine job, too," Jenna said. "Now then, why don't we see if there's any of that meat and bread I brought from last night's work. I worked up quite an appetite serving all those rich ladies and gentlemen."

"You didn't bring nothing from tonight?" asked Alice.

"I didn't bring anything. My plans were interrupted a little and I didn't have a chance to get near the food."

With the twins holding the candle and the lamp, she followed them down the long hall and into the small square room that they had chosen as their own. They had cleaned it as best they could, but there was nothing they could do about the cracked walls and scarred floor.

Looking at it, Jenna realized it was approximately the size of the sitting room where she had attempted to hide from Clay. The same size perhaps, but oh what a world of difference existed between the two rooms. She lived a strange existence indeed, shifting back and forth between the extremes of London life, belonging in neither place.

It had taken quite a bit of scavenging on the three floors of the old, rambling building for Jenna and the children to round up so much as a table and three chairs that were not broken down. She had taken the blankets from the lodging house when she rescued the twins the day of their father's arrest. She was barely ahead of the police, who had come to search the suspect's quarters.

She had heard that shortly after she left, a pair of men and one woman from another governmental agency had come around looking for the twins to place them in an orphanage until after the trial.

Barely in time had she saved the children from that

terrible fate. Like so many other unfortunates incarcerated before them in such institutions, forced to labor long hours in dimly lighted rooms over tedious sewing or cleaning tasks, they could die early, starving or succumbing to disease before a year had passed. If they somehow managed to survive, they might live the rest of their lives with poor vision and crippled hands.

No, such places were not for any human beings. Jenna could not save them all, but she had been determined to save her own loved ones. The threat of incarceration and perhaps a journey to the gallows had done nothing to stay her from that course.

For the eventual happiness of the children — for the return of their father which they wanted above all else — she would face the all-too-real danger of recognition in the fancy homes and the scrutiny of the few who still thought about the reward. She would find her rose-scented villain and somehow figure out a way to prove that he, not Morgan, had been the cohort of the dead Bertie Groat.

With the children in her charge, Jenna had found the glove factory an appropriate place to seek refuge, since it was here that she had heard the plotting. It had been abandoned for so long that scant attention was paid to its damp, musty interior. Thus far it had proven secure.

An added benefit had been the sewing machine they discovered in one of the storage rooms. A little oil that Jenna scraped into a small tin from a spill in the street and a great deal of dusting and manipulating with all the controls had got it to working again, and she had only to purchase the cheapest of woolen cloth to make her servant's dress, using her worn governess's dress as the pattern. The collar and cuffs she had purchased, along with apron and cap. She figured if they were crisp and clean without so much as a sign of mending, she could get by with the roughly sewn gown.

And she had.

But in all the jobs she had been able to get through the employment agency, none had yielded the man she sought.

Tonight had ended in far worse than mere failure. Tonight once again she had seen a side of herself she didn't like very much, a weakness for Clay that drove all rational thought from her mind. He respected her so little that he'd known all he had to do was touch her and she was his to do with as he wanted. She might not deserve his respect, but she wanted it as much as she wanted his love. Neither would she ever get.

On this damp and chilly night, a feeling that time was running out settled over her. Huddled around the table, she and the children made short work of the remaining food. Tomorrow she would simply have to break down and buy a few staples from her fast dwindling cache. And she needed to find another job, despite the danger of discovery and the insults she faced each time she moved among the upper classes. A different employment agency would be necessary, but was there really another one that placed temporaries into the richest homes?

Maybe she was searching the wrong places. Maybe the man she was after did not associate with the people she was watching, but then she remembered the fine cut of his cloak and the elegant way he had smoothed on his white gloves.

She remembered the autocratic tone of his voice.

He was a member of high society, all right. She would bet her life on it.

Jenna sighed. Betting her life was exactly what she was doing, every time she ventured out in the world.

271

* * *

That night, as she snuggled next to the twins, a pair of thin blankets under and over them, her thoughts went unerringly to Clay. At first the memories warmed her when she pictured the look in his eyes as he bent to kiss her. His cheek had been bristled and tan, his eyelashes thick and black as his hair, his hands strong and unyielding and splendid wherever they touched.

A sudden chill caused her to shudder. She must never forget that he had been after only one thing, the single bond that existed between them. He had been after sex.

Jenna supposed that when she finally dropped off to sleep, she would dream of him as she so often did. Instead she dreamed of a crowded city street that she knew was not London, and yet was not unfamiliar to her. Hordes of men, black skinned and white, rushed down the center of the street, in their raised fists bricks and clubs which they brandished in the air like mad conductors leading a mad band.

Their mouths were open and she knew they were shouting but the only sounds she heard were hollow echoes of drumbeats reverberating off the windowless buildings that rose on each side of the pavement.

Jenna viewed the scene from a high perch that floated in the air just out of reach of the highest club; she drifted overhead with the mob toward an expanse of tall green grass at the end of the street; the faster they ran, the farther away seemed the field, and then all at once, in a roar of wind and pounding of drums, they were upon it. A huddled figure lay in the center of the grass. Just as the mob fell upon him, she recognized her father.

"Jenna!" His frantic voice rose above the wind and drums.

She must save him, she must, and she reached

272

down to give him a helping hand, but she stretched too far and tumbled from her floating platform toward the erupting violence, falling down and down, the earth opening up for her, the crowds parting, and then she was in a void vast and dark, the air still and cold, her father far behind, with nothing to stop her fall and no one to answer her cry for help.

She jerked awake. Her breath came shallow and fast, and her heart pounded in her ears. Chilled though she was, she was bathed in sweat.

She lay quietly beside the sleeping children, the blanket pulled tight against her chin, and told herself it had been only a dream. But it had not been like any she had had before. When she thought of her father, she saw him among the orange groves or plowing a field, or even walking his young daughter down to the stream of water that ran through their farm, a fishing pole in his hand.

Vague images they were, but she could expect nothing else, having seen him for the last time when she was six. The same age as the twins, who were in terrible danger of losing their father, too.

Tonight she considered the way John Bailey Cresswell, Transvaal farmer and investor, widower and father, must have died. His end had come at the hands of a Pretorian mob, an innocent bystander caught in a tragic conflict of cultures and nations, tribesmen against settlers, British against Boers.

She had loved her father very much, and she realized that seventeen years after his death she continued to miss him with all her heart.

If she could have one wish fulfilled at the moment, it would be to have someone she could talk to about her strange and difficult life, someone to give her comfort, someone to hold her during the night while the wounds of the past healed.

By all rights, that someone should be the man she

loved, but the thought of sharing her secret suffering with Clay filled her with despair. She had gone to him once to seek help, on the terrible night when she feared her arrest was imminent; he had scoffed at the truth and insisted on falsehood.

That night she had met his sarcasm with sarcasm of her own, but in the aftermath she realized how much she had been hurt. The hurt lingered, as strong as anything else she felt for him, as strong as her desires, as strong as her love.

Chapter Twenty-one

Jenna spent the next morning repairing her servant's clothing and the afternoon braving a visit to the employment agencies she found listed in a day-old copy of *The Times* discarded in a refuse bin on Charing Cross Road.

The weather had cleared and was cool enough to justify the coat she liked to wear as it covered her plainly made dress. She had found the coat at a clothing exchange, along with the sturdy shoes and the plain straw hat she wore squarely on top of her upswept hair. Today she added a new touch to her appearance, a pair of wire-framed spectacles. So slight was the distortion of the lens that rarely did she have to peer over the tops to make certain she was headed where she planned.

The only document she had with her was the one she had forged painstakingly on the scarred table at the glove factory weeks before. It still carried the name she had been using when she first sought employment, Mary Roberts, since she had possessed neither the time nor the resources to change it. She hoped word of last night's debacle had not been circulated. Surely the duchess, unlike her domestic help, would be discreet.

At the first agency, she did not get past the woman secretary, whose squat, sturdy body was firmly planted behind a desk in the anteroom, effectively barring the main office from those she deemed unworthy to enter.

"Mary Roberts," the secretary said through tight lips, her eyes peering narrowly at Jenna's forged papers. She handed them back as though they were smeared with something foul and unmentionable.

"Nothing today. Do not bother to call again."

Jenna had been rejected before, but never with such disdain and speed. Shoulders back, she exited with all the dignity she could muster, but inside she was hurting. The word had already spread, probably originated by the butler in the Duke of Castlebury's employ. Mary Roberts had disgraced herself and embarrassed Her Grace the Duchess of Castlebury. From this day forward she was to be considered unsuitable for employment as a domestic; under no circumstances was she to be placed even as a temporary anywhere at any time.

Outside, she felt the warmth of a sudden breeze. Maybe she was simply suffering from paranoia. At the Deaf and Dumb Asylum she had done a little reading about such things, and right now, as best she could figure, she had all the symptoms of the mental disturbance. Which could mean that the world really wasn't after her — at least not at every level. One rebuff did not necessarily indicate that she would meet with widespread rejection.

The most immediate danger lay in overreacting.

No, she reminded herself as she walked along Oxford Street, the danger lay in the sharp eye of a policeman or in the curiosity of a reward seeker. As always, she ran a great risk of parading along the street this way.

The upturned faces of Alice and Alfred flashed across her mind, and Jenna quickened her step. They must always stay at the forefront of her thoughts.

As she made the rounds of the agencies, she gradually accepted the fact that she was just going through the motions of trying to get by, doing what she told herself she had to do. Expecting rejection, she found it, and as she walked out each door she dispiritedly marked another name off her agency list.

Having little money to waste on an omnibus, she walked from office to office, but she knew that fatigue was not the source of her malaise. Seeing Clay like that again and reacting with such abandon had killed something inside her, something she hadn't realized was still alive, something that not even the twins could rouse once it was gone. If she had to give it a name, she would call it hope.

A long time ago she had credited him with instilling that sustaining emotion in her, and now he had taken it away.

She ended her job search abruptly at the fourth agency on her list. The visit had started hopefully enough when she was readily admitted by the secretary into her employer's inner sanctum.

Sitting across the desk from a purse-faced man with slicked back hair and pencil mustache, Jenna watched him study her application form. *Mr. Goldsmythe,* read the sign propped in front of him.

"Mary Roberts," Mr. Goldsmythe said thoughtfully, tapping a pencil against his desk. He looked up and studied her. "Perhaps—"

She sat forward in the chair.

"One moment, please. I believe I have just the thing."

He made a wide circle around her and walked out the door. Alarms rang in Jenna's head, and she followed. Standing in the doorway, she saw him stop at the secretary's desk. Leaning low, he whispered something hurriedly.

On the wall behind the woman's chair was a telephone set. Consulting a scrap of paper in his pocket, he proceeded to turn the crank and speak into the mouthpiece. She couldn't make out his words, but she could guess at what they might be—and they had nothing to do with any employment that would be of benefit to her. Recognizing her from the long-ago posters, he was calling the law.

A second explanation struck her with equal force. Having learned her name from the duchess or someone in her employ, Clay sent out word that he was to be notified at once if Mary Roberts showed up asking for work, and that was exactly what Mr. Goldsmythe was doing.

The law, or Clay—the choices were equally frightening. Edging back into Goldsmythe's office, she grabbed her purse and coat and flew toward the outer door.

"Miss Roberts," Mr. Goldsmythe called after her, dropping the earpiece. He followed her down the front stoop and onto the busy sidewalk. "Miss Roberts, I believe I have something for you."

The shout followed her down the street as she wended her way past the other pedestrians. Goldsmythe most certainly did have something for her. More trouble and more heartbreak, two commodities she already possessed in equal and overabundant amounts.

That night she donned her rags for the first time in weeks and took to the streets to beg. She made enough money to stop by the street vendors and buy meat pies for dinner and a bit of bread for the morning, but there was little left over to add to her store of funds.

Long after midnight, as she was returning to the glove factory, she caught sight of a dark-haired woman in red laughing up into the face of a tall gentleman in evening clothes. The pair were strolling along Shaftesbury Avenue near Cambridge Circus. They kept to the shadows away from the lamp-posts, but she recognized the woman as Teresa Mims, from her laugh as much as from her irregular walk.

The light fell once on the man's handsome, mustached face. He looked familiar to her, but she couldn't imagine where she had seen him. Perhaps it was at one of the fancy parties where she had worked.

She supposed that Teresa had returned to her former profession, and her thoughts and sympathy went out to the husband she had betrayed.

In her room at the factory, worried that she would suffer through another nightmare, she found herself dreading to go to bed, but at last she gave in to exhaustion and slept without dreaming. She and the twins were awakened early by a pounding on the street-front door.

Motioning for them to stay under the blanket, she hurriedly slipped a gown over the petticoat in which she slept and made her way quietly down the dim and musty hall. A determined fist continued to pound, and the door rattled in its frame.

"Open up," a man shouted. "We know you're in there."

Jenna's breath caught, and she could not move. Her feet were cold against the wooden floor. The moment she had so long dreaded was here.

"Come on, open up. We've got orders to take the children. Be quick about it. Ain't got all day."

The children. A cold hand clutched at Jenna's heart, and she glanced back down the hall. Alice and Alfred were standing just outside their door, barefooted and wide eyed, their slender young bodies clad in oversized shirts that came to their ankles, Alfred's arm protectively embracing his sister.

The handle to the street-front door rattled, and a solid body landed forcefully against the door itself. Another few blows like that and the flimsy bolt and chairs that were supposed to protect them from the outside world would be breached.

Jenna knew she should be frightened for herself

and for the possibility of her own detection, but at the moment her fears were for her charges.

She smiled bravely at the two. "It would seem we've been found." She began to walk briskly toward them. "Let's make ourselves presentable for our guests."

"What's going to happen? Will they hurt us?" asked Alice. Her lips were trembling and her skin pale as the moon, but Jenna could detect no sign of tears.

"No, dear, they won't. But they most likely will ask you to go with them for a while."

She looked into their upturned faces but kept her hands clasped together behind her back.

"You must make me and your father very proud of you by going without so much as one tear or whimper. You have each other, remember, and that is more than many children have. I'll be after you to take you to a proper home as soon as I can."

She swallowed. "Remember most of all, that you must be very, very brave."

"Yes, Jenna."

"Yes, Jenna."

"And of course you know to agree with whatever I have to tell the people at the door."

This time they simply nodded.

She felt stupid and arrogant talking to these two small beings about bravery. In their brief lives they had been subjected to more trouble and conflict than the revelers who'd been drinking Castlebury champagne would ever know if they all lived to be octogenarians.

The door behind her opened with a crash.

Jenna reached for their waiting hands and turned to face whoever barged into their borrowed home. Privately she admitted that any advice she was tossing around about being brave should have been directed squarely at herself.

Much later, when the sun had set behind the somber buildings of the rookery and the air had turned from cool to cold, Jenna wondered how she got through the day.

"Name," the first man through the door had demanded. He had worn a brown suit and a brown bowler and a brown scowl on his face. He had not bothered to introduce himself.

Behind him had stood a second man, taller and wider and similarly dressed, and a woman also clad in brown. Her dress was heavy wool and full sleeved across the upper arms and made her appear as muscled as a stevedore. For all Jenna knew, she well might be.

"Mary Roberts," Jenna had replied and found the papers to prove who she was.

The three gave no evidence that they disbelieved her.

"What you doing with 'em?" He gestured toward the twins as though they had no name and no ability to hear. "Kidnapping's a capital offense in this country, don't you know?"

Heart in her throat, Jenna changed the subject away from hanging crimes.

"I found Alice and Alfred wandering the streets."

Behind her, the twins were silent.

"They were lost and afraid and I decided to bring them here."

He eyed her suspiciously. "You talk mighty fancy for a resident of the Dials."

Jenna pulled herself up proud. "I have worked in the finest homes in the city. Of course I speak well."

He consulted her papers. "That's what it says here, all right. Temporary domestic. Why temporary?"

"I prefer not to remain in one place too long. I prefer to move around."

His eyes roamed the cracked, peeling walls to right and left. "I can see where you'd want to come home to this."

"I do not plan to remain here, but employment has been difficult lately. When I found the children, not knowing what else to do with them, I decided that this abandoned building would be suitable for a short while."

"Short while indeed!" It was the woman who spoke. "The tykes have been missing almost a month. You should have brought them to the proper authorities right away."

And to the orphanage, Jenna could have retorted, *where they could slave for their keep.* She did not give voice to her thoughts.

The first man thrust the papers back at Jenna. "We got documents of our own that says we take them with us. Step aside and we'll forget bringing charges. Out of the goodness o' our hearts."

"I say we take her in," the woman said.

"Then you'll be handling the paper work," the man retorted.

The woman fell silent, a look of disgust on her broad, flat face.

Jenna found it difficult to thank him, but that difficulty was nothing compared to the impossible task of watching the twins dress, shake her hand goodbye, and walk out into the shadowed day, leaving Jenna standing alone in the hall.

The second man, trailing the others, did not speak until he was almost out the door. "I'll give ye a bit o' advice, miss. Ye'd best get yerself off the premises right away. The law'll be coming aroun' to make sure nothing's been 'armed. And the woman there, she'll be makin' sure they know about yer."

"How did you know we were here?" she had asked.

" 'ow we usually finds out things. A bobby picked up the rumor and passed it on."

A bobby. Jenna felt as though a loaded gun were pointed at her breast. Clutching her hands in front of her, she willed herself to remain calm.

"As to who was doin' the talking, 'ard to say. Some 'un seein' you come in and wantin' to come in hisself, more 'n likely, but you 'ad the door locked right proper against 'im. We'd been askin' around about the two."

"The children said something about their father being taken away."

"Charged with attempted robbery, 'e is. Tryin' to take the Queen's own jewelry, 'e was. 'at's why the little tykes got so much attention, bein' a royal robbery was the cause o' the troubles. I don't imagine those two'll be seein' their papa again."

"Is their papa all right?"

"Wouldn't know. Not part o' me job."

After he departed, the very shaken Jenna had taken his advice, gathered her meager belongings together, and dressed once again in her rags, the wide, old cap in place, strands of sooted hair falling about her face. Closing the door to the building that had so briefly served as her home, she made her way to the only place she knew to go, the Black Horse, a temporary hideout until she could decide what to do.

This time, after hiding her bundle of clothes behind a bin in the alley, she went in the front door, not standing upright as she would have preferred, but slump-shouldered with head bowed, her shawl pulled over her head and shoulders, her attitude one of defeat. In truth, with the twins gone to hardships she could too well imagine, the attitude required little pretense.

"Child," said Hector. He stood behind the bar, brutish in appearance as ever but with a kindly look in his eye, and watched as she walked around the tables toward him. At this morning hour there were no more than a half dozen customers scattered about the room, none of whom paid her any mind.

She was surprised by the smile of welcome that split his coarse-featured face. Kindness shining through the craggy lines made him handsome, and she cursed Teresa for leaving.

"Good to 'ave ye back, lass," he said as she came to a halt at the end of the bar.

She couldn't imagine why he was speaking to her, since he considered her deaf, but perhaps he was lonely for someone to talk to. It was a feeling she shared.

Taking up a rag, she began to clear and clean the tables, acting as though she had not been gone for weeks. He fed her a piece of cold mutton for lunch, and she kept at her work, washing glasses and clearing the tables as the need arose.

Night was falling when she caught sight of a frowzy-haired woman standing in the back doorway. Teresa had not left, after all. She must have been sleeping all day to make up for her exertions at night.

"Bloody bitch!" She turned to her husband. "Wot's Simple doin' here?"

Jenna cringed beside the table where she was working, but she kept on wiping.

"Doin' wot she ought," Hector replied. Mild as it was, it was the harshest thing she had ever heard him say to his wife.

"I want 'er out."

"She stays."

The tavern, more than half full of regulars, fell silent.

Jenna peered through her scraggly hair first at Hector, then at Teresa, who stood with hands on hips, a look of disbelief on her face.

"She wot?"

"She stays."

Jenna watched as Teresa tried to think. It was a difficult task, apparently, for it required wrinkling her face and biting at her lip. At last, she turned with a flounce and disappeared down the back hallway. Gradually the level of talk in the room resumed its normal loud volume, and Hector went back to serving ale behind the bar.

But he did not look at all happy. The smile was gone from his eyes.

Jenna only brought him trouble. And she had nothing to gain by remaining at the Horse, other than a temporary roof over her head. As soon as she was able to add to her store of money — and she determined to be especially pitiful looking each time she begged — then she would clear out of the tavern, out of Seven Dials, and out of town.

As she worked, a plan suggested itself to her. London was not the only place where the upper classes played. Bath came first to mind, but it was so far away and she shifted her consideration to the southern coast. Many of the wealthy and not-so-wealthy chose to take their socializing there.

She would work on the details concerning just how she would manage it, but her instincts told her that she was onto a good idea. And she knew just the place she would go. Brighton. She'd heard talk among the servants about some of the parties planned there. Not only was it time for The Season at the resort, but the name itself was cheerful.

Brighton it would be. Not knowing why, Jenna had a feeling that she would meet her destiny there.

Chapter Twenty-two

Jenna left London from Victoria Station on a rainy Sunday afternoon a week later, having enjoyed a run of good luck at a corner she occupied nightly on crowded Piccadilly Circus. In her beggar's rags, with her mittened hand upheld, she had not felt nearly so ashamed as she had on her earlier forays when she sought alms from the rich, not when the money would go for such a vital cause.

She felt good about the southward journey . . . almost hopeful, but she couldn't let herself go quite that far. At least her mind was partially at ease concerning the twins. Deciding she could not rest until she had done all she could for them, she had written to the Reverend Cox and given him what little she knew about the whereabouts of the children.

Please, she had concluded, *try to see that they are not abused. I know that you will do what you can. When time and circumstances allow, I will again write. Please keep this correspondence in confidence.*

As an afterthought, she had hastily scribbled, *You were ever my friend.*

She had, of course, received no answer since she had not included a return address, but she trusted him to do what he could.

Settling back in her third-class window seat, her gaze directed over her spectacles to the mist-shrouded scene passing by, her legs tucked tightly beneath the low-built accommodation, she brushed a cinder from her eye and, to herself, she dared a slight smile. Under her brown coat she wore a new—or at least not very old—soft green woolen gown with black velvet collar and cuffs (she had turned them and they looked good as new), and on top of her upswept red hair rested a forest green hat with a black feather that quivered when she moved her head.

Her purse and shoes were old but her gloves and stockings were new. She was proudest of that part of her clothing which no one would ever see—her petticoat and underdrawers. She had bought them in a small clothing store on Shaftesbury Avenue, and she was the first person ever to put them on.

On an overhead rack, stuffed between a canvas bag and a roped-together pair of much-used boxes labeled with a popular brand of snuff, rested her small portmanteau containing the servant girl's clothes; her money and papers were in her purse. She was the picture of respectability; when a bleary-eyed man with a bulbous red nose attempted to wedge his bulk onto the seat beside her and start a conversation, she let him know in no uncertain terms that she was not "that sort of girl."

He tipped his hat, said, "Well, ain't you the swell," and departed to seek friendlier company.

The narrow space was immediately taken by a thin, pinch-lipped woman of middle age who promptly closed her eyes and began to snore. Jenna felt a rush of gratitude both for the slender size of the woman and for the sleep that rendered conversation between them unnecessary.

She gave full thought to her destination. *The Times*—why, she wondered, did so many people simply toss their old newspapers in the street?—had reported a busy social scene under way in Brighton, verifying what she'd already heard from London domestics. Everyone considered fashionable, outside of the royal family itself, would be there.

London by the Sea, the reporter called the coastal town.

She would most certainly find employment. And if the villainous man that she sought was there, she would find him.

The only thing she had stinted on was food, and an hour out of London she felt her head reeling. She simply must spend whatever was necessary to get something to eat as soon as the train chugged into the station.

An additional half hour passed before her arrival. Portmanteau in hand, she made her way along with the other passengers down the length of the car and onto the platform. Cinders swirled in the air and stung her eyes, but she ignored them, caught as she was by the saltiness of the Brighton air. Since that journey long ago from the south of Africa, she had never been closer to the sea than the south bank of the Thames, and she was filled with both nostalgia and a sense of excitement.

She moved through the crowd in the general direction of the stationhouse, hoping to catch a glimpse of the water but not knowing which way to look. All she could see was an ocean of bodies, men and women and children, some ready to take the return ride to the fogs of the city and others eager for their holiday at the briny.

Adding to the congestion were piles of luggage and packages and cartons and even three caged dogs that had been riding, she supposed, somewhere in a special car.

She did not see one person who looked wealthy or interested in hiring a domestic to serve champagne. But of course such as they would be at the other end of the train near the first class cars. Porters would be taking their mounds of luggage to the Grand Hotel or one of the stately homes along the sweep of the Royal Crescent.

"Watch where ye're goin'," a man growled in her ear, and she realized she had swayed in his path.

She really must get some food.

On the street side of the station, strolling amongst the swarms of fun-seekers, she felt the warmth of the day. Suddenly her coat lay heavy on her shoulders and she wished she were dressed in a bright blue cotton gown with nothing more than a bunch of violets in her hair. At the edge of the street she spied a vendor selling ice cream. One small cup could not possibly sustain her for long, but oh how pleasant it was to give in to temptation.

She bought the cheapest cream available and, awkwardly holding onto purse and portmanteau, managed to take a lick. The sweetness dissolved on her tongue, almost painful in its coldness, but she had never tasted anything quite so good and downed the rest of the treat in short order.

Dropping the empty cup into a refuse bin, she smiled at a mother and child passing by, and they returned the smile.

Overhead stretched a sky deep and cloudless blue, and she heard the squawk of an unseen bird that she immediately associated with the sea. A gull, of course; she hadn't seen one since she was six, and she gave undivided attention to its swooping and soaring until it disappeared from view.

She needed to get right to the task of job-hunting; instead, clutching her belongings, she let the brisk, salt-laden wind guide her down the hill of Queen's Road all the way to the sea. Catching a glimpse of the gaudy Royal Pavilion, she decided the coast held far greater interest on this beautiful and promising day.

As she emerged onto King's Road, the thoroughfare that skirted the ocean, she let her eyes feast on the sight of smart carriages and cyclists, men and women both, moving along at a fast pace. To one side of them was the sweep of white-fronted hotels and Georgian houses, to the other was the promenade atop the high sea wall and, best of all, the rolling, enticing sea.

Making her way across the wide boulevard, she leaned against the railing and breathed deeply, filling her lungs with the clean salt air and expelling the fetid atmosphere of the Dials. Below the high concrete wall, children cavorted at the water's edge. In the surf both men and women splashed and swam as though they had not a care to trouble their minds. Gaudily striped umbrellas dotted the coarse sand; beneath them, singly and in groups, other men, women and children stretched out in various stages of repose.

Jenna took special note of the women and their brightly colored tunics which they wore over matching calf-length trousers, their hair bound in caps not so much different from the one she had used to hide her red hair.

After the gloom and stench of the slums, the stretch of sunkissed beach and cloudless sky seemed a bit of heaven. She longed to hurry toward one of the piers extending into the water, drop her pennies into the appropriate slot, and push through the turnstile. She wanted to sense the surge of the sea beneath her, to feel the spray on her cheek.

But she could not waste the money, and she consoled herself by finding an empty promenade bench facing the ocean and sitting with her face lifted to the sun, purse and portmanteau resting beside her. In a moment the burdensome coat joined the pile, along with the spectacles which she tucked into a pocket, and she gave a moment's longing for a parasol like one of the hundreds passing her by. Never contented, she thought with a sigh.

From the Palace Pier came the bright sounds of a

brass band. She drew in deep breaths of the salty, fishy air and watched the waves, watched the people, watched the gulls circling overhead. What she did not watch were her precious belongings.

The thief moved so fast he was no more than a blur, a young man in knickers and long socks, a cap pulled low on his forehead. He grabbed everything — purse, portmanteau and coat — and with them shoved under his arm, was a dozen yards away before she realized what had happened.

She bounded to her feet, screamed, "Stop," and lit out after him, holding her skirt so she would not trip, continuing to yell, her mind concentrated on catching the young man who darted so expertly among the pedestrians along the promenade, shoving aside any who might attempt to stop him.

Jenna's heart pounded in her throat. He was getting away.

He veered to the right, into the street, and without thinking or looking, she darted after him.

Too late she heard the whinny of the horse, the creak of the carriage, the shouted warning of the woman at the reins. A chorus of screams welled from the busy street and walkway. She felt a sharp blow to the side of her head. In the span of a single heartbeat, the day darkened into night and the sky filled with stars.

The next thing she knew someone was bending over her and she was fluttering her eyelids trying to determine who that someone might be.

"She's alive," a man said.

"Thank the Lord," a woman added.

She stirred. Hard cobblestones rubbed against her back. She was lying in the street, of all foolish things, right out where everyone could stare. She forced her eyes open all the way and saw a ring of faces hovering over her, the closest the man who had tried to sit beside her on the train.

She lifted her head and was struck with such pain that her eyes filled with tears, and she collapsed once again onto the harsh street.

"We need a doctor," someone said.

But doctors cost money.

She tried to tell them she would be all right, but no words would come out. If only the pounding in her head would cease, she could get control of herself and of this absurd situation.

She remembered a carriage, a horse . . . and then nothing.

"Let me through," a woman was saying. A woman with a soft but demanding voice. The voice made Jenna feel better.

"Out of the way. Let the poor girl have some air," the same woman said.

And then she was being cradled in arms as soft and caring as the voice, her head cushioned away from the cold, hard stones of the old street. She blinked and focused on the face now bent to hers. It was an angel's face, beautiful with its full lips and straight nose and fine blue eyes. Hair the color of gold provided a lovely frame.

But the woman was frowning.

"I'm all right," Jenna managed, but the words came out high and tight in a voice that did not sound like hers.

"My dear, I'm so sorry. You ran out . . . I couldn't stop."

Without warning the full scene came back to Jenna—not just the horse and carriage and the suddenness of night, but the thief, too, and the terrible, terrible loss.

"Oh," she moaned, giving in to tears, her eyes squeezed closed against the memory.

"There, there," the woman crooned, brushing a lock of hair from her face. "You'll be all right. Someone has sent for a doctor."

"No . . . no." Jenna could not keep the panic from her voice.

"Don't worry," the woman said. "I'll take care of you."

Against all reason, Jenna let the words soothe her. But all was lost. All was lost.

"I saw the whole thing," a man bragged somewhere in the crowd. "Little bastard got her purse and bag, he did, took off like a shot. Got clean away."

"Getting so that honest citizens can't walk the streets," another replied. "I hope someone's summoned the police."

The speaker might as well have stabbed Jenna in the heart. She felt as though she were stumbling through a horrible nightmare. Surely she would awaken and find herself dozing on the waterfront bench, her belongings at hand, her day once again full of promise.

She had allowed herself to feel good, to relax. She must never do that again.

Feeling good seemed as impossible right now as walking across the ocean. Despair swept over her. Many times before she thought she had fallen as deep as possible into despondency, but those times were nothing compared to now.

Maybe if everyone simply left her alone, she could lie here until her head quit hurting and she had drawn her last breath.

"Doctor," someone said. "Let 'im through."

"She's in pain, doctor," the woman holding her said. "Please be careful."

"I'll do what's necessary." The doctor's voice was brusque. "Here now, let me get at her. Stand back, give her some air."

He spoke with authority and Jenna, eyes still closed, sensed the crowd pulling away. She felt herself jostled as the comforting arms of the woman withdrew. A folded coat was placed under her head, and practiced hands unbuttoned her gown, felt at her pulse, probed for broken bones.

"Open your eyes, be a good girl."

She did as instructed and looked into a surprisingly kind face, wrinkled and pale, the faded eyes gentle and lit with concern.

The doctor touched the side of her head, and Jenna winced.

"Had a bit of a blow, you have. Can't see that much harm's been done but can't be too sure. What's your name, miss?"

Jenna tried to recall the name she had been using, but her mind was completely blank.

"I . . . don't know." She felt foolish and closed her eyes.

"Nothing to be alarmed about, nothing at all." The doctor looked around the crowd, which had dispersed only slightly.

"Who knows the lady? Anybody here with her?"

"Saw her on the train. Seemed to be riding alone, she did," a man said.

The angel who had cradled her so softly stepped to the doctor's side. "I'm Charlotte Rockmoor, doctor. It was my carriage that caught the girl. I'll take responsibility for her until we can find out whom we should notify. I have a home on Whitecastle Street. She's welcome to stay there."

"Best be careful," came a voice from the crowd, another man. "Taking an awful chance, you are, letting a stranger in your home like you're suggesting, hurt or not. Can't be too careful these days, that's what I say. Best let the authorities handle her."

A murmur of agreements sounded in the surrounding throng.

"The day I let such considerations keep me from helping an unfortunate young woman like this is the day I hang my head in shame," retorted Jenna's angel. She spoke up loud and clear, and no one ventured to present an argument against her stand.

"Good for you, Mrs. Rockmoor," said the doctor. "Pardon me, Lady Denham, is it not? Thought I recognized you. I think it's safe to move her. Like to get her rested so I can make a more thorough examination, though."

So it was settled, and there was nothing Jenna could do to change matters, nothing she could think of doing even if she had the strength. Head pounding so fiercely she thought it might split open like a melon, Jenna concentrated on one small thing to be pleased about. She had purchased a new petticoat and drawers.

Ignoring the suggestion of Robert the valet that he try the first-class accommodations of the London, Brighton and South Coast Railway, Clay chose to ride one of the earl's stallions down to the sea for a last brief visit with Charlotte before returning to Texas.

He didn't like trains, whether he went first class or hung onto the caboose. Besides, he needed to get out in the fresh air, and the only air around a railroad track was filled with cinders and ash.

He made several stops along the way, including one at the Surrey Inn, where he downed a glass of ale many long weeks ago. The same barmaid was working, and she greeted him with the same welcoming grin and, as best he could recall, the same welcoming hints as to how he could pass an hour or two.

Wondering what had come over him, he decided he still wasn't interested, and as soon as the stallion, a black named Midnight, was rested, he was on his way again.

Charlotte greeted him in the withdrawing room of her current residence on Whitecastle Street, Brighton, with a broad smile and a hug.

"Welcome, Big Brother."

Clay returned the hug. "You haven't called me that, Baby Sister, since you were in diapers."

"Nappies, Clay. In England they're called nappies."

"You seem to be up on the terminology." He stepped back and eyed her figure. She wore a pink gown that was tight at the waist and slender across the hips. "You're not working at making me an uncle, by any chance, are you?"

The smile on her face died, but only temporarily. She hit him in the arm. "Of course not. Don't be ridiculous. Why, William travels back and forth between London so much, we've barely had time—"

She broke off, her cheeks flushed. "That's neither here nor there. It's not bothering me nearly so much as it was."

She gestured toward an overstuffed chair by the hearth. "Sit and stretch those long legs of yours and I'll tell you what's been happening."

Clay knew when to follow an order. Tossing his hat onto a table by the door, he proceeded to loosen his string tie, sit low on his spine in the designated chair, and extend his legs, one dusty boot crossed over the other.

"Fire away," he said.

She rang for the butler, ordered a pot of tea and cakes, and made herself comfortable on the sofa where she could face him. "I have a guest in the house."

It did not sound like especially exciting news to Clay, but he tried to return his sister's smile with enthusiasm. He hadn't seen her this happy since before her marriage, and he didn't want to spoil her mood.

"A member of the royal court?" he asked.

"I don't know."

"You don't know?"

Charlotte shook her head. "No one does. Not even

she, although from the looks of her dress, I don't imagine she's got either title or money."

He could tell she was fairly bubbling over with the story, like a pot of stew hanging low over a hot camp-fire.

"A thief had just stolen everything she owned and she ran after him in front of my carriage and the horse reared and Doctor Emanuel thinks one of the hooves struck her in the forehead. It happened less than a week ago on King Street."

"Was she badly hurt?"

"Not exactly. She can get about, but she can't remember a thing about herself. Won't even talk to the police, saying she would be too embarrassed since there is nothing she could say."

Charlotte settled back on the sofa and waited for his reaction.

Clay tried to find something as exciting in the story as his sister, but he was damned if could see anything that could have set off Charlotte into such enthusiasm.

"So you took her in," he said. "How old is she?"

"Who knows?"

"Six? Twelve?"

"Oh, Clay, she's a grown woman." Her eyes glinted. "And beautiful. Everyone who comes down from London tells me you're only interested in beautiful women with red hair. Well, guess what color hair she has?"

He didn't have to be a genius to answer, "Red."

But he was not especially concerned. Maybe he would have been before the night at the Castlebury party. But no more. His Princess had not wanted to be found, he'd practically raped her to get her to admit who she was, and he was just about to get everything he wanted when—

He preferred not to remember all the particulars. He'd done a heap of explaining and apologizing to

Her Grace, but the grand old lady was not buying it. He had behaved abominably and done a weak female out of employment. And he had yet to hear from Alex and Libby, who'd have a word or two to say about their only son behaving in ways that didn't exactly cover him in glory.

He'd have a heap more explaining to do, all right, although he didn't know exactly what he would say.

A mystery woman showed up at the square one night to warn me away from some kind of danger she was never too specific about, then came to back to give me her virginity, then again with some wild story about being wanted for murder, backed off of that right soon and before skedaddling gave me the sweetest loving I've ever had, and when I found her again, naturally I went on the attack, randy bastard that I am.

He could see the expression on his daddy's face right now, and he could hear what his mother would have to say. She wouldn't be telling him anything he hadn't already told himself.

Somewhere in all those jumbled recollections were some clues as to just who his Princess really was and what was going on, but he hadn't figured them out just yet.

He'd for sure like to tell her he was sorry about what had happened—or almost happened—on that bear skin rug. Well, not exactly sorry, since he'd been so caught up in making love to her he hadn't been able to think straight, and the way he remembered it, neither had she. He hadn't exactly forced her into his bed.

But at that big party, with her trying to pass herself off as a maid—hell, for all he knew, that's what she really was—he'd been the one to start things, over some very pointed protests of hers, and for that he'd been hanging his head in shame. He'd be heading back to Texas with more than just regrets. He hadn't particularly liked himself for the past few days.

"—she has wonderful manners and the most delightful speaking voice."

Clay realized his sister was still talking, and he tried to be alert. Never could tell when Charlotte might ask questions.

"I'm sure she comes from a good family, but her dress was so shabby. Oh, Clay, she is the dearest thing. I've been buying clothes for her because the thief took everything she was carrying, but she keeps a running account of everything I've spent. She insists she'll pay me back. Of course, I don't always tell her the full amount. I just can't forget that dress she was wearing, and the shoes. Definitely not first quality. She did have on nice underwear. Nothing fancy, mind, but nice."

"Sure you ought to be talking to me about her underwear?"

"They're a large part of the few clues we've got. Besides, I'd be willing to bet you know almost as much about such things as I do."

"If Aunt Martha could hear you say that, she would box your ears."

"But she wouldn't say I was wrong."

"How long you planning on keeping this woman around?"

"As long as she will stay, or until she remembers who she is, which could happen any time. She got a little uncomfortable when she found out I'm married to an earl, so I decided not to mention anything about being the daughter of an earl, too. She seems to hold some resentment against those of us with title or money."

"But she hasn't turned down anything you've bought her, right?"

"Stop that, Clay. I won't hear such talk. I'll be getting enough of it from William when he finds out. I've bought her a few dresses and fed her and given her a bed to sleep in, that's all, but don't forget it was my carriage that ran her down when she was pursuing a thief. She's been good company for me, and as far as I'm concerned, that's repayment enough."

Clay felt put in his place, as only the women in his family could manage, and he nodded an apology. "Then how long are you planning on hanging around? Didn't you say the people who owned this place were in France?"

"Biarritz. They've extended their stay, and I've made an offer for the house. Or at least William has, through an agent in London. This is the first time I've stayed here, and I find I like it."

For a moment her eyes were shadowed and unreadable, then the light returned. Yes, he decided, she seemed happy enough, a far cry happier than she'd been the last time he saw her in London. Charlotte had a mystery woman of her own, and it was doing her good.

"How about you, Clay? I keep waiting to hear you're going back to Mason. There's a great deal of speculation about what's keeping you, including some from Mama."

"You all figure it's a woman, I imagine."

"We all do."

"You haven't heard from the Castlebury folks lately, have you?"

Charlotte shook her head. "Why?"

Clay caught the suspicion in his sister's eyes. So Her Grace hadn't spread the word. Good. She'd saved him from Charlotte's scolding. He'd made a mistake in bringing up the trouble matter at all.

"Tell the truth, Clay," she said, "how have you been passing your time?"

"Dinner at Claridge's, a couple of plays, but those things are so dadblasted silly that I gave up on them. Gambling a little, winning some, a round or two at the sporting club. Nothing you'd find to compliment

300

me on. I really came to say good-bye."

"Oh, Clay, you just got here. Stay a few days and meet my guest."

"If she can't remember who she is, what do you call her? Decided on a name?"

"She's considering several possibilities. She still gets headaches sometimes and I don't like to push."

"Since when?"

Charlotte ignored him. "Doctor Emanuel says her memory could return at any time, or maybe never. If it doesn't before long, she's promised to come up with something that she would like to be called. Maybe you can help us select a name."

"Maybe," he said, finding enthusiasm for the project hard to come by. He would definitely have to make his getaway as fast as he could.

Charlotte looked past him to the French doors that opened onto the garden. "Here she comes now. Just in time to join us for tea. I'll ask her to come in this way."

She sprang to her feet and circled Clay, opened the door, and called, "Hello."

"Hello," the woman answered, her voice drifting into the parlor along with a fresh, cool breeze. "You caught me by surprise standing there. Is there something I can help you with?"

Clay sat up and bent his knees. He placed his weight on the balls of his feet, and he listened with great care. Once again he was overhearing a voice he'd heard before.

"There certainly is," Charlotte said. "My brother's here. You're just in time to help me entertain him."

The voice grew louder as Charlotte's guest approached the door. "Oh, don't let me intrude."

"Nonsense. I've told him all about you, and he's waiting to see how he can help; I've ordered tea."

"Thank you, Charlotte. That would be nice."

"Your face has picked up a little color. Walking

about in the sun was a good idea."

"The garden is so lovely that it felt good just to watch the flowers grow. And the sun. I . . . I don't think I'm out in the sun much, wherever it is I'm from."

She did, indeed, Clay thought, have a most delightful voice, as Charlotte had pointed out. He'd thought so himself more than once, but it wasn't pleasing him very much right now. In fact, he was having a hard time believing what his ears told him, and he stood, his hands brushing at the dust his trousers had carried in from the road, his face grim.

He turned to watch her enter. Knowing already who she was, the sight of her hit him like the fall from a galloping cowpony and he had to hold onto himself to keep from letting loose with a curse word or two.

She was, he had to admit, the prettiest woman he had ever seen. Charlotte had bought her a pale green gown with a round neckline that let him see the familiar rise of her breasts. Familiar to the touch, that is, since he hadn't really had the opportunity to get a good look.

Her hair looked like a Mason County sunrise in the heat of summer, piled on her head the way it was and gently curled around her face. Her eyes were green and wide and her lips were the kind that made a man think of kissing. From the high forehead to the smoothness of her breasts, her skin looked like cream with a shot of brandy stirred in.

She stepped deeper into the room, the hint of a frown on her face as she adjusted to the dimness of the light. Slowly her gaze shifted from Charlotte to him.

Clay saw the recognition in her eyes, and the flash of fear. He took satisfaction. She'd damned well better be afraid. Amnesia, hell. She knew what she was doing. She was taking a sucker for a ride.

And Charlotte had been so happy. Clay had to get a grip on himself, seeing as how he'd never been more angry in his life.

Chapter Twenty-three

Jenna stood in sudden icy stillness, unable to believe her eyes. It could not be. She was having a nightmare of the most horrendous proportions. Clay was Charlotte's brother. And he was here, standing tall and straight and unsmiling not six feet away in Charlotte's withdrawing room.

No, her mind simply wouldn't encompass it. She had gone mad.

Dizziness overcame her and she felt her knees buckle.

"Clay!" Charlotte said.

Strong arms caught her by the elbows and she leaned toward a dark brown coat, a dark brown shirt, a broad chest, a dark and solemn face. It was Clay, and somehow she found the strength to pull away and stand under her own power. She stared at her hands, which were clutched together at her waist.

"Are you all right?" asked Charlotte, who hovered close by.

Clay had not said a word.

Jenna nodded.

"Help her to a chair," Charlotte said. "She's still very weak."

"No." Jenna spoke too loudly, but she couldn't help it.

"Now that's a word I've heard before," said Clay.

Jenna squeezed her eyes closed.

"Clay, what's got into you?" asked Charlotte. "Help her to a chair."

But Jenna couldn't accept the touch of his hand. And she couldn't look into his face again. The memory of the fury burning in his eyes still tore at her mind.

She made her way to the sofa before he could touch her again, and she sat with her head resting against the back, eyes closed, and wished she could die. Nothing in life seemed important enough to keep her breathing and thinking and hurting as she was doing right now.

Clay was Charlotte's brother. Dear, loving, generous Charlotte, who had given her friendship without question. Jenna had never had a woman friend before, and now she was about to inflict pain on the only one she had ever known. She knew Clay would not keep quiet. It wasn't in his nature. Any second the questions and the accusations would begin.

"Maybe she needs a swallow of water."

His voice was rich and deep and she heard the sharpness underneath his words. Did his sister?

"Good idea." Charlotte said, and she rang for a servant.

Jenna forced herself to sit upright, hands in her lap, nails digging into her palms hard enough to draw blood. She waited, but all was silence. What kind of game was Clay up to? Still playing her like a fish on a hook? She swallowed hard. He had such power to hurt her. And he was here.

He would never believe she had not known who Charlotte Rockmoor, Lady Denham, really was. Never. He never believed the truth.

Charlotte sat beside her on the sofa. "Are you all right? Should I call Doctor Emanuel?"

Jenna shook her head. "I'm all right." She smiled at Charlotte. "Truly. I'm just embarrassed for causing a scene."

She waited for Clay's response, which was fast in

coming. "I guess I took the little lady by surprise."

"Nonsense," said Charlotte. "Don't get into your head the sight of you brought on a fainting spell, Clay. You're not that special."

Jenna could have told her friend different. But she kept quiet, staring down at her hands and at the deep half-circles her nails had imbedded in the flesh. Surely the brother and sister sitting so close could hear the pounding of her heart.

Brother and sister! The realization hit her again, harder than it had when she had stepped inside the withdrawing room and met Clay's angry face. Sitting in a well-furnished room in a fine new dress and waiting for her world to fall apart once again, Jenna felt as though she were living out one of Dickens' most convoluted plots.

"Seems a little late for amenities," said Charlotte, "but this is my brother, Clayton Drake. You'll have to excuse his manners—he's from Texas. Clay, this is the young woman I was telling you about."

"Charlotte tells me you had an accident," Clay said, far too calmly. "What unfortunate luck for you. Never can tell in this life when things will sneak up on you. Don't you agree?"

"Oh, yes," answered Jenna, little above a whisper. *Come on,* she said to herself. *Get it over with.*

"Since when did anything ever sneak up on you, Clay?" asked Charlotte. "You always seem perfectly in control."

He let out a long slow breath, and Jenna could feel his eyes pinned to her. "Baby Sister, there are things about me you couldn't begin to guess. Probably about the lady here, too."

"Clay, is something bothering you?" asked Charlotte. "You seem—"

The door to the room opened, and a servant appeared, a wide silver tray in his hands.

"Oh, Bronson, put it here on the table beside me."

"Of course, madam."

306

Charlotte proceeded to pour Jenna a glass of water from a pitcher on the tray. Gratefully Jenna took it, holding the slender crystal with both hands to hide her trembling.

She took a small swallow. "Please," she said, "serve yourselves. I'll be all right."

The next few minutes were taken up with the passing of tea and cakes, both of which Jenna declined. To take more than a sip or two of water would have been like swallowing cotton.

Gradually her panic subsided, and she saw that she was not going to die on the spot as she had wished a few minutes earlier. Instead of sitting there so smug and determined, so close across from her that if she put out her foot she could have touched his boot, why didn't Clay say what he was thinking and put her out of her misery? She'd heard they shot horses with broken legs. Why not a woman with shattered nerves and a broken heart?

The answer lay in the question. He was *enjoying* her misery. Jenna looked up at him, caught the twist of his lips and the hard glint in his eyes, and knew she was right. She was perverse enough to draw courage from the realization. How dare he sit there, taunting her with his eyes when all she had done was love him?

If Charlotte had not been present, she would have told him just what she thought, but Charlotte *was* so close, so dear, so concerned, and she swallowed her aggravation as best she could, along with another sip of water.

"I didn't know you had a brother, Charlotte," she said, having to clear her throat only once. "And from Texas, of all strange places."

Charlotte smiled. "Clay and I were both born in Texas, but long ago I decided to settle here."

"You went to school in England?"

"As a matter of fact, I did. Clay may sound like a cowboy who never saw the inside of a schoolhouse, but don't let that voice deceive you. In his bucolic way, he's as sharp as an Oxford don."

That was something Jenna already knew, but the reminder brought her little comfort.

"You exaggerate, Baby Sister," said Clay.

"And he's rather nice looking, don't you agree? For someone who has spent most of his life on the back of a horse."

He was certainly everything Charlotte said, and more. Jenna knew her new friend was trying to make conversation, trying to make her feel at home, but such a feat was an impossibility. Jenna had seldom been more miserable in her life.

"You're embarrassing the little lady," said Clay laconically.

"Not at all," Jenna lied.

"Miss—" Clay began, then hesitated. "You'll have to excuse this country bumpkin, but I'm having a hard time knowing how to address you. Just bear with me, and we'll muddle along somehow, won't we?"

Country bumpkin indeed. "We can try," Jenna returned.

"Good girl."

Charlotte watched the exchange in silence.

"It seems to me," continued Clay, "that if we give you some choices, you might be able to get to thinking of a detail or two that'll mean something to you. You got a daddy, a mama, maybe even a husband and some kids? Couldn't have too many of those, unless you got started at a mighty early age."

He certainly was laying on the Texas accent thickly. Even Charlotte was staring at him in open puzzlement. Jenna put a polite smile on her face, but her cheeks hurt from the effort.

"Somehow I don't believe so," she replied. "I think that if there were anyone really close to me, I would have been thinking of him."

"Him?" asked Clay.

"Or her."

"Dr. Emanuel says it does work that way," Charlotte put in, continuing to look from one to the other, the puzzled look still in place. "Partial amnesia, it's called. A person can remember some areas of his life but not others."

"That could be a right handy condition, couldn't it?" asked Clay.

Charlotte snapped. "Clayton Drake, explain yourself. Whatever is wrong? You've been an embarrassment ever since my guest walked in this room, staring at her and asking questions without a thought to her discomfort."

Jenna accepted his challenge. "Are you suggesting that perhaps I have not lost my memory, Mr. Drake?"

"That would be most ungentlemanly of me. Beg your pardon." He glanced at his sister. "And yours."

"I should hope so," Charlotte threw back. "The poor dear has been injured. If you doubt it, talk to Dr. Emanuel."

"Perhaps," Jenna suggested, "he would like to inspect the bump on the side of my head. It's still quite prominent."

"Perhaps I would," he said, a glint in his gray eyes.

"This is the most bizarre conversation I have ever heard," Charlotte said, rolling her eyes. "You will not touch one hair on her head. I saw the accident. I was there in the carriage pulling back on the reins as hard as I could, but there was nothing I could do, it all happened so fast. The hooves of the horse came down so hard, I thought that surely—Well, you can well imagine what I thought. I didn't see them actually strike, but I saw the poor dear fall to the street. When she came to, she simply could not recall her name."

For just a moment, his eyes held a hint of the concern she had grown used to at the Black Horse. But just for a moment.

"I want her to get out more, to see some of my

friends and some of the others in the city. Maybe someone will recognize her, or she will recognize them. The doctor thinks it a splendid idea. Make yourself useful and convince her we're right."

He stood. It seemed to Jenna he towered about ten feet tall and took up all the air in the room.

"I intend to be helpful," he said. "As much as my sister. I just approach things a different way."

Now it was coming, Jenna thought, the revelation she had so feared the moment she saw him standing in the room. He'd been circling her with taunts the way she imagined American Indians had circled the early Texas settlers and he was ready to let loose with an arrow or two.

She simply wouldn't let him. She would break the news herself, although she did not know what she could say or how she would begin.

Shifting on the settee, she looked into Charlotte's warm blue eyes. She felt her own eyes watering, and she felt a sick feeling in the pit of her stomach, as well as an overpowering sense of regret. "There's something—" she began.

Clay broke in. "Let's not bother my little sister any longer." He extended his arm. "That sunshine outside looks pretty good to me, and I can see you're a woman who enjoys a walk down a garden path. Why don't we take a stroll? I can ask you a few questions that might jiggle something in that pretty head of yours."

So he wasn't quite ready to end the taunting. He preferred to circle her for a longer while. There were several things about Clay she would like to jiggle at the moment, but nothing that could possibly give him pleasure.

"I'm rather tired," she said.

"Of course she is," said Charlotte. "Except for the doctor and the servants, you're the first person that she's seen. Even the police passed along their questions about the theft through me. I can well imagine that you have exhausted her. Besides, she is in the habit of lying down for several hours before dinner."

"My mistake," said Clay, staring down at her from his lofty standing position. "Didn't realize you were still an invalid. You look so healthy."

Jenna gritted her teeth. There was nothing like a strong dose of Clay Drake sarcasm to give her strength. "Why thank you," she said.

"It was just a statement of fact."

"Of course."

Deep inside Jenna felt the rumbles of combativeness. Before long, Clay would let loose with a few facts and opinions, more of the second than the first, but she preferred privacy when the first explosions came. With the request to tour the garden, she decided he felt the same.

Setting aside her glass, she stood and faced him, or rather faced the parted coat and open throated shirt that he was wearing. Her eyes lingered a fraction too long on the brown skin and black wiry hair in the opening of his shirt. His neck was bristled, as was his chin, and he had the faint beginnings of a mustache over his lips.

His very grim lips.

She raised her eyes to his. "Perhaps you would like to meet me for a stroll before we dine. Then we can see what gets jiggled, as you so quaintly put it."

She smiled at Charlotte. "Thank you again for everything. You can never know how much I appreciate your kindness." She spoke from her heart. "No matter what happens, remember you will always have my undying admiration and affection."

For once Charlotte was speechless, and without so much as a nod to Clay, Jenna spun about, letting her skirt brush against him, and exited the room.

Jenna lay down for two hours, hoping to rest her eyes if not actually fall into a soothing sleep, but the entire time she found herself staring at the swirled ceiling of the chintz and lace bedroom that Charlotte had prepared for her.

The instant she left the withdrawing room, Clay could very well have told his sister everything he knew and suspected about her. Including the hot little session on Her Grace's bearskin rug. Jenna shuddered. Any moment she expected Charlotte to throw open the door and demand she leave the premises immediately.

She would be justified. In the five days she had been under the Rockmoor roof, Jenna had been given nothing but great kindness and concern and financial help, too, which she fully intended to repay. She hadn't worked out the details just yet on how she could manage that, but she would later when she had less on her mind.

The problem was that while she was regaining her strength, she was doing nothing about finding the man she sought. And she must get back to that search. Charlotte had wanted her to get out and meet some people. She would have to do just that.

Except that her life had become terribly complicated this afternoon. Surely there were only so many complications a woman could handle in her life. Today Jenna had passed her limit.

It seemed her brief existence on Earth had been little more than a series of shocks, beginning with the news of her father's death. From that long ago train wreck when she was six and continuing to this afternoon, the shocks went on and on.

After an hour and a half of studying the ceiling and thinking over the patterns of her life and waiting for someone to burst into the room and hurl imprecations at her, she allowed herself to consider that — ight have kept his mouth closed.

—, he was just biding his time.

— gave rise to another.

— ster's house, Clay wouldn't treat her

the way he had at the Castlebury home.

How absurd. Of course he would.

Surely she wouldn't respond in the same wanton way.

That one she was less sure about. She would like to believe she had enough control to tell him loud and clear that he was to keep his hands to himself, but since she had not once shown such control, she couldn't be sure.

If he must expose her for the fraud he considered her to be, she prayed he would do it in a way that would hurt Charlotte the least. If only Charlotte had told her she had a brother from Texas, she might have prepared herself—or run away.

But Charlotte had sensed her discomfort when she'd learned her new friend was Lady Denham, wife of an earl, and all conversation about Charlotte's private life had ceased.

Clay had once told her he was the son of the Earl of Harrow. Perhaps—

No, that was impossible. Not the Texan Clay.

Her thoughts returned to Charlotte. She couldn't tell her everything, but what to include and what to leave out? Which details would hurt the generous woman least?

Charlotte had always seemed familiar to her, as though they might have met some time in the past. Up until today Jenna had attributed the feeling to the blow she received on the head, or perhaps Charlotte simply reminded her of one of the women who used to donate time and money to the Reverend Cox and his school. One of the good ones who did not demand instant gratitude and obeisance.

Whether Clay believed her or not, she really had been injured, and she really did suffer from headaches when she got tired. If he questioned that portion of her story, she just might have to let him feel her bump.

Clay and Charlotte. Brother and sister, so different

in coloring, did not resemble one another in the least, except that they were both outspoken and liked to take charge.

Anna, the personal maid that Charlotte had insisted she use, entered quietly. "It's time, miss, for your bath."

She spoke softly, but then she always spoke softly, as though if she raised her voice she might harm her new mistress in some way.

Jenna wished there were more people like Anna in the world.

A hot bath really did make her feel better, and for once she let Anna go wild with her hair, sweeping it up into a topknot with a hundred small curls framing her face and the back of her neck. With Anna more concerned than ever about hurting her mistress, the combing and pinning took half an hour.

The dress she selected was her favorite out of the half dozen that Charlotte had purchased. A pale blue satin brocaded with white flowers, it had a low square bodice with shoulder straps and lace epaulets over elbow-length sleeves, the ends of which were frilled with lace and tied tight against her arms. Lace also trimmed the narrow waist, and when Jenna walked and turned in the dress, she felt like a queen.

Or, perhaps, a princess. She wondered how long it would take Clay to say something of the sort.

By the time she got down to the drawing room, he was waiting by the fire, a glass of brandy in his hand. Charlotte was not to be seen.

He watched her with hawk's eyes as she walked toward him. Heat rose in her as she looked at him looking at her, and her heart pounded as hard as it had ever done when he was near. Some conditions, it would seem, were not destined to change. Regret for so many things squeezed at her, but she pushed it away.

Tonight she held herself proud, not in the least a meek fieldmouse waiting for a predator to swoop down from the sky. For just a moment, she felt proud. Upstairs she had studied herself in the mirror and found that she truly looked beautiful. Never had she considered herself in such a light, and the knowledge gave her confidence.

For the first time since they had met, she and Clay were facing each other as equals, at least as far as outward appearance was concerned, and Jenna had decided long ago that it was appearance that counted above all.

Chin high, she came to halt in front of him, determined that if she could be nothing else, she could at least be a worthy adversary. "Good evening," she said.

"You really do look like a princess."

It had taken him less time to draw the conclusion than she thought.

"Where is Charlotte?" she asked, clasping her hands together at her waist.

"She'll be down in a while. I've been waiting for you." Again his careful eyes studied her hair, her face, and the details of her body. "It was worth the wait."

"Clay—"

"Ah, you admit to a certain familiarity."

"I assume that if I do not, you will throw me on the floor and prove in your Wild West style that I lie."

"The thought had occurred to me. I'm sorry you're giving in so soon."

"I've given in on nothing."

"Too bad, but then anything else would surprise me. And I assure you, Princess, I've had about all the surprises today that I care for. Baby Sister gave me hell after you left. It's a wonder you don't see the scars."

What she saw was a man in dinner clothes—a black coat and trousers, a ruffled shirt, a black cravat. He also wore a faint smile that did not include even a shade of humor. He had shaved, she noticed, and fool that she was, she would have liked to stroke his face and feel its smoothness.

In truth, there were several parts of him she would like to stroke, like his muscled upper arm and the ropey sinews across his back. She was more than a fool. She was insane.

"You mentioned the garden." Her voice was disgustingly thick.

"Yes. Less chance out there of being overheard."

"You think of everything."

He took a final swallow of brandy. She watched the workings of his throat. "If that's so," he said, setting the glass aside, "why are you always sneaking up on me?"

For that, she had no answer.

He put his hand to her elbow. She jumped.

"Something wrong?" he asked.

"If something wasn't wrong, I wouldn't know how to go on. Of course something's wrong. For one thing, I don't want you to touch me."

His eyes narrowed. "Why not?"

He was a devil. Not a hero, not an avenger, not one of the charitable souls of the world.

"If you don't know why not, then there were several nights in August when you weren't paying any attention to me."

"Oh, Princess, I paid attention to you, all right." His voice was low, deep and suggestive and as always when he took on that particular tone, it caressed her as warmly as his arms ever had. "The nights in August that I didn't think about you were the nights before we met. Let's go outside."

Jenna found his pronouncement thrilling and frightening at the same time. Keeping well in front of him, she walked on shaking knees through the French doors and took the first gaslit path that caught her eye. The garden was not nearly so elaborate as the Duchess of Castlebury's, but it was neatly laid out, with low-lying shrubs and beds of chrysanthemums and asters and a bank of oak trees. They did not stop until they were beneath the thickest-leafed tree, where they were not only away from prying eyes and listening ears, but they were also away from the light. The full moon halfway down the sky provided illumination, a soft silvery glow which did a great deal for the sharp-hewn face looking down at her and nothing for her racing heart.

She put two feet of space between them and faced him straight on. "There's not a great deal I can tell you that I haven't already said. For a while I really did forget my name." No need to tell him that the name had been false.

"But you've remembered it. Mary Roberts, isn't it? I believe that's what someone at Her Grace's said."

She looked into the dark.

"Now why do I get the feeling your name isn't really Mary?" he asked.

"Because it isn't."

"Ah, the truth. Do you suppose it could become a habit?"

His voice was hard. She turned back to face him. "Clay, I have never once hurt you in any way. Instead, I brought you pleasure and if you try to claim otherwise, I will know you for a liar."

The heat in his eyes was enough to melt the lace on her dress.

"I'm not claiming otherwise. The problem, Princess, is that you got under my skin. You had me jumping every time you said 'hop' and the only thing I wanted to know was which way."

"I didn't notice."

"You're the one that's lyin'. And you lied before. I half way bought the lusty rich girl story, but I'm not buying it now, nor anything else you're trying to think up, like falling on hard times and having to get a job. I'd just as soon believe that malarkey about the reward."

"You're just too clever for me, aren't you, Clay?"

"You'll never hear me claim that. I told you once a man does not like to be made a fool of, and, honey, you made me feel a lot of things, but in the end about all I had left was the suspicion that you had played me for a clown. All I needed was a painted face and some bells hanging down my tail."

Jenna lost all the confidence she had built upstairs, and she spun away from him. He turned her right back.

"I'm not through, and I'd regard it kindly if you would look at me while I talk. I'll do the same when it's your turn."

"You'll tell me, of course, when that occurs."

"Maybe if you'd said something about cutting out, I wouldn't have got myself all worked up about you. A simple good-bye is the way we do it in Texas."

"I—"

"Not just yet. You had me worrying about you, thinking all kinds of things might have gone wrong, and then you showed up at the duchess's party parading around in that costume—"

"It was the dress of a domestic. I was working that night."

"Maybe you were. Maybe the first lie you ever told me was that you weren't a servant. Care to clear up that little point right now?"

"You always want easy answers to hard questions, Clay, and I just can't give them."

"So I noticed. Despite that bump on the head, you're not a victim of amnesia, and you're not one of the society ladies or else Her Grace would have recognized you—she knows every one of 'em in town. I know a hell of a lot of things that you are not. Now it's time for you to tell me exactly what you are."

His voice was hard and cold and not in the least caressing. She felt pushed into a stormy night without protection against the rain, and instinctively she touched his arm. "Clay—"

"Don't try to sweet talk me, honey. Won't work this time. Not with Charlotte involved. I told you more than once to fill in this poor old ignorant cowpoke with a few words of truth. I'm telling you again, and if you didn't believe me before, you sure as hell better believe me now."

Chapter Twenty-four

"I'm looking for a man."

If Jenna had not been so distraught, she would have drawn pleasure from the surprised look on Clay's face.

"Now that's putting it plain enough," he snapped.

She took a deep breath. Perhaps her response to him had been ill considered, but standing there with the moonlight shining down on him, he looked so arrogant, so sure of himself, so censorial. For all his Texas ways, he still managed to represent all the haughty rich that she had been observing the past weeks, the lords and ladies and the untitled as well.

"You've criticized me often enough for being less than candid," she said, her head high. "And you're right. Sweet talk, you call it, but what you really mean is lying."

"You're the one telling Charlotte your memory's gone, and all because you're after a man. Here I'd been thinking what you were after was the money Charlotte's been spending on you."

"You can come up with something better than that. Maybe I'm really here to rob your sister of her jewels and I'm learning everything I can about her so my accomplice can break in and steal everything she owns. Maybe I plan on doing it myself."

"Maybe. There are only so many reasons you could be here, Princess, pretending to an ailment you don't have. I'm just trying to pick one of them, and I'd prefer one that wouldn't hurt Charlotte. I'd been feeling low as a snake for what happened at the duchess's, wishing I could apologize to you and make sure you were all right, but I gave up on that ever happening. So I ride down to find that like her brother, Charlotte's got a mystery woman. Then I find out our women are one and the same."

"I didn't know who she was," Jenna said, trying to break into Clay's harangue, but he did not pause.

"You skedaddled away from me without an explanation, and I'd like to be sure you don't do the same to her."

"I would never consider doing anything to hurt—" Emotion overcame her, and her voice broke.

"Don't try tears. They won't work. Not now."

He said the one thing that gave her strength—the one thing other than a kind word, which she knew not to expect. "I have no intention of crying. Not for you or for me. You're right. Tears don't work. They don't make me feel better. They only keep me from doing what I have to do."

"Which is find a man."

"Exactly."

"So you're sticking to that story. Got a particular man in mind or will anyone do? My room is on the right upstairs."

"Are you looking for a woman?" Jenna threw back at him. "Then don't judge me so harshly."

"You're not giving me a reason to do anything else. Not playing around with Charlotte's friendship the way you're doing."

"Hurting Charlotte is the last thing I want to do. She has been kinder to me than anyone I've met in the past few years, and her kindness came at a time when I needed it very much. I would as soon cut off my hand as cause her a moment's distress."

"Putting it a little strong, isn't it?"

"I'm learning from you, Clay, just how to express myself in the strongest way. For all your charm, you have a way of cutting a woman with words. You use them like a knife, twisting the blade when you know it's hit a vital spot, then—"

"Whoa. You're the one who came to me first, remember? Maybe you need a reminder."

His hands were on her shoulders before she could defend herself, and she found herself crushed against his chest, her arms caught in a tight fold between their bodies, her hands resting helplessly against his coat. The kiss came fast and hard, his mouth covering hers completely, his tongue working its way between her lips. She was jolted by the taste of him, and the moist warmth.

Worse was the surge of passion sired by his kiss. He was punishing her, not making love, and she was shamed by her momentary cravings. She struggled in his iron embrace, trying to twist her body away from his, but his hold strengthened. The more she fought, the more insistent became his demands, his hands stroking her back, holding her tight against him as though he wanted to press her body through the clothing separating them and let their hot skin touch.

He was a pleasure and a torment at the same time, an indulgence she could ill afford, and she knew the real battle was not with him but rather with herself. She was close to answering his kiss, to brushing her tongue against his, to letting her stifled sighs escape.

His kiss softened, as did his embrace. She took advantage and shoved away. Once again she had danced dangerously close to submission, ready to do his will if he pursued his course, and once again she knew shame.

They stood like two adversaries, staring at each other in the ghostly glow from the moon. She stood as tall as she could manage, and held her head tilted proudly, chin high. "Have you noticed, Mr. Drake,

322

that whenever you have approached me outside your bedroom there has been a need for force?"

"Persuasion, Princess. That's what it is called. And have you noticed I've never had to force you into anything? Not once we got things started. If I hadn't stopped, we'd be on the ground by now, and I don't think this is the time or the place."

She slapped him. The sound of her hand on his cheek rang in the air. He did not move.

"Feel better?" he asked, as calm and cool as she had ever heard him, and twice as arrogant.

She slapped him again. "Now I do." Which was a lie.

"Don't try it again. You got two shots at me, one for the duchess's parlor and one for right now."

"Which means I must wait for a third attack before I can take another shot, as you put it."

"I'll try to control myself."

"Please see that you do." She whirled away from him before he could see the hated tears welling in her eyes. A sharp pain throbbed in her head, so strong she grew dizzy. She swayed, and Clay was beside her in an instant.

"Princess," he said, his steadying hands on her shoulders. "Are you all right? Damn fool me, I forgot you've been hurt."

Jenna wanted his pity no more than she wanted his scorn, and she stepped away from his touch. "I'm all right." She turned to face him. "All I ask is for a moment of civilized communication between us. With words. No touching."

He rubbed at his face. "Seems fair enough."

"You asked why I am here. I can't tell you."

"What happened to wanting a man?"

"I said I'm looking for a man. It's not the same thing."

"A fine distinction, but I'll concede the point. You never did say if you had anyone in mind."

"I do. The trouble is, I don't know his name and I don't know what he looks like."

"Kinda the way I was with you before the duchess's party."

Jenna's cheeks warmed. "Not at all that way. I may be making a terrible mistake, but I'm going to ask for your help, Clay, and your trust. Most of all your trust. Do I have it?"

"Seems to me we've had this conversation before."

It wasn't an outright no, and Jenna hurried on. "I promise on my father's grave that I will be a friend to Charlotte and that I will leave as soon as I can. But first I must do everything in my power to finish the task that brought me to Brighton. And that is to find a man I heard planning a crime."

"Don't tell me. There's a reward out for him, and you want to collect."

"Are you going to listen, or should I just wait while you decide for yourself what I'm going to say?"

"For someone caught in a passel of lies, you have a clever way of making me seem in the wrong. Fire away. I'll do what I can to keep quiet."

Jenna knew it was the strongest concession she could expect. "You may have read about an attempted robbery of the Queen's jewelry. It happened at a children's garden party a few days after the . . ." She found herself blushing. "After the last time I went to Tunstall Square."

"I remember the night. The robbery I don't know about."

"A man was killed by one of the Queen's guards. Bertie Groat, a criminal from one of the slums." There was no need to add that Groat had been a regular at the Black Horse. As often as Clay had been to the tavern, he had probably never heard the name, although he'd seen Groat's scowling face a time or two.

"Another man was arrested," she went on when

324

Clay, for once, did not respond right away.

"Anyone I'm supposed to know?"

"A street juggler named Morgan. He'd been hired to entertain, and the police assumed he was in on the robbery."

"Now I suppose you're about to tell me he's innocent, and you want to spring him from jail."

"Why is it necessary for you always to lapse into sarcasm?"

"Damned if I know."

Jenna knew. He didn't believe her. She wasn't surprised.

"At least wait until I'm done before you call me a liar."

"I can do that."

He made her nervous, standing there so tall and dark and serious, and so close. He made her nervous, too, because she wanted very much—more than anything in the world right now—for him to accept everything she had to say and to provide her with the strength she wasn't quite sure she had.

She twisted her hands together. "Under very extraordinary circumstances which are not germane to the heart of the story—"

"That mean you're not going to tell me about them?"

She took a deep breath and hurried on, describing as best she could the overheard conversation between Groat and an unseen gentleman. She did not tell him where the conversation had taken place, nor how she had come to hear it, and she had no intention of doing so.

"Accounts in *The Times* mentioned Groat but did not include anything about a gentleman being involved. He was the one behind the plan. I know it. I heard him. Never once in that conversation," she concluded, "was Morgan mentioned, and I am certain he was hired only as a distraction. Unfortunately, the authorities believe otherwise, and he is now in jail awaiting trial while the real culprit goes his way among the gentry."

"What's this Morgan to you?"

"Nothing. I've never exchanged a single word with him."

As usual, Clay did not look as though he believed her. "Let me take a wild guess as to what all this is about. You want to find the gentleman thief, drag him before the police, and force him to confess so Morgan can go free."

On his lips, the plan sounded foolish but she had no choice except to say, "Something like that."

"How do you plan on catching him? You said he was unseen. At least that's the word I think you used. Got so caught up in the other details, I could be wrong."

"Don't be too humble, Clay. You remember everything I've ever said, and delight in reminding me. It was his face I did not see. I'm not entirely ignorant of his appearance. He's tall and thin and elegant, and he moves like a gentleman, with confidence and a long stride, and he's got a bald spot on the top of his head."

"Not much to go on."

"The best part is that I heard him clearly enough, and I smelled him, too."

"You smelled him? Wasn't he much on taking baths?"

"He had sprinkled himself with rose water, and he had a high, thin voice, almost like a woman's. I'd recognize it if I ever heard him speak."

She fell silent. She had said enough. Either Clay believed her or he did not.

He did not take long to respond.

"And that's what you were doing at the duchess's? Listening for a skinny, rose-scented dandy with a high voice?"

326

Put that way, her mission sounded even more foolish. "That's exactly what I was doing. I had hired myself out at several such parties, and all for the same reason."

"So you admit you're not really a servant."

Jenna waved her hands in frustration. "Is that all you want to know? Who I really am?"

"It'd make the rest of your stories go down a hell of a lot easier, Princess."

"Jenna." Without thinking, she blurted out the word.

"Run that by me again."

"I don't like the way you said Princess. You can call me Jenna."

He paused before asking, "Is that your name?"

"Yes." She could not regret having told him. The truth was, she wanted to hear her name on his lips.

"Jenna," he said.

In the dark she felt a tingle travel down her spine.

"It's got a nice sound to it." He was quiet a moment. "Jenna," he repeated.

The tingle repeated itself, too.

"Want to put anything with that? Something like a family moniker?"

Jenna Cresswell, born in the Transvaal, educated in an asylum for the deaf, lately of Seven Dials, a wanted woman who wants very much to be wanted by you.

She kept the words in her heart.

"I wouldn't want to overwhelm you with facts, Clay. Will you help me find this man? It would mean a great deal."

"I still don't get it. You say you haven't got anything going with the juggler."

"I most certainly do not!"

"Then he's your brother, or that Uncle Thomas you mentioned when you were playing the spoiled rich girl part. The one with the money. Oh no, couldn't be him, unless street jugglers make more than I think they do. Could be he managed to collect the thousand pounds that was on your head, but then that doesn't exactly figure."

"You're impossible."

"I'm just trying to put all your stories together and figure out what's the truth and what's not. It must be especially hard for you, considering your amnesia and all."

She lifted her hands in surrender. "You win, Clay. I'm a fraud and a liar and trollop and anything else you want to call me. I admit to all of them. But you are a very cruel man, and that is just as bad."

She brushed past him, tears dimming her eyes. For once, he did not try to grab her.

"Jenna."

Something in his voice made her stop, but she kept her back to him.

"You left something out of your story. Why didn't you go to the police and tell them what you heard?"

"Because—" But she had gone as far as she could with the truth. "Because I wasn't supposed to be where I was when the crime was being discussed, and to go to the authorities would only cause complications I'm not prepared to handle."

"And not because you killed someone and the police are really after you. That was one of your stories, as I recall."

His sarcasm inflicted a fresh wound. She was trying to be as honest with him as she could, and his skepticism hurt.

"I believe that it was, but of course you saw right through it. I wrote New Scotland Yard, but apparently they chose not to believe the letter because Morgan is still in jail. The reason he must be freed is that he is a widower with six-year-old twins who are dependent upon him. It is for them that I want to find the real culprit."

"You have the damnedest habit of throwing in details that are hard to swallow. Six-year-old twins?"

"Alice and Alfred. Think it over, Clay. We will talk in the morning. Right now I'm going back to my room."

She forced herself to turn around and look at him. With the moon behind a cloud, she could not see his face, and she wondered if the mark of her hand was on his cheek. She wondered if she had stung him as much as his harshness was stinging her.

"I'll tell Charlotte that I'm simply too tired to eat, which won't be far from the truth. Talking to you is like running a very long and difficult race."

"That's because you have to do so much thinking to keep up with what you've said."

"And with what you're going to throw back in my face. If your sister isn't down yet, please make my excuses for me. Tired or not, I do not believe I could sit across the table from you and listen to any more questions. You can tell her that, if you like. You can tell her everything you know and suspect about me, or you can do what I do. You can lie."

As she started to leave, Clay got in the last word. "Listen to me, Jenna, and listen well. Charlotte talks tough sometimes, but she's got a soft heart and she's had a rough time lately. I kept your secrets from the duchess, told her I was the one on the prowl and dragged you upstairs, and I'll keep your secrets for now. I'll do what I can to help, but remember I'll always be watching you."

Jenna woke from a restless sleep sometime after midnight. Fully awake, her headache gone, she sat up in the feather bed. Knowing her night's rest was at an end, she tried to prepare herself for a few hours of worry.

Five minutes passed. Five miserable, long minutes

in which her thoughts were in a tumble and her heart pounded at the memory of what had happened in the garden. She trusted Clay to keep her confidences a secret—he had promised and she believed him, despite his never believing her.

If only her fate did not repeatedly fall into his hands. He did not oversee her affairs any better than she did.

Jenna stood by the bed. Once before, on the third night she was under the Rockmoor roof and the first night she was free of pain, she had wandered outside. Roaming about the midnight streets of London in her beggar's garb had conditioned her to such periods of wakeful wandering, and she had been wanting to flee a troubled conscience that told her she should confess all.

She had found herself walking from the Whitecastle Street home toward the ocean. A more timid woman would never have attempted the trek alone, but Jenna was far from timid, and she had not been so careless as to remove herself from the shadows at the side of the street. As far as she could tell, she had made it all the way to the sea wall, down the steps, and to the water's edge without being seen. Certainly, no one had interrupted her walk.

The night had been cloudy and warm, without moon or stars and it tempted her to do a very foolish thing. Finding a lonely stretch of beach away from the piers, she had removed her clothes and, tiptoeing across the biting, coarse sand, she had gone for a late night swim.

Her father had taught her the skill in a Transvaal lake when she could barely walk, and she found that it came back right away. The ocean floor dropped off sharply in the area she had chosen, and she was able to stroke back and forth, working out her pent up energies without going far from the shore. After only a few minutes, her worries faded as she concentrated

330

on her physical exertions, on the push and pull of the water, and on the roar of the waves beating against the shell-strewn beach.

A half hour later, she had pulled on her clothes and, with her hair matted against her head and her dress damp against her skin, she returned to White-castle Street, where she slept the sleep of an innocent child.

This night, with thoughts of Clay tumbling in her mind, she decided for another midnight swim. By the time she let herself out the back door, the moon was down and the world seemed at rest.

All was as it had been before—the dark warmth of the air as she hurried toward the ocean, the caressing buoyancy of the water when she slipped into its depths, and the firm strokes that pulled her farther from the town. Even the sound of the waves against the shore was the same, only this time she was unable to clear her mind of worry.

My room is on the right.

How the words had hurt. Never would she betray Charlotte by going to her brother when she was under her benefactress's roof, and she could not betray herself by such wanton behavior, not anymore.

But she had wanted to. She had missed his love-making.

I'll be watching you.

But not to make sure she was all right. Anguish took hold of her. If she were without the worry of Morgan, she would just keep swimming all the way to Portsmouth, where she had first landed seventeen years ago. She would begin all over again.

Perhaps—

A hand gripped her ankle, then let go. She went under and came up spitting brine. Her feet touched the sandy ocean floor, and the water lapped just below her shoulders. She screamed, splashing as she did so to separate herself from whoever loomed dark and threatening beside her.

"Jenna!"

She screamed again.

Rough hands seized her naked shoulders and lifted her until she was suspended in the sea, her breasts exposed to the night air. She kicked and squirmed but to no avail.

"Jenna, it's me, Clay."

The words penetrated her terrified mind just as her fists pounded against a very solid and very bare chest.

She struggled to catch her breath. "Clay?"

"That's right."

She let the realization calm her . . . then she lashed out again, her fists flailing and splashing, but he did not move. The rolling wave lifted her in the water and she drifted against him. With a start she realized that he was as naked as she.

"Oh!" she cried.

"What in the hell are you doing out here like this in the middle of the night?"

She brushed matted hair from her face. His hands remained tight on her shoulders as once again her feet found the ocean floor.

"You followed me. You're spying on me."

"I said I would. It's the only way to keep you from surprising me. At least that's what I figured, but I sure figured wrong."

"I didn't hear you." Her breath came in gasps. "On the streets or on the beach or—"

"Don't feel bad about it. I'm a hunter from way back."

"You know where I am now. Go away."

She was finding it very difficult to keep her dignity with the waves washing her against him. Already the tips of her breasts were tight and erect.

Thank goodness the night was without light and the water deep, or he would be able to know, too. It was the kind of evidence Clay would do something about.

"Jenna."

His voice was husky. It wasn't necessary for her to see beneath the water to know that part of his body was also erect. She also didn't need a degree from Oxford to know where the night was fast heading.

"I'm finished with my swim. If you won't leave, then I suppose I will have to." She paddled away from him toward the shore.

"Too late, Jenna. You'd have to be a mighty fine swimmer to get away from me now."

Chapter Twenty-five

She had reached waist-high water by the time he caught her, his fingers clamping down on her wrist like tentacles from a creature of the deep and pulling her back against him. He twisted her to face him.

"It's been a long time, Jenna."

"It should have been forever."

"You don't believe that any more than I do."

In her heart, she knew he was right. Even the rhythms of the water's ebb and flow echoed her deepest thoughts.

I love you . . . love you . . . make love to me, Clay.

Her body, too, throbbed in the cadence of the flow.

She strained to see his face, but as they had done in his bed on Tunstall Square, they were about to make love in the dark. Her fingers outlined the damp contours of his upper arms. He was solid and sure, the one firm reality in the universe, a relentless force that, unwise as she was, she could not resist.

"I didn't expect you to follow me, Clay. Truly, I did not." As though the protestation would make what she was about to do all right.

"I know. But it doesn't make any difference, does it? Only, damn, I wish we had some light."

His words so echoed her own thoughts that she gave a small cry and threw herself into his arms. He crushed her against him, his mouth covering hers, his wet, hard body sending tingles of excitement through her, the water providing an erotic caress where she and Clay did not touch.

When he claimed the dark, moist interior of her mouth, the touch of his tongue against hers was electric. All the needs she had first experienced in his bed pumped hot and insistent through her veins. She grew dizzy with wanting, clutching with eager fingers at his wet, wondrous shoulders, matching his kiss with probings of her own tongue, biting at his lips when he withdrew.

As eagerly as she had given herself to him in London, she was many times over more eager to give herself to him now. She was someone she did not know, a slave to cravings of the flesh, a mindless wanton without conscience, without care. All the loneliness and despair, the worry and the travails of her life melted under the heat of his embrace and of the touch of his hands on her back and down her spine.

She rubbed her body against him, her lips trailing down the column of his neck and settling in the hollow of his throat. For once she was not reminded of the country; tonight she tasted salt and ocean water, but still she tasted his skin and felt the throbbing of his pulse that beat in time with hers.

His hands spanned her buttocks and with ease he lifted her in the water, pressing her close to his enlarged shaft. The ocean helped to support her as much as his hands and her arms around his neck. She drew incredible pleasure from the rhythmic rubbing of her breasts against his chest. She trembled, and she felt an answering tremble from Clay, heard a deep rumbling in his throat, felt the power of him enfolded in her arms.

With a shiver of delight, she realized she shared that power . . . the child of the slums, the fugitive from the law, the driven woman without a home, in most quarters without even a name. She was as powerful as the man she caressed because she could bring to him the same wild hungers, the same boundless pleasures that he brought to her.

He was not arrogant when he made love to her; he was gentle and forceful at the same time, but not cruel, and in this moment she felt a love for him wider and deeper than the inky sky that served as the ceiling for their worldly room.

She had known him only two short months, but already she knew her life would be forever empty without him.

Slowly his hands trailed up her spine, and he kissed her closed eyes, his fingers stroking her damp hair, her shoulders, and slowly, with excruciating care, he trailed back down, spreading his broad hands against her buttocks and holding her hard against him once again, showing her his need. Water lapped at her sizzling skin.

Her body throbbed in answer to his touch, and she felt such a need inside that she thought she would explode. A thousand pent-up worries and frustrations, longings and desires could be restrained no longer. Life held such little joy for Jenna, but at the moment she knew she was the richest, happiest woman on the face of the earth.

He bent his head to lave at the hardened tips of her breasts, and she dropped her head back until the ends of her hair trailed in the undulating ocean. The muted roar of the sea as it rolled, wave after wave, past them to the shore was as nothing to the pounding of blood in her veins, and the universe that stretched black and endless around them was reduced to the sliver of space occupied by her and Clay.

Together, they were as glorious as the unseen stars, as significant as the planets whirling past them in outer space, because of what they meant to each other in this fraction of time. As much as the separate pleasures Clay was bringing to her, the realization of her completeness when she was with him brought her jubilation.

How easy it was, buoyed by the water and by his demands, to wrap her legs around his waist and to lower herself onto his waiting shaft. What a strange and erotic sensation it was to feel below the surface of the sea his hardness rub against the throbbing bud of her desire.

Head bent, he pressed his lips to hers, his tongue tracing the outline of her mouth before dipping inside to claim her completely. She clung with all her might to him, her fingers digging into his shoulders, her breath hot against his unseen cheek. Primal urges swept through her. In the dark of the vast outdoors, with the timeless waves caressing, then rolling past them, Clay took them both over the brink of ecstasy.

Jenna held tightly to him as long as she could, willing the moment of ecstasy to last, knowing as she did so that all too soon they would break their embrace, once again two individuals at odds with one another, people with separate lives and separate dreams, and their harmony would be gone.

He broke the kiss, but he did not lessen his hold on her. Jenna hoped an impossibility; she hoped he never would. She loved him with a depth and strength of feeling that even she had not realized, and she knew that for all her proud words when she was away from him, without Clay she was hollow inside.

Arms and legs wrapped around him and eyes closed tight, she rested her head against his chest to listen to his strong, erratic heartbeat. She was a long time getting control of her own wildly beating pulse and of her ragged breath. Unable to release her tight hold, she took pleasure as long as possible in the slowly fading rapture that had exploded within her; she knew too well that loneliness would rush into the void.

"Jenna," he whispered, his voice barely above the noise of the water. "I want to hold you forever."

She kissed his chest where she felt the strongest beating of his heart.

"What would you say," he murmured huskily, "if I just didn't let you go?"

Tears burned at the back of her eyes. She knew he

spoke while still in the throes of physical love; he knew no other kind, at least as far as she was concerned.

And if, by some wild, impossible chance, he was falling into a more serious kind of love, the kind that meant commitment and honesty, what would happen when he learned the truth about her? Before she could begin to think of staying with him, she owed at least some time to the legal authorities of London, and, if a jury so ruled, she might owe them her life.

The most difficult thing she had ever done was to ease her hold on him and to let the water drift between them as she found her footing once again. She saw the outline of his shoulders and broad chest, the tapering to his narrow waist, the lapping of the water against the whorls of hair that lay damp against his tight abdomen. The water, she saw even in the dimness, hit him much lower on the torso than it did her. Even now, with the lovemaking past, she felt a longing for him.

But she kept her voice brisk, at a cost he would never know. "Then we would cause quite a scandal when the sun rose in the morning." She glanced toward the eastern horizon. "Which will not be very much longer, I'm afraid."

"You're a cool one, aren't you? Whatever else you are, you're not one to lose your head over a man."

The familiar Clay had returned, the one she could handle best, even while she felt her heart breaking.

She covered her exposed breasts with her arms. "I've learned to be realistic, that's all. And practical. Tell me, did you let Charlotte know any details about me?"

"I told you I wouldn't."

"So you did, but I wanted to make sure."

"That's my Jenna. Smart and practical. And right. The sun really is about to shed a little light on the water. Maybe we better hustle on back to our clothes and get to the house. And maybe you ought to start telling me how we're going to find this sweet-smelling bastard with the squeaky voice."

His fingers raked damp hair from his forehead.

"Damned if I know why, but I can't see my way clear to doing anything else but helping you out."

"I got a letter from the Duchess of Castlebury today." Charlotte smiled at her brother, who was sitting across from her at the dinner table of the Whitecastle Street home. Night had fallen, and they were gathered for the evening meal.

Jenna, sitting to her left, set down her glass before she spilled red wine across the white linen cloth. She did not dare so much as one quick glance at Clay; he would see the apprehension in her eyes, and he just might comment.

He had been behaving since their early morning return from the beach two days ago, but she hadn't struck up a conversation with him, not when they chanced to meet at breakfast, not in the parlor when they met with Charlotte before dinner, not even when he caught her in the garden one afternoon to determine that her headaches were gone.

He'd had the decency to stay away from the house much of the time, choosing to ride around the Sussex countryside instead.

He had ventured only one hastily written note which he placed beneath her breakfast plate the morning they returned from the beach: *Let me know what to do. And let me know when you'd like another swim.*

She had not responded.

Charlotte glanced at Jenna. "Too bad we can't get Her Grace down here for the ball Saturday night. She might recognize you. The duchess knows everyone in the south of England."

Jenna kept her eyes on her plate of untouched food. Charlotte was referring to what was to be her first outing since the accident, a grand party at the Albermarle Hotel. As slim as the odds were against her, she was determined to mingle among all the high-class guests. If her villain was there, she would find him. But not if the Duchess of Castlebury strode in and got a good look at her.

"Somehow," she said, "I don't believe that duchesses have played much of a part in my life."

"You could be wrong," said Clay.

Charlotte looked back at her brother. "The Duchess said you made an appearance at one of her balls. You didn't tell me."

"Didn't know you'd be interested."

"She's Mother's closest friend. Of course I'm interested."

Jenna felt a sick feeling in the pit of her stomach. The duchess had close ties to Clay and Charlotte; no wonder she had been so upset when she found Clay on her bearskin rug. Her apprehension grew over the letter, but her worry was for Clay. Just who was the mother of these two people who currently filled her life? Jenna wanted very much to know.

"How is Her Grace?" asked Clay.

Jenna would have preferred he ask about his mother.

"The same. Full of vinegar, as Martha used to say. Says she's slowing down, but it doesn't seem possible, not with everything she had to write about. Balls, card games, visits, even carriage rides. She makes me feel like the older woman, vegetating down here the way I've been." She sipped at her wine. "But of course, she's got a husband to stand beside her. His Grace sends regrets he had to miss the ball when you were there."

Jenna caught a rare bitterness in Charlotte's voice when she said the word *husband*. Lord Denham's name had not come up since early in her stay, when Charlotte had said he had business in London and would not often be down.

It had seemed a strange way to live in a marriage, primarily because she knew if she had been wed to Clay, she would have gone wherever he "hung his hat," as he put it, not wanting to let him out of her sight or touch for any longer than was absolutely essential. It was not a subject she had spent too much time pondering, since it was a subject filled with pain.

"When is old Bill going to put in an appearance? Didn't you tell me he might be here tonight?"

"He may arrive on the late train." Charlotte didn't sound as though she held out much hope. She turned to Jenna. "Never marry a man who devotes himself to business, especially when he doesn't believe you can add two and two. You'll never see him, and when you do, he'll be thinking of other things."

"What makes you think she's not already married?" asked Clay.

"No ring," Charlotte returned. "Although I suppose she could be betrothed."

"No," said Jenna without thinking. "I'm not betrothed." And then, because she owed Charlotte an explanation, "I believe that if I were in love with someone, I would feel a loneliness inside because he wasn't close by."

"Would you?" asked Clay.

Jenna could feel the warmth of the simple question, and layers of meaning she could only guess at.

"What has love got to do with betrothal, or even marriage?" asked Charlotte.

Neither Clay nor Jenna ventured an answer. The only thing that Jenna could be grateful about was that conversation concerning the letter had been dropped. Thank goodness the duchess had not described the scandalous events between Clay and a red-haired servant in an upstairs parlor, a servant who answered to a description that matched Charlotte's mysterious guest. Jenna was certain the incident had not been mentioned; otherwise Charlotte would have brought it up. She might even wonder if Jenna could be that servant, given the sharp exchanges that sometimes passed between her and Clay.

Charlotte was as smart as her brother and just as liable to say what was on her mind.

But talk of the letter had been dropped.

"Her Grace did mention one thing I found of passing interest."

Jenna's pulse quickened. She had relaxed too soon.

"It was about you, Clay."

As warm as the dining room was, Jenna felt a decided chill.

"What was that, Baby Sister?" He spoke casually.

"She mentioned that you had donated a rather sizable sum of money to the Deaf and Dumb Asylum in London."

The words were the very last Jenna might have expected to hear. She turned, wide-eyed and open-mouthed, to stare past Charlotte at Clay.

He winked at her, then smiled at his sister. "You put me to shame, remember, about not being much for charity. It seemed like a worthy cause. Besides, I wanted you to admit you might be wrong about my selfish hide."

"How did you ever hear about the school?"

"Asked Robert to find out if there was such a place. He's mighty handy when it comes to chores like that. Keeps him from fussing over my boots."

"Don't make the gesture sound less kind than it was. I remember you mentioned a deaf child you had seen in some tavern."

Jenna started, but neither of the others was watching her.

Charlotte continued. "She's the reason you put Robert on the trail. Don't deny it, Clay. You're not hopeless, after all."

"Now that's the first compliment I've had in a long spell. Tell you the truth, it was because of that little girl. Sent a letter to the folks that run the school asking if they could check into her situation and get her some help."

"She got to you, didn't she?" asked Charlotte.

"Kinda did, showing spunk in such a place and surrounded by the kind of people who'd slit your throat

342

for a shilling. Yeah, she got to me real deep, and I'm not talking about the money."

Jenna concentrated on stirring her food and dealing with the lump in her throat. Clay was speaking of her, if only he knew it. In one of her lives, she had managed to touch his heart, and she wished with every ounce of her being that she had done so all of the time.

"In case I haven't told you lately," Charlotte said, reaching out to pat her brother's hand, "I love you."

Jenna wanted very much to tell him the same thing. Like his sister, Clay was one of the good people with money, the unselfish kind. It seemed he was only arrogant with her, and it was entirely possible she was at fault.

The conclusion didn't do much for her self esteem, but it proved she had picked a good man to love.

She wished she could have been there when Reverend Cox learned the good news about the money. In a way, Jenna felt as though she had been partially responsible, and she felt a rush of pleasure. She owed the reverend so much.

Charlotte went on. "You haven't talked much about yourself at all, now that I think of it. I've hardly seen you, but then you always did prefer riding to sitting around the parlor and jawing."

She put a twang to the last word, and Jenna was reminded of her Texas roots.

"Not always," he said. "There are a few parlors and a few women I don't mind being around."

Jenna could feel his eyes on her. She felt a blush steal up her throat and face.

Tonight she was wearing the same blue gown she had worn on Clay's first night in Brighton, and Anna had arranged her hair in the same elaborate manner. She knew she looked at home in the elegant dining room, but under Clay's scrutiny she always felt ill at ease.

"There is one thing I haven't mentioned since I got here," said Clay. "Theodore caught a burglar."

Jenna almost blurted, *He did?*

343

"He did?" asked Charlotte in her place. She glanced at Jenna. "Theodore's a Bullmastiff."

"Oh," said Jenna.

"Someone tried to sneak over the back fence," said Clay. "Almost tore the poor bastard to pieces before Jimmy heard the ruckus and called the police."

Jenna swallowed hard.

"He's turned out to be a fine watchdog after all," said Clay. Jenna could hear the laughter in his voice, and wondered if Charlotte could do the same.

"I didn't know he was anything else," his sister said.

"There were a few times I wasn't sure," said Clay.

Jenna took a swallow of wine.

"You're not eating," said Charlotte, her attention directed to Jenna. "Are you feeling all right?"

"I'm fine, just not hungry."

Jenna smiled warmly at Charlotte, and Charlotte smiled back. Not for the first time, Jenna was struck by the familiarity of that kind and gentle look in her eyes. Somewhere, sometime she had seen Charlotte before, but where could it have been?

With dinner having drawn to a close, the three of them went to the withdrawing room. Clay had just poured himself a brandy and sherries for the ladies when the door to the room opened.

"William," said Charlotte, rising to her feet, her voice a little breathless, "you made it after all."

Seated on the sofa, Jenna looked over her shoulder at the man in the doorway. William Rockmoor, Earl of Denham, was tall, almost as tall as Clay. He wore a traveling suit of gray and sported a thin mustache on his handsome face. He smiled as his wife approached, as well he might for Charlotte looked lovely and graceful in a pale pink gown.

With a shock, Jenna recognized him. He was the gentleman who had been laughing with Teresa on a darkened street near Seven Dials. Charlotte's husband, a peer of the realm, was the kind who liked to buy his sex from a crude-talking prostitute rather than

344

remain faithful to his charming wife.

She had heard the whores at the Horse talk of such men.

But Charlotte, of all people, to have married one of them!

And then suddenly she realized where she knew her benefactress. Charlotte and William. She should have remembered their names. They were the couple who had given her a crown two months ago when she'd first tried begging at Piccadilly Circus. Or rather Charlotte — dear, generous woman that she was — had given her the alms. William had done nothing but complain.

How could she have forgotten? It was the same night she had returned to the Black Horse and Clay had appeared.

She felt Clay staring at her. She turned back to the hearth where he stood, started to speak, but what could she say?

Your brother-in-law betrays your beloved sister with the prostitute whose husband owns the Black Horse Tavern.

Remembering the conversations she had overheard among the rookery whores, she could have added that Lord Denham might very well give his wife a disease.

Clay would immediately start in with another round of questions, which she did not think she could forfend.

Clay bent to where she was seated and spoke into her ear. "You know William, don't you, Jenna?"

She had only one answer for him.

"I do."

Chapter Twenty-six

Jenna saw questions in Clay's watchful gray eyes, but Charlotte and her husband were upon them before he could respond.

"I've written William explaining your situation," Charlotte said. "The first day you were here."

William Rockmoor, standing behind his wife where she could not see him, glanced at the seated Jenna and his eyes made a quick survey. She could read nothing in his expression, but she felt Clay stiffen at her side.

"Lord Denham," she said in greeting. He returned her nod.

"Brother Bill," said Clay, "didn't think you were going to make it tonight."

A look of dislike passed across William's face. "Business. There are those who cannot spare the time for frivolities."

It was Charlotte's turn to stiffen. She turned to her husband. "Mending a marriage is hardly frivolous, William, unless it's one that does not matter very much."

The air crackled with tension. For once attention centered elsewhere than on Jenna, but she could not be grateful, not with Charlotte's eyes reflecting a

346

troubled heart. Jenna's own heart went out to her. She suddenly understood why she had been taken into the Rockmoor home and given such affection. Charlotte had been lonely and had reached out to a needy stranger.

"Please excuse me, Lord Denham," Jenna said, standing and setting her sherry aside. "I'm sure you would like some time alone with your family." Not waiting for a reply, she whirled and hastened through the door that led into the garden.

The hour was not quite ten, and a late moon bathed the beds of shrubs and flowers in a silvery glow. At regular intervals along the geometrically laid-out paths, lamp-posts shed circles of light. A fresh breeze stirred the leaves in the wall of oak trees at the back of the garden. Jenna stood beside the house and breathed deeply of the fresh night air with its scents of chrysanthemum blooms and the nearby sea. After the flare of tension inside, the scene of beauty beckoned.

But it could not bring her peace. Walking slowly down the nearest path, the night air cool on her arms, she hugged herself and thought of that night at Piccadilly, of the instant liking she had felt for the woman, even before the coin had been offered, and the strong dislike she had felt for the man. Her opinions had been strengthened tonight.

And then there was Clay, protective of his sister, watchful of her, as liable to say what was on his mind as he was to—

"You're getting downright predictable, Jenna. As soon as charming Billy entered, I figured you'd hightail it out here."

Jenna knew a moment of pleasure because he had followed her, but the moment did not last long. When Clay stole upon her this way, he always arrived with questions she did not want to answer, and with dangerous temptations she did not want to resist.

Slowly she turned to face him. He stood on the

pathway directly behind her, a dozen yards from the doors to the withdrawing room, his tall, lean figure blocking her view of the house. His face was caught in the diffused glow from a lamp-post beside him. The flickering light made much of the planes of his sharp-hewn face, the strong cheekbones, the deep-set eyes beneath a shock of black hair, the masculine chin and firm lips that always seemed about to smile—or to interrogate.

She rather thought tonight the interrogation would come before the smile.

"Hightail it? I suppose that means to run away."

"Anybody ever tell you you'd make a fine Texan?"

Jenna felt a twist of her heart. Only Clay could do that, and he never would.

"I felt a need for air," she said.

"You felt a need to run. William has that effect."

"I—"

Clay kept on. "Or maybe you just didn't want to explain how you knew him. He didn't seem to recognize you."

She had to give Clay credit. He didn't let her dangle long, wondering when the questions would come. As usual, she had to sift through what she could tell him, and what she could not.

"I hate it when you get to thinking like that," he said. "Usually means lies are on the way."

"If I tell you, it will only raise more questions."

"If you tell me what?"

"Where I've seen Lord Denham before."

"Honey, I've already got more questions than I can juggle." He paused. "Is old Bill mixed up in the other little problem you've got roaming about that pretty head of yours, like maybe he's the gent you're looking for? I don't recall him smelling like a rose, but then that's something I might not have noticed."

Jenna shook her head. "No, nothing like that." It was her turn to pause. "At least not exactly. I did see him one night when he didn't see me."

348

"One of those parties where you were passing the drinks?"

Jenna wished that she could say yes.

"No. It was on a street near Seven Dials. He was with . . . a woman."

"Must not have been Charlotte."

Jenna wished very much she could tell him the true identity of the woman, the coarse beauty who had rubbed herself against Clay at the tavern, the wife of the giant Hector Mims.

"She was a prostitute."

"Son of a bitch."

Jenna felt the same.

"Can't say I'm surprised, though. What brother Bill needs is a shot to the crotch. Gun or boot, doesn't matter which."

Jenna tended to agree and decided she was getting as plain thinking as Clay and his sister.

Clay looked at her thoughtfully. It was a look she did not like.

"Don't suppose you'd care to tell me what you were doing in that part of the city, or how you knew what kind of woman she was."

"She was . . . obvious. As for why I was there, I would tell you if I could."

Clay stepped close, so close she could see the texture of the skin pulled taut across his cheeks, so close she could breathe in the manly scent of him, so close she could run her fingers across his lips if she only lifted her hand.

"I'll tell you the truth about me right now. I'm thinking that you've led a hell of a life for someone who hadn't known a man until a couple of months ago when you crawled into my bed."

Jenna took a step backward, but Clay followed. She imagined she could hear the beat of his heart, then recognized the pounding as her own quickening pulse.

Clay's eyes darkened. "I'm thinking you look so

tempting right now with that blue dress hugging all the parts I want to hug and that silk skin and those full lips that stay parted just enough to let me slip my tongue inside to the sweetness of you. I'm thinking I'd like to run my hands over that dress and that skin, and I'd like to pull you down on the ground and do some things to you that we'd both enjoy a hell of a lot."

His words frightened and thrilled her, and heated her blood.

"I'm thinking I'd like to make love to you until the sun comes up, and then start in again, and not stop until you tell me what is going on with that crazy life you lead. And then keep on making love to you because I don't much care what it is you tell me, only that you tell me the truth and we can get these questions between us out of the way."

He paused. He had not touched her, not even with the lightest touch of his fingers, and yet she felt such a raging desire for him that she could barely breathe, could barely stand.

"Jenna, you're the finest lady in town tonight, with all those fancy curls and that fancy dress and that look you have in those green eyes, as if you're telling a man you wouldn't touch him if he begged you, but just in case you did, he'd know he was touched by the most desirable, beautiful, warm and wonderful woman he'd ever known."

He bent his head and brushed his lips against hers.

"And you'd be right," he whispered.

Jenna trembled. This time he did not have to crush her against him until she gave in to his wishes. This time she threw herself at him, wrapped her arms around his neck, and thrust her tongue into his mouth to taste *his* sweetness, to take as hers all the pleasures that he offered, to show him, without the words that were forbidden to her, how much she loved him and how completely she was his.

His arms enfolded her. She felt small and protected

and at the same time powerful and in command. The kiss was long and deep, but where it should have satisfied, it gave rise to stronger urges that drove rational thoughts from her mind.

It was Clay who broke away, his mouth leaving hers, his face still close and his breath hot against her cheek. She felt the rapid rise and fall of his chest and, with her mind gradually clearing, the unwanted return of sanity.

"Do you know what you do to me?" he said, his voice so thick and husky she could barely recognize it. "Another minute and I would have had you on the ground right here in the light and I wouldn't have much cared whether everyone in the house came out, I could not have stopped until I was inside you. I don't know who you are, not yet, but I know you deserve better than that."

Jenna pressed her cheek against the roughness of his starched shirt, unwilling for him to see the tears that welled in her eyes. As hungry as he had been to make love to her, he had also been protective. Clay was forever a mystery to her, with his combination of manly desires and unexpected considerations. If she had not already fallen in love with him when she watched him befriend a pitiful child, she would have fallen in love with him tonight.

They stood embracing for a full minute, with only the rustle of leaves and the rich musical call of a nightingale to break the stillness . . . and, as always, the beating of their hearts.

When at last they stepped apart, Clay grinned down at her, but he did not lose the smoldering in his eyes.

"You've lost a couple of curls," he said. "I could try to fix them, but if I got my fingers in all that, I'd be more inclined to pull out the pins than do any straightening."

"Oh," was all she could say, and then, after a moment, "I don't suppose that would be at all the thing for you to do."

"Not right away."

It was evident from his tone and from the look on his face that eventually he would get his fingers in her hair, and he knew she would not stop him.

"Then I'd best take care of it myself." She attempted a casual smile, but the result was feeble. "If you'll excuse me, I'll slip around the house and go in the front door. Please make my excuses to Lord and Lady Denham."

"Don't let Bill's title throw you into being formal. He doesn't have it coming." Clay stared at her in thought. "But you've got the right idea. We'll give 'em some time alone to fight things out, or however they choose to go about it. In one of your stories you mentioned riding. Remember?"

"I—"

"Explaining your rough hands, as I recall. Tell you what," he said, taking her arm and guiding her toward the side of the house. "Meet me at the stables as soon as it's light tomorrow, and we'll do a little exploring of the countryside. Maybe I can give you a pointer or two about sitting a horse. If a fine equestrienne like yourself won't take offense."

Jenna was speechless.

They rounded the house and Clay stopped at the front door, at last letting go of her arm. "Think I'll take a little walk to cool down. You get on inside and get some rest because tomorrow I'm planning on a long, hard ride."

He brushed his lips against hers, and she watched as his long stride took him away from her and into the dark. Dismay assailed her. One of her lies had truly caught up with her, and for once she prayed he knew it. Surely he would show mercy and be waiting for her with a broken-down nag.

Just as she had promised—or at least she thought

she had promised, but Clay had been such a fast talker she couldn't remember exactly—Jenna showed up at the stables in a divided skirt and matching coat Anna found for her among Charlotte's extensive wardrobe.

"Never seen her wear them," Anna had said.

Even the servants were conspiring to get Jenna on a horse.

Clay was waiting outside the stables, his gloved hands holding onto the reins of the largest animal Jenna had ever seen. Black as ink, tall as a tree, and with a chest three times the width of Theodore, the horse was a formidable brute. Jenna took a glance at his hindquarters; she knew enough about animals to know a stallion when she saw one. What she didn't know was how to climb on him and once she was there, how to remain.

"Good morning," Clay said cheerily. He wasn't wearing any kind of riding wear she had ever noticed on Rotten Row. No jodhpurs for him, just plain denim trousers, a plaid shirt tucked in at his narrow waist, a red scarf at his throat, the Texas boots she loved, and, tilted low on his forehead, a broad-brimmed hat right out of a Western novel. He was the best looking man she had ever seen and her heart turned several loops.

She stopped right in front of him, ignoring the round black eye of the stallion regarding her with scorn and the magnificent bobbing head. She shoved her own hat away from her eyes and announced, "I've never been on a horse in my life."

He grinned. "Didn't think you had. I was kinda hoping you told the truth before I had to pitch you on Midnight's back and scare it out of you."

Jenna was at once relieved and irritated. "You already scared me. Congratulations."

"Just tell me the truth and I'll treat you better."

He turned, hooked a finger and thumb between his teeth, and let out a whistle that would have summoned a half dozen bobbies had they been in the heart of London.

In Brighton he got one young stableboy with a mahogany-coated mare in tow.

"Jenna, meet Susan, your mount. Charlotte named her. You'll have to ask her why."

Jenna eyed Susan suspiciously. She had to admit the mare looked far more docile than the stallion, although she still had absurdly long legs and her back was higher than the top of Jenna's head. Handing Midnight's reins to the stableboy, Clay picked up Jenna by the waist and set her down on Susan's back, legs astride.

"That's Charlotte's gear," he said. "She can't stand to ride sidesaddle."

Since Jenna had no experience either way, she couldn't see that it made much difference, not when she was having to concentrate with all her might just to stay upright. Thank heavens for the knob right in front of her; it gave her something to hold onto.

"Let go of the pommel," ordered Clay.

It took her a minute to realize he meant the knob. "Why?"

"Bad form."

"Isn't it worse form to fall off?"

"You won't."

"Don't bet on it."

"Jenna, I'm the expert here, and you're going to have to do what I say if we're ever going to get away from the stable." He took it upon himself to remove her hands from the saddle and thrust the reins into her grasp. She held on to the leather strips as though they were attached to something more substantial than the mare's mouth.

To her surprise he took hold of Susan's bridle—he told her what it was called, along with several of its parts—and began to lead the mare around the yard in front of the wide double doors. Around and around he went, talking as he walked, Jenna rocking back and forth as though she were in a parlor chair only she was far, far above the hard ground, but at last she got the rhythm of the walk and found herself enjoying listening to his lecture about some of the terminology he thought she needed to know.

What a patient man, she thought.

"Time to head out," he said as he let go of the bridle. Taking the reins from the stableboy, he threw himself onto Midnight with such grace that she was dumbfounded, so much so that she forgot to worry about controlling her own horse. Susan took it upon herself to head for the street in a most irregular trot and Jenna was bounced around the hard saddle unmercifully.

Clay caught up with her and proceeded to explain how, by using words, reins, knees and heels, she could make the horse stop and start, only he called it "whoa" and "giddyup." It was a great deal to remember, but at last they were under way. They moved slowly down the street, Clay directing them away from the main part of Brighton. By the time they made their way to a pasture on a high hill above the houses, Jenna felt she had got the basics down without making too much of a fool of herself.

Clay said the lessons had just begun, and for the next hour she worked harder than she had ever worked in her life. At first hesitant, she found she wanted to please him with her progress, and gradually she realized that what she wanted just as much was to be able to ride. When she successfully completed a lope around the crest of the hill and reined to a halt in front of Midnight, she heard herself laughing in enjoyment. Clay's answering chuckle put a permanent smile in her heart.

With the sun halfway toward noon, Clay and Midnight led Jenna and Susan along a winding path to a stream on the far side of the hill. Dismounting, he tied the horse to a tree stump and turned toward her. Hands on her waist, he lifted her from the horse as though she were weightless, and he slowly let her down in front of him, let her body rub against his, watched her face as she slid down, and his eyes sparked.

"You're a devil," Jenna said.

"Yep," he said, letting go. Her knees buckled. He caught her before she could fall. Jenna felt as though she still had the horse between her legs, and her thighs pained her badly.

"You don't look exactly passionate, Princess," he said. "Damned shame, but that's the way it goes sometimes."

"You really are a devil," she said, pulling away from him. On shaky legs, she took the reins from his hands and tied Susan to the trunk of a sapling near the stream. The mare immediately submerged her nose into the moving water.

Clay watered his own horse, pulled feed bags from a bundle tied to his saddle, and slapped them on both mounts. Another bag came out, and he ushered Jenna to a shady spot beneath a stand of trees away from the stream. "Breakfast," he said. "Bread and ham. Hope you like it."

Jenna viewed it as a feast; stretching out in the soft grass, she wolfed it down. Not until she had taken off her hat and coat and brushed the sweat from her brow, using a shirtsleeve, did she notice Clay was watching her with great care, his own food untouched. She felt suddenly self-conscious and wished he would look somewhere else.

"You didn't have much of a ride this morning. I must have slowed you down terribly."

"Tell you the truth, Jenna, I don't know when I've enjoyed a morning more."

"You know something?" she asked, looking him straight in the eye. "Neither do I."

She could have looked at him forever, at his flashing eyes and the black hair that fell onto his forehead beneath the brim of his hat, at the tanned column of

356

his neck with its red bandana, at his bristled cheeks. But she couldn't let her eyes reveal what was in her heart, and she looked away. "Do you have a chance just to ride back in Texas or are you always going to or from someplace?"

"Oh, I ride. Downright slothful of me, I guess."

Jenna couldn't imagine Clay ever being slothful. "Tell me more about the Whiskey."

He did, filling in the details he had omitted back in his Tunstall Square bedroom, and she told him all she could remember about her Transvaal home. Sometimes neither of them spoke, but the silence between was never awkward, never unwanted.

"I'd like your opinion about something," he said at the end of one particularly long period without talk. "Charlotte said something about your not caring much for anyone with a title hitched to his name. Why?"

"I didn't mean Charlotte," Jenna replied hastily. "She's a dear person and would never let her position keep her from looking at a person's true worth. But it's just that I've seen far too many of the other kind, the ones who believe themselves more valued as human beings because they have money or because they're lords and ladies. They expect obedience and homage, and I'm just not willing to give it automatically. But not Charlotte," she hastened to add. "She's not that way."

"But most everyone else is."

"It's been my experience that they are. If I never saw another duke or viscount in my entire life, it would be just fine with me."

"You sound mighty sure. And maybe just a tad bitter."

"I have reasons."

He started to say something, then shrugged. "Well, I asked. Just glad you don't feel the same about Charlotte."

Jenna assumed the question had been put to her

because of his sister, and she hoped she had answered him satisfactorily.

"Have you decided what to do about William and the woman I saw him with?"

"I'm cogitating on it." When he didn't elaborate, Jenna decided not to probe and another silence descended. It wasn't until the sun was high in the sky that he unwound his long legs and stood, then reached down for her.

He pulled her up beside him and cradled her face with his hands. "One of these days, Jenna, you're going to tell me everything about yourself, not just the early years."

Then he kissed her, sweetly, tenderly, as though he loved her with a lasting kind of love, and Jenna responded in kind. He broke the kiss, and she stared at his lips, willing them to say words she longed to hear.

"We'd better be getting back." They were not the words she had in mind, but they carried a nice edge of regret.

She looked up into his eyes. "I guess we better." She forced herself to casualness. "I don't suppose there's a carriage you could order, is there?"

"No, Princess, you have to get back on the horse."

As much as she had enjoyed the morning, Jenna was too sore to take the remounting with enthusiasm, but she kept her soreness to herself—or so she thought.

"I've got some liniment your maid can rub on your backside," Clay said as he threw his leg over Midnight and settled back in the saddle. He grinned wickedly. "Better yet, I'll do it. You'll forget your aches soon enough."

"What a gentleman," she said, "but I couldn't put you to the trouble." She reined Susan toward the path and felt a sense of accomplishment when the mare went where she wanted her to go. Sore as Jenna was, the ride back passed too quickly and suddenly she was standing on shaky legs in front of the stable thanking him for his care, loving him more than ever, and wishing she could read what was going on in his mind. He seemed to be wanting to tell her something, but Lord Denham strode down the walkway from the house to the stables, and Jenna bid them both goodbye.

She was standing at the edge of the house when she heard the earl say, "Be careful, Clayton. Don't get yourself too involved. We don't know anything about her, and a man in your position can hardly afford—" He turned away, his voice lowered, and Jenna could not hear the rest. Nor could she hear Clay's reply.

She felt as though a cloud had passed over her sun. William Rockmoor sounded like all the aristocratic men she'd ever heard at the asylum and at the fancy parties where she had worked. She had no idea what he meant by a man in Clay's position—probably just referred to his wealth.

Jenna wasn't after his money. She wasn't scheming for anything to do with him, but oh how she wanted everything. For a while today she had thought he felt something deep and abiding for her; she wouldn't let an overheard conversation push the wish-thoughts from her mind. Today Clay had shown her a different side; he had enjoyed her company without the sex that usually ended their times alone. Not that he hadn't thought about making love. She'd caught a look in his eye more than once, but he had used restraint. So had she.

As she hurried upstairs, she wondered if she were not enmeshed in impossible dreams. She, a poor orphan raised in a charity school, she a wanted woman and a recent resident of the Dials . . . today she felt the equal of the handsome and obviously wealthy Texan. Maybe the dreams weren't so impossible after all.

Just as promised, Clay sent a jar of cream, a foul-smelling salve, to her room. If she hadn't felt a dire need for it, she would have pitched it in the trash.

Even soft-spoken Anna made a comment about the odor as she rubbed the ointment onto Jenna's shoulders, back and legs. Whatever was in it, it worked and Jenna was able to join the Rockmoors and Clay at dinner.

The first thing Jenna noticed was a bruise on Lord Denham's cheek; he explained he had walked into a door. Jenna drew her own conclusions: at the stable Clay had mentioned the prostitute and William had objected. She could see no mark on Clay.

With Charlotte and her husband being studiously civil to one another, she did not push to talk to Clay alone except to thank him again for the morning. The next day was Saturday, and it was time for Jenna's venture into Brighton society, which was gathering for a dance in the ballroom of the Albermarle Hotel. Clay sent her a note saying he would like to see her in private before the evening, but she got so involved in her preparations that she was unable to comply.

She took such care that when the hour for leaving approached, she was the last to come down, this time donned in an extravagantly expensive lambent green gown that Charlotte had insisted on buying for the occasion. Low-necked and tight at the waist, with a flowing satin skirt that accented the gentle roundness of her hips, it made her look as grand as the grandest lady she was likely to encounter.

It was a perfect compliment to her tawny skin and red hair, which Anna piled precariously on top of her head, adding five inches to her height. When she swept into the withdrawing room to the waiting trio, she got an admiring glance from everyone.

She sat beside Clay on the ride to the hotel, determined to make the rounds of every group of men she saw, regardless of what they thought her purpose, to eavesdrop and if necessary ask whether anyone knew of the gentleman that she sought. If she didn't find him, then she just might tell Clay everything and let him advise her what to do. She needed to trust him as much as he was trusting her.

He helped her from the carriage, and she looked with trepidation at the sweeping front stairs and the glittering lights inside the hotel foyer. Charlotte and her husband—tonight they were Lord and Lady Denham—went on ahead, but Clay put a restraining hand on her arm.

"Jenna, there's something I'd like to ask you."

She looked up into his dark, solemn face, wondering if she should allow herself to speculate on the question. It couldn't be the one she wanted to hear . . . or could it?

"What exactly do you know about me and Charlotte?"

No, it most definitely was not. She answered him with the same solemnity in which the question had been phrased. "I know you're Charlotte's older and only brother and she's your only sister, schooled in England although like you she was born in Texas. She is married to an earl and considers herself an Englishwoman, but her marriage seems none too happy. I know your mother is best friends with a duchess and that you must have a great deal of money, that you like to ride, that you like children and have a generous nature, that you don't seem to care for the aristocracy any more than I do, that—"

She broke off and looked away.

"Jenna—"

"It's Viscount Parkworth," a woman trilled behind them. "I can't believe my eyes."

Jenna glanced around and saw a redheaded woman dressed in purple standing beside her. She looked for the viscount the woman had been referring to, but Clay was the only man around.

"Clayton, I didn't know you were in town, the woman continued without so much as a glance at Jenna. "Thank heavens you're here. The season will be so much brighter, so much more fun."

Jenna felt Clay's eyes on her and she looked up at him. "Viscount Parkworth?"

"That's what I wanted to talk to you about today."

He was ignoring the newcomer, but she would not go away.

"Where are your manners, Lord Parkworth? Introduce me to your friend."

She glanced at Jenna, her cold eyes lingering on the piled-up red hair. "I'm Lucinda Armistead. I see the devil has found another one." She glanced coquettishly up at Clay. "You *do* have a penchant for titian hair, don't you? Now, how is your charming mother? Is she here, too? I swear, to have Lady Libby in town would be too much. I simply swoon at the thought."

Jenna's mind raced. Lady Libby. Wife of the Earl of Harrow. Clay was the son of an earl and a countess, a viscount in his own right. He had told her as much a long time ago in his bed, but it had not been a time for believing such a story. She believed it now.

Jenna felt her dreams crash around her. Clay would someday be an earl, and she had been wondering if perhaps once her troubles were past she could someday be his wife.

Jenna Cresswell Drake, Countess of Harrow. It could never be.

"You look pale, Jenna," Clay said. "I'll get you inside where you can lie down."

"I'm all right," she murmured, trying to pull away from his grasp.

"Oh, dear, is something wrong?" asked Lucinda.

Clay ignored her. Jenna felt lightheaded, and Clay said, "You look like you're about to pass out."

To her complete and final humiliation, he swept her in his arms. "I'll get a room where you can lie down."

"No." She shook her head vehemently, and the poundings in her head that had at last ceased during the past days returned with greater potency than before.

"Don't argue with me, Jenna."

With a scattering of people watching everything that was going on, including an openmouthed Lucinda Armistead, he carried her up the front steps and into the hotel.

Chapter Twenty-seven

After a brief stop at the desk, Clay took her to a room at the back of the hotel's second floor. She did not struggle in his arms; she did not have the strength, and she knew above all else that with the future Earl of Harrow carrying her upstairs — and all eyes upon them — she must not cause a scene. If she had any struggles left within her, she would save them for the room.

He carried her inside and closed the door with his foot, still cradling her close. She kept her eyes downcast, her head in the crook of his shoulder, her arms wrapped around his neck.

"Can you stand?" he asked, his voice deep and filled with concern.

She nodded, and he set her down. Hands lightly on her shoulders, he said, "You scared the bejeebers out of me, woman. I thought you were going to pass out."

Jenna felt like a fraud. The dizziness had been momentary, and even the pain in her head was lessening; it was the shock of her discovery, and the distress, that remained. She forced herself to look up at him. "Just a little light-headedness, that's all. Truly, Clay, it has passed."

"And I know what caused it. You really care if I've got a title hooked to my name."

"Miss Armistead took me by surprise."

Clay muttered something about Lucinda under his

breath, but Jenna missed the exact words.

"We should have talked today," he said.

"Really, Clay, it's none of my concern."

"None of your concern?"

"Not really. I've got a few prejudices, that's all, and I felt ridiculously stupid because I didn't already know."

She turned away. The room was large, almost as large as the bedroom at the Tunstall Square home, with a bed that was high and wide. The draperies were closed to the night air, and a single lamp was turned low on a bedside table. The light it cast was enough for her to see the bed and the chairs that sat in front of a cold fireplace on the opposite wall, and it was enough for her to see the look in Clay's eyes when she turned back to face him. It was the look of a man who, if not actually in love, most decidedly wanted to *make* love.

"I want you to lie down," he said.

She was certain that he did.

"Your sister—"

"I'm going back down and explain that you've had a little relapse and need to rest. She'll understand. And don't worry. There won't be a breath of scandal for you to worry about."

"For *me?*"

"Of course for you. And Charlotte."

Jenna understood. Any scandal attached to her behavior would reflect on the woman who had so readily taken her in.

But she also understood that he was genuinely concerned about her reputation, too. With all her being, she would have preferred to dislike him at this moment—because of the class to which he belonged, because of the dictates of society that put him beyond her reach. She could not. But she realized, more sharply than ever, the futility of her love. The hilltop where he had taught her to ride and where they had spent such innocent hours getting to know one another seemed a universe away.

Jenna made no protest when he helped her to the

bed and attended her lying on top of the quilted covers, her green satin skirt spread around her, a thick down pillow propped beneath her head. He did not touch her except to see to her comfort, but his hands tantalized her, and so did the curve of his lips.

He headed for the door, then glanced toward the bed. "Don't go anywhere until I get back."

Where would I go?

She did not put the question into words, and then he was gone. She heard the turn of the key, and she wondered if he were locking her in or locking others out. There was only so much a locked door could save her from. It could not save her from her thoughts.

She closed her eyes and gave in to a sweep of loneliness. Clay had never pretended to be anything other than what he was. She was the one who wove dreams out of thin air.

She lay very still and waited for him to return, little knowing how she would behave when he strode back to the bed. She estimated half an hour had passed by the time the key turned in the lock. Closing her eyes, she listened as he entered and closed the door. His footsteps were firm as he walked to the bed and sat beside her.

"Sorry to take so long." He stroked a wisp of hair from her face. "Not asleep, are you?"

"No," she said but she kept her eyes closed. "What did Charlotte have to say?"

Sensing a tension in him, she looked at his face.

"Charlotte and William were having a private discussion. Well, semi-private. Baby Sister isn't much on subtlety when she's riled, and her voice tends to carry."

"What was the argument about?"

"William was saying he needed to get back to London, and she decided he was making a mistake." Clay shook his head in disgust. "She's the one who made the mistake, a big one two years ago."

"Why didn't the earl stop the wedding? Did William convince him he would be a suitable son-in-law?

Does he have money?"

"Money wouldn't matter to either Alex or Libby."

But there were other considerations that would, a fugitive as a future countess surely being one of them.

Clay continued. "Charlotte pitched a fit to get her way. She's like that sometime, or at least she used to be. A couple of years with Bill have taken some of the starch out of her. She's stubborn and outspoken, but she's learned the hard way that getting what you think you want isn't always the best."

Jenna saw the seriousness of her friend's plight. "There can be no divorce for her, you know. William would suffer no real loss of prestige, but she would be ruined."

"I'm not sure she would mind."

"Not at first. But she eventually would."

"You're mighty worried about it."

"I've told you how I feel about Charlotte."

"So you have."

A silence descended between them. Clay's eyes never left her face. He sat close beside her and stroked her satin skirt. "This is the first time I've seen you in bed with the light on."

Her pulse quickened, and she felt familiar stirrings inside. But for her, circumstances had changed. Yesterday she had been fooling herself that she and Clay could find a life together, but she had not been considering all the facts, the important ones being that she was a fugitive on the run and he was a peer of the realm.

"Do you know how hard it is to keep my hands off you? Even yesterday, which was very special for me, Jenna, I thought a time or two about our stretching out in the grass and making long, sweet love to you. I've got a lot of wanting stored up inside."

She steeled herself against him. "You could have done what William does."

"And what is that?" His voice was deceptively calm.

"I mean you could have done what men of your

class do when they want a woman."

"You mean hire a whore?"

"You have a way of putting things plainly, but yes, that's what I mean."

What she really meant was that now, knowing who he was and how things must be between them, she would feel like the woman he had believed her to be — the birthday gift — on that night she first crept into his room.

"I didn't say I wanted a woman, Jenna. I said I wanted you. You might not think that's much of a distinction, but it's a big one to me. What's going on in that head of yours? I never know."

She twisted away from him on the bed. Her skirt caught beneath her, but he held onto it and would not let her straighten it, nor get away.

"Let me go."

"No."

"Clay, this is absurd. You brought me up here to rest —"

"You don't look overly tired. In fact, I'd say there's a lot of fight in you right now. At least in your eyes. You're not claiming a headache, are you?"

She tried to jerk the dress from his hands, but he stubbornly refused to let go, and she found it impossible to do anything else but lie awkwardly beside him on top of the covers, her skirt twisted to reveal her ankles and calves, her breasts heaving above the low-cut neckline, her hair falling loose.

"I'm trying to claim some dignity." She held her head high, as best she could.

Clay grinned. "Jenna, there's lots that's been said about making love, but I don't recall anyone claiming that it's dignified."

"And who says we're going to make love?"

It was a foolish question. Slowly his grin faded, and his eyes warmed. He continued to sit at the side of the bed, turned to face her, his coat and tie and high collar as neat as they'd ever been, but that was not the way she saw him, not in her mind. She knew already that he was all muscle and sinew and tight, warm skin, his legs long and lean, strengthened by the same taut muscles that contoured his arms, his back, his chest. Tonight she considered the texture of that skin and just how brown it must have turned on his ranch.

The color would have faded some, but not completely. She wanted to see for herself.

He could hold a hundred titles, but he was also a healthy, lusty man, hard like the Texas granite mountains he had described to her, hot like the Texas sun.

Like Clay, she wanted to make love in the light. She wanted to watch his eyes and his lips respond to her, she wanted to see his fingers caress her breasts and, more, she wanted to see the lone place on his body that she could not imagine, not even after the nights of careful manipulation with her hands.

She touched his face and felt a rise of passion as her body responded to him. What use did she have of dignity? With her pulse pounding and her blood thickening, and her breasts tightening, she could think of no use at all, nor could she consider the morality of what she was about to do.

He read the unmistakable signs of hunger, the eyes that devoured him, the parted lips, the shallow breath. Even the tips of her breasts were hard and visible through the double thickness of chemise and satin gown.

He released the hold he had on her skirt and pulled her back into his arms. She knew how he interpreted her actions, assuming they sprang from raw lust instead of overwhelming love. He wasn't completely wrong. One was involved as much as the other; she admitted to it as her fingers touched his lips and his throat, and began to work at his tie.

He pulled her to her feet beside the bed, and she was surprised when he let her undress him, surprised because she went so slowly, letting her eyes and hands discover all the hard planes and angles that she had explored previously only in the dark. He managed his shoes for her, and his socks and the catch at his waistband, but she did the rest. His skin was as brown as she pictured it, slightly paler on his legs and abdomen, but dustings of black body hair more than made up the difference.

She averted her eyes as she pulled the last undergarments from him, and then he was standing before her naked and, it seemed to her, glorious. She looked at his erection, swallowed hard, and lifted her eyes to his. The heat of his stare burned into her and she wrapped her arms around him, letting his hardness press against her still-clothed body.

His hands make quick work of the hairpins and curls tumbled against her shoulders. She felt his lips against the tangled mass. He moaned, and his hands made even quicker work of her clothes.

He stepped back to look at her. She was swept with shyness, but she would not cover the intimate parts of her body with her hands. She watched him as he looked at her . . . looked at every part of her, read the rush of passion in his eyes and recognized it as the same passion coursing through her veins.

The desolation and the loneliness she had felt such a short while ago burned away in the heat of desire. She was caught by a womanly yearning and, just as strongly, by his manly needs.

"You are a beautiful woman, Jenna. How you can manage to look shy and impatient at the same time I can't figure, but then that's just another mystery I'll have to explore."

The words hung in the air, and she had no reply. He stepped close and his hands kneaded her breasts gently, a thumb flicking across each tip until it hardened and the aureole puckered and darkened to a deep pink. Desire became a roar in her ears, a heavy pounding in her throat, a pulsing low and insistent that could not be denied.

"Clay, make love to me. Now."

The words were no sooner spoken than she was in his arms, her body pressed into his heat, his mouth covering hers in a deep and thrilling kiss. He broke the kiss, and with smooth, sure movements, threw back the covers and pulled her into the bed.

He loved her in earnest. Words whispered against her sizzling skin, hands stroking, lips exploring everywhere his hands wandered, his eyes always devouring her as though he wished to look at her forever.

All shyness gone, Jenna let her own eyes feast on his long, hard body, on the powerful thighs and calves, on his taut buttocks, on the muscles of his chest and back, on the column of his neck, and on his face, his lips, his eyes, the black hair, the bristles of hair on his cheeks.

She kissed his eyes and drew back to watch them darken. She parted his lips with her fingers, ran a thumb across the edge of his teeth, dipped inside to feel the roughness of his tongue. He bit the tips of her fingers gently, she chided him softly, and again she kissed his eyes.

There was an innocence to their lovemaking and a fiery knowledge as well. She was in turn soft and yielding and fiercely demanding as she stroked his body, pressing her lips against his throat, his chest. She parted her thighs to let his probing hand perform its wonders on her. Tonight's rapture, tinged though it was with a bittersweet realization of all the differences between them, was stronger than anything she had ever known, coiling tightly around her, binding her to him without reservation and without any doubt.

She knew full well what she was doing. She was glorying in the intimacy she had known with only one man . . . the only man she would ever give herself to. For all she knew, this would be the last time they would make love, and the knowledge drove her to daring. She held him, kissed him, and at last opened herself to him and welcomed his entrance.

His thrusts were quick and deep, desire spiraled, and they reached glorious ecstasy together. She held

371

him tightly, knowing that soon, much too soon, she would have to let him go. She held him tightly; desiring the impossible, she wanted to trap his heat inside her body so that she could carry it with her after he was gone.

She held him tightly because it was the only way she could tell him that she loved him.

Too soon he pulled away. Gone was the brief loving time of holding him close and listening to the rhythms of his breathing, pressing her lips against his chest and feeling his lips brush against her hair. She had thought they could lie in each other's arms all night long.

But like so many of her other wishes, this one was not to be. He kissed her once, sweetly, then rose from the bed and began to dress.

"What are you doing?" she asked.

"Going back downstairs. I don't want anyone speculating as to what's happening up here." He grinned down at her. "With a woman as beautiful and mysterious as you, they'll be on the lookout to see just when you return, and whether I'm with you when you do."

She felt abandoned; knowing she was irrational, she took offense. She did not care what others thought, not after what had just passed between them, and it hurt that he should.

She pulled the covers over her body and brought them close to her chin. "You seem mighty concerned about my reputation."

He buttoned his shirt. "Mighty? Why, Jenna Who-ever-you-are, you're beginning to pick up some of my bad habits." He looked at the wrinkled sheets. "And some good ones, too."

"I don't want to go back down there. Not now."

"Honey, neither do I, but I'd better put in an appearance. If you'd like, stay in bed for a while. I'll send Charlotte."

She watched as he worked at his tie and pulled on the cutaway coat. He looked every inch a viscount, every inch the son of an earl.

"Why are you being so careful?" she asked.

Once again he sat on the edge of the bed. "Don't get the idea I think we're doing anything to be ashamed of, but you know the way folks can be. You're the one likely to be hurt by talk, and once you get out of whatever it is you're trying to keep secret, I want you to hold your head high."

Jenna wanted to tell him that she was not ashamed, that she had been accused publicly of something far worse than making love, but she kept silent. The differences between them yawned wider than ever. Shivering beneath the covers, she watched in silence as Clay stood.

"Want me to strike a fire?" he asked.

She shook her head. "I'll be down before long. There's no need for Charlotte to come up here, but it's going to take me a while to get my hair pinned up again." She made herself sound as practical as he had a moment before. "You're right, Clay. We should not draw more attention to ourselves than necessary."

She saw the puzzlement in his eyes. "Why is it we're agreeing with one another and I get the feeling we're not talking about the same thing?"

"We are talking about the same thing. Reputations. You certainly have one to uphold far more than I."

"Who said I was thinking about me? I'm a crude and rude Texan, Jenna. Even Libby gives up on me from time to time."

Jenna could not picture his mother, but she suddenly remembered the Duchess of Castlebury striding into an upstairs parlor and catching her and Clay on a bearskin rug. It had been bad enough for a servant to cavort with a visitor from America, but with the son of an earl —

The situation was impossible. An accused murderess, a resident of the slums for the past year, a beggar on the streets of London — she had sought refuge in the home of the wife and daughter of earls. If word got out about Jenna's past, the news would of necessity reflect on the entire family, and she owed Clay and Charlotte more than that. Scandal of the proportions she would bring upon the Harrow name would haunt them for years.

She shuddered at the thought. As much as Jenna disliked the class system of her country, she was English enough to know just how bad her indiscretion had been, even if Clay did not.

And she had just enough pride left to look the Viscount Parkworth in the eyes. "Nevertheless, Clay, you do have a reputation to think about. And you're right — so do I. We've been self-indulgent tonight."

Anger flashed across his face. "Now that's one description I hadn't put to it. I thought we ware making love."

Jenna forced herself to smile at him. She liked him angry; she handled him better that way. He was tough, hardened on a Texas ranch, but she had been hardened in the slums of London and she would put her training up against his any day.

"We were making love, Clay. And now it's time to go back to the ball. Remember your sister. She's having a hard enough time managing an unfaithful husband without taking on the censure of her friends."

"I always said I liked a practical woman. Never thought I'd — " He waved a hand in disgust. "Aw, hell, you're calling the shots right now. I'll see you downstairs."

After he was gone, a coldness settled within Jenna, and she hurried to the adjoining bath. Filling the tub with hot water, she proceeded to soak her body and remove all traces of the past hour from her skin. When she was done, she set about pinning up her hair. In less than an hour after Clay had left, she followed his footsteps into the ballroom, sought out Charlotte who was talking with Lucinda Armistead at the edge of the dance floor, and announced she was feeling much better.

Catching Clay's eyes on her from time to time, she

proceeded to dance with a half dozen gentlemen, always listening for a high-pitched voice. But her thoughts kept returning to Clay. She could see how things were shaping up. Wealthy, titled men kept mistresses; he could very easily be considering setting her up as such for his pleasure when he was in England.

As Clay himself might have put it, like hell he would. For himself as well as for the view she must hold for herself, she could never allow such a situation to exist.

Forty-eight hours later, long hours during which she made sure she and Clay were never alone, the four of them attended another party, this time at the home of an acquaintance of Lord Denham.

"I'll need to make an early night of it," Denham announced as they were preparing to get in the waiting carriage he had summoned for the ride. "My train leaves early for London."

Charlotte did not respond. Whatever arguments she had to throw at him she must have already thrown, because Jenna noticed her eyes were rimmed with red.

Clay must have noticed the same thing, for he had a tight look about his face. But then he had worn a similar look ever since leaving her in the Albermarle bed.

The home to which they had been invited was on the Royal Crescent. Carriages were lined in front, and it took them several minutes to get inside. As soon as Jenna stepped into the entryway, her senses became alert. The scent of roses was everywhere. She turned to Clay and saw that he also noticed.

The flowery aroma was probably just a coincidence, she told herself, having lately decided the task she had set for herself was impossible.

The four of them were guided by a footman into a spacious sitting room. A scarf-covered grand piano occupied one end, a marble fireplace the other, and scattered in between were groupings of sofas and chairs. She estimated the number of guests who had already arrived at two dozen, all of them formally dressed, most of the women overjeweled for an at-home, but then she was hardly an arbiter of acceptable taste.

She saw right away where the scent of roses came from; vases of the flowers graced pedestals and tables in every direction she looked. She stepped ahead of the others.

"William, how good it was of you to come. I know what a busy schedule you keep."

The man's voice came from behind her. Closing her eyes for a moment, she remembered huddling on the floor of the abandoned glove factory and hearing exactly that same high-pitched tone.

Slowly she turned. Tall and thin, his features angular except for a pair of incongruously thick lips, his thinning hair carefully groomed, he stood in the doorway to the sitting room three feet away. One deep breath was enough to tell her the fragrance of his cologne; it blended with the rest of the room.

She did not recognize the face as one she had seen before, but she knew with absolute certainty that this was the man she sought. Darkness had protected him, but darkness could not hide his scent nor his voice.

Her eyes darted to Clay. Slowly she nodded. She had found her man.

Chapter Twenty-eight

Clay knew the search was over, even before he saw the look in Jenna's eyes. He liked the way she turned to him for help. He liked it a lot — and he liked having one of her stories proved. At least proved to him, what with the man in question reeking like a flower bed and sounding like someone had a grip on his throat.

Not that Clay had doubted there had been such a man. At least, he hadn't exactly, but he hadn't much cared. Whatever kept Jenna around was all right by him.

He'd been making plans, and he liked the current odds of seeing them through, no matter how she disliked his title.

But first to their host. Vincent Bartholomew, William had said in the carriage, a dabbler in investments who was the last descendent of old English family. Clay gave him a once-over and dubbed him Black Bart, mostly because of the color of his pomaded hair. All in all, he didn't look much like a desperado. Biscuit skin, body nothing more than skin over bones, eyes flat and sunken. The only thing plentiful about him was his mouth, which was as fat as a worm from a Whiskey Ranch creek bank and, come to think of it, the same color, too.

William performed the introductions, stumbling when he came to the female guest in his home, but his friend assured him he had already heard of the terrible mishap which had brought on her amnesia.

Vincent turned to Clay with a handshake about as firm as his lips.

"Parkworth, I've been wanting to meet you. Lord Denham had mentioned you were his brother-in-law."

As William should have done. He wouldn't have much of a bank account without the Harrow connection. With more time than duties on his hands in the city, Clay had done some checking to make sure his suspicions were actually true. Without Charlotte's money, which the law put squarely in her husband's possession, Brother Bill would have been hard pressed to hire the whore Jenna had told him about.

Lord Debtor, he was called in a few financial circles. Clay had enjoyed planting a fist in his face the other day when he'd made the mistake of badmouthing Jenna. William promised not to speak badly of her again.

"Bartholomew," said Clay with a nod, and let the greeting go at that. He wasn't much at talking to strangers except to get to the point of whatever business brought them together, but it wouldn't be the best strategy to lay things on the line right away. *You the one who set up robbing the Queen?* Black Bart might take offense.

Charlotte excused herself to join a group of ladies standing by the piano and asked if Jenna would go with her.

"In a minute," Jenna said.

Clay would just as soon she got out of the line of fire, or at least out of the middle of whatever approach he settled on. It wouldn't be shooting, unarmed as he was, and besides, they needed Bartholomew to talk, not turn belly up and expire. But Jenna wasn't one for doing whatever he wanted without asking questions.

Except in bed, which was a thought better saved for later.

The best he could hope for was that she didn't plan on causing a ruckus, not right away. Clay was having trouble enough acting civilized around William, and now he had another bastard on his hands. As far as he could see, one was about as bad as the other. Clay figured that once the "I-do's" were said, when it came to sleeping with other women — professionals or the kind that just liked to play around — a man was obligated to come up with an "I-don't."

He concentrated on Black Bart. "You get into London often?"

"I have a townhouse there." Bartholomew's eyes revealed a mild interest. Dark and sunken as they were, they looked like raisins in the dough-colored face. "Why do you ask?"

"Just wondering why our trails haven't crossed."

"Our trails — Oh, I see. How droll you are, Parkworth. I've been on the continent for the past few weeks."

"Business?"

"Pleasure." His fat lips twitched. "I did not care for the August climate of the city."

Jenna stirred.

"A lot of thieves running around, too." Clay kept his eyes on Bartholomew's face. "Early August, I think it was, someone tried to rob the Queen herself."

He saw what he was after in the depths of Black Bart's eyes. A flicker of recognition, an acknowledgment he knew exactly what his guest was referring to, but he'd see hell freeze over before he admitted it.

Guilty as charged. But it wasn't evidence that would stand up in court, and it wouldn't free the juggler Jenna showed so much concern about.

William broke in. "I didn't know you kept up with such sordid events, Clayton. You surprise me."

Clay gave a minute's attention to his brother-in-law. Bland and neat as usual, like one of the puddings his hostesses kept shoving his way, only he was wearing a look that said he didn't quite know what Clay was getting at and he'd be a damned sight happier if he would stop. Whatever crimes Bartholomew was up to, Clay doubted William was involved. Somehow he couldn't see Brother Bill having the gumption to plan a crime like the one Jenna had described, much less carry it out.

Clay shrugged. "Oh, I'm interested in criminal types." He looked back at his host. "In Texas we're given to bank and train robberies, and an occasional holdup. I've been curious if things are any different over here."

Bartholomew smirked. "Whitechapel murders interest you? Jack the Ripper and all that?"

"Really," said William, the look of unhappy puzzlement still on his face. "That's hardly a subject for polite conversation. We mustn't forget a lady is present."

"Don't mind me," said Jenna.

Clay shot her a warning look. If she read him at all, she would know he wanted her gone. As expected, she stood her ground. She looked lovely tonight, in a dress the color of bluebonnets, her hair worn looser than usual, her green eyes downright bright. She didn't look like much of a detective; mostly she looked like someone who would get in the way.

"Man talk," he said. "We have to mind you, or else you'd be bored. Why not see what Charlotte's doing? She's probably stirring up some kind of controversy." With his back to William and Bartholomew, he stared at Jenna long and hard.

At last she nodded, even though she did not look in the least bit pleased. "I believe I will join Charlotte. You will call if you need me, won't you?"

Clay winked. "Sure thing."

He watched her walk away, her body slim, her hair a mass of red, her hips swaying beneath the blue dress. Yes, sir, he had plans.

He turned back to the men. William still looked as though he didn't know exactly what was going on; the look seemed permanent.

"You said something about Jack the Ripper," said Clay. "He killed prostitutes, didn't he? Never was found. It's enough to keep men and women both off the streets."

"Really, Clayton," put in William, "I would prefer the conversation be about those cows you're so proud of rather than such an unpleasant subject."

"What subject is that, Bill? Prostitutes? Why, I'd be willing to bet a cow or two you don't find them unpleasant at all."

"What exactly is that supposed to mean?"

"Gentlemen," said Bartholomew. "If you have private matters to discuss—"

"I do not," William barked.

Clay shrugged. Black Bart was the fish he was trying to hook; he'd get to Bill later.

"I confess to being a mite short there with Bill," he said to his host, by way of apology, but he didn't give so much as a glance to his brother-in-law. "The truth is, I've got a thirst for some whiskey. Not brandy or sherry, you understand. Some rotgut would do, but I don't imagine you have a jug of that sitting around."

"Rotgut," said Bartholomew, who put a little trill on the first syllable. "That's a phrase one does not hear often. So descriptive." His smirk looked to be as permanent as William's distress. "I could check with the butler, but somehow I believe he would say no."

"Just a thought."

"I do, however, have a decanter you might be

interested in trying."

Clay saw he was speaking from pride. He took it as a flaw in the man's character, one he might start working on.

"Whiskey, you're talking about, right? Not sherry."

"And not brandy. This particular nectar is distilled from the finest grains in Scotland. You might find it pleasing to your palate."

"If you mean it'll go down easy"—Clay figured it wouldn't hurt to overdo the country-boy role—"I'm willing to give it a try. How about you, Bill? We could get us a glass and talk about women some more."

"None for me," William shot back. "I see you've invited a business acquaintance from the city, Vincent. If you will excuse me—"

He beat a hasty retreat into the sitting room, which was exactly what Clay was aiming for.

"Wait just a moment." Bartholomew followed William, spoke to one of the guests seated in the room, a middle-aged, blocky woman in a black dress, then returned to lead Clay across the hall into the library.

"My aunt," he explained as he gestured for Clay to enter. "She acts as my hostess when I'm in Brighton. A widow, rather tedious really, but then she serves her purpose, I suppose."

The room they entered was dimly lit and lined with shelves of massive tomes, all upright and neat and looking as though they'd never been read. The air was close and warm, and like the rest of the house it smelled of roses, only in this case the scent was stale. Clay felt an urge to open one of the windows, but decided maybe privacy was a better idea after all. Never could tell who might be roaming around outside and listening. Jenna was a name that came to mind.

Bartholomew walked ahead, fiddled at a table, then turned back and smiled. Except for the lips, he looked like a hungry timber wolf. The lips gave off signals he was a man who indulged himself. It was a combination that might lead a man to crime.

Clay gripped the cut crystal glass that he was offered and took a swallow. The whiskey went down smooth, the way a fine aged whiskey ought to. The wallop that followed said a great deal for the high alcohol content. Clay felt he'd been hit in the solar plexus with a velvet glove; it was not at all an unpleasant sensation.

"Good stuff," he said to his host.

"I sincerely hope you find it better than rotgut." Again Bartholomew put in a trill.

At a gesture from his host, Clay sat by the unused fireplace. Bartholomew settled in an adjoining chair.

Clay didn't waste words. "Back to that robbery I was talking about. The one involving the Queen. You got any interest in crime? You look like a man who might be."

"What is that supposed to mean?"

"Just what it sounds like. I'd say you're a man with a lot of interests." He let his eyes roam around the room. A hick from the sticks, who just happened to hold a title, that's what he was. He made himself seem impressed, especially by a pair of pistols mounted on the wall beside the fireplace and by a brass-handled sword that flanked the opposite side.

"All these books, bound to keep a man interested in most everything that comes along. Including an occasional bending of the law. No harm in being interested, now is there?"

"Of course not."

"I got a theory, Vincent. Don't mind if I call you that, do you? We're a hell of a lot more informal in Texas. Still a frontier in some ways. If you know what I mean."

"I'm not sure that I do."

"You know, shoot-em-up style."

Bartholomew's eyes widened a fraction. "You're carrying a weapon?"

"Now that's a question you don't ask a man. Not back in Mason." Clay knew a sheriff who would take issue with that particular remark, but Mason's finest law enforcement officer was far, far away.

"Parkworth, I find it most difficult to believe you're the viscount I have heard described in such complimentary terms. The earl has such an unblemished reputation—"

"Meaning maybe he's better'n me?" He leaned forward in the chair and frowned at his host. "Now, I'd like not to take offense, I'd like it a whole lot." He let the words sound like a threat.

"There was no offense intended. I was making nothing more than an observation."

Clay took a while to consider the remark, then nodded once. "Mighty fine. We're both men of the world, right? We've done some traveling, riding in different directions maybe, but traveling all the same. The minute I saw you I figured you were an hombre who liked to enjoy things. Kind of a kindred soul, you get my drift?"

Clay watched the play of expression on Bartholomew's face. There wasn't much to watch. The man was wary, but he was also intrigued by the confidential tone of the viscount's voice and by the strange things he was saying. Clay chalked up another character flaw. Black Bart was a snob.

Bartholomew sipped at his whiskey, but his sunken eyes were busy sizing up Clay. "You spoke of a crime. A robbery of the Queen, I believe. You mentioned it twice."

"So I did. It seemed to me that whoever planned to heist the old woman's jewels had a right fine idea, fearless enough to take everyone by surprise, and the promise of reward was great."

384

He could have sworn Bartholomew puffed with pride, but more than likely he just wanted him to.

"As I recall the news stories," said Bartholomew, "the police were not certain who was the intended victim."

It was Clay's turn to be wary. "Thought you claimed you didn't remember anything about that particular misdeed."

"You remember wrong. William was the one who responded."

Clay took another swallow of whiskey, stretched his long legs in front of him, and, with his glass held up for another shot, made an alteration in the way the talk was heading. "Brother Bill. He'd never consider the possibilities of living at the edge of the law, but then I always had doubts about what he wore dangling between his legs. Living dangerously can be better than taking a woman. Why, I can get a hard-on just . . . but then maybe I'm going too far. Difficult to tell with an Englishman just how honest he's willing to be."

He watched his host watch him. The thought had occurred to him that old wolf-face might be the kind who didn't like women, but he couldn't see that the man was looking at him with any particular interest other than trying to figure out what his unusual guest was up to.

Bartholomew unwound his gaunt body from the chair. "Difficult, yes. One has to be very careful in expressing oneself."

He brought the decanter to the table that sat between the chairs, poured two more drinks, then raised his glass in a toast. "Most unusual, Parkworth, most unusual to find a man of your position speaking in such a—shall we say candid manner?"

"You seen many cowpokes with a title running around these parts?"

Twirling the whiskey glass, Bartholomew shook his head.

"Damned right you haven't. The earl prefers to keep me hidden in Texas, if you want to know the truth." He lifted the glass, pretending to take a deep swallow, then shook his head. "Damn stuff's loosenin' the tongue." He put a slur to his voice. "Didn't plan on sayin' that about stayin' in Texas. My little secret." He laughed stupidly.

"Incredible."

Setting the glass on the table, Clay brought himself unsteadily to his feet and made an uneven way to the pistols. He ran his hand over the handle of first one, then the other. Sterling silver and elaborately engraved, they appeared to be at least a hundred years old.

He removed one from its perch and grinned back at Black Bart, who remained in his chair. He waved the pistol in the air. "You know, guns like this kinda remind me of jewels you see on a woman. Tempting, that's what they are."

"For stealing."

Clay chuckled. "For borrowing on a permanent basis."

"I suggest you do not try to take them when you leave, no matter how aroused you would be by the theft. They are in truth quite valuable."

He put Bartholomew squarely in the center of the sight.

"No, wouldn't try anything like that. Don't be nervous, Vincent. The gun isn't loaded." He returned the pistol to the wall and went for the sword, which hung on a matching plaque. Pulling it from its sheath, he waved the weapon in the air.

"Now take something like this. Don't have to fool with ammunition." He had an easy time slurring the last word. "It's ready to go right away."

"You're drunk, Parkworth."

"Maybe a little. It's just so damned good to be myself for a change. All that mealy-mouthed talking and playing the gentleman. That ain't what I am at all. Hell, I could tell you a few things that would curl your toes. Been hangin' out in the Dials. You ever hear of the place? It's in the city. Rough part of town."

"Seven Dials. Yes, it is a notorious slum. You truly do surprise me."

"Well, see, I was there one night. Been havin' a drink in one of the taverns and lookin' for a woman like the kind I'm used to back in Texas. Had a little too much, passed out and someone relieved me of my money. Came to and heard this bastard braggin' about how he was gonna kidnap some kid and rob the Queen."

Sword in hand, he made his stumbling way back toward his chair. "Whoever he was talkin' to called him by name. Bertie Groat. Funny kind of moniker that sticks with you, know what I mean? They talk funny in the Dials, but I got that name, by God. And," he added with emphasis on every word, "that ain't the only one I heard."

He lifted the sword and, standing over Bartholomew, touched the point to the man's throat, just above the edge of his high, stiff collar. "Wanna guess what the other name was?"

Bartholomew held still, his eyes unmoving in his pale, wolf's face. "Don't be ridiculous. How on earth would I know?"

"Now don' be thinkin' I don' know what I'm talkin' about. Vincent Bartholomew" — he made a mess of the name — "is a mouthful I ain't likely to forget. When I heard you were Brother Bill's friend, why, I said to myself, that's Bertie's friend, too. Only Bertie's dead. Read about it in the paper."

"I demand you remove the sword immediately." Somehow Black Bart didn't pull off the indignation he was after. "You're drunk," he added, sounding a trifle feeble for all the effort he put in the accusation.

Clay decided it was time for sobriety. "You'd be better off if I were, Vincent. Bertie Groat was very clear, and he was not, I assure you, under the influence of alcohol."

The change caught Bartholomew by surprise. Sweat broke out on his brow. "Impossible. Groat never knew my—" He stopped himself, but it was too late.

Clay smiled. He saw Bartholomew's hand edging toward his coat.

"Packing a gun, are you? Don't go for it. You're in enough trouble as it is without adding attempted murder to the charges."

Bartholomew caught him with a shoe to the groin. It missed its primary mark, but the flat sole struck Clay in the abdomen. Thrown off balance, he stumbled backward. The hand holding the sword flew to the right, and the blade struck the whiskey decanter. It fell to the floor with a crash.

The door to the library flew open, and Jenna rushed in. "Clay!" she yelled.

Bartholomew whirled on her, a snub-nosed pistol in his right hand. He pointed it at her heart.

"Get back!" Clay shouted, waving her away with the sword.

She was frozen in place.

The hammer on the gun clicked.

Clay moved fast, acting on instinct and fear for Jenna's life. He brought the sword down in a sweeping arc. The gun fired just as the blade struck Bartholomew's wrist, sliced neatly through, and kept on going, its tip tearing a hole in the carpet at Bartholomew's feet. In a spew of blood, the hand, still clutching the smoking gun, fell to the carpet by the tear.

Bartholomew clutched at the blood-slick stub, his white shirt turned crimson where he held the arm. He swayed once, his head turned to Clay but there was no recognition in his eyes, just uncomprehending horror.

Time stopped. The air echoed with the report of the gun and with Bartholomew's cry of anguish as he slipped to the floor, unconscious.

"Oh, my God," Jenna whispered.

"He was going to kill you." Clay threw the bloodied sword aside. He saw the mark of the bullet in the wall close to Jenna's head. A sickness hit him in the stomach, and the whiskey rose bitter as bile in his throat. He swallowed hard, his eyes still on Jenna as he repeated, "He was going to kill you."

Whatever else he wanted to tell her was lost in the noise made by the guests who were fast crowding into the hall outside the library door.

Chapter Twenty-nine

Clay knelt beside Bartholomew's still body, checking for a pulse at his throat. Jenna forgot the blood and thought of helping Clay as she rushed to his side, barely aware that there were others behind her.

"Is he dead?" she asked.

"Get back."

Ignoring the order, she knelt beside him, her blue skirt catching the flow of blood from the raw and terrible wound. She took a deep, steadying breath, but the smell emanating from the cut sickened her. "Is he dead?" she repeated.

Clay's head shook once. "The pulse is weak. We'll need a tourniquet."

Jenna grabbed for the nearest thing at hand, her petticoat, which like her skirt was stained with crimson. Her fingers trembled, and she cursed her show of distress. The cloth would not tear. Clay helped her, rending a long swath along the hem.

"Now get back."

This time she obeyed him, standing and stepping away from the spread of blood. She swayed and found herself enfolded in a pair of steadying arms.

"Don't faint," Charlotte ordered, sounding much like her brother. "I can't hold you up if you do."

"I won't faint." Jenna gradually became aware of a crowd of men flowing into the room, of harsh cries and questions filling the stale air. More than one turned away with a face as white as paint.

"My God!" one man kept saying over and over. It was a comment that echoed around her.

Bent over Bartholomew, Clay paid no mind to the crowd. Jenna shook her head, trying in vain to remove the ugly pictures in her mind.

"She needs fresh air," Charlotte said to the men behind her, and immediately a corridor opened for the two of them. In the hallway they met a phalanx of stark and curious faces. The sea of black suits and bejeweled finery into which Charlotte led her made the scene they were leaving all the more horrible.

With Charlotte's arm tight around her, they headed for a closed door opposite the library.

"What happened?" The question was shouted more than once.

"An accident," Charlotte said. "Please summon a doctor. Mr. Bartholomew has been hurt."

Staring at the closed door in front of her, Jenna saw the arc of the sword and the glint of lamplight on the sharp edge, as clearly as if the weapon were painted on the wood. She squeezed her eyes shut.

In the darkness behind her lids, the images of sight and sound all seemed to be one, the descending blade, the blood, the roar of the gun . . . and the scream. Jenna did not think she had screamed except in her mind, but the sound reverberated in her memory louder than the shot.

It wasn't because of the act itself, nor the blood, nor even the falling hand that she had felt such horror. She had seen the look on Clay's face, the revulsion in his eyes, the mouth tight, the skin, usually so tanned, pale and taut against his cheeks.

Between them had risen the sickly sweet stench of blood mingled with roses.

She had brought him to this. Brave, wonderful Clay with the warm look in his eyes, the wry twist of his lips, the scent of outdoors about his person. She had brought him to this act of violence, because she herself had committed an act of violence. She could see a thread connecting the two moments, the crack of a head on a marble hearth and the arc of a blade.

When she opened her eyes, she was in a small parlor, and Charlotte's arm was still around her shoulders.

Charlotte's gown rustled as she pulled away, and then Jenna was in Clay's arms, her head against his shirt, his hands stroking the silk that rested against her back. Charlotte busied herself by opening a window to bring a fresh breeze into the room.

"He tried to kill you, Jenna."

She forced her worst thought to words. "Is he dead?"

"Just unconscious. The doctor is on the way." He hesitated. "And the police."

Of course. The police would have to be called. In all the ways she had pictured finding the man who had plotted with Bertie Groat, she had been unable to imagine the details of his arrest and confession. No longer was her imagination necessary. The police were on the way. She discovered she was not afraid. Instead she felt relief. At last the truth would come out.

Charlotte spoke up. "Clay, what is going on? What happened in there?"

"He was going to kill her," Clay said. "He's a thief and Lord knows what else, and he was going to kill her." He held Jenna close. "Are you all right?"

Jenna nodded.

He kissed the top of her head. "And you were right. Before you came in, he'd just about confessed."

Her trembling started anew. "His hand, Clay." Her voice was little more than a sob, and she hated herself for her weakness. She pushed away and looked up at him. "It's all my fault. I was listening by the door. I heard the crash. If I hadn't come running in—"

"He would have aimed the gun at me instead of you. And he might have got off a pretty damned good shot."

"But his hand. I saw it. It just . . . just fell."

Clay took a deep breath. "Remember there was a gun in that hand. If you have to remember anything, Jenna, remember that gun."

"Jenna," said Charlotte. "Is that really your name?"

"It came back to her," said Clay, but he did not say where or when. "Just the one name. Jenna."

"It's a start," said Charlotte. "Now if I could figure out exactly what went on in that room—"

"I told you. Vincent Bartholomew is a thief and probably worse. I suspected it. Don't ask how, but I did."

"But he's William's friend."

"I doubt if your husband is mixed up in a life of crime. Where is Brother Bill, by the way?"

"He's seeing to Bartholomew's aunt." Charlotte sighed in exasperation. "I still would like to know just what is going on. How could you suspect a man of thievery when you just met him for the first time?"

"You're a mighty stubborn woman. I'll explain it to the police. They should be here shortly."

When they arrived, they would learn far more than they expected. Jenna pushed away from Clay and turned to stare out an open window. Her eyes fell to the purple-black stains lying damp and jagged across the bottom half of her blue silk skirt.

"Jenna," Clay said to her back, "there's no need for you to talk to the lawmen if you don't want to. I can handle everything."

She turned to face him. "But it's my story."

"They don't know that."

Charlotte stood before them, hands on hips. "Clay, would you please explain just how it's her story if she can't remember her last name?"

"No."

"Well, that's blunt enough."

"Do me a favor, Baby Sister, and take your cues from me. Listen and learn. That's the best advice I can give."

"Clay," Jenna said, unable to still a few of the questions burning in her mind, "do you think Morgan can be cleared?"

"Morgan?" said Charlotte.

"Jenna," said Clay, "I would imagine Bartholomew will be ready to clear anyone he can in return for some considerations on the attempted robbery charges. Remember, the Queen was involved."

"I hope you're right."

"The Queen?" said Charlotte.

"Ladies," said Clay, his eyes shifting from Jenna to Charlotte, "I'm going to repeat my advice. Listen and learn. And for God's sake, don't speak until or unless you're spoken to" — Jenna thought that particular warning was meant especially for her — "and back up everything I say."

A quarter of an hour later, the three of them, joined by William, were confronted by a pair of uniformed bobbies in the small parlor. The questions came after the officers had talked to the doctor and examined Bartholomew's wound for themselves.

"Nasty bit o' business," one of them commented after William escorted them into the room.

"Everybody else is gone," William informed the gathering. "At least most everybody. One of the women volunteered to stay with Vincent's aunt, and one of the men is accompanying him to the hospital. The doctor says he's in shock but should recover with no problems except," he said with a shudder, "for the loss of a hand, of course."

"Oh," said Jenna in a small voice.

"We'll discuss details later," said Clay.

"I've told you all I know," said William with a sniff. "I plan to put this entire sordid incident from my mind. If any of us is allowed to. The scandal—"

"We'll all manage to handle it," said Clay.

Jenna wished she could be as sure.

"Can we get on with the questions?" one of the officers asked.

Jenna steeled herself for whatever was to come. She fully expected the policemen to center their attention on her, to listen to her retelling just what she had heard in the glove factory and, more, to learn why she had been there to begin with.

But she did not give enough credit to Clay. She sat in wondering silence as he told of taking an instant dislike to Bartholomew and of deciding to play a game with him. A Texas game, he explained to the bemused officers, and went on to describe how he played the country bumpkin, gaining both the scorn and confidence of his host, and then started hinting that he knew the man was a criminal.

"Shouldn't have taken that sword from the wall," he said sheepishly, which was a tone of voice Jenna had never heard him use before. And he accused her of acting out roles!

"I guess I went too far. He pulled the gun and, fool that I am, I smashed a whole decanter of whiskey. The lady here—I'm sure you've heard of our mystery woman, the one who was hurt and can't remember her name—anyway, she noticed all the commotion and came in just as Bartholomew decided to draw iron."

"Draw iron, Lord Parkworth?" one of the police said. "You speak of the gun, is that right?"

"Right. Had no idea the bastard was armed. What

395

was I supposed to do, let him shoot her? Not a gentlemanly thing to do. We viscounts have had better training than that. He'd already as much as admitted to being behind an attempted robbery of Victoria herself. Somehow he got the idea I knew the name of his partner, and I guess somehow I didn't bother to tell him he was wrong."

The two policemen looked at one another, then back at Clay. It was clear they didn't know what to make of him or his story. Jenna was certain that put them in the same category as everyone else in the room.

With one exception. She knew very much what he was up to. He was covering for her, risking his own good name with half truths and outright lies. She had expected to be questioned, she had planned to tell what she knew, and of course, she had expected to be taken to jail.

But Clay had placed himself between her and the officers. At that moment she loved him more than she had ever done before, but it was a love scarred by guilt. Clay was everything that was good for her; for him, she was everything bad.

"We'll have to pass all this on to the inspector, you understand, my lord," an officer said.

"I'll be pleased to talk to him if you think that's necessary. Daddy raised us to be honest folk."

Charlotte was besieged by a fit of coughing. Beside her on the sofa, her husband sat open-mouthed.

"That would be the Earl of Harrow," an officer said.

"Right," said Clay.

For her part, Jenna sat still and did exactly what Clay had instructed them to do. She listened and she learned. She had turned to him for help and he readily gave it, to the point of committing an act of violence that had to be against his nature. He wouldn't blame her because he was not the kind to seek

396

blame, but she would always blame herself.

Too well she remembered the look on the faces of the men and women immediately after the terrible event. They would not soon forget what had occurred, even if they had not been eyewitness to more than the results, and they would remember that two members of the Drake family were involved.

She owed him a great deal, and she knew exactly how to pay. Her years had been filled with difficult decisions; tonight she made the most difficult of all. She would remove herself from his life.

The police left, promising to visit the Rockmoor home the following morning if there were any more questions, but it looked to them both as though the inspector would be concentrating on Bartholomew.

The four were silent on the ride home, even Charlotte stifling the questions that Jenna could read in her eyes. Jenna forced herself to stare at her own ruined skirt; she must remember the way Bartholomew's blood stained the silk if she were to have the strength to carry out her plan.

When they arrived at their destination, while they were still in the entryway, William announced that as planned he would leave early in the morning for London.

"Do what I can to salvage the family name," he said curtly.

Charlotte looked at him in disgust, but it was Clay who spoke.

"I don't see how that's so all-fired important right now."

"That's because you don't live in this country. I saw the looks people were giving each other tonight. I heard the comments, and they weren't anything I was proud to hear. Word will have spread before I can get to the edges of the city. Someone ought to represent the Harrows. I'll do what I can."

"William, that's the dumbest thing you've ever

said." Charlotte shook her head. "What are you going to do, run around from house to house saying Clay really didn't mean to lop off Bartholomew's hand, that he just did it because there was no other way of getting to the gun? That's the truth, all right, but it's not parlor conversation."

"Really, Charlotte," said William in disgust.

Jenna could see that with everyone's nerves on edge, a fight was on the way. She put a hand on Charlotte's arm. "We all need some rest. Decisions can be made in the morning."

Clay smiled at her. "Smart woman."

Jenna avoided his eyes. As smart as he was, he might read too much in their depths.

On impulse she put her arms around Charlotte's neck. "Thank you for your kindness and your affection and for—" Her voice caught, and she fought back the tears. She broke away and gazed into Charlotte's soft blue eyes. "I've never had a woman friend, not in all my life. Thank you for being that friend."

She pulled away before she broke down completely and, with Clay close behind, she hurried up the stairs.

Standing in the hallway, her hand on the knob to her door, she felt his hands on her shoulders. His thumbs massaged the taut muscles of her back, and his fingers worked at the crook of her neck.

"You're wound tight, Princess. Relax. It's over."

How wrong he was. He did not know that for her the worst was yet to come.

Crossing her arms in front of her, she covered his wondrous fingers with her hands. "Thank you," she said softly. "For everything."

"Seems to me I complicated things tonight."

She whirled around. "Not at all."

Gray eyes troubled, he stared down at her. "You're mighty quick to understand. That was an ugly bit of business. I'm sorry you had to see it."

Jenna remembered how Vincent Bartholomew had stood on the darkened steps of the glove factory and ordered the death of a deaf beggar child, the way he might have ordered the extermination of a household pest. He had sounded practiced and very sure of himself, as though other similar orders had fallen from those same thick lips on other nights.

Jenna had regrets for this evening's ugliness, but they were directed toward the memories that would trouble Clay, despite his toughness, and toward the scandal that would fall on the Harrow name.

"You did what you had to do. I needed a confession from Bertie Groat's accomplice. The twins needed it. Try to concentrate on them."

And then, lest he grow suspicious of her plans, she kissed him—gently, lingeringly, letting the touch of her lips on his provide the message that she could not put into words.

I love you, with all my heart and forever.

His thumb stroked her cheek. "Hate to keep bringing up the same old thing, but you think there's any chance I might meet these children you care so much about?"

"Maybe."

But Clay would never meet the twins, and she knew it, not with her plans to leave. Jenna looked up at him and saw trust, saw kindness, saw affection in his eyes. Suddenly fed up with her lies, she threw open the door to her bedroom and gestured for him to enter. "I've got something I need to tell you, and I don't want anyone to overhear."

"Jenna, you're tired and it's late."

"Inside."

He did not protest again. When they both in the room of chintz and lace with the door firmly closed, she stood straight and still in front of him. Moonlight in an open window provided a pale light, but

Jenna had no intention of striking a lamp. She and Clay had begun their relationship in the dark, and they would end it the same way.

"Please don't interrupt me until I've finished. In fact, I would appreciate it if you would sit and listen and not speak."

She sensed his hesitation, but, as she had requested, he found his way to the chair by her dressing table. She could feel his eyes on her as she stood in the dimness.

Not knowing where to begin, Jenna began at the point she had first begun to tell him lies; she began with the train wreck that sent her to the Reverend Cox and his school for deaf children, and for the first time she told him her full name.

"When I was twenty-one, the reverend found employment for me in the home of a wealthy financier, James Drury. I was to teach the Drury children, or at least so I thought, but my employer had other duties in mind."

Staring into empty space, she describe Polly's midnight summons, the confrontation, the shove. She did not spare herself when she told how, like a coward, she had run into the night and found refuge with the twins and later at the Black Horse Tavern in the disguise of a deaf-and-dumb child.

"It was you. I should have known."

Jenna hurried on. "You kept coming back to the tavern, and Teresa decided to take offense at your rejection. Bertie Groat was supposed to kill you in return for her favors, so I decided to warn you. When the police came around with word of a thousand-pound reward, I thought perhaps I would tell you the truth and you could give me advice."

"You were half right," Clay said. "You told me. But you got damned little in return for the confession."

"How could I expect you to believe me? I had

evaded the truth so many times—"

Her voice broke, and suddenly she was in his arms. "Don't bother to go on. I can figure out the rest. You heard the plans, heard Morgan was arrested, and came looking for Bartholomew."

"I didn't plan on the thief or running into the street or meeting Charlotte. Things just happened."

"Yeah, things just happened. Like old Clay coming along with an accusation or two."

"You came along and agreed to help even though you had no idea who I was or what you were risking. The best times of my life have been with you, and I don't mean just the lovemaking. I mean being with you, riding with you, listening to you talk. And in return, I brought you to tonight. I'm sorry."

The last was said with her final reserve of strength and she let herself rest against him.

His lips brushed her hair. "Is that all you are? Just sorry? I'd rather you say you're also in love." He pushed her back until he could look down at her face in the moonlight, his hands holding lightly to her shoulders. "At least I'm hoping so. Maybe I ought to prime the pump. I love you, Jenna Cresswell."

Her own love rushed warmly through her and she held his words in her heart. All that she had wanted he seemed to be offering—if only she could accept his declaration without question. So long had she wanted to make the same simple, thrilling statement to him, but all she could think of was that her story must have wrung his kind heart. He spoke the truth, as far as he realized it, but she must be a pitiful creature to him with her sad and twisted tale of troubles, and the words that had so often been on her lips would not come.

Clay was not done. "Don't think you're protecting me from myself by keeping quiet. If you can't make yourself tell me you love me, tell me that you don't.

I'll believe you either way."

Jenna gave up. "I love you."

Clay kissed her, broke away, then kissed her again before holding her tight, her head resting against his chest. "We'll get the best lawyers money can buy. That death was an accident and we'll prove it."

"And if we can't?" she couldn't keep from asking.

"Then we'll just do what you did before and we'll head for the hills."

Dismay dimmed her happiness. "To Texas? No, Clay. I can't run with you to your home. I couldn't face your aunt or your friends, not when we'd both be lying to them. I've had enough lies in my life already."

"Then how about the country where you grew up? You made it sound a little like Texas. We could start raising cattle there. The thing you've got to realize, Princess, is that we'll do what is necessary to make a life for ourselves."

Jenna clung to him for a minute longer, revelling in his words even as she knew that he was wrong. To leave with a cloud hanging over her head was to accept a life without promise, without grandeur. She could accept such a life as long as Clay remained by her side, for being with him offered a grandeur all its own, but she could not ask him to make such a sacrifice.

And she could not ask him to give up his beloved Whiskey Ranch. Eventually his love would die. Of all the terrible shocks that had assailed her during her life, that death would be the greatest shock of all.

At last she eased herself from his embrace. She felt cold inside, and dead, but she kept a smile on her face. "Maybe running won't be necessary. Let me think about all you've said, and we'll talk in the morning."

"You sure you're all right?"

"I'm all right." She took his hand and pulled him

to her bedroom door. Before she could change her mind about the course of action opening before her, she threw open the door. Light from the hallway spilled onto his face, and she let her gaze linger on his features. "I really am all right," she said to ease the frown lines between his eyes. Tiptoeing, she kissed him. "Goodnight."

Quickly she stepped back into her room, her back to the closed door, and she listened to his fading footsteps. She knew what Clay had in mind for to-morrow. He planned to go with her to the Brighton police and be there every step of the way while she threw herself into the gears of justice. Word of his involvement would be out within an hour, and the scandalous talk would begin, talk that would grow to unbelievable proportions if justice did not prevail and they truly did run away.

A chill wind blew in the window and she hugged herself, hugged the misery she would always carry inside, along with the memories of a far-too-brief happiness. She could not save Clay from everything, but she could save him from his own determinations. The best thing she could do for him, and for Charlotte, too, and in a way for the earl and Lady Libby, was to see that when shame did come upon her, they would not be tainted. Leaving was the one thing she could do that would repay them a little for all the problems that her ill-considered trip to Tunstall Square had wrought.

She had a little money that Charlotte insisted she carry. It would be enough to buy a third-class ticket on the early morning train, far away from William's first-class accommodations. By the time the servant Anna came to waken her for the day, she would already be gone.

Part Three

Home

Chapter Thirty

Jenna arrived at Victoria Station shortly after nine the next morning in the midst of a driving rain and hired a carriage to take her to the Deaf and Dumb Asylum. The housekeeper who met her at the door was a stranger to her, a gray-haired, rounded woman with a kindly look in her eye. Her lavender dress reminded Jenna of how the reverend never liked for any of the women in his employ to wear black.

"These children live in a soundless world, but they can see and they can smell. Let's give them pretties to look at and sweet scents to enjoy."

The housekeeper introduced herself as Ruth Severn — "Ruth, to you, my dear" — and delivered the bad news that the reverend was away at a church meeting, then insisted she come inside for a cup of tea "to take the chill off."

Jenna had a close schedule she had set for herself, but the kindly woman's offer was not something she could turn down. "I can only stay a few minutes," she said.

"Stay as long as you can, my dear," the woman said as she led Jenna to the small study that the reverend used as his office. "The reverend will be heartsick over missing you like this. Talks about you like you were one of his family."

Jenna hesitated to ask just what he had said, and whether or not the housekeeper had heard of her disgrace.

"Knows you're not guilty, he does," Ruth announced as if she could read Jenna's mind. "Should have come to him for help right away." With a brief nod, she left.

Alone in the study, Jenna looked with loving eyes at the room where she had come so many late nights to watch the reverend at his work. It was just as she recalled, with its shabby furniture and book-lined walls and warm, welcoming appeal.

The room was the same, but Jenna was not. Settling in the overstuffed chair that she used to crawl into on those nights, she brushed the moisture from her green dress, the one she had worn on the journey down to Brighton a few weeks before. All the bright, new dresses she had left behind.

Sad thoughts threatened, and she turned with relief when she heard the door open, expecting to see Ruth with the tea. Instead, she saw the grinning faces of Alice and Alfred Morgan.

"Jenna!"

"Jenna!"

Their voices blended, and Alfred added, "I *told* you she'd be here before long."

In an instant they were upon her, both scrambling into her lap, their tears mingling with hers, and this time she did not try to hold back her kisses and her hugs.

At last she sat back and looked at them. "You're getting fat."

"Am not," said Alice.

"Reverend Cox takes good care of us," said Alfred. "Got us out of that horrible place they took us to first and brought us here. Said he had heard that you was wanting . . . that you wanted him to see we got taken care of all right."

"That's what I wanted, all right."

"Guess who was here this morning," said Alice, a sly look in her eyes.

"I give up."

"Papa!" the twins said in unison.

"No!"

"Yes!"

The housekeeper entered with the tea and set it on the table beside Jenna as the twins began to babble at once about their father.

"It's true," affirmed Ruth. "Mr. Morgan was here no more'n a couple of hours ago, released from the robbery charge against him but he didn't know how or why. Visited with the children, then said he had some business to take care of, get set up with acting again or some such, and get a better place to live. With the reverend gone, I took it upon myself to listen in. Wouldn't be talking out of turn to let you know."

"No, it wouldn't," Jenna assured her.

"Children, let Miss Cresswell take her tea while it's hot," Ruth said. "There will be time enough to visit later."

But of course there would not, and Jenna gave them both an extra firm hug and another kiss on the cheek, then said she would be leaving in a few minutes but she would write them as soon as she could.

A cloud of distress passed over their young faces.

"Everybody keeps going away," said Alfred.

"I always wished I could get a letter," Jenna said. "Don't you feel the same way?"

The twins nodded.

"I can read it for myself," Alfred announced proudly. "I'm learning how to write, too."

"Me, too," said Alice.

After a protracted good-bye, Jenna was left alone with the tea. She found paper and pen on the reverend's desk. Her first idea was to write a long message describing her situation and what she planned to do, but she did not know where to begin and she settled on a brief note, expressing regret because she had missed him and thanks for all he had done for the twins.

As much as she longed to remain in the room where she had so often found sanctuary, other places and other matters beckoned. Ringing for the housekeeper, she thanked her for the tea and made a quick departure for the second of her destinations, the Black Horse Tavern.

By the time the hired carriage let her out on the street at the edge of Seven Dials, the rain had lessened. She looked around at what had been her home for so many months, at the dim and dirty street, at the brick front of the tavern with its swaying, faded sign, but she felt none of the nostalgia she had experienced at the asylum.

The front door was unlocked and she entered to see Hector standing by the bar, alone in the wide, dimly lit room with its round, scarred tables and straight-backed chairs and its worn wooden floor, and with its stale air redolent of ale and rum and old smoke, of unwashed bodies and lost hopes.

She stood straight, her red hair neatly tucked beneath the green hat that matched her dress, and she wondered how to let him know who she was.

He looked up, and his wide, coarse face broke into a smile. " 'opin' ye might return, lass. Yer a pretty un, ye are. Knew ye would be."

Jenna stared at him in open surprise. "You knew I wasn't a child? That I could hear and speak?"

He nodded his shaggy head, his face lined with sympathy. "Right away, soon as ye walked i' th' place. Yer business, it was. Recognized a troubled soul when I saw 'er. Ye got better at pretendin' as th' time went by."

"All that time you let me believe I had you fooled."

"Ye did, i' a way. Didn't 'ave no notion ye was a toff. Ye look fine, lass, fine."

"Why, Hector? Why did you take me in?"

"A man does wot 'e thinks best, lass."

A rustling in the back doorway caught Jenna's attention, and she watched as Teresa entered the tavern's main room. She was dressed in a loose, white nightgown, her black hair tangled and wild, and she wore a groggy expression as though she had been awakened from a deep sleep.

"Wot the 'ell's going on? Who yer talkin' to, fer gawd's sake, in the middle o' the night?"

"An old friend," said Hector, his eyes still on Jenna. "A lady." There was pride in his voice.

Teresa followed her husband's gaze and stood upright, smoothing her hair and blinking herself to full wakefulness. "A lady i' the Black 'orse? Wot'll 'appen next?"

"Hello, Teresa."

"Do I know ye? If you claims I took somefin' o' yers, it's a lie. Keeps me 'ands to meself, and that's the truth."

"You haven't taken anything from me," said Jenna and meant it. All the months she had resented Hector's bride because of the insults and the abuse seemed inconsequential now.

"Don't recognize 'er, do ye?" Hector glanced down at his wife. "That's coz ye never looked at 'er close. Ye needs to look at people, Teresa. Ain't allus wot they seems."

Teresa blinked. "Wot in bloody 'ell are ye talkin' about?"

"Look at 'er, woman."

Teresa did as he instructed, but Jenna saw that a week would go by and there would still be no recognition in those dark, blank eyes.

"You called me Simple."

Teresa's eyes slowly widened in comprehension. "Bloody bitch."

"That too."

Teresa looked back at her husband. "It's the dimwit."

"Or so ye thought, wife."

Teresa looked from Hector to Jenna and back

411

again. "Wot's goin' on 'ere?"

Jenna answered, although the question had not been directed to her. "I came to thank you for your kindness, Hector, and to say good-bye."

"Ye still runnin', lass, from wot's atter ye?"

"No, I'm not running any more."

Teresa spoke up. "She get some money off o' yer? Is that where she got the fine dress? Allus knew there was somethin' funny about 'er."

"Shut up, Teresa," ordered Hector, although there was no rancor in the words. "Ye've said enough."

"I'm turning myself over to the police," said Jenna. "There are charges against me that I need to face."

" 'at's wot I thought," said Hector.

"Bloody bitch," said Teresa.

"Shut!" This time Hector put force behind the word, and Teresa fell silent, her eyes round and her pouting mouth open.

"Hector, I'm sorry—" But Jenna could not finish the thought, could not say she was sorry for the woman he had married and for the betrayals he must know about. She looked from him to his wife and back to him, and she saw that he understood.

"No need, lass. I told ye a man does wot 'e thinks best. It's the reason I took in Teresa. I know wot she is—"

Teresa growled, but Hector went on.

"—but I also know it's th' lameness 'at's partly t' blame. She needs a 'ome. An' 'at's wi' me. Sorry I let 'er carry on so about ye. Didn't quite know 'ow to 'andle 'er for a bit."

He glanced at his wife. "She'll leave from time t' time, but she'll turn up agin. Like a bad penny, as th' sayin' goes, but th' thing is, she's *my* penny."

"Blimey," Teresa said.

Tears formed at the back of Jenna's eyes, as much for the bleakness of Hector's situation as for the forthright manner he was dealing with it. In a strange way he led a happier life than she, and she could learn a lesson from him.

"You've been a good friend, but I need one last favor. I need for you to summon the police."

"Are ye sure, lass?"

"I'm sure."

Teresa screeched, "I told ye I didn't take nuffin off o' ye. Wot yer callin' the rozzers fer?"

"For myself," Jenna said, and a sudden thought struck her. "You knew, didn't you, Hector, that I was the one those men were after."

"The ones wot offered the reward? I knew."

"But you didn't try to collect."

Teresa let out an ugly scream, and her face turned crimson. "Wot the bloody 'ell is goin' on 'ere? Ye could've turned 'er in fer a thousand pounds? Is 'at wot I'm 'earin'?"

"Ye 'ave a 'ard time doin' wot yer told, don' ye, wife?" said Hector. Moving his huge bulk away from the bar, he headed for the door.

When her husband had gone, Teresa turned on Jenna. " 'e's lost 'is mind, 'at's wot's 'appened." Her hands waved wildly in the air. "A bloody fortune for the likes o' ye."

Suddenly Jenna was fed up with the cruel and selfish Mrs. Mims.

"Keep it up and you'll find that nightgown down your throat, Teresa. You're a stupid woman, but not so stupid you shouldn't be able to understand one thing. Hector is the only good thing that has ever happened to you in your life. He loves you now, but that doesn't mean he will love you forever."

"Bloody—"

"Be quiet and listen. You keep abusing that man and one day he will toss you out on the street as you very well deserve. It's hard enough in this life to find someone to live your life with, someone who cares. Don't throw it all away."

Jenna knew her voice would break if she spoke

one more word, and she doubted that Teresa understood what she said. Before a response could be hurled at her, she whirled and without looking back left the Black Horse Tavern for the last time, leaving the way she had entered today, through the front door with her red hair shining and her head held high.

Down the street, she could see Hector's mammoth figure bent to a far smaller London bobby. Hiking her skirt, she hurried toward the pair. The sound of her footsteps drew their attention, and they turned in her direction and waited for her to arrive.

Nodding her thanks up at Hector, she spoke to the policemen.

"My name is Jenna Cresswell," she said without so much as a quiver in her voice. "I believe you have a warrant for my arrest."

Chapter Thirty-one

A fine, chilling mist was blowing against Clay's face as he made his way down Ratcliff Street. The hour was midnight, and he was in the part of London known as Blue Gate Fields, a slum that rivaled Seven Dials for decadence and poverty.

Residents of the Fields, more animal than human from their appearance, huddled by the side of the cobbled old street and in the doorways of the buildings that rose on either side. Ramshackle edifices they were, leaning inward and forming a dank tunnel of human despair.

Clay hadn't known despair could have a smell, but he knew it well enough now. It was an odor of rot and decay, of filthy bodies and festering sores. A rat had died in the eaves of the ranch house one fall while he and Aunt Martha were in San Antonio; they returned to the bouquet assailing him now.

A door to one of the old buildings opened, then closed, but not before he caught a glimpse of fringed lanterns inside, of cots and pipes and smoke. He also caught the unmistakable whiff of opium.

Worse, he decided. Blue Gate Fields was worse than Seven Dials, although before tonight he would not have believed such a thing possible.

The street was mean and ugly, but he did not walk down it unarmed. He had learned his lesson from Vincent Bartholomew. In the inside pocket of his coat he carried a snub-nosed pistol much like Black Bart's. He was ready to use it if the occasion arose.

The door he was looking for was in the next block. It sat in the middle of a two-storied brick building. Torn shades hung on the upstairs windows and let out a dim glow into the swirling mist.

Clay pulled his collar around his neck. A tingle of anticipation shot through him. He would not be turned away. He pounded on the door, waited half a minute, then pounded again.

The door edged open. "Awright, awright," a woman grumbled. Only her head was visible as she looked into the night. Clay stepped forward, into the light spilling onto the stoop from the inside.

"Ah," she said, drawing the syllable out. A smile split the white, furrowed face. The smile was snaggled, her few remaining teeth mottled and decayed, and her breath would have stopped a charging bull.

She opened the door fully; her mammoth girth filled the narrow hallway from wall to wall. Wispy gray hair bobbed in the dim light as she looked him up and down, her eyes dark buttons in the textured paleness of her face.

"You wouldn't be Gert, by any chance, would you?" As if anyone else could match the description Clay had been given earlier in the night.

"Ever'one knows ole Gert. And ole Gert c'n guess wot th' likes o' yer is wantin'. Got jus' t' t'ing to warm yer on a wet, cold night."

She stepped back, allowing Clay to enter. The air in the hallway held all of the ugliness of outdoors, with a layer of heavy incense added. Clay would have preferred standing in a barn that hadn't been cleaned for years.

"Joseph!" she yelled down the hallway. "Get yer arse down 'ere and pour the brandy. We got a gent come t' call."

"No brandy, thank you." Too well Clay remembered the first night at the Black Horse. "I'd rather get down to business."

The woman grinned once again. Imbedded in the mound of flesh that was her face, the smile was not a pretty sight. "Yer a man atter me own 'eart, 'at ye are. An' ye've come t' the right 'ouse. Wot e'er it is yer wantin' we got. Wimmen, o' course, but there's gents wot likes th' boys, too."

Clay had little interest in the bill of fare the madam had to offer. "It's a woman I'm looking for. A special one who goes by the name of Polly."

He could see the calculations going on behind the button eyes. "Polly'll cost ye extra."

"I've other women on the list. Polly's not the only one." Like hell she wasn't, but he didn't want Gert to know that. She'd make it impossible for him to get what he was after. "How much extra are you jawing about?"

"Ye sure talks funny fer a Lun'on gent."

"How much?"

"Two crown."

"One. And not a farthing more."

"Yer a 'ard man, that ye are." Again she looked him up and down. Her laugh came from deep in her fat belly. "I'll just bet ye are. A year ago I woulda taken ye on, meself."

"One crown," Clay repeated.

"In advance. I'll relieve yer o' the coin."

Clay gave her the money.

"Joseph," she yelled. A piece of plaster fell from the wall behind her. "Tell Polly she's got a gent waitin'." She looked back at Clay. "Gi' 'er time to get 'erself ready. Gent like yerself appreciates a woman wot's clean."

"I don't want to wait."

Behind Gert, a man appeared in the hall. Six feet, Clay estimated, just under his own height, but with upper arms the size of a hog's rump. His head had no more hair on it than did a grape, and a jagged scar pulled the left side of his face in two directions. An

417

interesting opponent, Joseph. The way Clay felt, he was ready to take him on. Jenna had been in jail three days, and that was three days too long.

"No need fer ye t' wait," said Gert with a sigh. "A 'ealthy one, yer are. Up the stairs. First room o' th' left."

She pressed her back to the wall and grinned as Clay eased past her in the narrow hall. "Gives a girl a thrill, it does," she said as her stomach brushed against his trousers.

Clay kept his own opinion to himself. Joseph stepped into a doorway as Clay passed. The scar gave the brute a permanent sneer, but his eyes, a pale blue, were without expression.

Clay hurried up the narrow stairs, stepping wide over a broken slat, and stopped before the door to Polly's room. He knocked once, then entered.

The room smelled little better than the downstairs. A bed and chair were the lone pieces of furniture; a threadbare rug covered the center of the floor. Light came from a fringed lantern attached to the wall. A window on the wall to his left, partially covered by a torn shade, was cracked to let in a whisper of air.

Clay concentrated on the woman who sat at the side of the bed facing the window. She wore a robe that hung loosely around her thin body. Her brown hair lay limp against her shoulders, and her feet were bare. She stared up at him with eyes that were dull and brown. He put her age at less than thirty, but she might have been an old woman, for all the life that was in her face.

"We don't see your kind much around here," she said, her voice as flat as her eyes. He wasn't surprised that she did not sound like a resident of Blue Gate Fields; it was what he had expected.

"Shows you how wrong an hombre can be. I'd have thought that working for a woman like Gert, you would see all kinds."

Curiosity animated her face. "Who are you? You don't sound like no English gentleman."

Clay let his eyes roam around the room before they settled on her. "And this doesn't look like a gentleman's parlor."

Her laugh came quick, sharp and bitter. "That's the bloody truth."

"You've traveled a long way in your life, haven't you?" he asked. "But then really not so far. By my reckoning, the Drury home is less than five miles away."

What little color she had drained away. She held her robe close against her chest. "How did you know about that?"

"I know a lot about you, Polly. I talked with the good widow."

"Good!" She looked away from him, her eyes narrowing as though she could see into the past. "Nothing good about her. May she burn in hell."

"You were parlormaid at the time of James Drury's death." He made it a statement; he didn't figure she would try denying what he already knew, but he also didn't want to waste time arguing.

She looked back at him, wary the way a trapped animal is wary. "I didn't have anything to do with it."

"I'm not here to charge you with murder, Polly. I don't believe there was a murder. Neither do you."

She chewed at her lower lip. "What's it to you to find out what I do believe?"

"You tell me what you remember. Everything. And then I'll decide." Again he looked around the room. "Whatever it is, it will get you out of here."

She hugged herself. "Don't be lying. This is a life not meant for no one, no matter what a girl has done. Mrs. Drury, the bitch, threw me out on the street without references. Said I made up stories about her husband, said he wouldn't never touch a woman. Fool. Just because he didn't touch her. No wonder. Like to freeze his hands off if he did."

"What happened, Polly? Tell me what you remember."

"You seem mighty anxious. I have a right to know why."

"The governess is in jail."

"Caught up with her, did they?"

"She turned herself in three days ago."

"Why she go and do something like that? I told her there wasn't any hope for the likes of us."

Clay had no quick and easy answer, and he let the question go. "I'm trying to get her cleared."

"She mean something special to you?"

"She does."

Polly gave him a closer inspection. "Some women has all the luck."

"She's not very lucky right now. Mrs. Drury is insisting that the police follow through on the old charges. She's a wealthy widow, and they're listening to her. I've tried lawyers, but things are moving too slowly. Now I'm trying you."

He didn't bother to tell her that she had no choice but to cooperate. The way she was looking up at him, anger and bitterness and an edge of something else in her eyes, something that looked like calculation, he figured she already knew the way the night would turn out.

"The old woman stickin' to the story she came up with?"

"She claims her husband called Jenna down to fire her. Said she was doing a rotten job of teaching their boys. Jenna got angry and shoved him."

"Uncivilized, that's what those two little bastards were."

"Kind of like their parents."

A half smile flitted on Polly's face. "Never thought of it that way."

"Tell me what you remember."

"You can't win with the old bitch. She's got the police believing her, and she's got money, too."

"Maybe I can. I'm a hell of a lot more determined than she is, and I'm mean in a fight. Richer, too, most likely. And I've got what we call an ace in the hole in a poker game. I've got a viscount title hanging on my name."

Polly looked at him in disbelief. "You're putting me on."

"Swear by my Texas ranch, it's the truth. Viscount Parkworth. It's not something I like to brag about, but it could have its uses."

"Fancy that. A viscount coming to me for help."

"The story, Polly. What happened?"

With a sigh, Polly closed her eyes. "Never thought to tell this to no one. Soon as I saw Jenna was gone, I got one of the footmen to go for help. A doctor come, and the coppers, too, right sharp like, askin' questions. Man as rich as Drury, someone's got to pay if he dies, especially the way he did, hittin' his head on the hearth and not natural, with his heart giving out in bed."

She shuddered and curled up at the side of the bed, her knees pressed against her chest, her eyes seeing sights that Clay could not see. He forced himself to stay quiet, but it was hard work.

"I come into the parlor just as she shoved him. Her dress was torn, and she had a scared look about her, like she was fightin' for her life. I knew what he'd been up to, all right, the old fart. Always wanting to get his hands on the new girls like a dog that marks his territory. She shoulda given in."

"She shoved him," Clay said, unable to keep from prompting her.

"Hard, too. Wouldn't have thought she would have the strength, little as she was. Drury fell, and you could tell by the way he was lying there, kinda twisted and still, that he wasn't never gonna get up again, not without someone helping him."

"And the governess?"

"I knew what would happen. Told her to get out, and she did. Came to see me once a few weeks later and I told her to get back to wherever she was hiding. The old woman had vowed to see her hang, and I couldn't

421

see any way of keepin' it from happening." She opened her eyes to the shabby room. "Thought at the time it were the worst thing that could happen to a girl, going to the gallows, but I was wrong. Let go, without papers, all of us were, and there weren't no men lined up in the alley waiting to offer us a marriage bed."

She fingered the dirty sheet on which she was sitting. "But the other kind was offered soon enough."

Clay was moved by the bleakness in her voice. "And you ended up with Gert."

"A girl does what she can to survive in this world. A girl does what she can."

"You should have told some of this story to the police."

"I tried, but there wasn't no viscount to make 'em listen."

"There is now. They'll listen to you now, I promise."

The wariness that he'd seen upon first entering the room returned to her eyes. "Don't have nothing to do with the rozzers. More than likely I'd just bring trouble down on my head, and I don't need no more trouble."

"A minute ago I said I would get you out of here. I don't mean just this room, I mean Blue Gate Fields. And I don't mean just for a day or two. I'm thinking of a permanent arrangement."

"Ain't nobody can do that."

"I can."

She studied him a long time. "We'd never get past that mountain of lard that owns the place."

"Gert smells bad, but if I hold my breath I can take her."

"And there's Joseph. He's a bad one. Keeps the gents from trying to sneak out without paying, the way some of 'em does, or from beating up on the girls, unless they paid special. I can tell you, once Joseph does a little carving with his knife, they don't try anything again."

"He ever cut any of you?"

"He don't have to. He gets his way 'cause we all remember that wicked blade he keeps under his sleeve. 'Cept for that new one last year. Meg. She got scared when he come in." Polly shuddered. "May she rest in eternal peace. She earned it that night, with the way he—" Her voice broke. "No one deserves to go like that."

"Joseph can't hurt you now, Polly. I've got a gun. If we have to shoot our way out of here, we're leaving."

Polly shook her head slowly. "You got a way about you that makes a girl believe. Anybody ever tell you that?"

"Not lately. But I've got hopes someone soon will."

"They got others like you where you come from?"

"Hundreds."

"Good." She stood and let the robe fall open to reveal a body more sunken than rounded. "That can't help but give a girl hope."

He gave her a few minutes to get dressed. She donned a thin cotton gown and a threadbare coat that would be enough to get her to the corner where he could hail a cab. He walked ahead of her down the stairs, then shifted places as they made their way down the long, narrow hall.

They passed a door opening onto a small parlor.

"Where ye think yer goin'?" a deep voice growled.

Clay saw the bald-headed Joseph snarling at him from inside the room, his beefy arms held loose at his sides. Behind Joseph, Gert watched. This time she did not have a smile on her face.

"You'd be smart to let us leave," said Clay, his own arms loose, his right hand ready to go for the gun.

A quick movement, and suddenly Clay saw the glint of a knife in Joseph's hand.

He waved the blade in the air. It was an adequate substitute for words.

But then so was the pistol. Clay brought it out fast, making sure both Joseph and Gert had a good look.

"Get the bastard," ordered Gert from her protected position.

Joseph growled.

"Wait by the door," Clay ordered Polly.

He took a side step in her direction just as Joseph came at him, knife pointed at his gut. Clay shot him in the chest. The roar of the gunshot echoed around them, but Joseph kept coming, momentum and fury carrying him onward despite the direct hit, the blade wavering in the air. Clay's fist crashed into his face. The knife caught on the sleeve of his coat, ripping through the fabric and narrowly missing his skin. Joseph stopped in his tracks, his pale eyes blinking in disbelief. He looked down at his chest, at the blood spreading across his shirt.

He fell, and the walls of the parlor shook.

Clay looked over his still body. Gert's eyes were trained on the gun.

"Next," he said.

She shook her head. Her fat cheeks wiggled like jelly.

When he turned to Polly, he saw in the dim hallway light a small smile on her face. He hustled her out the door. At the corner he hailed a cab and waited impatiently while an ancient nag clopped along the cobblestones slowly toward the curbside, a dark carriage to the rear.

Clay helped Polly inside and gave orders to be taken to the nearest police station.

"Cor, not many as asks for sech as that," the driver said from his high perch.

Clay settled back on the seat as the carriage jerked into motion. Beside him, Polly shivered, and he rested his arm lightly around her shoulders to give her warmth. She did not protest, but she kept herself still and quiet.

His thoughts turned to the reception he would get when he finally saw Jenna. Thus far she had refused to see him, but she wouldn't get away with that for long.

The past three days he'd been following leads that would take him to the Drury parlormaid, imagining a

424

thousand tortures Jenna was going through, fighting the urge to shoot up the jail and set her free. He'd even considered shooting a lawyer or two who had told him what he was trying to do couldn't be done.

Arresting an innocent woman for a capital crime—hell, any crime—was civilization at its worst.

Jenna would be grateful for all he'd done, that's for damned sure, but gratitude wasn't what he was after. She'd talked about loving him, but if she thought sneaking away and leaving him to go out of his mind with worry was showing love, she wasn't thinking clearly. Or else she'd decided she felt differently.

It was time for him to lay down a few of his own laws. It was time to find out just how matters stood.

Chapter Thirty-two

Jenna exited the police station in the early morning on what would have been her fourth day of incarceration.

"All charges dropped," one of the officers on duty had announced when she was brought from the dark cell off one of the building's corridors. "Got word no more'n a few minutes ago. No reason to hold you now, Miss Cresswell. You're free to go. If you'd like to wait for someone to get you, just take a seat."

"Thank you," she said. She knew who might very well be on the way. Clay had sent word days ago that he wanted to visit her, but she had refused. To see him in such a place, to explain why she had left Brighton, to return to that cell after bidding him good-bye — she could not bring herself to such a scene.

She did not know exactly what had prompted her release, and neither did the officer, but she was certain that Clay was the cause.

As she stepped outside the station, she passed a pair of uniformed policemen and a scowling man she recognized as one of the inspectors who had questioned her the first day. They hurried inside without giving her a second glance, and Jenna truly felt free. Ragged clouds over the buildings to the east glowed red with the morning sun. She smiled into the brightness.

She looked up and down the busy London street with its carriages and pedestrians, half expecting to see Clay.

He would be along shortly, she was certain, and she was debating whether she ought to wait. Elated as she was, she could almost believe that all her troubles were at an end, that a happy life might await her after all. Whatever happened between her and Clay, she didn't want this particular confrontation to occur near a jail.

In the distance she heard a young male voice crying out above the early morning noise. One of hustlers who sold the penny scandal sheets, she decided. The sheets came on the streets fast after an incident occurred or a bit of gossip was uncovered by one of the unscrupulous newsmen who printed and distributed them. She couldn't make out what this particular young man was saying, and she gave her attention to finding a carriage for hire.

The voice grew louder, and despite her lack of interest she heard *viscount* clearly.

She knew with dread certainty just which viscount was meant.

"His Lordship frees accused murderess!"

The youth was close behind her. Jenna turned and watched as a half dozen men and women thrust coins into his hand and grabbed at the sheets of newsprint. Fearing what the story would say, she became one of his throng of customers. With the paper crumpled in her hand, she signaled for a carriage. Not until she was sitting back on the narrow seat headed for Old Kent Road and the Deaf and Dumb Asylum, did she glance at what she had bought.

It was all as she had expected, black and white and glaring with half-truths and innuendos about how Clayton Drake, Viscount Parkworth, Texas farmer and only son of the Earl and Countess of Harrow, had fallen in love with a fugitive from justice and when she was thrown into a "rat-filled, damp cell with other cutthroats and assorted miscreants," he had used his power and money to see that she was free.

Specifically, he had traveled through the city's worst slums until he found a prostitute who once worked alongside his true love. Over the protestations of the family of the victim and of "certain elements of the law that do not like undue influence being used in the pursuit of justice," he had located a magistrate who would issue an order to free his lady love.

Jenna translated the story: Clay had found Polly and at last a court official had listened to her story and believed it.

The only portion of the story left out was the violence that had occurred in Brighton.

Jenna winced especially at the caricature of Clay astride a fire-breathing horse, guns blazing, as he rode up the steps of an edifice clearly marked NEWGATE PRISON. She had never been near the place, but the worst offense was the way Clay was made to look like a buffoon.

And all for love, the story stated.

Clay had told her once that a man did not like to be made a fool of, and she had succeeded in doing just that in the most public of ways. Even his mother came in for a comment or two about her unorthodox manners and speech.

Everything that Jenna had dreaded — the public humiliation and scandal that would fall on Clay and his family because of association with her — was coming about. She had once thought she did not care a fig for members of the aristocracy, but she cared very much for one in particular and, almost as much, for his family and his heritage and their right to dignity and pride.

By the time the carriage arrived at its destination, Jenna was distraught to the point of breaking into tears. Paying the driver with the last of the coins she had brought with her from Brighton, she stumbled up the steps of the school.

The housekeeper opened the door, took one look at her, and helped her inside. "My dear, whatever is wrong? No, don't speak. I'll get you some tea. The reverend's here today, thank the Lord."

She escorted Jenna into the study, telling her as they

walked down the hallway that the twins were on an outing with their father today. Reverend Cox, seated at his desk, looked up from his work. "Jenna," he said as he rose and started toward her.

He was exactly as she remembered him, tall and thin, his hair gray, his face kindly and lined with the cares he had taken on himself through the years.

Jenna had been determined to be cheerful and brave, to let him know immediately that she was not a source of worry for him, that she had gotten herself into more trouble than anyone could ever imagine and that, while everything was not exactly as she would wish, her problems were ones she could work out without troubling him.

She looked into his gentle eyes and felt the tears come.

"Oh, Reverend Cox," she said with a sob, "I've made a most terrible mess of things."

By late morning she had told the reverend almost everything about the past year and two months. He had known about the incident at the Drury household since the day after it happened—"An accident, I always knew," he said solemnly when she tried to describe the scene—and she had told him of the intervening time.

She had not lied. She had held nothing back, not the Black Horse Tavern or Whitecastle Street or the way she fell in love. It had not been necessary to tell him everything about her relationship with Clay, but she had seen that he understood.

"You said earlier, Jenna, that you had made a mess of things. That is not true. You did what few others would have done. You're a remarkable woman, the woman I knew you would be when you first arrived at the asylum, trapped in a soundless world with no friends and no family. You were a brave little thing, and I expect you to be brave now. Tell me. What did you do to help those two hungry, bereft children?"

429

"I watched over them and eventually begged for money to help them, but I had no choice, and others were begging, too."

"Just answer the questions. What was it you did when you heard about their father's imprisonment?"

"I began looking for the man who could free him."

"And what did you do when you realized you were in love with Mr. Drake?"

"I—"

"You made certain that you would see him again. Surely even you can draw conclusions now as to what you should do."

"What, go after him again? The circumstances have changed. I have brought shame to him. You saw the scandal sheet."

"You saw trash. It belongs in the refuse bin, not in your memory."

The reverend had a way of putting things that gave Jenna heart, but she could not so easily be convinced.

"Clay moves in a different world from mine, whether he realizes it or not. I wouldn't belong."

"Pish tosh. You know what I think? I think you're a snob."

"Me?"

"Yes, you. From everything you've said, I gather that you hold little respect for the upper class. Only Parkworth himself and his sister have drawn kind words. What about the men and women who donate to the asylum, both with time and money? And there are others who, while not favoring charities in particular, do manage to live exemplary lives or, at worst, rather ordinary ones. You can no more say that they are a cruel and selfish lot any more than you can say that the residents of the slums are slovenly rogues."

He spoke the truth, clearly and bluntly, as he had done so many times before. Always he understood the human heart. She must make him see the hesitancy that remained in hers.

"I know I was wrong to judge a class of people the

430

way I did. But Clay is still the son of an earl, and his wife will one day be a countess."

"I think you would make a splendid countess. And what is far more important, so does he. Perhaps you have been listening to your own inner voice of reason for so long that you did not really listen to what he had to say."

A knock at the door brought a pause to her protests, and she looked up at the housekeeper. She had only a moment to notice the woman was dressed in sky blue today before hearing the words, "You've another visitor, Reverend Cox." Ruth stepped aside.

Clay strode into the room. He wore the brown coat and trousers he'd been wearing the first time he visited the tavern, and the boots. The only differences Jenna could see were the shadows under his eyes and the set of his lips. A small sound escaped from her lips and her heart reached out to him, but she shrank back in her chair.

He did not look her way, nor respond to her gasp.

"Good afternoon, Reverend Cox. I'm Clayton Drake."

The reverend stood to shake his hand. "Good afternoon."

"I'm sorry to intrude unannounced, but I've only just got free. I had a little trouble in Blue Gate Fields during the night and had to get some matters cleared up."

He spoke quickly, with no rancor or agitation, but still he had not looked her way. Jenna sat with pounding heart and shallow breath as she stared up at him.

The reverend started toward the door. "I'll leave the two of you alone."

"Not necessary," said Clay. "What I've got to say isn't especially private, and I'd just as soon you heard it right." At last he turned to her. "The lady here has a habit of taking things the way she wants to take them, and not hanging around to discuss whatever's eating at her."

"You have a point, my lord."

"I see she's told you the viscount business."

Through her shock at his sudden appearance, Jenna experienced a ripple of irritation and she found her voice. Standing, she said, "It is not necessary to talk about me as though I weren't in the room."

"Oh, I know you're in the room, all right, Jenna. I know every time you're in a room. Or have you forgotten?"

Too well Jenna remembered how he could sense her presence in his darkened bedroom. "I haven't forgotten."

"Thought not. Have you forgotten what we talked about down in Brighton the other night? You know, about my loving you and you loving me."

"Clay — "

"Yes or no."

Jenna took a deep breath. "No."

"Were you lying? Yes or no."

"No," she said softly.

"Now these are some no's I don't mind hearing. The only thing I can figure is that you hold my family against me."

"No!"

"Then prove it." He reached into his coat pocket and pulled out an envelope, which he thrust into her hand. "Alex and Libby are back in town and they've been planning a little get-together for a hundred or so of their friends over on Tunstall Square. There's your invitation, hand delivered by their son and heir, Viscount Parkworth, maybe someday Earl of Harrow but he hopes not for a few decades. It'll get you in the front door with the rest of the gentry and it'll get you a trip down the receiving line. Charlotte will be there, and so will the earl and Lady Libby."

"But Clay, you don't understand. Already stories are circulating — "

"If you're talking about that printed garbage, forget it. I didn't think it was a very good likeness of me, anyway, on the back of that horse. And whoever drew it got

432

the bridle and bit wrong."

"But Clay—"

"I'm not listening to arguments, Jenna. I'm done with that nonsense. You love me, you want to be my wife, then you mosey in the front door with your head high and you take your place by my side. I'm not such a country bumpkin that I don't realize clothes could be a problem. Charlotte's sending over some duds later. You can do with 'em what you want."

"But Clay—"

"Nope, don't want to hear it. If you don't show up, I'll figure you just don't love me as much as I love you."

He glanced at the reverend. "Sorry to take up your time and involve you in some personal matters."

"It was no sacrifice on my part, my lord. You are welcome here anytime."

Clay nodded, took one long look at Jenna, a look that turned her insides to pudding and set her heart to racing, and then he was gone. She felt as though he taken the air from the room when he left.

She sank back into the chair and stared up at the reverend in disbelief, her head reeling. "I was trying to tell him that I was wrong. That maybe we can work things out if we try."

"It is possible, Jenna, that your young man has decided it's too late for maybe."

"Do you suppose?"

"Anything in this world is possible. Did I not teach you that?"

"So you did." Jenna felt a growing excitement. "Too late for maybe, you said. I definitely agree." Her chin tilted a degree higher. "The only way I can tell Clay is to go down that receiving line. I don't think—no, it's definitely not an unreasonable request."

"That's my Jenna."

"It's not going to be easy, of course."

"If you faced the streets of Seven Dials, you can face anything." He hesitated. "About the borrowed dress—"

"Don't worry about it. I'm always borrowing from

433

Charlotte," she said, a note of regret in her voice.

"Perhaps you won't have to this time." The reverend's eyes twinkled. "I do believe it is time I told you a special bit of news I've been holding back. You mentioned a pair of policemen who twice came looking for you at the tavern, the second time with talk of a reward."

"Yes, that's a curious thing. I asked the police if Mrs. Drury had made arrangements for the money to be offered and they didn't know what I was talking about."

"As well they shouldn't. Matthew Primm and Ebeneezer Crock are not policemen. They were hired by me."

"By you? I'm touched that you wanted to find me, but where would you ever get that kind of money?"

"It wasn't my money I was offering, Jenna. It was yours."

Jenna shook her head. "I don't understand."

"Of course you don't, and I will not keep you in suspense one moment longer. A year ago I received a letter from an attorney in Portsmouth. He was looking for the only child of John Bailey Cresswell, late of the Transvaal."

"But why would he—"

"He had been in correspondence with an investment firm in Pretoria. After you left, your father saw that he might not be able to emigrate just when he planned and he—I believe the term is liquidated his assets and invested everything in a gold mine."

"I never knew that."

"No one did. An investigation of the mining company turned up records of the investment. The particular mine which drew your father's attention proved exceptionally profitable. And everything he earned has been drawing interest during the past seventeen years."

Jenna looked at him in stunned silence.

"Simply put, you are a rich woman, Miss Jenna Cresswell. A very rich woman, indeed."

Chapter Thirty-three

Music poured onto the street in front of the Earl of Harrow's Tunstall Square home, and carriages lined the cobbled street. It took Jenna's rented brougham a quarter of an hour to make the last block, a quarter of an hour during which she fidgeted with the neck fastening of her circular black mantle, drummed her fingers on the seat, thought of a thousand things to say to the Earl and Countess of Harrow and rejected every one.

Beneath all that wool, she was overdressed, that was part of the problem. Blue silk gown with puffed sleeves, a lace insert that ran down the front of the skirt from waist to hem, and a squared bodice embroidered with pearls and sequins. Pearl drop earrings, too. She had never worn earrings in her life.

The reverend's housekeeper Ruth said she had done "right well" in finding such a dress so quickly; the kindly woman had even helped pile up her hair in knots and loops and curls.

"Working with the good reverend and children all day, a woman forgets how nice it is to tend to womanly things," she had said with a smile.

Jenna was tending to womanly things right now . . . the most womanly thing of all, and that was going to her man. She hoped he would not turn from her in disgust, but if he did it would be no more than she deserved.

The carriage came to a halt and the footman scrambled down to open the door. Head high, she stepped into the cool, dry night.

"We'll be waiting for word, Miss Cresswell, when you're ready to leave," the driver said from his perch. In the bright electric light from the lamp-post at the Harrow front door, she could see the admiring look in his eye.

"Thank you," she said, then turned to her fate, which at the moment consisted of walking up the front steps where she had been turned away her first night on Tunstall Square. This time she would not cower in the dark.

She strode up the front steps and stared at the brass knocker as she listened to the music coming from within, and the lighthearted laughter.

She thought of a lifetime without Clay, and she brought the knocker down with a bang. The footman Jimmy, dressed smartly in black and white, answered the knock and she strode past him into the foyer as though she belonged, her black mantle flowing behind her.

Another sharply dressed servant met her, his gloved hand extended. She looked at him blankly.

"Your invitation, miss," he said.

"Of course." With a smile, she pulled it from her reticule and gave it to him. Stepping ahead of her to the door that led to the ballroom, he announced in a stentorian voice that carried over the music, "Miss Jenna Cresswell," then moved aside.

Jenna looked into the glitter and the lights, blinded a moment, then saw that in the crowded room with its black-suited men and brightly-dressed women, all talk was gradually ceasing and all eyes were turning to her. Even the couples on the dance floor paused; only the musicians kept at their task.

The scandal sheet must have made the rounds, but Jenna decided that walking the few yards to the receiving line was no more difficult than going out that first night to beg. With head held high, just as Clay had instructed, she covered the distance with a steady and, she hoped, graceful step.

She would face the receivers one at a time and not worry about who was next . . . or who was waiting at the end and what he might say and do. If she gave much thought to a particular man, she would truly disgrace herself, rush up to him, and tell him she loved him with all her heart and should never have left Brighton or the jail this morning or done many of the things she had done.

But that would not do. One at a time, that was the way.

At the head of the line stood the Fourth Earl of Harrow, Alexander Drake, tall and lean and erect and looking very much like his son. His dark hair was streaked with silver and the expression on his face—one of affectionate humor—was one she recognized.

He took her hand in his. "Miss Cresswell, I am happy to make your acquaintance at long last." His gray eyes twinkled as he spoke. Oh yes, he was very much like Clay.

"And I yours, my lord," Jenna returned.

He turned to the slender woman on his left. Her fair hair was arranged simply in a topknot off her neck, and there were smile lines around her blue eyes and her mouth. An older version of Charlotte. Most definitely.

"My dear, this is Miss Cresswell."

"Lady Harrow," Jenna said, feeling as though she were back in school and taking some kind of very difficult examination.

"They're all watching," the famous Lady Libby said.

"I beg your pardon?"

"Everyone in the room is watching." To Jenna's absolute amazement, the countess gave her a wink. "Let's give 'em a show. After all you've been through,

437

you deserve it."

So saying, Libby embraced Jenna, squeezed tight, then stepped back. "I knew you'd be here. Clay would not fall in love with anyone who could hurt him the way you would have if you'd stayed away. Does that make sense? Alex says in my dotage I sometimes ramble on."

The Earl of Harrow laughed.

Lady Libby grinned. "Welcome to the Harrow Hall of Horrors. Get through the next few minutes with all the gawkers standing around, and you can take on the meanest Texas bull. Including my son."

Jenna was certain that no potential daughter-in-law had ever been welcomed in a more unorthodox manner.

"Mother, you'll scare her off."

Jenna turned to Charlotte, who awaited her next. "No, she won't."

"Good for you," the countess said.

"Lady Denham," Jenna said, trying very much to be proper, but she was unable to avoid copying Lady Libby's wink.

"Lady Charlotte, I'll have you know. I decided that since I was no longer going to be married to old Bill, I might as well return to the name that was mine before. Don't look so surprised. I sent my soon-to-be-former husband packing. I should have done it long ago, only you know how stubborn we Drakes can be. And proud, I'm afraid." She smiled at her mother. "The best part was that no one said they had warned me."

"Later, Charlotte," Lady Libby said. "I'll get to that later."

Jenna had never seen Charlotte looking so happy. She had a glow about her that warmed the room.

"That's a beautiful dress," commented Charlotte. "I didn't send it, did I?"

"Later, Charlotte," said Jenna. "I'll tell you later."

Suddenly she was standing in front of Clay, and

everything else faded from consideration. His suit and hair were black, and his white shirt looked pure white where it touched the brown skin of his neck. As always, a lock of hair fell across his forehead, and his eyes glinted down at her and his lips parted, and Jenna could say only, "Hello."

"Hello."

"I moseyed."

"So I noticed."

"And I'm not going to turn tail and run."

"What are you doing, Princess, trying out your Texas talk?"

"Maybe. Oh, sorry. I wasn't going to use that word. Everything is going to be definite answers tonight. Yes, always, never, no."

"Sounds good to me." He glanced around them, gave a quick smile back down the receiving line, then took her by the arm and led her to a small, open alcove where they could be observed but not overheard, passing on the way the Duchess of Castlebury, who gave them an approving nod.

Holding onto her hands, he said, "Now then, what are you saying yes to?"

"Do I love you? That would get a fast and positive reply."

The glint in Clay's eyes heated. "What about always?"

"And I always will."

"Never."

"I've never met a more wonderful man."

He growled. "You're making it mighty hard for me to keep my distance from you, Jenna. I almost hate to ask what no might mean."

"No, I will not run away again."

"Now that's the best answer of all." His gloved hand touched her lips. "Seems to me you ought to get something in return. Yes, I want you to be my wife, and I will always be there to take care of you, and never will I

439

feel any less than the love that is in my heart right now, and no, I most definitely will not listen to any arguments about whether you will fit in back at the Whiskey. You're going to fit in just fine."

"You're making it mighty hard for me to keep my distance from you, Clay."

"Then let's dance. That's one thing we haven't tried."

With her arm looped in his, he took her onto the dance floor. A song was just ending, but one look from Clay and the orchestra leader once again took up the baton. Music filled the room. He took her into his arms and whirled her around and around. Though he was much taller than she, he made her feel graceful and willowy and very much the belle of the ball.

After a couple of trips around the floor, he slowed the pace, held her close, and said, "There are a few details I might ought to mention, seeing as how I don't plan to rope you into anything you won't like. I've booked passage in two weeks for Galveston. Won't be any problem to add the name of my viscountess to the booking. We can get married before we leave. That way Alex and Libby and the reverend and whoever else you want to invite can view the proceedings."

"How can a girl object to that?"

"You're gonna love Texas."

"I'm certain that I will. It's not so different from the Transvaal. Remember, I was born on a farm."

"Yeah, I remember. And you were raised poor, I know. No more malarkey about aristocrats and having money and not having money, right?"

"Right." Jenna couldn't hold back a grin. "I won't give you any trouble about my poverty. It could be you don't know everything about me as well as you think you do. It could be, Clayton Ernest Drake, Viscount Parkworth, that I've got one bit of information you don't know anything about."

"Probably more than one, Confound it, honey, with

440

you staring up at me that way with those wide green eyes and that mouth curved so sweetly, I give up on being a gentleman. It's not worth it."

Clay stopped in the middle of the dance floor and with the band playing and everyone watching, he said, "I love you, Jenna Cresswell, and I'm filled with happiness because you have consented to be my wife."

He sealed the declaration with a long and satisfying kiss.

Epilogue

Mason County, Texas
November, 1897

Jenna Cresswell Drake, Viscountess Parkworth, saw her new home, the main house of the Whiskey Ranch, when the open carriage in which she and Clay were riding came upon a rise. The stone structure sat on a far hill a mile away and beckoned her as no building ever had.

The day was cool and clear; above them stretched a sky as blue and wide as he had described, and on both sides of the winding road lay the rugged Hill Country of central Texas, with its scrub oaks and mesquite and granite boulders giving texture to the rolling land.

The time was mid afternoon. They'd arrived in Mason by train last night, and they'd left at daylight. In between those times Clay had initiated her into the comforts and pleasures to be found in the town's finest hotel, known appropriately enough as the Mason House.

But only after he had roused the proprietor of H. Zork & Company to measure her for her wedding gift, a pair of ladies' Western boots in brushed calfskin. They were promised within the week.

Clay was eager to get her under her own roof. At least that's what he said. She knew he wanted to be there himself.

With the Whiskey in view, she expected to be forgotten for a while, but she caught sight of Clay out of the corner of her eye. He was watching her watching his country. Their country, she corrected. She knew he wanted her very much to be at home.

"I love the land already," she said. "But then I knew I would."

"Good for you."

"You know, Clay, I can't keep from thinking about Polly."

"Polly?" he asked in surprise. "I told you she was immigrating to Australia."

"Looking for someone like you, I believe you said."

"When did I say that?"

"You hinted. I don't blame her. I just don't think she can find anyone half so splendid. You helped pay her way, didn't you? Don't deny it. Charlotte told me."

"Baby Sister always did have a tendency to talk too much. Helping Polly was the least I could do. Her testimony got you out of jail and kept me from shooting my way in to get you."

"Would you really have done that?"

"We'll never know for sure, now, will we? You just keep on believing I would."

A lump formed in her throat. She squeezed his leather-gloved hands, which held onto the reins, and she turned her eyes once again toward the house. She did not look in another direction, even when the carriage took dips and turns that removed the structure from view. She did not look away when the carriage was making a long descent from the main road toward the barn which sat fifty yards from the ranch house.

Clay had explained the first ranch house, one much closer to the barn, had burned shortly after he was born; this second had been built farther back, on a rise that allowed for a fine, wide view.

On the porch stood a woman—tall, white-haired, and of "comfortable proportions," just as Clay had described to her during the ride.

She spared one quick look at her husband. The love in the eyes looking back at her caused a catch in the beat of her heart.

"Aunt Martha?"

"Aunt Martha."

He reined to a halt near the front steps and helped Jenna from the carriage. She was wearing a forest green mantle with a matching hat, and beneath the mantle a gabardine dress of lighter green that she had purchased for the journey.

She made her way slowly toward the steps, wanting to give Clay time to greet his beloved Martha, but he was having none of it. He pushed her on ahead.

"Careful with the girl," Aunt Martha chided as she came down the steps to greet the pair. She looked from one to the other, then settled on Jenna. "No need for introductions. You're the one that civilized him, aren't you?"

"I don't know whether I did a good job," said Jenna.

"You did a fine job," she said with a bob of her head. "Got a letter from Libby. She thinks so, too."

"She was very kind to me in London. Both she and the earl made me feel as though I belonged."

"Of course you do, child. Clay wouldn't marry anyone who didn't."

"Are we going to stand here jawing all afternoon, or are we going to get a proper greeting?" asked Clay.

Martha went for Jenna first, hugging her against her soft bosom. Both of the women were sniffling by the time they pulled apart.

Martha gave Clay a similar hug, then stepped back. "You two tired? The way I remember my marriage, you might not have been getting much sleep."

Jenna saw right away that this latest addition to her new family was just as outspoken as the rest.

"We're fine," she said.

"Good. Let's get your luggage inside and sit a spell

444

for some visiting. Then, if you don't mind," she added with a glance at Jenna, "you can turn a hand in the kitchen and we'll get us some food."

"That sounds wonderful," Jenna said, and meant every word.

Admitting to a worry about how Martha would welcome another woman into the home which she had run for so long, she knew in her heart that with affection and understanding, they would meet no difficulties they could not overcome.

After a supper of ham and fresh-picked tomatoes and thick slices of cornbread slathered with butter that Jenna helped churn, Clay introduced her to the ranch hands and neighbor Andy Taylor, who had ridden over for a short visit.

"She's prime, Clay, prime," Andy announced.

Jenna knew he meant it as a compliment, even as she decided he needed to learn a thing or two about the subtleties of talking to women. Clay had told her his friend never was much good at wooing, and she could see why. She decided Andy Taylor's education, subtly approached, would be a worthy project.

After Andy left, Clay walked her down to a creek that meandered along the base of the hill behind the house. Their way was lighted by a canopy of stars and a full moon, and for good measure Clay brought along a lantern. They came to a pool hidden by trees and shrubs. Resting the light on a flat rock, he pulled her into his arms.

"Welcome home, Mrs. Drake."

"I feel welcome, Mr. Drake."

"Not yet. I haven't made love to you under your own roof."

"It seemed a little early to go to bed."

"Princess, it's never too early to go to bed. If you think Martha is going to be watching the clock, forget it. As a matter of fact, she told me tonight she plans a trip down to San Antonio in a day or two to buy some winter clothes."

"I won't have her run out of her own house."

"She's been looking for an excuse to get down there for a long time now. Couldn't leave until I got back. She's got several friends in Mason who go with her from time to time. Don't deny her any fun."

He kissed her. "And the same goes for me."

"Love *is* fun, isn't it, Clay? I never knew that. It had been so long since I laughed for the sheer pleasure of laughing. Then I met you."

"That's as nice a compliment as I've had in a long time."

"I complimented you last night in bed, didn't I?"

His eyes darkened appreciatively. "That wasn't because I made you laugh."

She felt a tingle of delight remembering exactly what he had done.

"No, you didn't make me laugh."

"You're quite a woman, Jenna Cresswell Drake. Using so much of your money the way you did, donating to charity, making sure that Hector Mims is taken care of, and the reverend, and Morgan with his twins. My only objection is your putting Charlotte in charge of handling your investments."

"She'll do a splendid job. She'd heard too often that she didn't know anything about business, but once I got to talking to her, she was advising me so fast I had to ask her to write everything down."

"She always could talk."

"What she said made sense. But you know what convinced me beyond any doubt that she was money smart? She confided that before she wed William, she made an arrangement with the earl to turn over only a portion of her endowment as the wedding settlement. Just in case William, who as her husband would take control of her property, really was as bad as Libby said. Once the divorce is final, she'll have the rest of her inheritance."

"Good for Charlotte. Should have had more faith in her. I sure can't argue with your reasons for putting her in charge."

"So why the objection?"

"You've practically made her a banker. My own sister!"

"Yeah," Jenna said with a grin and a touch of a Texas twang.

"You're a soft-mouthed filly, that's what you are."

"Definition, please."

"You don't take to the bit. Just what are you planning on making of yourself?"

"So many things. I want to learn to ride better so I can keep up with you. I want to care for your home and learn all the things I need to know about the ranch. Most of all, I want to bear your children."

"You're not—"

"Not yet. I hope we have a dozen boys who look exactly like you."

"Now that's an unsettling thought. I'd just as soon we had a few little Jennas running around, if you don't mind. And if we're gonna have that kind of family, maybe we ought to get back up the hill and get started at this end of it. It would seem downright appropriate if our first child was conceived the first night we spent on the Whiskey Ranch."

SURRENDER TO THE PASSION

LOVE'S SWEET BOUNTY   (3313, $4.50)
by Colleen Faulkner

Jessica Landon swore revenge of the masked bandits who robbed the train and stole all the money she had in the world. She set out after the thieves without consulting the handsome railroad detective, Adam Stern. When he finally caught up with her, she admitted she needed his assistance. She never imagined that she would also begin to need his scorching kisses and tender caresses.

WILD WESTERN BRIDE   (3140, $4.50)
by Rosalyn Alsobrook

Anna Thomas loved riding the Orphan Train and finding loving homes for her young charges. But when a judge tried to separate two brothers, the dedicated beauty went beyond the call of duty. She proposed to the handsome, blue-eyed Mark Gates, planning to adopt the boys herself! Of course the marriage would be in name only, but yet as time went on, Anna found herself dreaming of being a loving wife in every sense of the word . . .

QUICKSILVER PASSION   (3117, $4.50)
by Georgina Gentry

Beautiful Silver Jones had been called every name in the book, and now that she owned her own tavern in Buckskin Joe, Colorado, the independent didn't care what the townsfolk thought of her. She never let a man touch her and she earned her money fair and square. Then one night handsome Cherokee Evans swaggered up to her bar and destroyed the peace she'd made with herself. For the irresistible miner made her yearn for the melting kisses and satin caresses she had sworn she could live without!

MISSISSIPPI MISTRESS   (3118, $4.50)
by Gina Robins

Cori Pierce was outraged at her father's murder and the loss of her inheritance. She swore revenge and vowed to get her independence back, even if it meant singing as an entertainer on a Mississippi steamboat. But she hadn't reckoned on the swarthy giant in tight buckskins who turned out to be her boss. Jacob Wolf was, after all, the giant of the man Cori vowed to destroy. Though she swore not to forget her mission for even a moment, she was powerfully tempted to submit to Jake's fiery caresses and have one night of passion in his irresistible embrace.

Available wherever paperbacks are sold, or order direct from the Publisher. Send cover price plus 50¢ per copy for mailing and handling to Zebra Books, Dept. 3444, 475 Park Avenue South, New York, N.Y. 10016. Residents of New York, New Jersey and Pennsylvania must include sales tax. DO NOT SEND CASH.